Quarry

A Collection of Short Stories by A. Wayne Ross

Allen Wayne Ross
4/05/2014

Table of Contents

Blue Hole

Prologue

"Get the pistol. End this misery," the voice inside was saying. Richard felt conflicting voices urging him in polar opposite directions. The presence of such two large voices inside his already overcrowded and aching head was too much to bear for long. One voice saying finish it. The other saying no. His frustration grew. A frustration he had never before encountered.

He sat on the edge of the bed and reached into the nightstand where he kept his small Charter Arms thirty-eight caliber revolver. He slid it out of the weathered brown leather holster and held it in his right hand. Gripped it. Stared at it. Rubbed his calloused thumb up and down the wood grip and the cold steel barrel. Cold like Richard had never felt, cold that reached deep into his tortured mind and curled icy fingers straight into his soul. He pushed the release with his thumb, flicked open the cylinder, and stared dumbfounded at the five shiny full metal jacket bullets. They were waiting for him to make a decision. He snapped the cylinder shut. Touched the cold steel again. Felt the icy fingers again. They were somehow comforting, soothing, like a cold beer can against your cheek in hundred degree heat.

"Be a man. Do it!"

Richard now had the barrel jammed against his chest. The barrel, cold enough to pass through his thin shirt, again offered him odd comfort.

"Do it." What is there to live for? Enough of this shit. You've done everything in life that you wanted to. Why stick around? One too many of everything; disappointment, pain, loss. What is left to live for?"

Richard jammed the pistol even harder into his chest. Held his breath, clinched his eyes shut, pulled back on the hammer.

The voices were whispering to him feverishly. Do it, don't. Do it, don't. The pleading so passionate he could swear he felt hot breath against both ears.

Richard was shaking now. Sweating and crying large hot tears that left a stain on both cheeks that could have come from hot springs. His roaring mind grabbing onto the thought that it would all be over in just a fraction of a second. No more Richard. No more pain and heartache. No more anything. And the comforting thought that it would be better for everyone. That the time had come.

"just do it. Do it. All that's left is to pull the trigger. Just the slightest pressure. Barely a millimeter. A gnat's eyelash. Do it. Squeeze the trigger," the voice urged.

Chapter 1

Richard St.Clair was always rushing, so the red lights flashing in his rear view mirror were no surprise. It was embarrassing though since Richard was speeding all over town attempting to acquire enough signatures to file his petition, on time, to be listed on the ballot for the position of Mayor. The red streaks on the road made by the flashing lights were almost as bright as the color of Richard's cheeks. Almost.

As Mayor, Richard would be in charge of the police department and the Police Chief who had just emerged from the police cruiser. Richard watched in the side view mirror as Chief Darryl Bollinger squared his hat and rearranged his gunbelt under his considerable paunch. Richard allowed himself a private grin at the slow saunter of the Chief as he made his way for to Richard's driver's side window.

"Mr. St.Clair," the Chief drawled, "I hope you don't mind being pulled over."

He grinned a bit, turned his head and spit out a great wad of snuff. Richard wondered, not for the first time, how the Chief kept his white shirt white as the Chief seemed to have the ever present wad of snuff jammed behind his lip and was constantly spitting out long brown streams of tobacco juice. The red lights gleaming off his gold Chief's badge made it look a bit like a party favor; sparkling and dancing.

"I heard you were running for Mayor," the Chief managed, between tobacco spits. Richard was silently thankful the wind wasn't blowing.

"I thought perhaps we could get a cup of coffee and chat." Richard felt obligated to the Chief for not writing him a ticket and surprised by the invitation and the fact that the Chief even knew who he was.

"Sure, Chief. How about Moe's Diner? We can even get a couple doughnuts."

A slight smile touched the Chief's lips, but never went near his eyes.

"That's funny. I like a Mayor with a sense of humor. See you at Moe's," said the Chief as he turned away and headed for the squad car. He let fly with another stringy wad of tobacco juice without ever breaking stride.

Richard walked into Moe's Diner just slightly ahead of the Chief. The smells of grease and coffee assaulted Richard's nose as the two men made their way past the lunch counter and its cracked red cushioned stools, past the cluster of tables and toward one of the half a dozen or so worn and cozy looking booths against the far wall. They were barely seated when the waitress appeared, order pad at the ready. Like the Chief, she wore white. In place of a badge, she sported a hair net. The Chief ordered coffee, black and ordered it with a jut of the chin suggesting he thought ordering black coffee made him tough. He grinned when Richard ordered tea.

"I like to keep tabs on who's running for Mayor. Looks like this election is down to you and Denny Horton. Denny's wife is already on the town council, and between you and me, she's a real pain in my ass, so I'm not feeling any desire to have him be my boss. You, on the other hand, I don't know anything about. How do you feel about us police? Do you know what your duties will be if you are elected? And most importantly, what kind of changes am I in for?"

Richard took his time before responding, and answered in his newly assumed politician's voice.

"I studied pre-law in college with a minor in law enforcement. Plus, while I was in college, I was a part-time police officer right here in Ganister under Chief Brandon, your predecessor. So, I have a tremendous respect for the job. My goal is not to make a lot of changes but to keep things running smoothly. My ultimate goal is to use this as an entry into the larger world of politics so I can quit selling insurance. The position of Mayor of Ganister is not my ultimate career goal."

"As you may or may not know, you will be responsible for the Police department's budget, and that sack of shit borough manager seems to get it cut back every year," Chief Bollinger responded immediately and with not just a pinch of venom, "I need more part-time and full-time officers, and by God, I need a raise. I can't live on this salary. Are you gonna' be fightin' for us or is it gonna' be the same old stuff?"

"Well Chief. May I call you Chief?"

"That's what I answer to."

"I hope to work towards improving the police department, and I would be glad to pursue a raise for you, but, first I have to get on the ballot and get elected. Till that happens, there isn't anything I can do."

The Chief sat silent for a few minutes and sipped his coffee. Then he looked Richard right in the eye and announced, "I think I like you. You're sure as hell a better choice than that Horton fellow. What do you need yet to get listed on the ballot?"

"Actually, I was just running around town trying to get the final signatures."

"Well let me give you a hand. Do you have an extra petition?"

"I just happen to have one Chief, and would really appreciate your assistance. I need to get them filed next Wednesday at the courthouse."

As soon as Richard handed a petition to the Chief, the Chief removed his pen from his pocket and signed it. Richard was impressed and pleased.

"Let me see a few people, get you a few signatures, and I'll get this back to ya'."

Richard's shoulders relaxed as he felt a wave of relief. He was tired of knocking on doors and wasn't sure he was going to find enough local Republicans to sign the crazy petitions to get on the ballot.

Richard thought about his lovely wife, Pamela, on the way home. His slacks were already uncomfortably tight when he came through the door. There was no need for Viagra in this household. He enticed her back to the bedroom, kissed her first on her full, soft lips then on the nape of her neck below her ear. As his lips moved down her neck, his hands moved under the blouse and worked on the hooks of her bra. With the loosened bra giving him access, he softly caressed her fabulous warm, soft breasts. Unable to resist he lifted her blouse and kissed her breasts while his roaming hands made their way down past her smooth, flat stomach and under the waistband of her skirt and bikini panties until he felt her soft, fine pubic hair between his fingers.

They made love until they were sweaty and no longer able to go on.

Chapter 2

The Chief left the restaurant, sat in his police cruiser, and using different ink pens and pencils filled in a dozen different signatures on Richard's petition. He needed Richard to be Mayor. He also believed in always having the upper hand. A little leverage! He smiled as he signed the petition, thinking, once again, he would have his boss right where he wanted him. After all, it was by having something to hold over the heads of those in control of his future that he had held onto his position of Chief and obtained the salary he knew he deserved. His favorite leverage was the various "favors" he bestowed upon the councilmen.

Councilmen who were in charge of hiring and firing police personnel. At any given moment he could always count on at least two of the present councilmen to vote in his favor on any matter that might arise. All he had to do was protect them from various embarrassments. As long as there were rebellious teenagers, there were embarrassed parents. All he had to do was keep a keen eye on the councilmen's kids and always be there to lend the helping hand when one of them got into trouble. Sweet, sweet leverage. He knew you made your own luck and took advantage of every opportunity, so it was with this in mind that the Chief signed the petition for his soon-to-be new boss. His new boss because the Chief wanted him to be. He almost looked forward to the first time the new mayor gave him grief and the Chief could show off his leverage, his forged signatures. Plus he was sure to dig up some skeletons in Richard's closet. The Chief was quite good at that. But then, most people were good at the things they enjoyed.

"Darryl, is that you?" the Chief's wife asked as he came in the door.
Darryl squinted his eyes at the sound of her voice. Sweet, complacent, thoroughly irritating.
"Yeah, it's me. Who the hell did you think it was?" he answered in his most sarcastic voice, "Where's my beer?"
"I'll get it Darryl," she said and he lowered his hefty load into his lazy boy recliner. He heard the refrigerator open and close as he picked up the remote control and clicked on the television. The Chief shifted impatiently as he waited for his cold beer and finally settled into the worn and molded spaces of the chair. He ran his hand lovingly across the faded leather arms and glanced around the cluttered room. He thought it might feel good to sweep his thick forearm across one of the shelves and bring those goddamn Hummel figurines to destruction. His stressful, dangerous job had paid for the crowded high end furniture and those silly knick knacks ordered in from all over the world.
"Beer, woman," he yelled, pissed off now.
"Coming Darryl," she said as she entered the room, "How was your day dear?"
"Same old shit. When's supper?"
"Did you get to meet with the guy that's running for Mayor?"
'Yeah."
"So what did you think of him?"
"Typical asshole. Just so he stays out of my way and my business, he'll be alright."
"He's not going to cause you problems, is he?"
"Not me, woman. I'm made of Teflon. Now feed me."

Chapter 3

Richard felt practically giddy as he opened the door to
retrieve the Ganister Bulletin, the local newspaper and he
knew this day, November 7, 1984, would start out as no other.
The final election results could be found there. Of course, he
knew the results from the night before, but somehow, the
written word would make it official, would make it real. There
it was, the morning's headline:

"REAGAN WINS RE-ELECTION"

Richard was a bit embarrassed to find he was disappointed.
He casually glanced around to be sure no one else was
watching him.
"What did I expect?" he mumbled to himself. After all the
election of the country's Commander in Chief was probably
bigger news than the results of the Ganister Mayoral race. He
read past the pork-barrel Congressman and was unsurprised
to see the sleaze had kept his job. The local State
representative was voted in once again. No surprise there.
"He'll probably die in office," Richard grumbled, trying to
find his own name in print.

"St.Clair wins Ganister Mayoral race!"

"Hey Pamela," Richard yelled, "Come check out the paper,
your husband is officially the new Mayor of Ganister!" As
always Richard watched her walk into the room. She never
failed to wow him with her red hair, long legs, and perfect
breasts. Her nipples pressed against her tee shirt and it took a
moment for Richard to pull his eyes away. He slid them
slowly up the smooth curve of her neck to her heart shaped
face, devoid of all make-up at this hour. He knew in just
minutes she would be perfectly dressed and expertly made up
to start her day as a mortgage underwriter.

"You realize," Pamela said, "that now the phone is going to ring even more. Every little problem will get dropped into your lap. I can't believe you actually wanted this position." Surprised Richard looked into her eyes for the tell tale sign of her joking. But the tiny crinkles at the corner of her eyes were absent. Richard couldn't help but think about how supportive Pamela had always been. Even when he went to racing school and invested in a formula race car she was supportive. Even when he actually began racing, she had been supportive. In fact, she learned to check tire pressures and time laps for him. Her reaction to his win now felt like cold water in his face.

"Pam, you knew I might actually win this race." Richard prepared himself for a disagreement and he didn't even understand what had changed. The phone rang. Perfect. Pamela just rolled her eyes.

"See what I mean?" she said, turning on her heel and storming off.

"St.Clair residence," Richard said as he picked up the phone.

"Richard," replied the familiar voice on the other end, "Why the grumpy voice? I just read the newspaper.. Congratulations Mr. Mayor."

Richard smiled into the phone. His best friend, Bobby, always managed to pull a smile from him.

"I was just calling to be sure we're on for lunch today now that you're a big frog in a little pond," said Bobby.

"Well, of course, I wouldn't give up our lunches just because I'm now the big kahuna in the borough of Ganister. In fact, I'll probably need more of them."

Richard hung up the phone and went to find Pamela. He was surprised to find her yet undressed, staring into their full length mirror, in just panties and bra. Richard found himself suddenly no longer irritated at her at all. He stepped across the room and behind her, cupped her breasts and nuzzled her neck.

"What's on your mind?" Pamela asked in a low sexy voice.

"Thought we might play mortician, and bury a stiff," Richard replied playfully.

"Funny man, but, didn't we just get out of bed?"

"It's your fault for being so sexy."

Richard led Pamela back to bed. Pamela's bra and panties flew through the air landing softly on the carpet.

Richard felt himself relax as he pulled into the parking lot of the familiar little diner just outside of town. Close enough to be convenient, but outside the dry town limits, it was a favorite of those who wanted something besides iced tea with their food. Richard liked it more for the homemade pie served with a good six inches of meringue. There were fancier eateries along Route 866, but the one story brick diner was clean and inexpensive and the waitress knew both his and Bobby's "regular" orders. She also knew to seat them in the booth in the far back corner. Richard sat, as usual with his back to the wall. He was seated only moments when Bobby walked in. Shorter and slim and with a beard that made him look older than he was. To the casual acquaintance, Bobby looked like the local dentist he sometimes was. But Richard could see in Bobby's walk the skilled killer that he was. The killer that had saved Richard's life in the Vietnam war. In 1970, they had parachuted into Cambodia to hike through the jungles and the rice paddies to stop the North Vietnamese from pushing southward toward the Rocket City which was to become the U.S. base of operations. Of course, according to the politicians, there were no U.S. soldiers in Cambodia. The objective was to hike through the jungles and rice paddies into "the Parrots Beak", that point where Cambodia and Laos meet Vietnam.

Richard spent the endless hiking hours daydreaming. About home. About women. They hiked over the hills, laden down with heavy packs, sweltering in the hundred plus degree temperatures and praying for the rainy season to end. He stepped around a moss covered tree and suddenly there was a rifle barrel pointing right at his chest. His own rifle barrel pointed down at the ground. Not exactly the way he'd been trained and a definite way to get dead. There wasn't time to think, still his mind raced, struggling desperately to find a solution to this new situation he had found himself in. His only thought at the moment was that he was between a sweat and a panic as time stood still, Richard expecting to feel the sting of being shot and never leaving this god-forsaken jungle. As if in answer to a prayer two red blossoms appeared on the North Vietnamese's forehead and he fell over on his back in the mud before Richard even registered the sound of a gun firing. Richard looked up to see his buddy, Bobby, in full camouflage and with the slightest of smiles on his face, his rifle smoking and still at the ready.

As Bobby walked toward the booth, Richard thought how at home he had looked in the jungle, how competent and confident. It was all about survival. Bobby did more than survive, he accumulated quite a few ribbons and medals, though he just mailed them home, and forgot about them. Bobby slid into the booth and the waitress came immediately to take their orders. Richard playing it safe, always ordered the chicken sandwich while Bobby, the adventurous one, always ordered the special.
"So, Mr. Mayor, what's going to be your first official act? Some big ribbon cutting for a new mall or meeting with the Governor?" Bobby asked good naturedly.
"Well, after I get sworn in, then I have to go swear in the fire department chief. Then right away the first borough council meeting. Not sure what to expect there. If I survive that I hues I'll just have my police officers go out and arrest all the bad guys, then I can go to Aruba on vacation. How does that itinerary sound?"

"Well, Mr. Mayor, what do you intend to do about the drug problem in this town?" Bobby asked.

"Bobby, this is a small town. How do you propose to catch anyone with drugs? Undercover cops? Everyone in town knows everyone else. They sure as hell know who they can trust and who is a cop. You can't do any undercover work because everyone in Ganister knows exactly who is a policeman, who is a police sympathizer, who is related to a cop, or who is from the outside of town and therefore, very suspect. I do intend to check in with the State Police and Blair County detectives. Not much can be done beyond that."

"Just so you know, if I ever catch anyone giving drugs to my kids," Bobby said, "You'll be having me arrested cause they'll be dead." Bobby looked up and into Richard's eyes as he said it. Richard knew immediately that Bobby was serious. Dead serious.

"Thanks for the tip. Now, seriously, do you have any good advice?"

"If it was me, I think I would talk to Roger, the old Mayor. He's in our Masonic lodge, though he doesn't usually make the meetings. But, I'm sure he can be a big help when you start dealing with the council members and the police officers. Just call him up."

"Finally, a good idea. Thanks, bro," Richard replied, "So who's a good first candidate for drug dealer in Ganister?"

"Could be the mailman for all I know. I actually haven't been hunting one."

"Well, just for you," Richard tells him, "My first act as Mayor will be to have it checked out. You having pie today?"

"Well yeah. Why do you think I'm here? Certainly not for the company. How's business, anyway?" asked Bobby.

Richard stayed busy enough with his insurance agency. He had built a nice specialty business by travelling throughout western Pennsylvania and Ohio dealing with lumberyards;

insuring them, inspecting them, and trying to make the insurance company a profit, so they could reward him with a nice fat bonus. These days the bonuses were hard to come by. A new company was beating down the prices and stealing some prize accounts.

"Well, I just had a call from the home office last week. Seems they heard there was a pyromaniac running loose in Erie, Pennsylvania. He seems to be concentrating on lumberyards, so they called to get a quick notion of how many of the lumberyards we insured up there. Fortunately none of the ones we insure have burnt yet. I made some calls and found out that one of our insureds had been contacted by the Erie police and were to set up a round-the-clock surveillance team to try to catch the pyro."

"If he torches one of your lumberyards, what do you stand to lose?" asks Bobby.

"You mean other than my career?" Richard asked.

"Yes, I mean in dollar terms."

"We have several insured for over a million dollars each, but that is spread over four to six buildings. Still, wouldn't be any fun for the company to stroke a check like that."

"Kiss your bonus goodbye," Bobby said with a smile on his face.

"Which means no vacation in Aruba. Who will keep my stool warm at the Aruba Beach Club bar at happy hour? And Pamela could really use some down time," Richard quickly responded, "And no more racing weekends. How about you, buddy? What's new in your world."

"Same old stuff. I sure miss the old action days. Scaring little kids seated in a dentist chair with a drill is just not as exciting. Maybe Ollie North and the boys can get a good war, excuse me, police action, going in Nicaragua, and I can re-up, and take care of business."

Richard could almost see Bobby's mind going back to the jungle. "Don't you get enough of that going hunting?"

"Not the same, brother. Not the same. Need some bad guys to shoot at to make me feel alive. Besides with nightmares I have left over from Vietnam, I don't get to sleep more than four hours a night anyway. Need something to do to fill the time."

"Maybe I'll put you on the police force and you can collar the bad guys. "

"And work for Chief Bollinger? That would be the day. You'd just use me because I know everything that's going on."

"You're Dan Rice." Richard had picked up this silly response which he tended to overuse, but at least it made people laugh. He preferred it over actually saying "Damn Right". They slid the check back and forth a few times, paid the waitress and left the restaurant. Richard slid into his new Volvo and yelled over to Bobby.

"Tell Claire I said hello."

Bobby was just climbing into his own vehicle, an old Chevy pickup he uses on his farm, hauling his dogs around and four wheeling through the woods and fields.

"You do the same to that good-looking Pamela," Bobby replied then began laughing hysterically.

"What?" Richard asked, confused, but unable to keep his own smile at bay.

"You're driving a Volvo?"

"Yeah, it's a great car."

"It's an old man's car. That's what grandpaps drive. The ones that like to get on the roads when everyone else is hurrying to work so they can poke along twenty miles UNDER the speed limit and hold everyone up. They try to see how long of a string of cars they get behind them. They're like a moving chicane."

"Since when do you know racing terms like 'chicane'?" Richard asked.

"I got skills. I know things. You may be the 'Hot Shoe' but I know stuff."

Richard shook his head, impressed and watched as Bobby finally climbed into the faded red truck with its dents and scratches.

As soon as Richard got back to his office, he took Bobby's advice and called Roger Thompson, the soon-to-be former Mayor.

"Mayor Thompson," Richard said when Roger answered, "I hope I didn't catch you at a bad time."

"No, now's good. Just daydreaming about what I'll do with the free time I'm about to have."

"I wanted to call, and ask your advice for when I take office."

"First thing is keep both eyes on Chief Bollinger, and Ned Mahoney, the borough manager. Either one of them will stab you in the back anytime you turn around. Bollinger needs to protect his position, and Mahoney just wants everyone to know that he runs the town, contrary to what the voters think."

"Have you had any serious problems with Chief Bollinger?"

"Well," Roger hesitated, seemingly choosing just the right combination of words, "the guy is made of teflon. Everytime I think I've caught him with his hands in the cookie jar, he comes up with the most realistic, believable reason, then reminds me that he is in the police union and may need to contact their attorney. I know for a fact that he has several of the councilmen in his pocket. He caught one of the councilmen's juvenile boys out drinking and handled it all on the hush hush, so that councilman now protects him with a passion. You can't even say a bad word about the Chief in front of him. Another one uses him to protect him while he runs an illegal fireworks business every year before the Fourth. The guy makes quite a chunk of change every year selling illegal fireworks and the Chief looks the other way," Roger says.

"What's the story on Mahoney?"

"He tries to control the police department by controlling the budget. None of the council people have enough know how to prepare the budget so they leave it to Mahoney. He doesn't like the Chief, so he keeps cutting back the budget so they can spend the money on the sewage system, which is under Ned's supervision."

"Isn't there any way to get through to Ned?" Richard asked.

"You'll have to play hardball. The only ammunition the mayor has is the mayor signs the budget. No signature, no budget. But, trust me, Ned, will not let you forget that without a budget the borough stops. The borough stops, the borough workers don't get paid. You don't want those misfits on your case. So, like every good part-time mayor, you learn to take the path of least resistance. Just sign the budget, and forget the hassle. It's not like this is a major career. Then hope the Chief doesn't go ballistic."

"I guess I should have spoken with you before I put my name on the ballot?"

"If you had, you wouldn't have put your name on the ballot. Hell, you're married, if you want a hassle, just go home and you'll find one ."

"Well, thanks for all the information brother Thompson. I appreciate it."

"Good luck to you. I hope you come out of this with less gray hair than I got."

Chapter 4

Richard left his swearing-in at the State Representative's office to meet with Chief Bollinger before his first Council meeting in a below zero cold snap. Another one.

"Beautiful day," he grumbled as he pulled his coat tighter around him. The grumbling and the crackling icy snow under his feet and the monochromatic gray sky above made him wish for spring. Or Aruba. Thinking of Aruba made his mind drift to swimsuits and Pam. Oh, how he loved Pamela's swimsuits. Always a two piece, always just a wee bit skimpy. He ducked back into the State Representative's office and asked to use the phone.

"Pam?" he said.

"Anything wrong, Richard?

"No, just wanted to hear your sweet voice and tell you I'm thinking of you. I'm on my way over to the Chief's office for my first meeting with him and then on to the Council meeting. Wish me luck."

"You'll do fine, Babe. Just be yourself.

"Okay, I'll 'squeeze' you later. Maybe we should have a fashion show tonight. You could model your bikinis. Get ready for Aruba."

"Or maybe, we'll just have a fashion show without the bikinis. Bye."

The chief was waiting for Richard, in his office, a small room with just enough space for two desks and two tiny jail cells.

"Good afternoon, Your Honor," drawled the Chief as he stood from behind his desk and reached out for Richard's hand. He drew out "Your Honor" into four syllables making it sound like curse words. Bollinger's handshake was sloppy and he held it for an extra few seconds.

"Afternoon. How's everything, Chief?"

"Well, I have the police report ready. Your predecessor just read it at the council meeting instead of having me go in and read it. How do you want to handle it?"

"That sounds all right to me. I have to be there anyway. May as well as have something to do," answered Richard.

"Mayor Thompson always made up the schedule too. The guys are wondering whose working when. Any idea what I should tell them?"

Richard could see firsthand now how the Chief had survived through each change of mayor. It was Bollinger who was the constant.

"How often is the schedule made up?"

"Mayor Thompson did it each week," Chief Bollinger said.

"How about if we make up two schedules and just rotate them unless we have a holiday or something special? Let me know who works how many hours and any special requests and I'll get the schedules made up before the council meeting."

"You're the boss, Your Honor. Any chance I'll get a raise this year?" Richard knew the Chief would not let him forget this particular item.

"I haven't got into the budget yet, we'll see."

Just then another officer came through the doorway. His uniform was as neat as a pin, shoes spit shined. He had intelligent eyes and was wearing a bullet proof vest under the blue uniform shirt.

"Mayor St. Clair, this here's Assistant Chief, Galen Farr," said the Chief.

"Very nice to meet you Mayor St.Clair," says the Assistant Chief, and they too shook hands. Galen Farr had a firm handshake and Richard thought about what his father used to say about handshakes, how you could trust a man with a good firm handshake. Richard's mind wandered from the room to his deceased dad. He thought of his father's "rules" and wondered if he'd have the chance to enforce them on his own future children.
Rule one: don't ever lie to me. Rule two: do what your mother tells you to.

"Well, it's nice to meet you, Assistant Chief Farr. How long have you been on the force?" Richard asked.

"I've been here about eight years now. Hopefully one day I'll land a Chief's position somewhere."

"Are you wearing a vest?" Richard asked, curious.

"Yes, I was rousted by a gang of men one night and spent a few days in the hospital. Ever since then I don't take any chances. I like the job, but, I don't care to go home in a body bag. There are a lot of nuts out there. Tonight will be especially bad. Full moon tonight. Brings out the crazies."

"It sure does," added the Chief. " Everytime there's a full moon, our number of calls practically doubles. I usually put an extra man on for the full moon, but Mayor Mahoney wanted to save some payroll dollars since he was leaving office. I think he wanted to make a good impression on you, Your Honor."

"Well," answered Richard, "if you need an extra man, bring one in. If it is a budget concern, we'll chop some time out somewhere else." And with that, Richard's first official act as Mayor was done. Off to a great start. Spending money already.

"Chief, Assistant Chief, have a good evening. I'm off to meet with the Borough Council. Wish me luck."

"You're gonna' need more than luck, Your Honor," says the Chief.

"You'll do fine Mayor St.Clair," said the Assistant Chief.

Richard felt like he was strapping himself into a race car as he slid the seat belt of his Volvo around him. The uncertainty of what would be expected of him, of how he would perform. His heart rate rose as it did the first time he was buckled into a real race car. He would never forget that day, being buckled in with the five point harness so tight he fought to breathe. Getting the car up to speed and start pulling G's through the first turn. Suddenly the safety belts felt loose as he started sliding around the cockpit. His heart rate increased again as the car started sliding up the track toward the concrete wall. His heart increased again as he got as close to that concrete wall as he could stand. He had a decision to make; face his fear and keep his right foot planted on the accelerator or ease up. Richard heard his father's voice then, "when in doubt, floor it." Richard floored it. His fears were left in the dust.

It was time to face those fears again. It was time to live on the edge again but this time in the world of politics. Small town politics, but politics nonetheless.

Chapter 5

Richard entered the mostly empty room for his first ever Council meeting. Only a few dozen or so folding chairs facing the council table were occuppied. At the table sat Ned Mahoney, borough manager for over ten years. As usual, he was blandly dressed in white shirt, a corduroy jacket with patches on the elbows and a plain tie. Richard found it difficult to believe this man was as indispensible to the council as he had heard. Also at the table sat the Borough Solicitor, Joel Trigiani, and three council members. The two council members that former Mayor Thompson suggested were tight with Chief Bollinger; Chuck Walsh and Bob Kemp, and Charlotte Horton, the third person seated at the table, who had been heard around town and around the council table suggesting someone besides Bollinger should be sporting the gold badge.

Ned Mahoney introduced Richard to the council and the few citizens in attendance. Richard promised to do his best by the borough and thanked all who had voted for him. Ned brought the meeting to order. The usual items on the agenda were dealt with quickly; the plowing of streets, personnel problems, summer project planning and committee reports. The budget for the year was reviewed by Ned, approved unanimously by council members and handed to Richard. He placed it on the table in front of him and listened quietly to the continual chatter.

As the next order of business, Richard was called on to deliver the police report for the prior month. He talked about the number of arrests, the number of citations issued and the total payroll used. The report was accepted by the council.

"You'll need to sign the budget before the end of this meeting, Mr. Mayor," said the solicitor, "wouldn't want the borough to come to a halt."

"I will first need to review the Police departments' portion of the budget, and I would like to know what the tax effect on the citizens of the borough will be for the budget as presented," Richard responded.

Borough Manager Mahoney quickly responded. "We have had to cut the Police department budget by ten percent, but we were able to bring the budget in at the same end results as last year which means no tax increase for our citizens. The citizens of Ganister had made it clear that they cannot handle any tax increase, so we did our fiduciary duty and maintained the same budget as last year, without cutting any essential services. Of course that required the police budget being slightly reduced. "

"Then where was the ten percent spent that was taken from the Police department?" Richard asked. Thanks to the former mayor, Richard already knew the answer.

"We had to increase the budget for the sewage department, and the street departments," answered Mahoney.

"We have a problem then," Richard replied with as much sympathy as he could muster, "the police department budget needs to stay at last year's level. The department is barely able to protect and serve the citizens of our fine borough as it is, and a cut in the budget will severely hamper those efforts. I'm afraid the police department budget must stay the same as last year or the budget does not get signed!"

Mahoney jumped to his feet and addressed the borough solicitor in a rising voice, "can he do that? This will bring all borough activities to a halt tonight. No borough employees will get paid." Mahoney already knew the answer to the question before he asked it. He had made this same stand several times before as a new mayor came into office. What Mahoney really was doing was marking his turf. Like a dog spraying his urine around his territory. Because, just like the Chief, Mahoney expected to be a constant regardless of how many mayors or council people came and went. Other council members joined in the fray, commenting to each other how inconsiderate it would be to bring the borough to a halt over a few dollars. The reporter for the Ganister Bulletin actually woke up and began scribbling notes. Solicitor Trigiani quietly consulted Richard.

"What will it take to get the budget signed?"

"I've already told you. Perhaps if the borough comes to a halt for long enough, we will save enough money to get the police department budget back to where it was," Richard replied. Time to put the pedal to the metal, Richard thought. If he didn't make a stand now he would forever be under the thumb of the council. Meet pressure with an equal amount of pressure, Richard's father always said.

"That will never happen," remarked councilperson Horton.

"Then I guess I may as well go home," Richard said, rising from his seat. The borough solicitor stopped Richard from leaving, had a quick huddle with the council members, and made the change.

So it's begun, thought Richard. He knew some citizens would be pleased he had stood up to the council and some would be incensed he had not been more cooperative. So it was in public service.

Assistant Chief Farr approached Richard as Richard headed for his car.

"How would you like to do a ride along with me one evening?" asked Galen.

"That's probably a good idea. I haven't been in touch with that side of things for a few years. Not since I was a patrolman while I finished college. I'll give you a call towards the end of the week, some evening after my wife goes to bed, and you can pick me up."

"Great. Just give me a call," said Galen, as he got into his police cruiser.

Richard smiled as he got into his own car. He was pleased with himself for drawing a line in the sand. His first official day was done and Richard found himself thinking about Pamela. He drove a little faster, careful to stay within the town speed limit and imagined the feel of her. All soft and smooth. Her cologne faint and sweet. That musky, woodsy, citrus smell of the Alfred Sung cologne Richard responded to. The curves of her breasts falling against his body.

Richard hurried inside to find her asleep.

Chapter 6

Pamela's breathing was soft and even beside Richard. He reached out and softly stroked her relaxed face. He moved his hand down to the exposed top of her breast that spilled from her cotton nightgown. Cotton. Had they really been married long enough for her to wear cotton? She still looked ravishing. He again stroked her smooth face and marveled how she looked much the same tonight as she did on their first date. Well, an impromptu date, but a date nonetheless. Richard was a sophomore in high school. A newly popular sophomore as he was the first to be first string on the varsity football team. He was already flying high from a victory against the team's biggest rival and was leaving the locker room when he spotted her. Such a vision! Short skirt, sexy long legs. Beautiful. Even the deep furrow between her eyes and her pouty lips gave him a thrill.

"Have you seen my brother?" she asked Richard, placing a hand on his arm. He shuttered involuntarily as what felt like electricity ran up that arm and down his spine.

"No, he was one of the first to leave. Said he had a date," Richard answered.

"He was supposed to take me home!" She said, casting her eyes downward.

"I'll take you home Pamela." Richard said quickly, anxiously.

"You don't even have your driver's license yet, do you?"

Richard blushed slightly.

"No, but you don't live far and I can still walk." Pamela laughed and nodded.

They chatted and laughed together and by the time they reached Pamela's home they were holding hands. Richard turned quickly toward her at the front door and leaned in for a kiss before he lost his nerve. She didn't pull back, but kissed him full on the lips. A kiss that sent vibrations through him, that kept his feet from touching the pavement all the way home, a kiss he would never forget.

Richard sighed, closed his eyes, but sleep escaped him. His mind freewheeled from his first day as mayor to Pamela's breasts to his best friend, Bobby. He felt the tiniest twinge of quilt about knowing the things he knew about Bobby. Things Bobby didn't know Richard knew. Like Bobby's frequent hunting trips. He went hunting, all right. But not for game. The prize for Bobby was big time drug dealers. Richard had actually seen Bobby blow a hole through a drug dealer and then casually dispose of the body. And he did it all with the blessing of the Colonel who had approached Bobby after a

Vietnam tour with a mission Bobby could not refuse. An undercover unit designed by the Colonel and endorsed by the President. A unit whose sole purpose was to stamp out the flow of drugs into the country. Richard often wondered about Bobby's motivation. Just the thrill of the kill? Richard didn't think so. Perhaps it was the thought of some low life drug dealer getting his hands on the beautiful daughter Bobby so adored. In any case, Richard noticed Bobby was spending more time close to home these days and fewer days on "hunting trips" out of state, hell, even out of the country. Richard felt sleep finally approach with his resolve to keep Bobby even closer in his sights. If his best friend could keep such secrets from him, there might be more Richard would want to know.

Chapter 7

On a late Thursday evening, after 9:30 PM, Richard called Assistant Chief Galen Farr at his office and asked him to pick him up for the drive-along when Galen had the opportunity. Only a few minutes later, a police cruiser pulled up in front of Richard's house.

"So, Assistant Chief Farr," Richard asked after the normal exchange of pleasantries, "who do you think is the local drug pusher?" Richard was anxious to get some answers before his next lunch with Bobby.

"Well, the Chief would like everyone to think it's the new pizza shop owner. But I'm skeptical. I know we get free coffee and pizza there. He likes us to stop in cause it keeps the young kids from congregating and raising hell, so he bribes us with free food. Seems like a nice enough guy."

"So has anyone seen any drugs coming out of there? " Richard asked.

"Not that I'm aware of, but the Chief was suspicious of that also. In fact, he won't accept the freebies. Won't even go in the place. Just cruises around it, checking it out."

"Maybe you could keep your eyes and ears open since you do go in. It certainly is where the young folks go."

As they cruised around the borough, Galen explained all the usual nightly duties: checking business doors, watching traffic, and even directing traffic so the second shift at the plant could get home a few seconds quicker.

The cruiser's radio crackled and sputtered to life with a request to respond to a domestic disturbance call on the far side of town.

"So, Mayor, want me to drop you off at home?"

"No way! I'll ride along with you."

When they arrived at the scene, Assistant Chief Farr notified the State Police that he may require back-up as the small borough of Ganister had only one squad car.

Richard watched from the car as Galen walked up to the older mobile home and across the built on front porch. Richard strained to see across the bushes in bad need of trimming and all the junk piled high on the porch. An obviously inebriated man stumbled onto the porch. He swayed back and forth and even poked the Assistant Chief in the chest with a bony finger. Soon a woman in a dirty dress and straggly hair also came out onto the porch.

Before Richard could even blink, Galen had the drunk cuffed and stuffed into the back of the police cruiser. All the way to the hospital where the necessary blood specimen would be taken, the drunk spouted off obscenities and threats. He threatened the Assistant Chief, his mother, his spouse, his children, anyone who might even know the Assistant Chief casually.

"Call the Chief. The Chief looks after me. He'll be pissed if you don't take me back home. Call Bollinger, you asshole," the drunk continued between fits of threats.

"Call the Chief."
"Call the Chief."

"Call the Chief." The drunk's mantra.

After a quick trip to the hospital, the drunk was locked away in the county lockup and the Assistant Chief and Richard continued their patrol in the newly appreciated silence of the patrol car. The squawking of the police radio broke through the silence after just a few minutes.

"Assistant Chief Farr, please call the county lockup." Farr pulled over and made the call.

Once the call ended, Assistant Chief Farr turned to Richard, his face revealing disbelief and astonishment.

"Guess what the county found out about our drunk? He has outstanding warrants in California. And he's still screaming that the Chief be notified. That the Chief can explain all of this. Interesting, huh?"

"Has this ever happened before?" Richard asked, curious.

"Not to my knowledge, but I'll check it out," Assistant Chief Farr responded. Richard saw the suspicion on his face, his police instincts kicking in.

After a few more hours of patrolling, Richard was ready to call it a night and asked to be taken home. As they pulled in Richard's driveway, Galen turned to Richard.

"Mayor, I would really appreciate an opportunity to be Chief, if the chance comes along. I feel I can do a more professional job. I don't want to be speaking behind the Chief's back, but his backwoods manner doesn't do anything for the image of the department."

I'll keep that in mind Assistant Chief, but at the moment it doesn't look like Chief Bollinger is going anywhere. Oh, and keep me posted on the drunk. I'm very interested in why he wanted the Chief called. Thanks for the ride around."

He quietly entered the house and managed to get into bed without waking Pamela. He snuggled up against her and the feel of her smooth skin and her sweet smell left him wanting her to awaken. He fondled her gently, hoping she would wake up and turn to him, but she didn't. She moved a bit farther from him on the bed and pulled the covers up to her chin.

Chapter 8

"Morning honey," Richard murmured sweetly into Pamela's ear. Her head came close to clashing into his when she whipped it around to face him in the bed. Her lips were drawn down into a tight line.

"Don't morning me. How long were you out last night?"

"I'm sorry I tried to be quiet when I got in."

"Well it didn't work. I suppose you are going to be doing this every evening now?"

"No dear probably not again for a long time."

"I really needed a good night's sleep last night. I have a doctor's appointment this afternoon, not to mention a ton of work on my desk that has to be cleared off." Pamela growled as she continued rifling through her closet for something to wear. She held each garment up to her before tossing it on the bed. The discard pile grew larger as her face turned redder.

"On top of everything else," she cried, " I don't have a thing to wear! I'm getting fat! You're out half the night! This sucks."

"You look fine, Pam," Richard blurted out, Just think it's only two months till we're off to Aruba!"

"Oh great!" Pamela growled, "I'll probably get harpooned in my black and white Orca bathing suit. I'm not going. I may never leave the house again." Her voice was thick with tears now; reminding Richard he should learn to keep his mouth shut. He just watched her as she finally selected a dark blue suit and quickly dressed.

"Why are you seeing a doctor anyway?" Richard asked.

"Just female stuff," Pamela said between sniffles, "don't worry about it."

"Is your thyroid acting up again? Seems all the women in your family are always changing their thyroid medicine."

"Again, just female stuff. I gotta' go. I'm going to be late for work." Pamela stormed out, leaving Richard with nothing but worry for her. And a large pile of clothes on the bed.

Richard was relieved to find a calmer Pamela that evening.

"How was your doctor's appointment?" Richard asked, hoping to open a dialogue with her. "Is everything okay?"

"Yes, it's okay. I really don't want to talk about it. And I decided to go to Weight Watchers tomorrow to sign up. I need to start feeling better about myself," Pamela answered with a sad and tired smile.

Richard helped her make a light supper and after they chatted for a while, watched a little television and went to bed. Pamela was asleep within minutes!

Chapter 9

Chief Bollinger felt his blood pressure rise a little more with each sentence he read of Assistant Chief Farr's report the next morning. Seems his friend had not only fallen off the wagon, but had also landed in county lock-up. He was still steaming as he followed the county officer into the visitation room after locking up his office, driving to the county lock-up, signing in and handing over his gun belt.

"Chief," his friend smiled and tried to get up but he was handcuffed to the metal table he was seated at.

"Ronnie, what the hell did you do?" the Chief asked in a sharp but low voice.

"I had a little too much to drink Chief, and that bitch started nagging at me." Ronnie looked down at the table as he said it.

"We talked about this. You promised me you'd behave yourself. You keep this crap up and you're gonna' cause us both a lot of problems." the Chief lectured. One thing about a captive audience, they had to listen.

"But Chief..."

"No butts," the Chief growled, "you listen and you listen good. You plead guilty at the hearing. You apologize, and you promise never to do this crap again. I'm gonna' talk to the judge about your outstanding warrant. But if this happens again, they are just gonna' send your ass back to California and throw you in their jail." The Chief straightened up and stormed out the door.

"Asshole," the Chief mumbled. The Chief thought he may have to send him back to California where he came from. He couldn't let Ronnie screw up a good thing.

Shit, the Chief thought to himself as he drove back to Ganister. *I got a wife with expensive tastes, don't make enough damned money, and now this asshole wants to mess with my extracurricular income. It took a lot of years of planning and hard work to get to this point. If he screws up once more he's gone. Won't be the first time.* A smile crossed the Chief's lips as he remembered another associate. *Jackass actually thought he could skim money off the top. Guess I showed that asshole. Wonder how he's making out in the big house with the missing fingers.*

"Woman, where the hell's my beer." The Chief yelled as he crossed the threshold of his house.

"Coming dear."

"What the hell are all these boxes? You buying more shit from that TV show?"

"But I got some great buys, Darryl." she answered defensively and handed him a beer.

"Yeah. Well, quit spending all my dough. Think it grows on trees?"

"Darryl. Please. We have plenty of money. Can't take it with you. Relax, dear. Drink your beer."

Chapter 10

It was several weeks before Richard heard from Assistant Chief Farr. Richard was heading out the door to meet with Bobby when the phone rang.

"Thought you might be interested in knowing, our drunken disorderly got thirty days in the slammer. I'm told the Chief went to see him the day after we took him there. I'm also told he quit talking after the Chief left," Farr said. Richard could hear the suspicion in his voice.

"Pretty interesting the way he demanded to see the Chief, then the Chief shows up. What do you think is going on there?" Richard asked although he thought he already knew.

"Not sure yet, but up until that night we had been having two to three burglaries per week. They completely stopped after that night. Haven't had one since."

"Any way you can find out a little more about what the connection is, if any?" Richard asked.

"Be glad to check on it Mayor."

Richard extended his thanks and hung up, thinking how most coincidences were anything but.

He walked out into the dreary weather. Nothing but brown trees and gray skies. He spent the ride over to the diner thinking about Pam. It seemed he spent every free moment thinking about her, worrying about her. Her beautiful face seemed to hang to her waist these days. The shine had left her eyes and her depression had become somewhat palpable. He hoped the Aruba trip would help her. He knew how hard it was to be an outdoorsy person and get through a northern winter. The snow crunching underfoot as he walked across the parking lot to the diner door reminded him of just how much winter was left. Such a cold, hollow sound.

"Hey Bobby. Good to see you. What's new and exciting?" Richard called as soon as he saw Bobby sitting at their usual booth.

"Well, the Pennsylvania Game Commission knocked on my door yesterday," Bobby answered without even looking up.

"What did they want?"

"He sure wasn't there just to show me his badge." Bobby said, his voice dripping sarcasm. "He wanted to know who vandalized their turkey traps that they had set up."

"Where were these turkey traps?" Richard asked, his curiousity piqued.

"Down in my lower field. The assholes put them up one day when I wasn't home. They never asked permission. Just put traps all through my field. I didn't know who did it, but, I didn't give a shit either. When I found them, I busted them up."

Richard managed not to laugh, but couldn't help but smile as he thought about Bobby bitching and growling and kicking the crap out of the turkey traps.

"What did you say when he asked?"

"I told him the truth. Told him he had no business putting them on my property especially without first asking permission. I told him when I found them I kicked the shit out of them."

"So is he going to haul your ass to jail? Maybe he'll send a warrant over to the department and I can ride along when the Chief goes to pick you up. That would be cool. Me in the front seat, you in back behind the wire screen where the back door handles won't even open the doors. "

Bobby gave Richard a crooked smile, "No, he asked permission to put them back."

Richard laughed, but Bobby was stone faced serious. " I asked him why they were trapping turkeys. He told me they were going to trade them with some Game Commission in Michigan or Minnesota or one of those frozen tundras. So, I asked him what they were trading for? Know what he says? He says, 'fish'.
He said they would get a truck load of fish to put in the Conemaugh River. Fish that actually eat pollutants and could clean the river naturally."

"That sounds like a good plan, and here you are demolishing their traps."

"I said he could put them back, but, with a couple conditions. I told him they need to not destroy my field; can only use the lower field, and I would appreciate if they notified me when the fish came so I could be there to watch. I'm curious what kind of fish these are and what they look like." Bobby shook his head and changed the subject.

"So, how are you making out with your firebug in Erie?" Bobby asked Richard.

"Well, there's good news and bad news. The good news is they caught the kid." Richard hesitated, just long enough to drive Bobby a little crazy. "The bad news is, he burnt down the lumberyard that we insured, while they were there. The idiots almost got burnt up too. Can you imagine? Cops doing surveillance to catch a firebug and he lights up the building they're watching from."

Again Bobby shook his head in disbelief, "You're putting me on. I thought the Game Commission had cornered the market on intelligence or the lack thereof. "

"I wish I was putting you on. That will be a half million dollar fire."

"Since they caught him, can you get any money back?"

"He's a juvenile, no way to subrogate. Plus it will take forever for a court case, and proving he actually struck the match is tough to do without an eye witness. Even though the cops were there they aren't eyewitnesses. Guess my bonus just went up in smoke."

"How's the Mayor thing going?" asked Bobby.

"Let me just say this, if local politics is so full of arm twisting, I can only imagine how bad it is on a higher level. First thing, the borough manager..."

"Who, Mahoney?"

"Yeah, he wants to cut my budget right away, so he and I had to have a showdown. Now I'm on their shit list. He'll probably have his plowboys skip my street next time it snows and I'll be up to my ass in white stuff. Then I find out the Chief may be doing a little illegal protection on the side. I was riding one night with the Assistant Chief, Farr, you remember him, don't you?"

"Yeah, I've met him once or twice."

"Well, we're cruising the borough and get a call for a domestic disturbance. Anyway, long story short, we end up hauling this drunk up to county lockup and he starts yelling to see the Chief. We didn't really think much of it, but, after the Chief read Farr's report, he went to county to see the guy. And we find out there is an outstanding warrant for this dude from out in California. So I'm really wondering if the Chief knew about the outstanding warrant. And with the way the Chief knows everything that goes on, I can't imagine he didn't know about the warrant. If he did know, what does that say about the Chief."

"Sounds like the Chief just got caught with his hand in the cookie jar. Why don't you just fire his ass?"

"First, I've got no solid proof. Second, he's got the majority of council in his pocket. And council has to do the hiring and firing."

"I thought you ran the police department?"

"I did too, until I read the Borough Code. They wrote that thing with checks and balances. The Mayor directs the activities of the police officers, but, only the council can hire and fire. That's why old Mayor Thompson said the Chief was made of teflon. Nothing sticks to him. But sooner or later something will show up, if he is in fact bad. Who knows? Maybe he's a good guy?"

"We talking about the same person?" Bobby asked, "Oh yeah, before I forget. I had a client the other day who said your Assistant Chief had an illegal sawed-off shotgun mounted on the wall of his apartment. What the hell kind of department are you running? "

"That's interesting. I'll ask him about it next time I see him. Thanks for the tip. I think."

Lunch was served, but the conversation never slowed, full mouths and all.

"So Bobby, not to change the subject, but I need you to do me another favor. Pamela is in a funk. She always gets this way during the winter, and I don't blame her for that, but this time seems to be much worse. She went to a doctor, but she won't say what she found out. I thought maybe when we come in for our checkups next week, you could see if you think there is anything weird going on. I know the other women in her family have thyroid problems."

"Well that could certainly do it, especially on top of this rotten winter. But, come on, everyone's depressed right now. You should see Claire moping around the house. But, I'll ask her. See what she says. If I were you though, I would just relax and be patient with her."

"You the man. Whatever you say," Richard always relied on Bobby's better judgment.

"Yeah right", said Bobby as he checked his watch, "whoa, I gotta go. I have a checkup scheduled at one o'clock. I gotta get back to the office."

"Take off. It's my turn to pay anyway."

"Thanks, bro. See you next week."

"Take it easy. And don't speed through my town or I'll have the Chief jail your ass."

Richard felt better driving home, his spirits lifted after a good lunch with a good friend, and he had even gotten some new and interesting information about Assistant Chief Farr. Richard thought it might be time for another ride-along and some questions for Farr about a sawed off shotgun.

Chapter 11

Richard hung up the phone after his conversation with Assistant Chief Farr. He and Farr had settled on a 9:30 pm pickup. Richard knew Pamela would be in bed by then and he was trying to be sensitive to her mood. The house had never been so clean. She was either cleaning when she was home or she was in bed sleeping. Richard couldn't figure out how the house could need that much cleaning with just the two of them living there and both of them working all day.

Farr was right on time and Richard was ready and waiting at the door.

"How's it going Assistant Chief Farr?" Richard asked.

"Town's pretty quiet so far. Any place in particular you want to go?" Assistant Chief Farr asked in an "aiming to please" voice.

"Just carry on. I do want to ask you something though." Richard said, anxious to get the unpleasantness over with and hoping it was a baseless rumor, although Bobby was not one to spread rumors.

"Shoot, figuratively speaking," Farr said with humor in his voice and a smile on his face.

Being direct and with eyes peeled for body language, Richard said, "I heard you had a sawed-off shotgun."

Assistant Chief Farr's face reddened, and hesitantly he answered, "Yeah, I got it mounted on my wall."

"Where did you get it?"

"We had it at the station left over from a case. I asked the Chief and he said go ahead and take it."

"Really?" Richard asked, just barely surprised.

"Yeah, I probably shouldn't have it, but it stays on the wall. Nice decoration. Stop by my place sometime, I'll show it to you."

The police radio began to bark. "County nine one one to Ganister one, come in."

The Assistant Chief answered the call, and was informed there was a serious two car accident on Route 866 at the edge of the borough. Farr confirmed that he would respond.

"Do you want to go along or should I drop you off at home?" he asked Richard.

"Just drop me off, Assistant Chief, body parts do not excite me." He thought how Bobby would want to be the first one there, if he were here. Of course, Bobby had been an EMT while in college before Vietnam. He would always have a gross story about body parts to share with Richard. Richard knew Bobby knew these stories disturbed Richard. Richard also knew this was why Bobby told them.

It was still early when Richard got home, but Pamela was already in bed. Richard undressed quickly and slipped in beside her, his bare chest and legs conforming to her soft, but covered, form. She stiffened, turned her face to look at him and graced him with 'the look'. The look that says, *touch me and you pull back a bloody stump where your hand used to be.* He rolled on his back and grabbed the remote control and flipped through the channels until he found something quiet and boring. And not the least bit sexy.

The following day Richard took a few minutes to call the Blair County barracks of the Pennsylvania State Police. After asking about the sawed-off shotgun, he was directed to a detective Brown. Detective Brown gave a not-so-theoretical answer to Richard's theoretical question.

"All guns from cases are to be destroyed, at the State Police barracks, following the conclusion of the case. Any person having said firearm in his possession could in fact be arrested. Can you give me specifics?"

"Can this be handled within the department?" Richard asked.

After a very pregnant pause, Detective Brown answered, "Well, alright, as long as the theoretical shotgun shows up at the barracks to be destroyed and some type of consequence is suffered by the guilty party."

Richard thanked the detective and hung up. His mind wouldn't stick to the situation at hand, determined instead to think about more important things; Pamela, Aruba, racing. In fact today would be a great day to go for a drive out on the ice and snow covered highways where he could practice his driving skills. Driving in the snow and ice was similar to running the turns on a road race course. Richard allowed his mind to conjure up the coming spring and the lure of the race track that came with the warming temperatures. He thought it was time to start working on the Formula Ford in the garage. Get it ready for the first race in spring. Richard didn't mind getting dirt under his nails as he performed all the basics; changing the oil, bleeding the brakes, going over the car completely to check that every nut and bolt were tight. Being mechanically challenged, this was about all Richard could do. That didn't bug him as he would rather be driving anytime.

His mind left the track and he considered the current situation. This part-time Mayor thing was sure keeping him busy. The question weighing on his mind: Who was the guilty party? The one in possession of the shotgun or the one who allowed him to have it, or both; and how was other case evidence being handled? Richard knew how important this was, one thing he remembered from his criminology classes. When he got back to Ganister he would first review the evidence procedures with the Chief, then make some inquiries about the shotgun. Most importantly, he needed to get the Assistant Chief to bring the shotgun up to the State Police barracks to be destroyed. And he needed to keep this quiet. Richard wondered if it was better to air your dirty laundry or keep it in the closet and quietly solve the problem. Thoughts of a headline about this in the Ganister Bulletin had Richard leaning toward solving the problem quietly.

Richard made the appointment with the Chief upon returning home and asked him to have Assistant Chief Farr join them. A room within the borough building served as both the police department and the Chief's office. The building apparently had never been changed since it was built in the 1950's; two story red brick, insufficient lighting, high ceilings and baby poop green walls. The police department was adorned with the usual black block lettering on the window of the office door. The room was uninspiring with dark wooden chairs and several old, wobbly metal desks.

"Good morning, Your Honor," the Chief drawled as soon as Richard arrived. Richard believed the Chief's smile was bordering on a sneer.

"Morning Chief. Morning Assistant Chief."

"So, Your Honor, to what do we owe this pleasure?" mumbled the Chief as he looked around for something to spit his tobacco juice into.

"Well, I think we have a situation." Richard said, skipping small talk, "Galen, as we discussed earlier, you said you have in your possession a sawed-off shotgun."

"Yes," Farr answered quietly. Richard noticed the perspiration starting to build on his forehead, small bubbles of unease ready to start streaming down his reddening face.

"How did this sawed-off shotgun come into your possession?" Richard asked.

"It was in our evidence room, and I asked the Chief if I could have it?"

Richard turned his attention to the Chief. The Chief's drawling did nothing to hide the newly tensed muscles in his neck when he shrugged and answered, "Well now the case was long over. Farr asked for it, so I gave it to him."

"Where exactly was the shotgun being kept?"

The Chief squinted his eyes slightly at the question and Richard saw the tell tale perspiration bubbles building on the Chief's forehead while the Assistant Chief let out a long held breath.

The Chief looked down to his left, "We keep all evidence in the empty cell, Your Honor."

Richard's criminology classes had also taught him that most lies come when the person is looking left. A look to the right usually means they are looking for a reason.

"Was or is the cell kept locked?"

"Hell no," said the Chief. "Ain't no-one in here but we cops. No need to lock the cell. Not like there's a prisoner in there. We no longer keep prisoners, they all go to the county lockup."

"Chief, are you aware there is a state policy that any weapons used in the commission of a crime, following the completion of the case are to be destroyed at the state police barracks?"

"It was just a rusted up piece of shit," the Chief answered angrily. "Probably won't even shoot."

"Well, I've been in contact with Detective Brown of the PSP. Someone could be arrested for this. That's not going to happen because I don't wish to air our dirty laundry in public. So, Assistant Chief Farr will contact Detective Brown form the PSP as soon as this meeting is over, make arrangements to take the shotgun to them and witness it's destruction. After which both of you are suspended for two days without pay."

The air in the room seemed to disappear and was replaced by such quiet that Richard could hear the Chief's double time heartbeat as the Chief leapt from his chair and was instantly in Richard's face, spitting tobacco juice everywhere, but never missing a beat.

"What do you mean two days without pay? Who's gonna' work? What makes you think you can get away with this? I'm in the union. I'll be calling the union attorney before you're out the door. And the borough council will sure as hell hear about this."

Richard refused to back up even a step, even with the hot nasty tobacco juice sticking to his shirt and chin.

"Chief, you do what you have to do. I'm doing what I have to do. Assistant Chief Farr, what do you have to say?"

"Nothing, mayor, you're the boss," Farr said with obvious relief. "I agree I was in the wrong and I sure don't want to be arrested."

Richard pushed on although he was beginning to think the Chief might have a stroke. Richard marveled at the color of the Chief's face and neck. He finally understood the reasoning for the name for that color; Rose Madder.

"Also, Chief, from this minute forward, you will lock the cell that holds any evidence. You will go through that evidence making sure it is clearly marked and logged into a log. You will destroy any items that should be destroyed. You will be solely responsible for the evidence and the key to the evidence cell, and if there is a repeat of this, you will be solely responsible and it will cost you your position."

It didn't take Richard long to find out within two hours of his departure, the Chief was back on the job. With pay.

Richard knew a Councilmen had to be behind that. Richard also knew the Assistant Chief stayed home with the exception of his trip to the State Police barracks, with shotgun in hand, to witness it's destruction. Richard had been summoned for a meeting with the council.

Richard's phone rang early the next morning. He scooped it up quickly, wondering what had happened now to merit such an early call.

"You're dead you bastard!" said the unknown caller.

"There's no fence around me. Come get me," Richard fired back. The caller hung up. Richard closed his eyes and tried to remember the voice. It was too quick, too early, and Richard was too mad. Who the hell? Maybe the Chief? Maybe the Assistant Chief? Maybe that drunken disorderly friend of the Chief's? Oh, hell, maybe the tooth fairy? Richard wished to hell he was heading for Aruba instead of facing another fine day of miserable weather, an upset wife, an unhappy council, a pissed off chief, and now, an unknown caller full of threats and venom.

Richard stopped by to see the still-working Chief later that day to run the call by him and gauge his reaction. The Chief's face revealed nothing as Richard told him his story but he offered to have a tap put on the phone. Richard declined and left the building. The cold air whipped through him and he was grateful for the in seat heaters in his Volvo. Nothing like a warm ass to improve your mood, he thought. While waiting for the windshield to defrost, he decided to call Bobby to fill him in as soon as he got home. After making a large mug of hot tea for himself, Richard called Bobby and thanked him for the information on the shotgun, let him in on what he had learned from the State Police detective, and told him about the meeting with the Chief. Bobby was quiet until Richard reached the part about that morning's phone call. No use having a junk yard dog as a best friend if you didn't keep him apprised.

"Let's find this coward and make him pay," Bobby growled into the phone.

Chapter 12

Richard woke to a ringing phone and wondered if he would be assaulted with more threats when he picked up the receiver. Although part of him would welcome the opportunity to respond to the dark caller, he was still relieved to hear Bobby's always chipper voice.

"Richard, pick me up at my office on the way to lunch, will you? My daughter needs the truck."

Richard didn't understand how Bobby could always sound like he was in a good mood regardless of the time of day or how little he had slept the night before. He had told Richard long ago that he still suffered from bad dreams from 'Nam and slept only three or four hours a night. Richard knew Bobby had done a lot of killing in Vietnam and apparently even the best soldiers had to justify their actions in their own minds. Richard remembered the drill well; kill the enemy. That's your job, your duty. Protect your country and all it's inhabitants. Done. Seems pretty cut and dry. But then there are the inhabitants of your country that object to the war. Object to the killing. Object to your duty. Then seeing your friends killed in front of you and knowing it could have been you. That if you hadn't been a hair quicker or a tad smarter, and sometimes just plain lucky, you would have been the one shipped home in a flag draped box instead of being the one left standing alive. That you were the "lucky one". The one still having nightmares and cold sweats. Richard couldn't help but wonder how Bobby kept his cold efficient soldier under his good natured exterior. That always ready, always capable defender behind an easy smile.

That smile greeted Richard when he picked Bobby up.

"What's with the shit eating grin?" Richard asked.

"Just thinking how cool it is to have a mayor for a chauffeur."

"So, how's the insurance business, Richard?" Bobby asked as they pulled away from the house.

"I told you they caught that firebug in Erie, right?"

"Yeah?" Bobby said, clearly interested.

"Well, he was a juvenile, so the State, in their infinite wisdom, took him from his father who apparently had sole custody of the kid. Then the State placed him in a foster home."

"Yeah? So?"

"So the foster home happens to be right next to a lumberyard."

Bobby laughed heartily. Richard joined him.

"Amazing," Bobby stated, shaking his head.

They were just settling in to their favorite booth when Richard saw their favorite waitress, Irene, making her way over to them with their regular drinks in hand.

He smiled at her as she crossed the floor. Every time he saw her she seemed to have her dark hair piled a little taller on her head. She placed Richard's Mountain Dew in front of him and Bobby's unsweetened iced tea across the table.

"The Special as usual for you, sir?" she asked Bobby, "and a chicken sandwich for you?" she next addressed Richard with pad, pencil and shorthand ready. They both nodded and she tucked the pencil back into her hair. Richard wondered if she ever lost it in there. He watched her as she turned and headed back to the kitchen and marveled how she was so thin she almost disappeared when she turned sideways. She had to be at least sixty and it was obvious to Richard that waitressing was a profession to her. Efficient but friendly. Fast but thorough.

"So what's new in the borough, Mr. Mayor?" Bobby asked.

"I feel like I need to take a Dale Carnegie course. I'm sure not making friends. Like I told you the other day on the phone, since you told me about the shotgun, I gave the Chief and Farr both two days off without pay. Farr didn't say anything, just did as he was told and moved on. The Chief called everyone he could find and the borough council, who gave me the 'Only We Can Hire and Fire' speech, put the Chief back on the job with pay."

"And you let them get away with that?" Bobby had stopped eating and looked directly at Richard.

"Nothing I can do about it," said Richard, "the Chief still calls me 'Your Honor' but it's sarcastic."

"So do you think the threatening phone threat came from him?" Bobby asked.

"Not sure. Oh, I know what I wanted to ask you, since you have your ear to the ground. You know quite a few of the Ganister EMT guys don't you?"

"Most of them. Why?" Bobby asked with raised eyebrows.

"Pamela and I were going to visit her family last weekend. We left late Friday evening so we could be there first thing in the morning. We were going over Cresson Mountain on route 22 and there was the Ganister ambulance sitting on the top of the mountain. That's quite a ways out of the borough. Any idea what they do there? It was around midnight when I saw them."

"That is strange. Let me do some checking for you. Anything else I need to do for you? You run the police department and I get all the work to do. How much do they pay you anyway? I need to get my share."

"Not enough, Richard answered, "May as well be charity work. Wouldn't be bad if the Chief weren't always on the defensive. What's the problem with you doing my legwork? Shit, you don't sleep anyway. You may as well have something to do."

"I have a wife and daughter you know," Bobby answered, "they expect to see me on occasion.

"Yes, but they probably sleep at night. Unlike you."

"You're right about that. It's just me and the dogs in the early mornings. Speaking of which, remember I told you the Game Commission was going to let me know when they had the load of fish from up north? The ones they traded my turkeys for?"

Richard smiled as he responded, "They weren't exactly your turkeys."

"They were trapped in my field. That makes them my turkeys. Anyway, they stopped early last Saturday morning to say they had the fish and were taking them right down to the river. So I followed them down."

"Well good, so you got to see the new fish get put in the Conemaugh River?"

"Yes," Bobby said before he started to chuckle. "They dumped the entire load from this truck in the river. It wasn't fifteen minutes and they started popping up to the surface."

"What?" Asked Richard, " too much pollution for them? They want out?"

"No, they were floating belly-up. Our intelligent game commission put them in a river that was more than thirty degrees colder than the water they were shipped here in. You have to slowly bring their temperature down to match the river before you dump them in that cold water. They killed all the fish they traded my turkeys for. Can you believe that? I told them don't trap anymore turkeys on my property."

"Well, there's no sense being stupid if you don't show it off every now and then. Maybe they can get a refund?" Richard said barely able to keep a straight face.

Irene was johnny-on-the-spot with large pieces of pie while Richard and Bobby were still enjoying a chuckle at the Game Commission's expense.

"Guess what Mahoney did. The last snow we had, he had the plowboys plow my street first. Then skip the other close streets and go across town and plow. Everyone is bitching that I'm getting preferential treatment and taking advantage of my position. That bum did it on purpose to get even for the budget thing. Do you believe that crap?"

"That's politics. If you can't run with the big dogs, stay on the porch." said Bobby while sporting a huge grin.

"Well, master," Richard said with an exaggerated bow, "Your car and chauffeur await. Where shall I drop you?"

"To the office, James," Bobby replied in a bad British accent..

A black, sporty Camaro Z-28 shot past them like a bat out of hell followed by the Ganister police cruiser in hot pursuit. It's red lights flashing, it's siren shrieking.

"Let's go check it out," Richard said as he glanced to Bobby. Not waiting for a response he stomped on the accelerator and the tires squealed as they fought for grip on the asphalt. The turbo roared and Bobby was pressed back into the seat. After a moment Bobby looked over at Richard with a wicked grin.

"This isn't grandpa's Volvo, is it?"

Richard grinned. "Not exactly stock. Had the pressure turned up on the turbo. Bilstien high performance struts all around. Thicker sway bars. Strut tower brace. Vented disc brakes. Just a few goodies that every respectful road racing car needs."

"I'm impressed, and you certainly caught up to the police cruiser, but...."

"But, what?"

"But, the police cruiser is losing the Camaro. He's going to get away."

"Not today my friend," Richard said, his eyes twinkling, his smile broadening, "Not today."

Richard was practically riding the bumper of the police cruiser as they approached a sweeping left hand turn. Richard whipped the Volvo out and passed the cruiser as it braked for the curve. He stomped the accelerator and before long he reeled in the Camaro.

"Impressive, Hot Shoe," Bobby chided, "now what? You caught him. What are you gonna do with him?"

"Point View is coming up. He'll have to slow up for the curve or go off the road. Either way, it's good for us."

"How do you figure?"

"We're going to pass him on the curve then block the road," Richard stated very matter of factly.

Point View came up quickly. The bright red brake lights of the Camaro lit up immediately. The nose of the Camaro dipped and Richard planted his foot on the accelerator.

As casually as if he was on a Sunday drive he glanced at Bobby.

"It's all about the apex. Every turn has at least one apex. Hit the apex right and it's full throttle through the rest of the turn."

The expression on Bobby's face told Richard he was impressed, but Richard didn't miss how white Bobby's knuckles were hanging on. Richard jammed on the brakes, whipped the steering wheel first left then quickly right and the Volvo slid sideways to a stop blocking both lanes of Route 866. The Camaro was already squealing to a stop and a very irate large bearded man was jumping out and headed for Richard's car. Richard unbuckled the shoulder belt and jumped out of the car, leaned casually against it and waited for the rapidly approaching madman.

"You son of a bitch," the madman was screaming, "I'm gonna rip you a new asshole!"

"Whoa. Whoa. Whoa," Richard said as he held up his hands in a gesture of defeat. Bobby was coming around the back of the car preparing for the upcoming battle.

"Calm down," Richard said in a soothing voice now looking up into the man's face as he was practically standing on Richard's toes.

"Calm, my ass, you're gonna die, you mother.....'

"Stop." Richard yelled in his face. The big man backed up, looking surprised.

"I can't fight you..." Richard began.

"It's a little late for that," the hulking mass said.

Richard saw Bobby waiting and watching from the corner of his eye.

"I can't fight you because I'm a racer. These hands are delicate and precious."

The big man squinted his eyes and cocked his head in confusion.

Richard kicked him hard in the crotch.

"But, I can kick your ass, you big goof."

The big man fell to the ground holding his privates and whining while his eyes turned upward. A siren undulated through the still air, growing louder with each second. The police cruiser slid to a stop behind the Camaro and the Chief rushed over.

"Mayor, what the hell are you doing?" the out of breath chief asked.

"Your job, Chief. Cuff him and stuff him. I have to take Bobby to his office. He's late for a teeth cleaning." Richard said as he and Bobby turned back to the Volvo.

Richard took one last look at the big pile of pain lying on the asphalt and being cuffed.

"Come on, you big pussy," he heard the Chief say, hauling the guy up to his feet and leading him to the cruiser. "Don't you know you can't run from the Ganister police. We always get our man."

The Chief shot a long stream of brown tobacco juice and Richard drove away.

Chapter 13

Richard grimaced as he answered the phone and heard the Chief's patronizing, sarcastic voice. "Your Honor," the Chief began, "I need some more man hours. We need to stake out the pizza shop. Assistant Chief Farr told me you were asking him about that guy, and I think he's dirty."

"What have you got on him so far?" asked Richard.

"Nothing yet, but my gut tells me he's dealing drugs," the Chief replied.

"Have you conferred with the County detectives? They have a drug unit." Richard was greeted with silence and remembered former Mayor Thompson's warning that whenever the Chief wanted a raise or more man hours he would contrive a big drug bust was just around the corner. All he needed was more money.

Finally, the Chief answered, "Yes, they think he may be worth watching."

"There's nothing in the budget for surveillance. You'll just have to do the best you can." Again, silence from the Chief.

"Thank you, Your Honor," he finally said. It came out as "Think Yew, Yere Awner."

Richard hung up the phone and scratched his head. Decision time. If he failed to authorize more budget and there in fact turned out to be a source of drugs in the borough that could have been halted and wasn't, he would be doing a grave disservice to the citizens of Ganister. On the other hand, if this was just another ruse by the Chief to obtain more money for hours and therefore, more favors then Richard needed to nip it in the bud. *This is like running a corporation,* Richard thought to himself, *with stockholders nagging at you for better results. Budgets, money, drugs, man hours. If only I was a drinking man.*

"Time to go see Carmine," Richard mumbled to himself. He called Bobby to see if he wanted to tag along.

"Yo Bobby, how about going to lunch with me at Rizzo's?"

"I got customers today. Two fillings and a cleaning. Besides, what do you want to go there for? What do you have? A death wish?"

"I need some info. Everyone thinks this pizza guy is a drug pusher; the Chief, the assistant chief, hell, maybe even you. Maybe he is a drug pusher. But how do I get evidence? The Chief hasn't come up with any yet. Where's it going to come from? Great gobs of goose grease, that's where. Everyone knows Carmine Rizzo is and has always been the local mafia don. Hell, he's been around since my dad's days. My dad may even have done a few favors for him for all I know. What? Are you scared?"

"This is stupid, Richard, but I can't let you go alone. You may end up in the quarry, swimming with the fishes. Hell it's close enough to Rizzo's restaurant and far away enough from Ganister. And deep enough that a pair of concrete boots would keep you from ever making it to the surface again."

"Okay, let's go," Bobby said in a resigned voice.

Richard picked up Bobby and headed up the mountain. Richard enjoyed the nice twisty road up to about twenty eight hundred feet elevation, great place to put the car through its paces.

"Bobby, do you mind if we stop at the quarry for a sec? Talking about it today made me want to see it."

"Sure," Bobby answered with a grin, "might as well pick out a burial spot."

About three miles outside of Ganister, Richard turned the car onto a well-worn packed dirt road. The no longer used limestone quarry was barely visible from the road and even then was surrounded by large leafy full grown trees. It was bigger than two football fields end to end and was over forty feet deep. Vehicles and mining equipment still littered the bottom to be found only by the scuba divers who practiced there. Richard parked the car sloppily on the side of the road and he and Bobby both got out. They made their way along the craggy edges, holding on to outcrops of foliage protruding from the cracks between the sharp jagged slabs of stone that lead down to the incredibly clear, smooth water which was marred only by reflections from above. The quarry was constantly fed by an underwater stream and was consistently cold, deep and clean. In places the stony sides stood at a seventy degree slant and demanded you pay attention to where your feet were at all times.

"That looks like a nice resting place over there," Bobby said and pointed to a particularly sharp edged slab that fell off into the deep blue.

Richard's mind meandered back to his youth. The quarry. The blue hole. A lot of his youth and education was spent right here on these ledges. A lot of his education, his real education began right here. He learned to swim from his father here. He bonded with his family here; swimming, bathing, laughing. He got lots of exercise here. Hell, he even lost his virginity here. Ah yes, the Curtis sisters. Several years older than Richard and his brother. Ornery girls. Horny girls. And all girl. Slim bodies. Big breasts. At least they looked really big to a young, inexperienced Richard. They teased for a bit but it didn't take much encouragement till they had Richard and his older brother in the soft grass at the far end of the quarry teaching them about the birds and the bees. Of course, it was a quick lesson, at least for Richard. And later, Pamela. The Blue Hole was special for Richard and Pamela also. The many starlit evenings spent parking. Kissing, fumbling their way around until they became experts at the art of caressing. The windows of Pamela's car steamed up quickly as they tore clothes from each other's bodies and by the time they sat up in her back seat sweating and panting, a blanket may as well have descended over the car for all they could see. On the warmest of nights, they would race each other to the water's edge and watch each other undress with ever increasing excitement. The cold dark water did nothing to thwart the growth Richard experienced as his eyes followed the glimmering , moonlight filled droplets of water creeping sensuously down Pamela's naked body. Oh those lucky, lucky drops of water feeling her soft....

"Let's go," Bobby said, snapping Richard back to the present.

Just a few miles down the road they turned into the parking lot of Carmine's Steak and Seafood restaurant and were momentarily asking the huge bartender for Carmine. He flexed his biceps without ever looking up from the newspaper he was reading. Richard could see now why there was never any talk of trouble at the restaurant.

"Who's askin'?" he said defensively.

"Richard St.Clair. Mayor of Ganister. I believe Carmine knew my father, Howard," Richard answered.

The bartender looked up then, his black eyes narrowed at Richard as if trying to decide whether to shoot him, beat him, or get Carmine for him. He pushed himself off the counter with leg-sized arms. Richard still couldn't tell if this guy actually had a neck.

"I'll see if he's in the mood," the bartender said, clearly irritated. He went through a door behind the bar and was back in short order.

"Carmine will see you. Go back through the kitchen," he said as he gave them the once over. Richard wondered if he were being measured for cement shoes.

Carmine was standing with his back to the wall in a black suit, a white shirt that strained across his considerable girth and a conservative tie. He ran a pudgy hand through his thinning hair and stood up to his full height of about five foot seven.

"Mr. Rizzo," Richard said as he entered the kitchen, "Richard St. Clair. How do you do sir?"

"Who's your little friend?" asked Carmine with a tip of his head toward Bobby.

"Mr. Rizzo. Bobby Morrow" Richard answered.

"He your muscle? He's not very big." Carmine was still sizing up Bobby.

"He makes up for that with a bad temper. Kind of like a junkyard dog."

"He packin'?"

"My guess would be yes, but I don't know for sure." Richard said, then turned to Bobby.

"You packin', Bobby?"

Bobby just smiled at Carmine.

"Put it on the table," ordered Carmine.

Bobby gave Richard a glance then pulled out his Glock and placed it on the table. Carmine's lips turned up and formed something between a smile and a grimace.

"I knew your dad, Richard. He did me a few favors. He and his brother were big beefy guys. They came in handy sometimes. He ever mention that?"

"Only that he knew you, and my brother and I should contact you if we were ever in trouble. He also said not to tell our mother," Richard said.

"Good man, your old man. Sure could drive a car." Carmine said looking into the distance and smiling slightly.

"So," he said, once again focused on Richard, "What are you here for?"

"Well, as you probably know, I'm Mayor of Ganister."

"I know that. I keep up on things. What do you want to drink?"

"We're fine. Thanks anyway."

"You come talk to Carmine," Carmine said, "you have a drink. Want what your old man always had?"

"Yea, a beer and a shot. That'll do. Bobby will have the same."

"Now you're talkin'. Gino get these fellas a beer and a shot. They want to chat with me. Start a tab for them. They can pay when they leave." Carmine waited until the bartender left.

"Okay kid, speak."

"Everyone seems to think the new pizza shop owner is pushing drugs. I was wondering if you might know, just whether he is or not?"

"We don't do drugs around here. We're an old fashioned business. In fact, I think those pushers are scum. I heard about this new guy. Comes from New York. Makes a half decent pizza."

"Can I then assume he's okay?"

"Someone's probably got their reasons for sending you that direction. Be a great thing to have you look in one direction while someone else is bringing in the goods."

"Don't suppose you'd give me a name?"

"Don't suppose," Carmine quickly replied while he admired his fingernails.

"I thank you for your help." Richard said as he was rising from his stool. Gino appeared with drinks on a small tray and placed them on the table before quickly retreating. Naturally there was an extra drink for Carmine.

"Always like to help the civil servants. Just a charitable old man, I guess," was Carmine's reply. He turned to Bobby.

"Mr. Morrow, here's your gun. I know you were a war hero. Was always curious if you were the real thing, or just another one of those guys that got shot in the ass, then got a medal for it."

Bobby returned his gun to inside his belt in the small of his back and looked Carmine straight in the eye, "Still wondering?"

"You got balls kid, I'll give you that much. You ever need work, you come see me."

"Thanks, Mr. Rizzo. You ever need dental work, you come see me."

Carmine laughed. A big full belly laugh.

"Don't forget to pay for the drinks when you leave. Gino's got your bill," Carmine said still smiling.

"So what do you make of that?" Bobby asked Richard once they were back in the car.

"I think Carmine was trying to tell me there's someone else we should be looking at."

"Who?"

"Damned if I know. I'm still wondering why you thought the Pizza guy was the one."

"Just seemed like he blew into town and was in a good situation to be a pusher."

"Maybe that was originally his plan and he met Carmine?"

"Well at least I know that if the dental practice doesn't work out, I could talk to Carmine about a job. Probably be better hours. Might even get major medical and dental coverage with him."

Richard looked at Bobby and replied, "Funny man. I'm almost sorry I introduced you to him."

"He likes me," Bobby said, "Oh yeah, on that other thing you asked me about. The ambulance sitting on top of the mountain? I'm told they are part of a group of ambulances with the main office in Indiana. Guy I talked to said they meet once a week to pass supplies on to each other."

"What they never heard of UPS?"

"Doesn't seem very cost effective does it? Another g I heard. The Chief's son is an EMT. Seems he's the one ways makes the pick up."

"Didn't know he had a full time job." Richard said and wondered if he had ever actually met the Chief's son.

"I didn't either. All I ever heard about him was he drank too much. Not about to get arrested though, with daddy being the big man in town."

"Okay, here you go Bobby," said Richard as he pulled in front of Bobby's office, " go clean some teeth. And, thanks for going with me to see Carmine."

Chapter 14

Assistant Chief Farr sat in his car watching the house. Though still on duty he traded the police cruiser for his personal vehicle in an effort to not be noticed. The residence he was watching was the drunken disorderly that he had taken to jail the previous month. Since the jailbird had been released the burglaries had resumed.

Stake-outs being what they were, Farr was prepared with the required thermos of coffee and bag of doughnuts, along with his black coat, black ball cap, and his long lensed camera. So far, Farr had spent three nights watching and waiting which meant his odds were getting better. Perhaps tonight was the night.

As Farr was about to dip into the doughnut bag for the third time, the side door to the house opened. Barely visible was a person all dressed in black, leaving the house and heading for the old pick-up parked in the driveway. The person opened the pick-up door and slid in behind the steering wheel. Farr took note that the interior dome light did not go on when the door was opened. The pick-up started and pulled onto the street, Banks Street, and headed west. Farr waited till the pickup had a good head start then pulled out after it. The pick-up turned north at the next intersection, then made a left at the next corner and continued west on West First Street. A few blocks down the pickup pulled into the lot of the Musselman's Grocery store, and parked at the far end of the lot near the rear entrance. Musselman's was the only local grocery store left in town, as Ganister, like all the small towns in the area, lost shoppers to the big malls located just fifteen miles away. Everyone wanted to shop at the big box stores, and the local stores were having a problem competing price wise.

The suspect left the pickup truck and began walking south behind the store and over the railroad tracks. Farr watched then parked and began following on foot. Somewhere near S. Ligonier Street, the suspect disappeared. Farr continued down the street another three blocks then headed for the alley behind the street and reversed his direction back toward his vehicle. Farr stopped often in the dark alley to listen. Dogs could be your best friend in times like this as they would start barking should a stranger come near their residence, so Farr listened and waited. Listened and waited. There it was, about a block away, a single dog barking, then a second joining in. That would narrow down where the suspect probably was. Farr waited a little more then began very slowly moving toward the noise. The barking had subsided as owners came out and took their dog in or hollered at them to be quiet. There across the alley, in the second floor window was a light. Not a room light but a small light moving back and forth. Probably a flashlight. If so, this could be his guy. Farr watched the house and with his right hand checked to make sure his police radio was turned down. Now would not be a good time for a radio transmission to give away his location. Farr moved a little closer, crossed the alley and stepped just into the back yard of the house he was watching, next to the garage. There was a bass boat parked there which gave Farr good cover and yet allowed him good sight of the home. If all went well, the suspect would be caught red-handed with plenty of loot. And again, he waited. Was quiet and waited.

After about an hour, Farr began to get antsy. Had he missed him? Did he exit another door. Was it even his suspect. Farr started to move away from the garage, heard a sound, and stopped. It was a very low moaning sound. It seemed to be coming from the other side of the house so Farr quietly moved that direction. There was an object, a person lying on the ground. Farr caught another movement out of the corner of his eye. There was another person clad in dark clothes running into the next yard and heading for the alley. Farr checked the person on the ground. He turned on his mag light and focused the beam onto the person on the ground. It was in fact, his suspect, with his hands bound with a black plastic tie. The suspect had duct tape over his mouth, and another black plastic tie around his ankles.

Farr took out his police radio and made the call for backup. Then made a separate call to the Chief. Farr wanted to give him the news before the suspect started howling for the Chief himself.

As soon as Farr put away his radio, he began searching the suspect. Besides a wad of cash the suspect had several rings and necklaces on his person. If the homeowner could identify these items as their own, Farr would have his collar. Bag'em and Tag'em.

Soon, red flashing lights were heading down the street towards Farr's location. Farr handed off his suspect to the uniformed officers and checked out the house. The doorbell went unanswered. Neighbors confirmed the occupants were on vacation. Farr went inside. The house was empty and Farr checked all the doors and windows. Then he went back to the station to type up his report.

Early the next morning the Assistant Chief Farr called the Mayor to relate the previous night's events.

"So, Galen, you mean that someone else was there also

and was able to catch your thief before you could?"

"Seems that way, Mayor."

"Any clues as to who it could have been?"

"I barely saw him; just a shadow, so I can't even speak to his size or anything. He or she was just a black blur. The only clue I may have, is the knife I found. It could belong to the perp, but probably the phantom vigilante."

"Where was the knife?"

"Well it was lying next to the perp. Could have fallen out of his pocket. But I doubt it, unless he stole that along with the jewelry."

"What kind of knife?"

""Pocket knife. Well worn, but in great shape. Extremely sharp. Had a Special Forces logo on it. That's why I don't think it was the perp's. To my knowledge he was not in the military. I am double checking that, but it's still possible he stole it during one of his midnight romps."

"Huh. Special Forces logo? Interesting."

Chapter 15

Richard barely had time to process this new information before Bobby called.

"Yo Mr. Mayor, what's happening?"

"Well seems we arrested a burglar last night.

"That's what I heard. Who made the collar?"

"Beats me. Seems he was gift wrapped and left for Farr on the lawn like a bag of trash."

Bobby laughed. "Listen, I've been making some inquiries about your ambulance question you had."

"The Assistant Chief told me they picked up their supplies that way from another squad." Richard advised Bobby.

"Well, that could be true, but, I think something more is going on."

"Like?"

"Like there may be drugs involved," Bobby replied.

"How did you hear that?"

"Doesn't matter, but, I expect to get some more information soon. I'll let you know when I have it."

"Hey, Bobby, did you lose your Special Forces knife?"

"Yeah! How did you know?"

"Doesn't matter."

Bobby grew silent and begged off the phone.

Chapter 16

Richard was watching Pamela sitting next to him at the dinner table from the corner of his eye. He noticed her pale complexion looked almost waxy and the usual sparkle of her eyes was gone. He reached out for her hand and had just brushed her fingertips when the phone rang. The caller was the patrolman on duty.

"This better be good," Richard growled into the phone.

"Sorry to bother you, your honor," the patrolman said, "I just picked up a couple of teenagers and dropped them off at the Ganister hospital for blood tests. They are either drunk or on drugs. I called the Assistant Chief for further instructions and he said to call you."

"Why me?"

"Well one of the teenagers is Carol Morrow and the other one is Gina Rossi."

"Shit," Richard mumbled. Carol was Bobby's daughter and Gina, Carmine Rizzo's granddaughter.

"OK, thanks for calling." The receiver had barely hit the cradle before the phone rang again.

"I'm on my way to pick you up." Bobby said and immediately hung up.

Richard turned from the phone to see Pamela staring at him.

"Sorry, Babe. I'll be home as soon as I can."

Pamela nodded slightly and waved in his direction before turning back to her cooling dinner.

Within the half hour Bobby and Richard were questioning the girls at the police station where they had been brought after the blood tests. Richard felt his heart melt looking at the two of them. Two beautiful teenage girls, both shaking slightly and looking drawn, scared and sick. They told their story once more; Carol met Gina at the Pizza shop. They both got several slices of pepperoni pizza and a coke. They sat in a booth, just the two of them and did girl talk. They went to the restroom, together. They returned to their booth to finish their meal and shortly after began feeling strange and left the pizza behind to go home. They both swore to all that is holy they were not drinking alcohol or using any drugs. The patrolman stopped them soon after they left the pizza shop, before they reached their vehicles because they were weaving down the street.

"The blood test results will be in tomorrow," the patrolman said.

"Fine, we'll be taking the girls home now," Bobby stated and began guiding the girls toward the exit of the police station. Nobody made a move to stop him.

Bobby dropped Richard off and as he walked through his front door, Pamela held the phone out to him, "It's for you. Carmine Rizzo. What's going on?"

"I'll tell you after I speak with Carmine," Richard answered.

"Mr. Rizzo," Richard said after taking the telephone from Pamela, "I take it you heard about Gina?"

"That's right," Carmine said, slipping an extra syllable in and merging the words together to form "thattsaright".

"What's going on?" he demanded.

After listening patiently to Richard repeat the information he knew, Carmine took control of the conversation.

"Who did this to my granddaughter? She don't do no drugs, and she don't do no drinkin'. She's a good girl. Either you find out who did this to my Gina or I will. My guess is you no like the way I handle this so you may want to get your cops off their asses!"

"Carmine, I promise you the police department will get to the bottom of this. Please bear with me." The phone clicked in his ear before the last sentence was out. Either Bobby or Carmine handling the situation on their own gave Richard cold chills. They both felt the same about family. Taking care of family was number one on the lists of those men. That was a rule. Nobody messed with family. Richard hoped he could get to the bottom of this mess before one of them did and if he couldn't, he hoped whoever was responsible had a funeral director on speed dial. Richard called Chief Bollinger to review the situation with him and let him know that Bobby Morrow and Carmine Rizzo would both be going all out to find the guilty party. Neither man believed their young family members had intentionally taken drugs or alcohol. The Chief had better get to the bottom of the puzzle before they did. The Chief assured him he had his own connections and would begin looking into it immediately.

Pamela listened intently as Richard shared the story with her as she was readying herself for bed. Richard saw a flash of what could have been pity race across her face.

"No rest for the wicked, huh?" Richard asked.

"Or even for you," she responded with a slight smile, then turned over and turned out her bedside light.

Richard was having his first cup of morning tea when the phone rang.

"Mayor St.Clair, this is the Assistant Chief. The Ganister hospital called this morning with the lab results. It appears the Morrow and Rossi girls had ingested Rohypnol. It's known on the streets as the date rape drug. It appears it is easy to get and is a small pill that dissolves in liquid. If mixed with a sweet drink, the naturally salty taste is masked. The effects are felt within thirty minutes. Just makes you feel like you're drunk."

"So now we know what, but do we have any leads on how or by whom?"

"Not yet, Mr. Mayor. Still talking with anyone we can learn was at the pizza shop that evening."

"Well, keep on this Galen. This is extremely important. If we don't find out who did this real soon, we are going to have some serious problems with the families of both those girls. And we really don't want Carmine Rizzo taking things into his own hands. That would create another mess to clean up."

Bobby, with his unnerving ESP, called just after Richard hung up.

"Richard," Bobby said, not bothering to introduce himself, "do you have any lab results yet? I want to know what happened to my Carol."

"Just got off the phone with Galen. The hospital called this morning. Both girls had ingested Rohypnol."

Bobby was quiet for a moment.

"Rohypnol. The date rape drug," Bobby said quietly. Quietly and dangerously.

"Does that mean someone had plans for raping Carol or Gina? This has just escalated to a brand new level, Richard. Any clues of who may have done it?"

"No leads yet, Bobby," Richard answered, "but the guys are working on it. Top priority. They'll find out who's involved. You take care of Carol. I'll keep the department working on this."

"Your guys had better find him fast, Richard. I will not sit back and let this happen to my daughter, and you know I mean that," Bobby said in an increasingly harsh voice. Still quiet, but now showing anxiety.

"Bobby," Richard said in what he hoped was a soothing yet authoritative voice, "please, give me some time on this."

"Yeah, well, keep in mind you have more than me to worry about. I may give you some time, but do you really think Rizzo will?"

Richard knew Bobby was right about that. There would be no holding Rizzo back. Rizzo or all of his connections. The word would already be on the street and everyone would be wanting to kiss Carmine's ass and buy themselves some favors by fingering the guilty party. And then that guilty party would probably be wearing a body bag instead of this years latest fashions, assuming his body was ever found. Jimmy Hoffa may be easier to locate. And Carmine's message would be clear; you don't mess with his family.

"You are right, Bobby, but I need some time. I understand that Carmine is probably already way ahead of the police department, but this can't become a three-way race. You need to sit tight for a little bit. Take care of Carol. And, please, if you learn anything new from Carol that can help in the investigation, call me. Don't go off half-cocked and take things into your own hands.

"I'll give you a couple of days. After that, I'm on the case. And if I find him, you never will."

"Yeah. Trust me, I will take care of this for you. I owe you."

Richard hung up and allowed himself a deep sigh before he called Carmine. He hesitantly dialed Carmine's number at the restaurant. The phone rang only once before it was answered by Gina's father.

"Yeah, what have you got?"

"Mr. Rossi, it's Richard St.Clair. I want you and Carmine to know that the police department is doing everything it can and will find the guilty party. By the way, did you know it was me calling or who were you expecting to have called?"

"You do what you gotta do. I'm gonna do what I gotta do. You find out what my girl was slipped yet?"

"Yes, the lab report just came in this morning. Both girls had ingested Rohypnol. On the street it's ....."

"I know what it is, Mr. Rossi growled, "Some bastard is gonna pay for this. He'll wish he was being raped cause that'll feel a whole lot better than what he's gonna get.

"Mr. Rossi, can I speak with Carmine?" Richard asked.

"You can speak to him all you like, but he feels the same way. There ain't no changin' our minds."

Richard waited. He heard Mr. Rossi ask Carmine if he wanted to talk with him.   Carmine's voice became louder as he came toward the waiting phone.

"I'll talk to him, but only because he's Howard's kid." A split second later he was talking to Richard.

"St.Clair, what do ya want? We're busy here." Carmine announced in his usual no nonsense style.

"Mr. Rizzo, I know what you are thinking. I just called to keep you up to date in the police investigation and to implore you to please give the department some time to get this guy."

"You heard Gina's old man. And rest assured, we will not be put off or swayed from takin' care of family business. This was our girl, not yours. Imagine if it had been your sister. You think your old man would sit back and do nothin'? Hell no, so don't even waste your breath. You do what you gotta do and hopefully we won't have to bang horns. Gotta go."

And with that the phone line went dead. Richard was left listening to a dial tone and his own thoughts.

"No way this isn't going to get ugly," he mumbled, shaking his head.

Chapter 17

Pamela sat in the stark quiet, sanitary white walled waiting room. Waiting. Nervously looking at her wristwatch every few minutes, then every few seconds. She had purposely made the first appointment of the day so she wouldn't have to wait. So she wouldn't have to think about it all day. So she could just get on with it. And yet here she sat. Sat and waited.

"Mrs. St.Clair," announced the medical assistant.

"About time," Pamela said quietly to herself, without moving her lips, like a ventriloquist.

"Room A, please Mrs. St.Clair. The doctor will be with you shortly."

Pamela entered Room A. It looked like the waiting room in miniature. The only thing different was the examining table in the middle. It was a metal frame softened only by a thin plastic mat and adorned with a bleached white flimsy paper sheet. It seemed more conducive to torture than to healing. Pamela sat on the edge, the paper sheet crinkling with complaint as she did. She waited.

Pamela had first noticed the lump in her breast about a week earlier. She had been showering and, as she did every month, did a self breast exam. Breast cancer ran rampant in her family and she wasted no time scheduling a mammogram and consequently a biopsy. Now she waited. Waited for the results. Waited for the doctor. Waited to see if her life would get back to normal. Waited.

The exam room door opened and admitted a professional looking doctor. She was not the surgeon who had performed the biopsy.

"Good morning, Pamela," she said with a slight smile, "How are you this morning?"

"A little anxious," Pamela responded.

"I'm sure you are. Let's just get right to it, shall we? The lump was not benign. With your family history of a high incidence of breast cancer, I recommend we move quickly. There are basically two ways we can go but I think the lumpectomy is the prudent course of action."

"Excuse me doctor, but we are talking about my breast, and my life. I know the statistics. One in eight women will develop breast cancer. A tumor doubles in size in less than two years. And some families, like mine, with a history of cancer are at higher risk."

The doctor stared at her silently, eyebrows raised.

"So," Pamela continued, "I prefer to have the masectomy. Remove the breast. In fact, with my family's terrible history, I want to remove both breasts to prevent me from being back here next year or the year after. I don't want to live in fear of this monster!"

The doctor waited until she had finished and calmed down before she asked her, "Pamela, have you discussed this with your husband?"

"Not yet, but...."

"Don't you think you should before making such a radical decision?"

"Doctor, I've seen what chemotherapy did to my mother and sister. And for what? They ended up repeating the process several years later. And, eventually, the cancer wins. So, no, doctor, I will take the more radical road so I won't be wasting the next couple years wondering when the next lump will show up."

"But Pamela, your husband..."

"Doctor, Richard is MY husband. He will either accept and respect my decision, or he's not the man I married. We won't have a marriage anyway if I'm dead, will we?"

The doctor remained quiet while a composed and confident Pamela continued, "You schedule the procedure; I'll speak with my husband."

Chapter 18

Richard sat quietly at the kitchen table. Pamela had left for work and the kitchen smelled of fresh coffee and her sweet soap. Richard's head felt heavy and his shoulders sagged from its weight. He closed his eyes and tried to remember the last time they had been intimate. The last time they had even had a substantial conversation. He shook his head slowly and wondered if he had missed something. Some kind of hint. Did he say something, not say something? Do something wrong, not do something right? Was he too self involved? He stood and walked over to the stove, pulled his favorite mug from the cupboard and put on water for tea. As the water heated, he ran a calloused thumb over the surface of the mug. "BIG KAHUNA" in bulging black letters against an Aruba beach backdrop. Richard smiled at the memory of the morning Pamela had presented him with the mug. They were in Aruba and she served him tea in bed. Tea with whipped cream. Actually, Pamela with whipped cream, tea with sugar. Still smiling, he glanced out of the kitchen window and noticed w inter was finally coming to an end. The snow was gone, the sky was bluer. No new problems had erupted. Yet. Richard had heard that Bobby's circle of questioning about the incident with his daughter, Carol, had widened around town. Carol had recovered and her world seemed to be back to normal.

Richard jumped slightly when the phone tore him away from his thoughts and his tea.

"Your Honor, how about you coming out to the quarry?" Chief Bollinger asked.

"What's up Chief?" Richard asked.

"I'd rather not say on the phone. But you may want to get out here. You want to be kept up to speed on everything so you may as well be in on this from the start." the Chief continued, the sarcasm thick as sap.

Richard drove the couple miles out to the quarry, the four ways flashing on the Volvo. As he rounded the last curve, the blue lights flashing from multiple police cars seemed indecent against the perfect sky. He pulled in behind the Chief's car and saw the ambulance and the coroner's wagon. Even the State Police had put in an appearance.

"What's going on Chief?" Richard asked as he was still sliding out of his car.

" We found the owner of the Pizza shop."

"What are you talking about?"

"Well," the Chief explained, " I had a call from an informant who said we could find the Pizza man at the bottom of the quarry. So I didn't waste any time. I called the scuba rescue boys from the State Police. They came down, swam around, and sure as shootin' they found a body tied to a cement block down in the deep blue water." The Chief tilted his chin toward a thick, slick black body bag still resting on a stretcher. It was obviously occupied.

"Who was the informant, Chief?" Richard asked.

"No idea. But I'm glad I followed up on this." Said the Chief as Richard looked at him closely. He knew no more details would be forthcoming and that another raise request would probably be on his desk in a day or two. The Chief finally returned Richard's stare.

"The Coroner will be able to confirm whether it was a murder and not a suicide," the Chief said.

"Not very likely someone tied a cement block to their feet and jumped in the quarry, now is it Chief?"

"Not likely," the Chief conceded, "I happen to think it's quite a coincidence that it's the pizza shop owner in that body bag over there. Where's your buddy Bobby?" Richard watched the smirk cross over the Chief's lips.

.   "How would I know," asked Richard, "and why do you care?" Richard wondered if the Chief would actually accuse Bobby outright.

"Well my first guess would be that Carmine Rizzo or your best friend, Bobby did this," the Chief replied. Another smirk. This one made even uglier by the tobacco juice shooting from the Chief's mouth.

"You might have to make some new friends, your Honor."

Richard figured the Chief would drag Bobby into this just for being Richard's friend. But then again, he may have a point. Bobby was certainly capable of ultimate retaliation. So was Carmine or Mr. Rossi. And it did have the look and feel of a stereotypical mafia style killing. Damn, Richard thought, a murder in Ganister and on his watch. There hadn't been a murder in Ganister in several decades.

"I want to talk to your friend. Today. I suspect you will be calling or seeing him, so tell him not to go anywhere, you understand me Mr. Mayor."

Richard nodded curtly and wasted no time climbing into his car and spinning off, the gravel shooting out from under his tires. At that moment, Richard was grateful for the racing school training.

Chapter 19

The early morning brought winter back in lieu of the promise of spring that had been hinted at only a few days earlier. Thin, scraggly snowflakes clung to the windshield briefly before being tossed aside by the wipers. With the bun warmers built into the seats of the Volvo on and the heater blowing full blast, Pamela and Richard were slowly warming up as they sped down the highway toward Pittsburgh International Airport and the paradise that lay at the end of the flight. The desert island of Aruba. Once they left the airport in the flying can it would take only four and a half hours to get to the good life. As they did every year, Pamela and Richard wore shorts and tee shirts under their winter clothes so by the time the plane touched down they were ready for the tropical weather that would greet them as they stepped from the plane.

They, along with an entire group of traveling snowbirds, were soon hurrying through the Queen Beatrix Airport, through Immigration and Customs and heading for the waiting taxi cabs to whisk them from the winter doldrums.

Richard's pace and excitement built as the cab took them into Oranjestad, up L.G.Smith Boulevard to the Aruba Beach Club timeshare. The check-in seemed to take hours instead of minutes as the sun glinted off the water and left small, bright patches on the shining tile floor of the lobby. Richard almost sprinted to the room, dragging Pamela behind him and was soon decked out in his favorite blue trunks. He turned around to grab a large beach towel as Pamela emerged from the bathroom in a one-piece black swimsuit.

"When did you get that swimsuit, Pamela?"

"Before we left." she said curtly, leaving no room for conversation.

"But where's the bikini?" he plunged ahead anyway.

"Not in a bikini frame of mind, Okay?"

Richard nodded slightly, reached for her hand, and they left the room and stepped onto the beach. His senses were overwhelmed. No matter how many times he came here, it was always overwhelming. And wonderful. Endless hues of blue took his breath away; the sky and water, the fanciful beach umbrellas. The fine, white sand was soft between his toes and the grays of Pennsylvania started to melt. He picked up the scent of pure air, sunscreen and mangoes. His ears were so ready for the laughter of the sun worshipers and beach bar visitors and the melodic and constant crash of waves on rock and sand. His face and arms warmed quickly in the tropical sun and his hair tosseled about his head in the persistent tradewinds.

Richard settled into a beach hut and, as usual, spent the afternoon reading a Jeffrey Archer novel and trekking across the sand into the inviting, clear blue Caribbean Sea every few minutes. Pamela began her process of baking in the sun. Even though she preferred full sun to Richard's shade, he knew he would end up darker than her at the end of the week as his olive complexion turned the rays of sun into bronze where Pamela's fragile complexion bred freckles.

Richard let his guard and his mind down for awhile. He slipped into the normal routine of Aruba. The long afternoons on the beach, the 5:00 clean up for dinner, the oh, so comfortable silence between him and Pamela. Just the occasional "are you going in the water?" and "are you getting hungry?" He was so relaxed and lazy and warm it took him several days before it dawned on him the normal routine was not so normal this year. Normally Richard and Pamela's sex life increased in direct proportion to the melting away of the winter doldrums. Yet, the usual lovemaking had not yet occurred. Pamela's festive and sexy bikinis had not yet made an appearance. She had spent only the first day baking in the sun and since then had shared his hut, and his space, yet seemed so uncomfortable when she caught him leering at her. He stayed quiet about the changes. For four days he stayed quiet.

"Pamela," Richard asked on the last full day of fun in the sun, "everything okay with you?"

"What do you mean," she asked, raising her head off the lounge chair and looking directly into his eyes.

"Well, you know, it's been quite a while since we, you know."

"Can we talk about this later?"

"If you prefer, or we could go to the room now, for a little afternoon delight," Richard answered with a sly grin.

Pamela stared at him for several moments.

"We better talk, "she began with a sigh, "you know I've been seeing a doctor."

"Yes," he said in a whisper, his eyes questioning more than a little afraid.

"Well," Pamela said hesitantly, "I don't know how to tell you this, but.."

Richard didn't know what the rest of the sentence would be, but he did know nothing good ever started with those words. He sat up straight and moved a few inches closer to her.

"Pamela?"

"Oh hell, Richard, I don't know how to tell you this."

"Just say it Pamela, what is it?" Richard asked in a concerned voice.

"I have breast cancer and I've decided to have both breasts removed so I don't have to worry about this again." Pamela said quickly, shakily and averted her eyes from Richard's.

"Pamela," Richard said in a soft voice, jumping from his lounge chair and curling up next to her. "Babe, I'm so sorry. Why didn't you tell me this before? We'll beat this thing. You and me together, we'll beat this. I'm here for you. I love you."

"You're a boob-man, Richard. I'm not so sure you'll even stick around when I'm boobless."

""I'm a Pamela Man. Always."

Richard held her close for long minutes while the

Caribbean sun dropped from the sky in dazzling shades of gold and yellow. It lay like a giant egg on the horizon and still they stayed still holding each other in silence. the sun slipped slowly down past the waterline. Richard wondered momentarily if there would be a green flash, the one that occurs when conditions are perfect. No green flash tonight. Tonight the conditions were anything but perfect. And still they stayed.

Richard wasn't scared of not being able to "stick around" if his wife were suddenly without breasts. He was scared of having to go on without her. Her beauty was inside, the lovely exterior, just a bonus.

The ringing of the happy hour bell roused him from his thoughts and his lounge chair. He rose and extended his hand toward Pamela. Although he didn't drink much, the bar was beckoning him tonight.

"Hey babe," he said, "want to go to the bar and get a drink? Maybe a margarita or mango daiquiri?"

"Actually Richard," she said softly, "I need to be alone for a little bit. I'm going to take a little walk down the beach."

"I'll go with you."

"No, I really need some alone time. I'll be right back," she said with a slow, sad smile.

Pamela grabbed her beach towel, tied it around her waist, put her water bottle and book in her bag, and slowly turned toward the gently lapping Caribbean Sea before Richard had a chance to protest.

Richard watched her walk away, her red hair in soft tangles in the breeze, her long legs red from the sun's assault, somehow finding her even under the beach hut's protection.

"I love you, Pamela," Richard whispered.

Chapter 20

Pamela had leisurely walked along the water's edge for a half hour or so, stopping every few minutes to stare out at the dark water. The only way to know where the water ended and the new night sky began was by the jewel-like stars that dotted the sky with no competition.

Suddenly, a sweaty hand slammed over her mouth squeezing it closed and cutting off her voice and most of her breath. Another hand yanked her back roughly as an arm encircled her towel wrapped waist.

"Stay quiet and you won't get hurt, bitch," a voice whispered roughly into her ear. The hand over her mouth pressed harder against her. The sweaty hairy arm around her waist turned into a roaming hand with rushing fingers that worked their way up her torso until they forcefully grabbed her breast.

"Sweet," he whispered. His voice was low and growling. Hateful.

"We're gonna have some fun. Just be a good little bitch and come back a few steps to that private beach hut." He roughly lifted her from the soft sand and turned her away from the lapping sea, forcing her back toward the dark beach.

Pamela bit the nasty hand squeezing her mouth while at the same time bringing the heel of her right foot forcefully into the villains' crotch. Having the family jewels smacked around caused the sweaty arms to release Pamela just enough for her long athletic legs to make giant leaps across the soft sand. The sweaty hand was able to grab her necklace and hang on to it until the chain snapped and let him crouching there with just the necklace in his hand.

Like a gazelle running from a cheetah, Pamela wasted no time putting a lot of sand between her and the still doubled over, predator. She was panting when she reached Richard at the beach bar.

Richard took one look at her and his eyes widened. He grabbed her arms to keep her from falling and she crumpled into his arms. He held her for a few moments before holding her back to get a good look at her, but kept his hands on her arms to steady her. His eyes went from the deep scratches on her neck to her exposed breast.

"Pamela, what's going on? Where's your towel? Why are your boobs hanging out?"

She pulled away from Richard, tucked her breasts back into her suit, and leaned close to him to whisper in his ear.

"We need to go. Now!"

Richard left his stool and drink quickly, encircled her waist with loving arms and they made their way back to the room.

Chapter 21

Richard felt numb on the trip home. Pamela's hand felt chilly as it lay limp in his hand. He was unsure if it was her hand that was chilly or just another part of the pervasive cold in his heart. Normally, the trip home was crowded with smiles and suntans. With enough surf, sea and Caribbean spirit to erase all traces of a nasty Pennsylvania winter and refresh the soul. Richard and Pamela would walk into their home ready to welcome the work and challenges facing them. Not this year. The nightmarish quality of the last 24 hours followed Richard onto the plane, into the car and up the steps to the house he shared with the woman he adored. The woman he would always adore. The woman he could not live without. The warm and inviting home felt cold to Richard. Cold and quiet and empty. It felt sad. Like it knew the man entering was not the same man who left a short week ago.

Pam retired silently to the bedroom as Richard brought in the luggage. He made a cup of hot tea for himself and settled into his chair. After a few moments he picked up the phone.

"Can we meet for lunch?" he asked Bobby.

"Sure. When and where?" Bobby answered. His cautious tone let Richard know that Bobby knew this would be no ordinary lunch. That something serious brewed.

"Moe's Diner. Noon," was all Richard said and hung up the phone.

"How was Aruba?" Bobby asked as he slid into the booth across from Richard.

"Aruba was..," Richard hesitated, "Sunny, beautiful, horrible."

Bobby let the smile drop from his lips.

"What do you mean? What happened?"

Richard swallowed hard and took a deep breath before he answered.

"Pamela finally told me about her doctor's visits," Richard said in a shaky voice, "She has breast cancer. She's getting a double mastectomy."

"Whoa." Bobby said quietly, "How can I help? Are you okay?"

"But wait, there's more," Richard continued with a sarcasm that was out of character,
"While we were in Aruba, some bastard attacked her on the beach!"

"What? Any idea who? Did you catch him? Was she hurt?"

"She was just shaken up. She didn't even want to notify the Aruba police. The pervert is nursing some sore nuts today."

"Where were you?"

"Waiting at the beach bar for her. She wanted some alone time after telling me about the cancer. She never got a look at him. All she knows is he was tall, skinny, white, had hairy skinny arms with a tattoo on his right forearm of two snakes wrapped around a pole," Richard said.

"I'm so sorry, buddy," Bobby said. His face told Richard he understood, was sincere and concerned.

"Please let me know whatever I can do to help," Bobby continued.

"Oh, I'm not done yet," Richard said. His upper lip curled in a smirk and he looked Bobby directly in the eyes. He waited until the waitress took their orders and left the table before continuing.

"The Chief thinks you are a good candidate for dumping the pizza man into the quarry."

"You're shittin' me" Bobby said staring back at Richard.

"Chief called me the moment I got in the door this evening. Said he had enough on you to put you away."

Richard waited a few moments before continuing.

"So, Bobby, my question is.........did you?"

"No," Bobby said without hesitation, without blinking, "If I was sure he was the one who drugged my daughter, I would just put a bullet in his head. Right between his eyes. Double tap. I don't think he was stupid enough to do that in his own store. I think it was someone else. I just don't know who yet. So, no. I had no reason to kill the man."

Richard nodded slowly. He knew Bobby would not hold the question against him. He also knew Bobby just told him the truth.

Chapter 22

Richard's patience had reached an all time low and before he even brushed his teeth the following morning, Richard called the Chief.

"Chief," Richard began in his best authoritative tone, "two things; one, you be damn sure before you continue accusing Bobby Morrow of the homicide that you have some solid proof, second, I expect you to consult with the County District Attorney before you proceed any further."

"Look Mayor," the Chief replied, his tone matching Richard's, "I'm the Chief. I'll conduct my investigation as I see fit. And when I'm ready, I'll arrest whomever I think is good for this crime."

"Well, as I said, you better be damn sure before you make any more accusations against Bobby because damaging his reputation could be costly if you're wrong about this. And so far, I don't see where you have anything more than circumstantial theories. The real danger with you becoming so fixated on Bobby is you could be overlooking a better suspect."

"I get that he's your buddy, but, if I get any hard evidence, he's goin' down. Friend of yours or not, Mayor. And you won't be able to stop me," the Chief said. He was obviously irritated.

"Listen to me Chief, make sure you run whatever you have by the DA."

"You listen, Your Honor," the Chief said loudly, "I run this department. Not you. In fact, you're only Mayor of this town as long as I say you're Mayor. I'll have your ass out of office so fast you'll never know what happened."

"You need to back off Chief, who the hell do you think you are?" Richard asked, his own voice rising.

"Well Your Honor," the Chief said sarcastically, his drawl not so pronounced now, "You back off and let me run my own department or I go to the county election board and tell them how a dozen of the names on your petition were not only faked but done under duress." The Chief sounded proud and more than a little victorious.

Richard laughed heartily.

"Think this is funny, do ya?" the Chief said in a low dangerous voice.

"Actually, yes, I do. I assume you are now telling me that you didn't actually get me real signatures on my petition to get on the ballot for mayor. Is that what you're telling me Chief?"

"That's exactly what I'm sayin'. When I blow the whistle, you're out of office."

"Chief," Richard said, all traces of laughter gone, "the only thing keeping you in a job right now is the fact that only the borough council has the authority to fire you. Trust me, if it were up to me, you'd be gone."

Richard slammed the phone down. Richard knew the Chief had it in for Bobby and wasn't open to other possibilities, his mind was made up and closed for further discussion; he was overlooking something or someone. But what or who? Bobby didn't do it. Bobby was capable of doing it, but he hadn't. This was the one thing Richard was sure of. So who did? And why? The pizza guy was relatively new to Ganister. Did someone know something about him? Something about the pizza shop? Something about the pizza guy's past?

Questions built up in Richard's racing mind. He knew he was going to have to find some answers. But who could provide those answers? Who could help him find someone who could provide those answers? Richard made a mental list. The county district attorney? The state police? The assistant chief? Bobby? No, cross Bobby off the list. Bobby was in deep enough. Mr. Rizzo? Rizzo was certainly well connected. But he was also a possible suspect. Richard decided on Assistant Chief Galen Farr.

"Galen," Richard said when the assistant chief answered the phone, "Are you up to speed on the pizza man homocide?"

"I've been reading the Chief's reports and I've kept my ear to the ground. What's up Mayor?"

"I'm afraid the Chief has blinders on," Richard responded, "He wants to nail Bobby Morrow and I'm afraid because of that that he is overlooking other things. Could you do a complete background check on the pizza man for me?"

"I'd be glad to," Galen responded quickly, "Would be nice to be doing some real police work for a change."

"Well have at it. And be thorough. This guy hasn't been in Ganister very long and he might have come with some baggage that could shed some light on this case. Also, if you can, please find out if old man Rizzo or his son-in-law Rossi could have something against this guy. We need to find out if they are potential suspects or not."

"I'm on it Mayor, but my gut tells me it looks too convenient for Rizzo or Rossi. It looked like a mafia type thing, but those guys wouldn't be so sloppy this close to home. Unless they were sending a message, but I still don't think they would do the cement shoe thing. Makes for good movie material, but not so believable in real life. Anyway, I'll check it out and I'll get back to you."

Richard figured the Assistant Chief would be on this task like white on rice, he had real ambition to wear the gold shield. Still, this could go bad for Bobby. Richard was anxious to help Bobby out of this mess. And he needed to do it quick so he could focus on Pamela.

Richard decided to trek up to Rizzo's mountaintop restaurant for a stiff drink, and hopefully some answers.

Chapter 23

Richard pulled into the gravel parking lot at Rizzo's, got out of his car, locked it, and made his way into the bar area instead of the restaurant area. As usual, Rossi was behind the bar and nodded at Richard as he pulled up a barstool. It was early afternoon and there were only a few people in booths, and one other at the bar. Rossi made his way down the bar, wiping the polished wood until he arrived in front of Richard. Then he stood there, crossed his huge tattooed arms, and stared at Richard. Waiting for Richard's drink order. Richard ordered a margarita. Rossi turned toward the shelves to grab the appropriate bottles, but not before Richard caught the slight roll of Rossi's eyes.

"Want to run a tab?" Rossi asked as he placed the drink in front of Richard.

"Yeah, I......."

"You find the sonofabitch that drugged my girl yet?" Rossi interrupted.

"Not yet, though some people think you already found him. Found him and outfitted him in cement shoes to go swimming with."

Rossi met Richard's stern gaze. Rossi leaned across the bar and Richard met him half way. When Rossi spoke, his mouth was so close to Richard's ear that his breath tickled.

"The pizza man didn't drug my girl. My family is like a pack of dogs, we don't shit where we eat. You get my meanin'?"

Richard pulled back slightly but kept his voice low.

"I get your meaning. How can I be sure it's the truth.?"

"You know it's the truth because I say it's the truth. If I get the guy before your keystone cops do, I'm gonna send a real message. Nobody screws with my family."

"Rossi, you heard Mr. Rizzo, we get to handle this within the law."

"Yeah. Well, we'll see." Rossi said and headed back down the bar to check on his other customer. Richard figured the conversation was done and was surprised when Rossi came back toward him after pouring a beer for the only other customer at the bar.

"Tell you what Mr. Mayor, I'll point you in the right

direction, you see if you can handle this situation."

Richard contained his excitement. Could Rossi really have some information?

"Rossi, are you holding out on me? Do you know who drugged the girls or who put the pizza man to the quarry?"

Rossi was silent for a Minute, studying Richard in intently with his dark eyes.

"Maybe yes, maybe no," he said.

"Which is it?"

"Could be the same fool did both deeds. Could be your Keystone Cops are protecting him. Could be you are protecting him. Could be I just might double tap the bastard." Rossi said his mouth barely moving, his eyes intent and fierce.

Double tap. Richard knew the term. It meant two bullets right in the victim's forehead. Two shots. Double tap. The danger in Rossi's eyes was almost palatable.

"Mr. Rizzo here?" Richard asked quietly.

"Yeah, he's here." Rossi said and went back to wiping down the bar, "Not sure he wants to talk to you."

"Well could you find out?"

Rossi didn't respond but he did go into the back.

Richard heard the conversation beyond the open door.

"The St. Clair guy is here. He asked to see you."

"Where is he?"

"End of the bar. Can't miss him."

"Tell him I'll be there when I get there."

Rossi reappeared from the back. "Sit tight," he s aid to Richard and walked away.

Richard did. He nursed his margarita and waited for Rizzo to make an appearance.

When Carmine Rizzo made his appearance, it did not go unnoticed. Although his customers were few at this time of the day, they were quick to acknowledge his presence with greetings of "How you doin', Mr. Rizzo.", "Good afternoon, Mr. Rizzo", "So nice to see you, Mr. Rizzo". They did everything but kiss his ring. Richard followed suit as Carmine approached him.

"Mr. Rizzo, how are you today?"

"St. Clair," Carmine mumbled, "Whadda' you want?"

"I was chatting with Rossi. He insinuated that you may know something about the girls getting drugged or the pizza man's death. That true?"

Carmine stared directly at Richard for a moment before answering with the slightest shrug of his shoulders.

"Please Carmine, let the police handle this."

Again, Carmine stared directly at Richard. He looked around the bar, moving only his eyes, and came around the bar to sit beside Richard. When he spoke, it was in a low, contained voice.

"Tell you what I'm gonna' do here. I'm gonna' give you one piece of the puzzle. You take care of bizness real quick like, or me and the boys are gonna' take care of it. Our way. I haven't even told Rossi or my own daughter yet. I'll give you forty-eight hours, then." Again, the shrug.

"First tell me why you haven't told Rossi or your daughter yet."

"Rossi'll go kill him. Then I have to get a new bartender." *Apparently Carmine had a practical side.*

"So, Rizzo, who did what?"

"It's all tied together."

Richard was tiring of pulling all these teeth. He kept his frustration at bay and continued the questions.

"You mean the girls getting drugged and the pizza man wearing cement shoes are related?"

"Someone wants to be Ganister's drug kingpin." Rizzo said in a low, measured tone.

"Who"

"Look real close to the Chief." Carmine said, then stood and walked away. Richard had been dismissed.

"What the hell does that mean," Richard mumbled to himself. He left the bar and headed home. He had some calls to make and a wife to see.

Chapter 24

Late afternoon shadows reached across the lawn toward Richard as he stepped from his car and headed toward the front door of his home. Spring had gone into hiding and the air was crisp, the weak sun low in the sky. Richard was grateful for the warmth of the house.

"Pam?" he called out as he hung up his coat and put his keys in the small bowl right inside the front door. That had been Pamela's idea. And a good one at that. No more scurrying around in the mornings looking for car keys. When no answer came, Richard made his way down the hall to the bedroom they shared. Richard had decorated the room himself, at Pamela's request, and it portrayed a Caribbean dream. Soft blues and greens, white shutters and curtains, gleaming hardwood floors, and large prints of the amazing beach in front of their Caribbean condo adorning the walls. The room oozed comfort and peace and yet Richard felt anything but as he gazed down on a sleeping Pamela. The white down comforter was pulled up to her chin and a slight sheen of perspiration gave her face a waxy complexion.

Richard felt a wave of love and dread come over him. He slipped out of his shoes and crawled in next to her, pulled her close with one arm and buried his face in her neck. She moaned and stretched a little, turned away from Richard, and pulled his arm closer around her waist.

Richard awoke with a jerk, sweating himself, and jerked his head around to look at the clock. It was 11:00 PM Pamela was sleeping soundly, but apparently had been up. Her hair was still damp from a shower and she had changed into her sleep shirt. He kissed her tenderly on her cheek and slid quietly from the bed. After splashing cold water on his face and downing a tall glass of iced tea, he hunkered down to make his phone calls.

"Galen," Richard said as the Assistant Chief answered the phone, "sorry to call so late. Is there a list of everyone that was at the Pizza Shop the night the girls were drugged?"

"Sure thing Mr. Mayor. Hang on while I look in the file."

Richard screwed his fists into both eyes and yawned while he waited for Galen to come back on the line.

"Here you go," Galen said, then read Richard the short list of just six names. Two were young girls. The remainder, guys. One name in particular jarred Richard awake.

"Thanks, Galen," Richard said, "Have you made any progress with the inquiries?"

"I haven't found anything negative on the pizza man yet. He stayed out of trouble. He actually moved to Ganister because his wife's family used to live here.

Richard thanked Galen once more, hung up the phone, and immediately picked it back up to phone Bobby.

"Bobby, sorry it's so late. I need to run something by you. I met with Carmine Rizzo today. He claims neither he nor any of his people had anything to do with the dead pizza man. He also said he knew who did do it. On top of that he said the pizza man's death is related to the girls being drugged. He gave me a clue; the guilty person is close to the Chief. I wasn't sure what he meant by that, so I called Assistant Chief Farr and got the list of everyone that was in the pizza shop the evening the girls were drugged. Guess who was on that list?"

"Holy shit!" Bobby said when Richard told him, " But why? And why the pizza man?"

"Don't know the answer to that yet, but hopefully I will soon. In the meantime you steer clear of the Chief. I'm gonna' have the Assistant Chief keep checking around. I'll let you get to sleep buddy. Talk to you tomorrow." Richard hung up the phone. It was barely in its cradle before it rang. Richard picked up quickly, not wanting Pam to wake up.

"Mayor St. Clair," the Chief said, "since you want to be kept up to speed on all aspects of the investigation, I thought I'd give you a call. I want to show you something that just came up. Can you meet me at the quarry?"

"Sure," Richard answered, "When?"

"Fifteen minutes." the Chief said and the phone line went dead.

"Damn," Richard said to nobody and grabbed his coat. He hated to leave Pamela so late, but he was curious and needed this case to be solved. Minutes later he was driving toward the quarry.

Chapter 25

The evening air was chilly and Richard was grateful for the windbreaker he had slipped into before leaving the house. His car was still running, the headlights pointing to the top of the path leading down to the diving cliff and on to the water's edge of the quarry. Richard sat staring at the path with his car door open, wondering what this trip was all about. Richard looked at the Chief's car parked across from him and wondered if the Chief had actually found some solid evidence.

Richard found it hard to reconcile the beauty of this place with the crime that had ended here. Memories swam in front of him, dancing in the headlights of the car, making him feel lightheaded and nostalgic. His brothers and sister and father here with him on Sunday mornings. The "Blue Hole" his dad called it. Water so blue and so pure it was once considered as a possible water supply for the borough of

Ganister. The idea was scrapped due to overwhelming projected costs of running pipe. Richard learned to swim here. By accident. Richard was playing in the small, shallow area while his older brother swam close by where the ledge dropped off to about 48 feet. Richard heard his older brother begging his dad to throw him into the deep blue but Richard got grabbed instead. He remembered flying through the air, his dad yelling, "Oh shit, that was Richard". Richard hit the water hard and seemed to descend forever, holding his breath as the water got darker and colder. He kicked and finally broke through the surface before he ran out of air. his dad let out a whoop of relief, laughed and said, "Now would be a good time to learn to swim, Richard. Just kick your feet, put your arm out and pull it back, one after the other. You'll be alright. I'll come get you if you need me". So Richard learned to swim.

Now here he was, at this favorite place, and it seemed so sinister. He looked around cautiously as he walked slowly over to the path. He looked over the limestone walls and the deep water and sky. They were all black. The usually colorful scene was monochromatic, the bird calls gone and replaced by crickets and the call of the bullfrogs.

"Chief, it's Richard, you down there?"

"Down here, Mayor," called the Chief from below, "come on down."

Richard grimaced, not happy about trekking down that path in the dark. In dress shoes. With no flashlight.

"On my way Chief. Sit tight."

Richard began the shuffle down the path, sliding more than walking in the loose gravel. As he neared the end of the zone where his headlights aided his way, the Chief shone a flashlight on the path for him. Soon, he was at the dive spot standing near the Chief. There was someone else there, too. In the dark, Richard couldn't tell who. The silhouette was about the same height as the chief, skinny, and smoking. The tip of the cigarette burned a blemish into the perfect blackness.

"Chief? What's going on? What have you found? Couldn't this wait until morning?" Richard fired off without waiting for a reply.

"Well Your Honor, I really just needed to chat with you," the Chief spat the words with the same enthusiasm he spat tobacco juice.

Richard shook his head slightly in disbelief, and spat his response to the Chief, "We could chat in your office, Chief."

The Chief smiled without any sign of humor.

"Yep, that we could. But I don't think you understand the situation, and I thought you might get a better grasp of it out here."

"So there's no new evidence in the drowning murder?" Richard glanced around him and realized he was in a dangerous position. Nobody knew he was here.

"Mr. Mayor, you've become a pain in my ass. Just who the hell do you think you are?"

"What the hell are you talking about Chief?"

"I'm talking about you interfering in my job. I'm the Chief. I run this town. You're just a flash in the pan around here. You'll be gone in a few years. I'm here for good and I don't appreciate your interference."

Richard managed a chuckle.

"So, what? You brought me out here to beat the shit out of me? To persuade me to just let you do whatever you want?"

"Well, your honor, that's one way it could go. The other way is you could take a swim tonight." The Chief's head moved slightly to the side and Richard's gaze followed. He saw some objects on the ground, but they were not clear in the moonlight. Richard's mind filled in the details; rope, chain, cement blocks perhaps.

Richard jerked his chin toward the silhouette standing apart from the Chief.

"So, who's your mystery date, Chief?"

"That's my boy. You know him. In fact you've been having Assistant Chief Farr nosing all around about him." the Chief growled, "You got some nerve checking on my family. That's why your buddy Bobby is gonna' take the fall for the drowning."

Richard stood still, his back to the path and facing the water. The chief was facing him on his right and the mystery son was standing to Richard's left. For the second time in the last half hour, Richard's memory took control of his mind...

"Where you been, Richard?" his father asked before Richard even got through the front door of his childhood home.

Richard looked up into his father's eyes. His own eye was swollen and starting to color.

"Downtown," Richard mumbled.

"What were you doing downtown?"

"Just hangin' out," Richard answered. He figured a half truth was better than no truth at all. He had been just hanging out with his friends at "Mouse's", a little country store and one of the only places to go in the sleepy town. A fight between Richard and an upper classman ensued in the alley beside the store when the classmate followed Richard out, taunting him, threatening him because Richard had been awarded the older kid's position on the football team.

"Charlie, my barber just called me. Again, what were you doing downtown?"

Richard nodded but kept his head lowered.   Richard closed his eyes briefly. Charlie's Barber Shop was across the street from the alley. Charlie was dad's barber. And a good friend.

"I got in a fight." Richard answered quietly.

"Well, I guess it's time I gave you the rules on fighting. First rule on fighting, you don't ever start one. Got that?"

"Second rule on fighting, you don't ever back away from one." Richard looked up now, staring at his father in surprise.

"Third rule on fighting, they may be bigger than you or more of them than just you. While they're running off at the mouth, you hit them hard and fast in their most vulnerable point. Kick them in the nuts if you can. If they outnumber you, always go after the leader first. He'll be the one with his chest puffed out and his mouth running. Any questions?"

"No, dad."

"Good. Get in the kitchen, your mother's holding supper for you. And this talk it's between us, you don't share it with your mother. And that black eye of yours came from a doorknob."

Richard focused on the situation at hand now. Maybe he could lunge at the Chief and the son and knock the three of them into the water. Maybe one or both of them would crack their skulls on the limestone on the way down. Maybe. Unfortunately they were standing too far apart to grab them both. Richard didn't even know if he would make it to the water without hitting the limestone. It was dark; the cliff walls go down at an angle. Richard wished Bobby was here.

"Doesn't this seem desperate to you Chief? Luring me out here. Threatening me? What possible good could come from this," Richard asked quietly, careful to keep the panic out of his voice. Richard glanced over at the son's silhouette and saw a slight little red dot appear on it. Richard recognized it as a laser sight. Relief flowed through every cell in Richard's body.

"Chief, you don't think I'd be stupid enough to come out here alone, do you? You might want to check out sonny boy's new accessory."

The chief jerked his head to look at his son.

"What's goin' on here?" The Chief asked, his own voice rising in concern. The silhouette spoke for the first time.

"Dad what the hell's happenin'?"

"Just relax son. I'll take care of this."

The sound of a fast approaching car broke the tension of the moment and all three men turned to look up at the top of the gravel path as headlights came into view. Car doors slammed and several pairs of feet could be heard.

"What the shit is goin' on here?" Carmine Rizzo boomed.

"Glad to see you Carmine. It's Richard St.Clair."

"I know who it is. You and that fat pig of a Chief. I assume the skinny one is the fat pig's son. What I want to know is what your doin' on my goddamn property?"

Richard started a slow stroll toward the path.

"Well Carmine, I do apologize for trespassing," Richard said as he climbed the path toward Rizzo, "the Chief asked me out here to see some new evidence."

"That right?" Carmine asked.

The Chief had taken a step toward the path, his shoes crunching the loose gravel.

"Just stay where you are Chief." Carmine said, "now's a good time to sort all this out."

"What do you mean?" the Chief asked.

"I mean, you or your boy move Chiefy, and the kid gets it. That little red dot'll blossom all over his head. And then he won't have any head. So you two just sit tight. You, St.Clair, I'm gonna handle this now. I don't appreciate my granddaughter gettin' drugged. I don't appreciate gettin' questioned for a murder I didn't do. And I really don't appreciate my quarry bein' used as a garbage dump."

"How did you know anyone was here, Carmine?" Richard asked.

"It's my quarry. I know everything that goes on here. The farmer on top of the cliff? Terry? He keeps me informed. He saw the Chief and the skinny kid come. He saw them carrying the cement blocks down the path. So he kept watchin', see? What with the shit that's been goin' on here. Then he sees your car pull in and recognized you as our fearless mayor as you was gettin' outta the car." He poked Richard in the chest with a thick finger. "I'm kinda disappointed in you, St.Clair. Your old man woulda' figured this out long before now."

Richard looked at him, his eyes questioning.

"What did I miss, Carmine?"

"For starters, you or your Keystone Cops shoulda checked the county records and seen that I own this place. Would I dump a body in my own quarry? Whatta ya think I am? Stupid?"

Richard stared at Carmine. He hadn't even been sure Carmine knew this many words. The man had always kept to himself.

"And not one soul ever bothered to ask farmer Terry up there if he mighta' seen anything?" Carmine continued.

"Is there anything else you know that you want to share, Carmine?" Richard asked, "Like maybe why the Chief and his son felt the need to show me the quarry at night."

"That's the easiest one of all," Carmine answered, "his kid brings in drugs usin' the ambulances. His kid drugged my granddaughter and that other kid. Thinks he's gonna be some kind of big shit. But you know what?"

Carmine shifted his gaze and voice toward the Chief.

"You know what Chiefy? Your kid crossed the line. He shoulda never pissed with my family." Carmine turned his head and addressed his son-in-law.

"Whatta ya think we should do with that skinny-assed kid?"

A low gravelly voice replied, "the cement blocks are here, he's here, what say we just see how strong a swimmer he is?"

"Well as fun as that might be," Carmine replied, "Not in my quarry. Maybe we should just let Richard's pissed off friend take care of him."

"Who's the sniper, Carmine?" Richard asked, once again looking at the red dot on the silhouette's head, and thinking he may already know the answer.

"Your friend Bobby was more than anxious to stop by when I called him and told him how stupid you were bein'. He told me, all he ever does is pull your ass outta' the fire. That right St.Clair?" Carmine asked, amusement playing briefly over his face.

"Yeah, Carmine, that's about right. I just hope he has enough control to not squeeze that trigger too hard right now. His trigger finger gets antsy some times. Seems to have a mind of it's own."

"He's a pro, pros don't waste bullets on piles of shit." Carmine answered.

"So, Chief," Richard yelled down the path, "You want to make a statement?"

Silence.

"Get your asses up here," said Carmine. The demand was met by the crunching of gravel.

"Keep in mind, Chiefy, there's a crazy man over there with you and sonny boy in his sights. I wouldn't push my luck if I were you as long as that little dot is clinging to my kid's head."

Carmine turned to face Richard. "St.Clair," Carmine said in a low, authoritative voice, "think you can take over now without screwin' it up?"

Richard nodded although there was no solid evidence. Just opinions from Carmine and the Chief of Police as a suspect. Richard was sure he had an alibi lined up.

"Guess you and your boy better get back to town, Chief," Richard said as the Chief and his son got to the top of the path, "and I'll be making a few inquiries to substantiate Carmine's claims. "

"Thanks Carmine." Richard called out to Carmine's retreating back. Moments later Carmine was being driven away by his son-in-law.

Bobby appeared by Richard's side dressed in camoflauge and carrying his laser scoped rifle.

"Thanks, buddy," Richard said, giving Bobby a quick hug and longer handshake, "I'm glad you didn't take the shot."

"I thought about it. Just wasn't worth it," Bobby said.

"You want to follow me to the police station?" Richard asked.

"Naw, I'm going back to bed. You're on your own. Keep your eyes on those two. Don't do nothing stupid," Bobby answered then turned to go. He stopped after a few steps, pulled the rifle up to his shoulder and aimed at the Chief's car.

"No! Don't," Richard called out, but there was a slight popping sound as the rifle with a silencer on the end spit a bullet in the direction of the Chief's car. The driver's side mirror shattered and disappeared. The brake lights came on quickly and went off just as quickly as the Chief dropped the hammer on the gas pedal and shot out of sight and around a curve.

"Bobby. What the hell is wrong with you?" Richard spit out.

"Relax, that piece of crap isn't going to do anything. It was just a warning shot and he knows it. If I was serious his melon would have exploded all over the interior of his car. That wiseass needs to know that we know all about him and we ain't going to take his shit." Bobby responded calmly and casually as he lowered the rifle and walked away, disappearing into the darkness.

Chapter 26

      Chief Bollinger's pulse was accelerated as was his car as he sped away from Bobby Morrow's rifle. He had briefly considered stopping and confronting Bobby about shooting off the side mirror on his car. He reconsidered when he saw how casually Bobby lowered his rifle and took a few steps in the direction of the police cruiser. When Bobby and the quarry disappeared from view, the Chief's pulse settled and he replayed the evening's events in his mind. His lips formed a crude smile. He stuffed snuff into his lip, slowed his car a bit and cracked his window to let a little cold air in. *Yeah*, he thought, *those bozos are so sure they've got me by the short curlies. Right.*

      "Well, what do we do now, dad," the Chief's son whined.

      "Shut the hell up, I'm thinkin'." The Chief's son slid lower in his seat, crossed his arms and pouted.

      Chief Bollinger put his window down further and spit tobacco juice into the cold air. *So, a mafia kingpin accuses me of a crime*, he thought, *so what? Mr Mafia was gonna' trot into court to tell his story? Slim to no chance of that happening. And Mr. Big Shot Mayor may know what really happened. Could he prove it? I'll still take care of that bastard. Maybe I can't get him to the quarry again, but there are other places. Maybe use Your Honor's little wifey-poo as bait, maybe use that son of a bitch Bobby.*

      He glanced over at his pouty son staring out of the passenger's side window. *Little smart ass is too blatant in his activities, he would get caught. Time for a long talk with sonny boy here. Now would be a good time, but I need to come up with a plan first. Sonny boy may need to leave town, maybe leave the state for awhile. The Mayor may try to get a confession from my boy. My boy may talk if rattled enough. He's not the sharpest tool in the wood shed. Then all my hard work and my beautiful little empire would come tumbling down. The Mayor may go to the State Police with the information he already has. I could call in some favors for solid alibis. If something happened to the Mayor, it could throw the investigators off my trail and on to someone else's. Maybe big shit mafia guy. I can figure this out. It's gonna' be frickin' fine. Might even be fun.* The Chief threw more snuff in his mouth and smiled a juicy smile.

Chapter 27

Richard's mind was reeling all night long. He found if difficult to believe the Chief could be involved in something so blatant and his son seemed too stupid to put something like that together. Then again, Richard believed Carmine was telling him the truth. So, what now? Richard didn't have the ability to investigate. Assistant Chief Farr probably wasn't up to the task either. Investigating your boss, for Assistant Chief Farr would be difficult to say the least. Richard dialed the State Police.

"Detective Brown? Richard St.Clair, Mayor of Ganister, got a minute?"

"Mayor St.Clair, how is everything in Ganister? I've been following your excitement in the newspaper. What can I do for you?"

"If you've been following the murder, then you may know why I'm calling." Richard said.

"Let me guess, the Chief is in over his head but he doesn't want to lose face so he had you call for assistance."

"Almost."

"I heard through the grapevine the Chief thinks your buddy is a good suspect." Detective Brown said.

Richard smiled. A detective is always fishing for information.

"Well the main reason I'm calling is not to see if you can assist, but to see if you could take over the investigation," Richard said.

"Whoa!" Detective Brown quickly responded, "I don't need to step on anybody's toes."

"The thing is, Detective; an accusation has been made that the Chief and or his son may be involved. I'm not sure I can hand it off to Assistant Chief Farr because he may not be in a good position to investigate. Would you be interested?"

"Those are some serious allegations, Mayor, and if substantiated, the shit would really hit the fan. Let me check with the district attorney, and I'll get back with you. But you do realize that if I take over the case, the chips will fall where they fall. You may not like what I find out."

"Whatever direction it takes, we have to know."

"Alright Mayor, I'll call you back as soon as I call the District Attorney." Detective Brown hung up quickly while Richard held on to the phone pondering if he did the right thing. This could get real ugly for the borough.

The phone rang almost immediately.

"Detective Brown here, Mayor. I've been given the green light from the D.A.. I'll be taking over the investigation. I'll be there first thing in the morning. I'll be grilling the Chief, his son, and your friend Mr. Morrow first. Then we'll see where this thing goes."

"I understand Detective Brown. Just do what you have to do. We need to get this thing tied up here."

Richard hung up the phone again, closed his eyes for a moment and took a deep breath.

"Here we go," he mumbled.

Chapter 28

Bobby Morrow found his daughter, Carol, sitting on the edge of her bed crying. Crying, loud and hard. He crossed the threshold to her bedroom and sat beside her on the bed.

"Carol, what's wrong sweetie?"

"Dad, we need to talk. I've kept something from you. I thought it might not be anything, but now I'm scared." Carol managed to get out between sobs.

Bobby slid closer to her and put his arm around her shaking shoulders.

"Carol. You know you can tell me anything. You should know that I'm always here for you. You know that, right?"

Carol looked him straight in the eye. She took a deep breath before she spoke.

"Daddy, I missed my last period," she said and immediately started sobbing again.

It was Bobby's turn to take a deep breath.

"Any idea when this happened?"

"Gina and I lied." Carol said.

Bobby's voice and face hardened slightly.

"What exactly did you lie about, Carol?"

"The evening we got drugged, there was more to it than that. But Gina and I made a pact to never tell anyone. After we drank our cokes, and we both started to feel funny, Gina went to get something out of her car. Well, the Chief's son was there in his EMT uniform. He asked me if I was okay? I said no, that I felt strange all of a sudden. He said I should go with him out to the ambulance and he would give me something to make me feel better." Carol stared at her father until he nodded for her to go on.

"When we got in the back of the ambulance, he started to hug and kiss me. And the thing is, I didn't mind. I think I almost wanted him to do more. And before I knew what was happening, he was pulling down my jeans and my panties. He undid his belt and took down his jeans and underwear. Then we laid on the gurney and he slid his penis into me," Carol was stumbling through the story now, her face red and splotchy, and the tears still flowing.

"It was horrible, Daddy. It was horrible because I was liking it. I didn't try to stop him or anything. And then Gina was banging on the ambulance door and then she opened it. The Chief's son jumped up and then Gina laughed and pointed at him and said, "where'd you get that little dick?" and she just kept laughing. He yanked up his pants, dragged me up, pulled me up by my arms and yanked up my pants then shoved us out of the back of the ambulance, threatening to kill us if anyone ever found out."

She looked up into Bobby's face; she was holding on tightly to his arms, leaned in and put her head against his chest.

"Dad, I'm so sorry. But I can't stand that guy. I can't believe what happened, but I was hoping since he had just stuck it in me for only a minute that nothing would happen. How can I be pregnant? What am I going to do? How can I get through school?" Her sobbing intensified against his chest and he let her cry for a few minutes. Finally, he pushed her softly away to look at her. He kept his arms around her and his voice soft.

"If you like we will get you an abortion. Your mother and I can take you into Pittsburgh and have a really good doctor perform the surgery. There is no need for you to ruin your life over something that you had no control over. But why didn't you tell me sooner dear?"

"Because I was afraid you would do something to him. Not that I care about him, but I couldn't bear the thought of you going to jail for hurting someone."

Bobby hesitated.

"First we'll take care of you, then we'll deal with that schmuck."

"Please dad, I'm begging you, don't do anything you'll get in trouble for," Carol said, "Mom and I need you."

Bobby nodded slightly, kissed Carol on the forehead and left the room.

Chapter 29

Chief Bollinger was not surprised when Detective Brown of the State Police turned up at the Ganister Police Department early the next morning.

"Chief Bollinger," the detective said, staring intently at the Chief, "I'm sure you can anticipate my first question, but allow me to ask it never the less. Where were you on the evening the pizza shop owner was found at the quarry?"

"I was at home," replied the Chief, quickly, defiantly, but also calmly and in an accommodating tone.

"I am sure, Chief, that you, yourself, have heard that same response in answer to the same question many times. So can anybody verify that?"

"My wife and son."

"And, I'm sure, Chief, that of all the times you have heard that response, you were immediately suspicious?"

"Sure. What's your point?"

"My point is that, like you, the response makes me a little suspicious also. We both know that family will stick up for each other. Is there anyone else who may be able to corraborate your story?"

"Only the fact that the Assistant Chief called me here at home, after he had received the anonymous tip that the pizza man was swimming with the fishes at the quarry. As good as I am, I certainly can't be two places at one time."

"And you will also swear that your son was at home with you the entire evening?"

"Of course," the Chief said, smiling, "it was his night off from the ambulance."

"When you did arrive at the scene that night, did you immediately take over the investigation?"

"Of course," the Chief replied hesitantly, " This is a small department. I am ultimately responsible, not to mention the most experienced man on the force. So, yeah, you bet your ass I took over the investigation."

"And were you able to find any clues at the scene as to who may have committed this atrocity?" Detective Brown asked, still staring intently at the Chief.

"Look Detective, I know you think we're just a bunch of country bumpkins, but I know a murder when I see one. This guy didn't tie himself to a cement block, then tie his hands together, then throw himself out into the middle of the quarry. Even a nutcase can't do that."

"Again, did you find any evidence that may lead to the perpetrator?"

"Well, seein' as we can't pull fingerprints off a wet rope or cinder block and seein' as the victim is on the dead side and can't tell us who did what, all I have is circumstantial evidence at the moment." the Chief answered sarcastically.

"And what, pray tell, is the circumstantial evidence?"

"Detective, we have long suspected the victim of being a source of drugs in our community. And recently, that is the establishment where the Morrow girl appears to have procured some drugs. So we feel sure it was drug related and..."

"When you say 'We', Detective Brown interrupted, "whom are you speaking of?"

"I mean 'me'. Of course, the Assistant Chief agrees."

"And so along that line of logic, do you have any suspects?"

"First in my book would be Bobby Morrow," the Chief answered, "he's overly protective of his daughter, and probably has the means. Everyone knows he was a big shot war hero in 'Nam."

"Anyone else Chief?"

"Well it certainly fits the Mafioso mold, doesn't it? Maybe this guy was cutting in on old Carmine's turf. He sure looks like another good suspect to me."

"Can I have a look at all the daily patrol sheets from the evening before the incident to about a week after?"

"Sure," agreed the Chief.

"Including yours, Chief?"

"I got nothin' to hide. I'll get them all for you."

"Thank you."

"Anything I else I can do for you detective?" the Chief asked in his most obliging tone.

"Just one thing; your son. Is he working now or where can I find him?"

"Yep, he's workin'. You'll find him over at the ambulance station."

"And I assume when I ask him the same questions I asked you, I'll get the same answers?"

"Guess you'll have to ask him the questions and find out. Don't see why the truth would change none," the Chief answered.

Detective Brown slipped into his well-worn overcoat and turned toward the door. He put his hand on the door knob but looked back over his shoulder.

"By the way, Chief, I'll be obtaining a warrant to look over yours and your son's bank records."

"Good then you can tell the Mayor I need a raise since I don't earn shit around here."

It was a short drive to the ambulance station and soon Detective Brown was facing a basic concrete block building painted white with a large metal garage door and a small entrance door next to it.

The detective entered and stood before a small glass window with a hole cut in it to speak through. A young bleached blond sat behind the counter, chatting on the phone and snapping her gum. Her eyes caught the detectives but she turned slightly to the left and kept talking and chomping. Detective Brown rapped his knuckles on the glass. The blonde rolled her eyes and hung up the phone.

"How rude! What do you want?"

The detective flipped open his badge and slapped it against the window.

"What I want is you to let me in. Now," he barked.

The blonde pushed the buzzer which allowed the door on the detective's right to unlock and he entered. Facing her now he announced, "I'm here to see Chief Bollinger's son. Where is he?"

"Oh my god, what did he do?" she asked in surprise.

"Nothing you need to be concerned about. Where is he?"

"Probably in the garage. When the guys are not out on a call they usually hang around back there doing guy stuff."

"Thank you. You have been most helpful," he responded sarcastically. But the blonde smiled warmly.

"Oh you're so welcome," she cooed, "I always help policemen."

The detective rolled his eyes and headed toward the back. The guys were indeed doing guy things. Drinking soda, telling dirty jokes and in general just wasting time.

"Which one of you is Billy Bollinger?"

A tall, thin wiry guy telling the jokes looked over at the detective.

"Me, who's asking? No, wait, let me guess. Your Ed McMahon and I just won the publishers sweepstakes. Did you bring me flowers? My check?"

"You dad didn't mention you were a stand-up comic, Billy," Detective Brown said, humorlessly.

"How would he know? He couldn't laugh if you paid him to. Way too uptight." Billy said, looking at the other guys in the station and laughing.

"I'm Detective Brown. Pennsylvania State Police. You and I need to go somewhere private and have a little chat."

"Here's cool detective. My bud's don't mind." Bill said, jerking his thumb over his shoulder at the other guys.

"I mind. Come with me."

Billy rose from his perch and as he walked toward the detective he held his wrists together in front of himself. Grinning and talking loud enough for his audience to hear he said, "Don't you wanna' cuff me detective? After all I'm a bad dude." Everyone in the station, save the detective, laughed.

"I don't think I'll need to. If you give me any shit, I'll just shoot you." Again, everyone in the garage laughed, except for the detective. And Billy. Billy's pace picked up and he suddenly looked serious as he followed the detective to the State Police car.

"Get in the back," Detective Brown demanded. He then began the line of questioning he would use over and over.

"Billy, where were you the night the pizza shop man was killed?"

"I was at home with the old man and my mother. We were watchin' TV."

"And can anyone confirm that?"

"Well, yeah, the old man was right there next to me on the sofa. What are you askin' me for?"

"I'm asking a lot of people. Sometimes to eliminate suspects, sometimes to get more suspects."

"Well why would I want to off the pizza man? He's got the only good pizza in town! Man, I hate the thought of driving fifteen miles just to get a decent slice of pizza." Billy said, smiling. He looked around but there was no audience.

"Ever take any drugs, Billy?"

"What the hell does that have to do with anything?" Billy snapped.

"Just asking? Well do you?"

"None of you damn business. Look, you asked me where I was, I told you. Are we done here?"

"You got a girlfriend Billy?"

"You're pretty nosy aren't you? Why do you wanna' know?"

"Just curious, do you?"

"Not at the moment. Why? You got a daughter that needs lookin' after?"

"You're a funny guy Billy. Guess the reason you had to stay home and watch TV with your old man was because you can't get a date," the detective said with a smile.

Billy flew forward on the rear seat and smacked the wire partition in the police cruiser with both hands.

"What's your problem man? I can get a date anytime I want one," Billy spat, his spittle lit up like ice flakes on the wire.

"So you have a steady girlfriend?"

"Not at the moment," Billy said. He relaxed and sat back against the seat.

"I'm between women, know what I mean?"

"Who was the last one, Billy?" the detective asked his voice calm and steady.

"Not that it's any of your business, but I was datin' Jill Jenson."

"That's the gas station guy's daughter?"

"Yeah, so?"

"So, how come you two are not still dating?"

"I didn't want to be tied down." Billy quietly replied, looking down into his lap. All his bravado seemed to be gone.

"Thanks for your time, Billy. You can go now." Detective Brown got out of the car and opened the back door for Billy.

Billy left the police cruiser and lit a cigarette before he went back into the garage. The guys were watching and waiting as he entered.

"Dumb as only pigs can be. Can't figure anything out for themselves. They got to come to me for help to find the killers," Billy said, smiling once again for his audience. His audience laughed.

Detective Brown stopped briefly at the gas station.

"Mr. Jenson, Detective Brown of the PSP. Got a minute?" he asked, offering his hand.

"Sure, detective," Mr. Jenson answered, offering his own hand in return. The two shook briefly, "What's up?"

"Your daughter used to date Billy Bollinger?"

Mr. Jenson rolled his eyes and blew out a disgusted breath, "Yes, she was rebelling. The more we told her she couldn't, the more she thought he was the best thing since sliced bread."

"They still see each other?"

"No way! She finally wised up."

"Anything in particular happen between them that you know of?"

"Well yes, but I'm really not comfortable telling you about it."

"Maybe I could speak with your daughter, then?"

"I'd just as soon you didn't." Mr Jenson said. He removed his cap, scratched at his scalp for a moment, slid it back on and continued, "She said he was completely into drugs and he tried to force himself on her once. My daughter's a good girl, detective. She's still a virgin. She insists she will be until her wedding night. Her mother and I have no reason to doubt her."

"She tell you anything else about the drug use?"

"No. Only that he always had a lot of money to throw around. I think that's why she dated him, in fact. They used to go to all the fancy restaurants. Hell, her mother and I can't afford to go to those places."

"I may need to speak to her in the future, Mr. Jenson."

"Well I'd just as soon no one even mentioned that bum Bollinger's name to her, but she's a good girl. If you need to talk to her she'll talk to you."

The detective smiled, nodded and offered his hand again, "Thanks Mr. Jenson. Have a good day."

Detective Brown jotted down a few more notes before heading across town to Bobby Morrow's dental office. The office was housed in an old Victorian style house and had become a dental office only after being the home of one of the founding families of Ganister and then, the local mortuary.

Detective Brown approached the receptionist sitting behind a sliding window. It opened immediately when he reached the counter.

"Yes, do you have an appointment," the bright-eyed smiling receptionist asked.

"No I'm afraid not, I just came to see Mr. Morrow."

"I'm afraid you'll need to make an appointment, he's rather busy today." she responded through a set of perfect teeth and with a slight cock of her head showed how disappointed she was for the detective.

Detective Brown flipped open his badge and placed it directly in front of the receptionist.

"Please tell Mr. Morrow that Detective Brown of the Pennsylvania State Police needs to speak with him," the detective said in a low, confidential voice.

The smile disappeared quickly from the receptionists' face.

"I'll let him know right away sir," she said, jumping up quickly and sliding the glass window closed. Detective Brown watched her retreating back before sitting down and settling on a magazine. Within minutes, the side door opened and Bobby Morrow appeared, his eyes searching the waiting room full of patients.

Detective Brown stood and nodded slightly toward Bobby.

"Detective, please come in," Bobby said pleasantly. He led the detective to his private office, offered him a seat and took his own seat behind a well-organized desk.

"What can I do for you, detective?"

"Just doing some legwork on a case. Need to ask you some questions."

"I'm happy to help you, detective, but I do have a waiting room full of patients. Do I need to rearrange my schedule?"

"I don't think we'll be more than a couple minutes right now."

"Good," Bobby responded, "Let's get started. The Mayor told me you may stop by."

"I assumed he would. You and the Mayor good friends?"

"No. We're best friends. We met in the military. Spent all our time in 'Nam together. Been best friends ever since."

"Okay. So the evening the pizza shop owner was found in the quarry.."

"The Blue Hole," Bobby interrupted.

"Yes, the Blue Hole, that evening, where were you?"

"Well I was at a lodge meeting early that evening."

"What time was that?"

"We start at seven o'clock. It's about a thirty minute ride from my place. The meeting ran till around ten o'clock. Richard, the Mayor, and I hung around and shot the bull for another fifteen minutes, then I went home."

"I assume someone can vouch for you."

"Sure, there were probably two dozen guys at the meeting, they all saw me and there is no slipping out of there."

"Why is that?"

"Because in the Lodge, we go into an inner room, when the Master calls the Lodge to order the door is locked behind us and stays that way until the Master calls the meeting closed. The only way out is to have the Pursuvant knock on the door and the Tyler on the other side of the door has to unlock it."

"After you left the lodge meeting, you went directly home?"

"Sure. That's my time to spend with my wife and daughter. We watched a little TV, then my wife and I went to bed and I read for a little while."

"And the Mayor was at the Lodge meeting the whole time also?"

"Sure, he has to be, he's the lodge secretary."

"Okay," the detective said, standing, "Thank you Mr. Morrow; I won't take up any more of your time right now. I may have more questions for you later."

Bobby stood also, handing the Detective a business card, smiling.

"Here's my card. Feel free to call me anytime. And by the way, when was the last time you had your teeth cleaned?"

"Been a while," the Detective said, smiling back at Bobby, "Maybe I'll call and get an appointment once this investigation is over."

Chapter 30

Chief Bollinger drove over to the ambulance station full of determination and a sense of urgency. He pulled up to the garage door and honked the horn of the police cruiser. The garage door started up and the Chief saw a group of young men standing there looking out. He motioned to his son who walked to the passenger side of the cruiser and got in.

"What's up dad?"

"You and I have to talk, Billy"

"About what?"

"The time has come for you to leave town," Chief Bollinger answered in a low, serious voice, his eyes never leaving those of his son.

Billy shook his head slightly and barked a quick chuckle.

"What are you talking about, man? I can't leave town! I got a great business going here."

"Yeah, well I can't protect you anymore. And if that detective digs any further he's gonna' come up with some things that you won't be able to explain away."

"But, I've been careful, just like you said, dad."

"Well, Brown has already talked to that Jenson girl and a couple of your buds. Trust me, this guy is good. He'll put it together like a hundred piece jig saw puzzle and I won't be able to help you. You need to go stay with your sister in Florida for awhile. There's a motorcycle repair trade school there. It would be the perfect reason for you to leave town. A little career change."

"But dad," Billy said, whiney now, "I make good money here. Lots of money. I ain't gonna' just give that up."

The Chief swung around in his seat to face Billy and forcefully grabbed his shoulder. When he spoke again, his voice was dangerously low and his words measured.

"Look, son, your friend from California already has the mayor and council suspecting me of all kinds of shit. If you get connected to drug running I'm done in this town. Correction, I'm just plain done. Now, be a good boy and go pack your bags."

He let go of Billy's shoulder and knew he had gotten through. Billy Bollinger jerked away, snarled and climbed out of the cruiser.

Chief Bollinger watched him walk back into the ambulance garage before blowing out of the parking lot.

Chapter 31

The gavel cracked loudly down on the oaken black, sounding nearly like a gunshot. The wielder of the gavel stood tall and erect, immaculately dressed in a black tuxedo with crisp white shirt and black tie.

"Gentleman," the well-dressed Master spoke, "I now declare this master masons lodge closed. Please inform the tyler."

With that, the other gentlemen, all in dark suits, arose and moved towards the now open door. Richard and Bobby were among the first to leave and once outside the meeting room, conferred quietly

. "I've learned quite a few things recently," whispered Bobby to Richard, "first of all, would you like to take a guess at who spent time in Aruba the same week you and Pamela were there?"

Richard jerked his head toward Bobby, but managed to keep his voice low, "Who?"

The other lodge members were streaming out of the meeting, but neither Richard nor Bobby made eye contact with any of them, instead remaining huddled close together and speaking quietly.

"My sources tell me the Chief's son had just got back from there just about the same time you did and with a new sunburn. So I asked if he had any tattoos. Seems he has two snakes on his forearm curled around a pole."

"That son-of-a-bitch," Richard hissed, "you think he's the one who attacked Pamela? Think he targeted her? Knew who she was?"

"I wouldn't doubt it, Richard. Small town. Seems he's also sportin' some new jewelry. An old coin necklace that he came back from the beach with. Wears it on a chain around his neck."

"I'll kill that bastard. That was my father's coin. When he passed away, it was given to me. I didn't know at first what it was until I met Steve Littman in the Caribbean. He's a jeweler from Philadelphia that now lives in the islands. He assured me it was a Brazilian Rial. He even gave me the approximate year and value for it. It's worth a lot of money, so I had in mounted on a necklace and gave it to Pamela. It was torn off when she was attacked. Pamela was more upset about losing the coin than being attacked."

"Now that we know where it is, buddy. How about I go get it back for you?"

"I appreciate that Bobby, but this is something I want to take care of myself. I'm gonna' fix that little bastard good."

Bobby placed his hand on Richard's shoulder.

"Listen to me, Richard, before you do anything. There's more. Billy is without a doubt, trying to be the big drug dealer in town. I'm making arrangements now to have him taken down for that with the feds."

"So, you're finally admitting to me, your best friend, that you're on the fed's payroll?"

"I'm not admitting anything, but you know I'm not going to let him run free and do any more harm to my girl. He picked the wrong girl to mess with, and the only reason he's not already six feet under is because I promised my family, and I promised you I wouldn't go after him. This is different. I'll gladly watch his skinny ass being carted off to prison."

"Bobby, don't make any calls just yet. I intend to get Pamela's necklace back first. After that, he's all yours."

"Hey, Richard, Bobby, you guys going to join us for some strawberry shortcake, or are you guys gonna pow-wow all evening?" Richard turned his head as he heard Roger Thompson who was coming from the kitchen area.

"Yeah, Roger, we'll be right there," Bobby responded.

Richard had already decided he would go home early, but the thought of strawberry shortcake made him hesitate. *Just a quick bite,* he thought, *strawberry shortcake and good news for Pamela. This night just kept getting better and better.*

Chapter 32

Ganister was just a small town. Small, old fashioned, quaint. The main road heading into town was State Route 866 which became First Street when it crossed the borough line. When First Street met High Street, the main business district, the intersection was still controlled by only four way stop signs. There were no stoplights in this borough. At least once a year, the question of adding a stop light was brought to the Borough Council. The Council always referred to the state survey showing the number of vehicles passing through the intersection and the costs that would be involved in adding a stoplight. The installation and ongoing costs of the electric bill could just not be justified.

There was a Speedz convenience store with gas pumps on the northeast corner of this intersection. Speedz started as a mom and pop, or more specifically, pop and sons operation and had grown over time to become a standard in Pennsylvania towns and even crossed into a few other states. The stores, once small brick buildings selling only necessities such as cigarettes and milk grew into inexpensive gas stations with convenience stores selling everything from sandwiches to novelty lighters. All the stores sported large bright red awnings over the gas pumps with the bright white Speedz logo.

Richard was at pump number two pumping high test gas into his Volvo when he saw Chief Bollinger's son in a car packed to the gills drive down High Street and make the turn onto First Street, heading out of town.

Richard felt the blood rush into his ears, leaving only rage and a roaring sound when his heart slowed a bit.

"Hey Billy!" Richard yelled at the top of his lungs, "Billy, you get back here." Richard watched Billy turn his head, look at him, flip him the bird and speed away, still smoking without missing a beat.

"Son-of-a-bitch," Richard spat. He immediately hung up the gas nozzle, quickly screwed the gas cap back on and jumped into his car, squealing the tires as he raced off after Billy. Richard was out of the borough before he caught sight of Billy and went into full race car mode to close the gap between them. He watched the apexes of the turns to carry his speed through the turns, tires squealing. Richard's speed and rage carried the blood through his body quickly enough to make his head pound and his heart race, but his mind was processing thoughts even quicker. *I'm gonna catch the little bastard*, Richard thought, *I could run him off the road easy with just a gentle nudge on the rear corner. But, Billy the kid might get killed that way. I only want to kill him if I can wring his scrawny neck with my bare hands.*

Just a few miles later Richard was right on Billy's bumper even though Billy was furiously trying to fend him off, spending more time driving in the middle of the road then in his own lane. Richard sped up a little and gave Billy's bumper a gentle tap. Just to let him know he was there and that there was no escape. Richard knew how to get Billy to stop; fake coming around one side then cut back the other way and get alongside him, preferably in a turn. The Point View Bridge was coming up in less than a mile and there was a left hand turn on the far end of it. Having practiced his race car skills on that bridge, Richard could tell by headlights if anyone was coming in the other direction. Plus most people didn't go screaming over that bridge at full tilt. Richard wasn't most people.

As the two cars approached the bridge, Richard saw Billy's brake lights flash briefly. Richard made his move. His newer Volvo had little in common with the former square boxes of earlier models. The new and improved Volvos were turbocharged and had great weight distribution allowing for excellent drivability and with great speeds. Richard made his fake and when Billy moved to the right to keep Richard from passing, Richard sped right around him. As soon as he got in front of Billy, Richard hogged the road forcing Billy to slow down. Finally Billy pulled to the side of the road. Richard quickly placed the Volvo in park, pulled on the parking brake and jumped from the car.

As he marched up to Billy's car, Richard pulled out the small Charter Arms 38 special he had been carrying ever since receiving the death threat on the phone. Billy just sat behind the wheel of his car, looking straight ahead, his fingers white knuckled on the steering wheel. Richard tapped on the side window with the gun barrel.

"Put down the window," he demanded.

Billy turned his head to look at Richard, his face white as a ghost and when he spoke; his voice was a few octaves higher than normal.

"What the hell is wrong with you man?"

"You and me are going to talk, now wind down the goddamn window," Richard replied in a voice that demanded compliance. Billy did as he was told, his hand shaking and sweat gathering at his temples.

"My old man is gonna' hear about this. You're going to be in some serious trouble, man," Billy said in an unsteady voice.

"You're going to answer my questions, so just shut up and listen," Richard started, just stopped cold when he saw the sun glinting off the gold chain around Billy's neck. Richard grabbed it with his free hand and jerked it roughly from Billy's neck, breaking the links of the chain.

"You little bastard, this is my wife's Brazilian Rial necklace, where the hell did you get it?"

"Uh, a friend of mine found it and gave it to me," Billy answered after a few moments hesitation.

Richard nodded then shoved the short cold steel barrel of the 38 harshly into Billy's forehead.

"Think about your next few answers carefully 'cause they may just be the last words you ever speak," Richard spat.

"Now, again, where did you get the necklace? You were in Aruba, yes?"

"Yes, yes," Billy sputtered, his hands up in surrender, his voice pleading as he continued, "I took it from your wife, but, I swear I had no intention of hurting her."

Again, Richard nodded and pushed the barrel of the gun just a little further into Billy's forehead.

"Next question, where do you get the Rohypnol?"

Billy looked surprised, but answered without hesitation.

"From the ambulance suppliers."

"And you slipped it to the Morrow and Rossi girls?"

"Yes, but nothing happened, I swear."

"Where are you heading now?"

"My dad's making me leave town. I'm going to stay with relatives in Florida. Please. Please don't hurt me." Billy pleaded, sweat running between his blood shot eyes. Sweat, tears and snot running down his nose. They offered the only hint of color on his otherwise pasty white face.

"Change of plans, Billy-Boy. You're gonna' go on back home and tell your daddy we just had ourselves a little conversation. Then tell him to call me, got it?" Richard shoved the pistol even further into the white skin of Billy's forehead, pleased to see a little round bruise forming there. Then he walked away from a weeping, shaking Billy, holstered his pistol and strode back to his waiting Volvo.

"Pussy," he mumbled under his breath. The image from the old John Wayne movie jumped into his Richard's head, where John Wayne said to the bad guy, "I ought to hit you. But I won't. The Hell I won't!"

That was all it took for Richard to march back to Billy's car.

"Now what?" a dejected Billy asked.

"I almost forgot, this is from Pamela." Richard shot the open palm of his left hand hard into Billy's nose. Blood flew everywhere.

"Damn," Billy screamed in obvious pain.

"You should have never touched my wife!"

Richard turned and walked casually back to his car.

Chapter 33

"Colonel," Bobby said when the phone picked up after the first ring, "It's Bobby Morrow. I need to report a situation."

"What's up, Bobby?" the colonel asked in his usual low, businesslike tone.

"I was watching one of our subjects tonight, the Chief's son. I figured if Detective Brown put any heat on the Chief or his son they might do something."

"And, so did they?"

"It appears the Chief was getting Billy out of town. I watched them load his car with far more things than anyone would take on a vacation, so I hung with him. I lost him at the edge of town 'cause I passed him so he wouldn't suspect a tail, figuring I could pick him up again down the road a little piece. Since we now have enough on him to bust him for dealing drugs, I thought I better bust him before he left town. At the same time, I wanted him out of the borough away from daddy's protection."

"Are you sure the witnesses you have will testify against him?"

"I'm sure, Colonel. Plus, I have witnessed nearly every aspect of this thing. He drives the ambulance once a week out of the borough to make the drug pick up. Then he brings it back to town, at taxpayers expense and sells it to the locals. They feel safe buying it since they all know he's the Chief's son."

"Yes, but don't forget we want to catch some bigger fish."

"I have no doubt I'll be able to get him to rollover on whomever he buys from. Then we'll just keep working our way back up the line. But I first need to get him on ice. So, when he didn't show, I doubled back. Found his car off the highway down in the bushes."

"What did he do? Wreck?"

"Not exactly. He's dead, all right, though. Someone put two new holes in his head. Double tapped. "

"No shit! Did you see anyone around the area? See anyone leaving?"

"No sign. Whoever did him, made quick work of it. Got him stopped. Somehow. Offed him. Then disappeared."

"Well," the colonel said, "I won't say they didn't do us a favor. Apparently he stepped on some toes, you know what they say, payback's a bitch."

"Yeah, but I sort of wanted to do that piece of shit myself. After all, it was definitely him that raped and drugged my daughter; then he tried to attack Richard's wife. But first, I wanted this drug supply chain shut down."

"So the Chief is aware his son is dead? Will he be snooping around?"

"He'll know any minute now. As soon as the car accident is reported, the ambulance will be rolled, and rest assured, they will notify the Chief right away."

"Will the Chief be investigating? Is the 'accident' within his locale?"

"The accident is outside the borough so the State Police should be handling it, but, you know how cops stick together. Plus, I'm sure he'll do plenty of investigating on his own."

"Maybe you need to check into Billy Boy's death a little closer. Check for DNA on the body. Try to find a passerby witness. But, be careful Bobby." And with that, the phone line went dead. Bobby wasn't offended. It was the colonel's trademark. When he's done talking, he's done. No goodbyes. No catch you laters. No kiss my ass. Just a dead phone line.

Chapter 34

A chill passed through Richard's body. "A goose just walked over your grave" his grandmother would have said. He clasped his hands tighter together in front of himself and wondered why funeral homes were always freezing cold. He had stood at attention in numerous funeral homes since the time he was a young boy. His grandfather died at a young age, then his grandmother, followed by Richards' favorite uncle and immediately after that, his sister. The St.Clairs learned about death at an early age. Still, he never got used to the cold. It bothered him even more than the overwhelming aroma of competing flowers in small spaces.

Richard jumped slightly when a hand landed on his shoulder. He turned.

"Bobby. Thanks for coming buddy."

"Richard I am so, so sorry. I thought after the operation they had gotten all the cancer. I can't believe Pamela is gone. I'm just so sorry, Richard. Is there anything we can do for you?"

Richard shook his head, fighting back tears as his eyes moved from Bobby to Bobby's wife Claire and his daughter Carol. Richard felt guilty at the jealousy he felt for this intact family as the women took turns giving him hugs and kisses on both cheeks. Finally they moved on toward the casket while a stream of people stopped to shake Richard's hand and offer condolences. After a while, Richard moved forward himself to gaze upon his newly departed wife. She still looked beautiful, her red hair perfectly made up like she'd have wanted. *Didn't even have a chance to lose her hair*, he thought. Bobby came to stand beside him.

"She looks lovely, Richard."

"Yeah, but she doesn't look like she's sleeping. You know, people always say the dead look like they're sleeping. But they're wrong. Even with the make-up, she's so pale, so still."

The two of them stood silently for a moment, looking down at Pamela in her new dress and her favorite Brazilian Rial necklace. Richard caught Bobby's head spin quickly to look at him but Richard didn't respond. Instead, he turned slowly away from Bobby, shook some more hands and offered himself up for some more hugs.

Soon, Claire and Carol Morrow left after stopping once more to speak to Richard. The three of them hugged and cried. Then the women slowly let go of Richard and made their way toward the exit of the funeral parlor. Little by little, Richard's friends left. Bobby stayed behind until the visiting hours ended and he was alone with Richard.

"Richard," Bobby said, as he approached Richard once again, "anything I can do? Anything at all?"

"No. Thanks."

"Do you want me to drive you home?"

"No. I've got my car. I'll be alright."

"I think we should talk, Richard."

Richard finally let go and started to sob.

"I can't believe she's gone, Bobby." he managed between great bursts of tears, "I can't believe she's really gone."

"I know Richard. It's not fair. She was a lovely person. A good person. Fortunately, you got to spend quite a few years with her."

"I am thankful for that Bobby. But what will I do without her?"

"You go on Richard. She would want that. You think about all the good years you had with her and you move on."

"Just not sure I want to go on without her, Bobby."

Bobby was silent for a few moments and Richard felt the heat from Bobby's eyes warming tiny spots on his cold face.

"Listen, Richard," Bobby finally said, not unkindly, "Now's probably not the right time, but I need to ask you something."

"What Bobby?" Richard asked, returning the heated stare.

"I saw that Pamela was wearing her necklace."

"Yeah, I was able to get it back for her. A parting gift, you could say."

Again Bobby hesitated before continuing.

"How did you get it back Richard?"

"Not here. We'll go to my place and talk."

They took their separate cars to Richard's house. Richard couldn't speak for Bobby, but he sure didn't feel like making small talk. They arrived within seconds of each other and Richard unlocked the door and stepped inside. The silence was overwhelming and the chill in the house complete. Richard had never really known what the term 'emptiness' meant. He knew now. It meant no Pamela to snuggle up to at night. It meant he was now really, truly alone, Pamless. It meant no tinkling, musical, Pamela laughter. No Pamela ever again. No Pam. No Pam. No. Pam. His trance broke as Bobby spoke and the tears began to roll once more.

"Richard, I know this is a horrible time. I don't mean to bother you, but this could be really serious. How did you get Pamela's necklace back?"

Richard turned slowly and looked Bobby in the eye. He felt angry, but resigned. Restless, but exhausted. He turned his tired, red eyes toward his friend.

"Since you told me the Bollinger kid had it, I've been keeping tabs on him. I was filling up my car at Speedz's when I saw him go by. I yelled at him and he shot me the finger and hellfire shot through me. I chased him down, made him stop his car. I tapped on his side window with my 38 Special and he rolled it down. I jammed the revolver into his forehead until I had his attention, until I thought he might wet his pants. I knew he was scared shitless, but I didn't give a damn. I asked him some questions and he admitted attacking Pamela. He admitted slipping the drugs to the girls. I ripped the necklace off his neck and I left. That what you wanted to hear Bobby?"

"Richard," Bobby placed his hand on Richard's forearm, "Did you kill him?"

"What?" Richard wasn't sure he had understood the question.

"No, Bobby, I didn't kill him. I wanted to. I wanted to so much. He deserved it. He raped your daughter, he attacked my wife. My now deceased wife," Richard said, stopping to take a deep breath. "I wanted to, but I didn't. I knew we had him, he was going to go to jail. So I let him live."

"You didn't try to shoot him?"

"No, Bobby. I just told you! I jammed my pistol into his forehead, left a nice round bruise. That's all! I never laid a hand on him. Well, I might have broken his nose just a little."

"How do you break a nose just a little?"

Richard lowered his eyes and landed on the floor near a chair and on the corner of a book Pamela had been reading. Again his eyes welled with tears.

"I hate this house Bobby," Richard said changing the subject.

"No, you don't. You and Pamela loved this place and put so much into fixing it up all special with all the beach stuff and everything. This house is full of memories of all the good stuff."

"It's not good anymore. It's cold and lonely."

"Richard, you gonna' be alright here tonight?"

"Sure, I'll be okay. You go on home. Spend some time with Claire."

"Man, I hate to leave you all alone."

"Appreciate it. You need to to go home. I'll be ok."

Bobby nodded slightly, sighed in resignation.

"All right. You call me if you need anything, buddy. I'll see you in the morning before we go back to the funeral home."

Richard smiled, let Bobby out and closed the door behind him. As Bobby's car backed out of the driveway, Richard dropped to his knees, covered his head with his arms in retreat and sobbed.

Chapter 35

"Get the pistol. End this misery." the voice inside was saying.

Richard felt conflicting voices urging him in polar opposite directions. The presence of two such large voices inside his already overcrowded and aching head was too much to bear for long. One voice saying finish it. The other saying no. His frustration grew. A frustration he had never before encountered.

He sat on the edge of the bed and reached into the nightstand where he kept his small Charter Arms 38 pistol. He slid it out of the weathered brown leather holster and held it in one hand. Stared at it. Rubbed his calloused thumb up and down the wood grip and the cold steel barrel. Cold like Richard had never felt, cold that reached deep into his tortured mind and curled icy fingers straight into his soul. He pushed the release with his thumb and stared dumbly at the five full metal jacket bullets. They were waiting for him to make a decision. He clicked the magazine shut. Touched the cold steel again. Felt the icy fingers again. They were somehow comforting, soothing, like a cold beer can against your cheek in 100 degree heat.

"Be a man. Do it."

Richard now had the barrel jammed against his chest. The barrel, cold enough to pass through his thin shirt, again offered him odd comfort.

"Do it. What is there to live for? Enough of this shit. You've done everything in this life that you wanted to. Why stick around. One too many of everything; disappointment, pain, loss. What is there left to live for without sweet Pamela?"

Richard jammed the pistol harder into his chest. Held his breath, clinched his eyes shut, pulled back on the hammer.

The voices were whispering to him feverishly. Do it, don't. The pleading so passionate he could swear he felt hot breath against both ears.

Richard was shaking now, sweating and crying large hot tears that left a stain on both cheeks that could have come from hot springs. His roaring mind grabbing onto the thought that it would all be over in just a fraction of a second. No more anything. No more pain and heartache. No more Richard. And the comforting thought that it would be better for everyone. That the time had come.

"Just do it. Do it. All that's left is to pull the trigger. Just the slightest pressure. Just a millimeter of an inch. Do it."

Richard bolted up on the sofa, sweating, crying. The recurring dream more real than his own sick reality. Richard wrapped his arm around his new best friend, his new lover, and sunk deeper into the sofa. Most nights were spent with this new friend, this poison in a bottle that would comfort him through the night. He wiped the snot from his nose and jerked his head up when he heard a hot metallic click. Like the sound of a hammer being cocked on a pistol. He looked down at his hand, the one not gripping the whiskey bottle, just to make sure he wasn't holding his dream pistol. When he looked back up, he just made out a figure standing in the weak morning light. A figure standing in his doorway, holding a pistol pointed right at him.

"What the hell are you doing here?" Richard slurred.

"You killed my son you bastard."

"Like hell I did. What gave you an idea like that?"

"His paint is smeared all over your front bumper. Tell me, Richard, did you really think you could get away with this?"

"Yeah, I stopped him. Yeah, I bumped him with my car. Yeah, I sure did want to kill his punk ass. I wanted to so bad I could taste it. But I didn't kill him."

"Don't believe you, Your Honor, no doubt in my mind you're responsible for his death."

"That rotten son-of-a-bitch deserved to die. He raped Carol Morrow. He attacked my wife. So yeah, I wanted to blow what few brains he might have out the back of his skull. But I didn't."

"And I'm just supposed to take your word for it? You wanted to so bad, but didn't?"

"I don't give a shit what you think, Chief," Richard said, rising from the sofa and striding up to the Chief. When

his nose was almost touching the Chief's, Richard stopped. He stared at the Chief, grinding his teeth, and in a loud, not quite steady voice continued, "You here to arrest me Chief? No? Didn't think so. You want to shoot me, Chief? Go ahead, be my guest. I don't give a shit. Suicide by cop is my favorite anyway." Spittle appeared on the Chief's face and Richard was pounding on his own chest, growling now, "Come on, asshole. Come on! Coward!
Shoot me."

The Chief lowered his pistol and took a few steps back. Richard closed the space between them and shoved the Chief, screaming now, "Come on! Come on! Do it! Do it! Whattaya waiting for coward?"

"Drop the gun Chief." said the calm, authoritative voice of Detective Brown from behind the Chief.

"Drop it now, or I'll drop you." demanded Bobby Morrow. There were two guns trained on the Chief.

"Stand down, Chief," Detective Brown spoke again in a voice not to be ignored.

The Chief turned his head and Richard grabbed his gun, twisting it from his hand and shoved him backward once more. The Chief tripped, went down hard on his back. Richard stood over him, pointing the Chief's own gun at his head.

"Richard ," yelled Detective Brown. "put the gun down, now."

Richard looked over at Bobby who offered him a single nod. Richard threw the gun down, striking the Chief and drawing blood from his temple.

The Chief sat up, ran his hand over his temple, and stared at the blood on his fingertips.
His eyes never left Richard, but when he spoke it was to the Detective.

"Detective Brown. I'm glad you're here. I came to arrest the Mayor for the murder of my son. There are paint marks on the front bumper of his car that I know will match the paint from my son's back fender. He as much as confessed to me that he had a gun to my son's head."

"I'll look into it Chief."

"I want that son-of-a-bitch to fry," the Chief continued, "he killed my son."

"Chief, the feds appear to have built a case around your son for the delivery and distribution of drugs."

The Chief looked over Detective Brown's shoulder and for the first time acknowledged Bobby Morrow.

"What the hell is he doing here?" the Chief asked.

"Chief, Mr. Morrow is an undercover federal agent. He has proof against your son," Detective Brown answered.

"Bullshit," the Chief declared, "he's the Mayor's friend. The Mayor's accomplice. Hell he probably helped the Mayor kill my son. Now that he's dead, they just want to use him as a scapegoat."

"There's more, Chief," Detective Brown stated, "I have a federal warrant for your arrest."

Bright red splotches crept up the Chief's face. He looked at Detective Brown, his eyes uncomprehending, scared, angry.

"What the hell is going on here? He's the one needing arresting," he screamed, pointing at Richard.

"Come on Chief. Don't make this any harder than it has to be. You are under arrest for the murder of Guido Pacelli, the pizza man, for harboring a fugitive, for knowingly allowing your son to sell drugs in the borough you're sworn to protect, and now, for breaking and entering and possibly threatening bodily harm to the Mayor."

"Get outta' my house, Chief," Richard barked, glaring at the Chief, "I can't stand the sight of you no more."

The Chief stared at the floor looking beaten and tired. Tobacco juice dripped from his mouth.

"I sure as hell didn't kill my own son. That son-of-a-bitch there done it," the Chief declared in a defeated voice.

"He killed my boy," the Chief continued, his voice lower now. His face crumpled, appeared to cave in on itself as he fell to his knees, on top of the gun Richard had thrown at him.

"Gun," Bobby yelled.

Both Detective Brown and Bobby fired at the Chief. As the smoke and cordite smell cleared Detective Brown walked over and rolled the Chief over with his foot. In the Chief's right hand was the service revolver, hammer cocked, ready to roll.

Bobby felt the Chief's neck for a pulse. Nothing. He nodded at the detective and Richard.

Richard was the first to speak, "Guess Teflon doesn't protect like it used to."

Chapter 36

Richard stood unsteadily at the top of the quarry, at the very edge. He stared down into the Blue Hole, memories and visions swirling together, causing him to become dizzy, even more unsteady on his feet. They were all beautiful, the memories, the visions. Richard's father smiling and laughing, swimming in the deep blue. Richard and his siblings splashing around, joking, learning all they needed to know about life. About relationships. About beauty and about companionship.

And beautiful Pamela under the moonlight at the top of the quarry. Lying on a blanket and counting the stars while making plans for her wedding and for her life with Richard. Kissing Richard on his neck and giggling. Wrapping her long,

long legs around him and moaning when he licked her nipples and slipped a hand under the elastic of her panties. The slight chance they would be caught by some adventurous teenagers bringing both of them to a quick, satisfying release.

And now the state of his soul was like that Blue Hole. Cold, bottomless, emotionless. Richard sucked the last of the whiskey from the bottle and swung it into the quarry. He watched it sink into the deep clear blue water. Richard pulled his revolver from the holster, considering the idea of a little target practice. He snorted to himself, at himself. His father's voice whispered in his ear, "Come on, Richard. Man up, pull yourself up, and dust yourself off. Get on with it, you're a better man than this."

Richard jumped slightly when a heavy hand fell on his shoulder. For a moment he thought it was his father. He turned quickly to see Bobby standing behind him.

"I never even heard you, man. You're like a cat," Richard said.

"What's up? You planning a long walk off a short pier?" Bobby asked and patiently waited for Richard to speak.

"The booze isn't working. It doesn't lessen the pain one iota."

"So you have a plan B?"

"Pamela had a directive asking for her ashes to be scattered in the Caribbean Sea in Aruba. Immediate plan B is to board a plane."

"Then what?"

Richard shrugged and turned his head once again toward the water.

"Well at least you have a short term plan B." Bobby replies, "But when you get back, there's still one loose end to tie up."

"What's that?" Richard asked.

"Someone shot Billy Bollinger."

"Figured it was you, Bobby."

"Wasn't me, you said it wasn't you. Hard to commit suicide and pull the trigger the second time."

"Bobby, watch my lips" Richard stated, "I don't care anymore. Let Chief Farr figure it out."

Bobby was silent for a few moments. He stared at Richard.

"Richard, until the killer is caught, you'll be a suspect."

"Still don't care. Couldn't have happened to a better guy."

"Look, Richard, I care. First of all, I don't want people thinking my best friend did this. Second your political days will be over. And third, I report to people who demand answers. So far, the only one reported leaving the scene was you."

"Sure, I was there. But, how many people wanted to kill Billy Bollinger? Me, you, Rizzo, Rossi, Gina, Carol, screwed over drug buyers, probably a bunch more."

"Let me take your gun in and run ballistics on it, then. Just to rule you out."

Richard turned and stared at Bobby.

"You want my gun?"

"Yeah, to rule you out as a suspect."

Richard slowly pulled his gun from the weathered holster at his waist. He held it out, studied it. It had been his father's and Richard had acquired it after his father's death. He turned toward Bobby and held the gun out. As Bobby reached for it, Richard changed directions and threw the gun far out into the Blue Hole.

"Richard, what the..."

"I told you I didn't shoot him and I've never lied to you. Now it's just another secret the Blue Hole will keep."

"Richard," Bobby said in an exasperated tone, "you're making it damn hard for me to believe you are innocent!"

"Bobby, a wise old man once told me, 'Never kick a sleeping dog.'"

"What the hell does that have to do with anything?"

"Why can't you just believe me, when I tell you I didn't off the piece of shit."

"I want to," Bobby answered, "but you're sure showing all the signs of hiding something."

"Bobby you're my best friend, and again, I tell you, I have never lied to you. That should be good enough."

"It's good enough for me. But it won't be for everyone else."

"Bobby, that gun cannot go through ballistics."

"Why? If you didn't shoot Billy Bollinger, why?"

"Do you remember what Carmine Rizzo said the first time we went to see him?"

"I don't remember anything about your gun."

"He said, my dad did favors for him. Nothing specific, and I have no idea what kind of favors he was talking about. But, just in case, my dad's gun will NOT be going through ballistics. End of story."

Another Blue Hole

Chapter 1

Richard St.Clair ambled into the Ganister Police department. Assistant Chief Galen Farr who was sitting at the Chief's desk reading the newspaper, with his feet comfortably on the desk, jumped to his feet when the intruder entered, dropping the newspaper onto the open box of doughnuts and nearly spilling the steaming cup of coffee.

After a brief hesitation, Assistant Chief Farr spoke, "Mayor, you alright?"

"Yeah, why?" came the response.

Galen Farr hesitated again. The reason for his confusion was the man standing in front of him. Richard St.Clair was wearing several days worth of facial hair, sloppy blue jeans, a wrinkled shirt, and hadn't appeared to have combed his hair in days. His normal appearance would have been quite the opposite. Normally he was clean shaven, sporting a button down shirt with colorful necktie and khaki pants. And his hair would have been combed.

"You look different, Mayor," was all the Assistant Chief could say.

"Yeah, whatever," Richard began, "you look like you're making yourself at home at the Chief's desk."

The crimson color spread across Galen's face as he appeared to be looking for an answer, however, Richard didn't give him time to speak as he continued, "look, raise your right hand and repeat after me."

The Assistant Chief did as he was told and raised his hand. "I solemnly swear to uphold the laws of the United States of America, the Commonwealth of Pennsylvania, and the Borough of Ganister. I will do nothing to tarnish the position of Chief of Police of Ganister. So help me God." After the Assistant Chief said the words, Richard St.Clair tossed him a gold badge, "Congratulations, you're the new Chief of Police." Galen Farr stood quietly admiring the gold badge, then rubbing it vigorously against his shirt to bring out the shine, "Thank you, Mayor."

"Listen, Galen, I'm leaving town for a few days. Don't do anything to embarass me. Don't do anything to cause me any grief or make my phone ring. Okay?"

"You can count on me, Mayor," the new Chief stammered as he took off his old silver badge and pinned on the new gold one.

"Where are you going Mayor?" Galen inquired.

Richard looked down towards the floor and responded in a hushed voice, "Pamela's will stated her ashes were to be put in the Caribbean Sea. I must honor her wishes."

Richard's wife Pamela had recently passed away following a brief struggle with cancer which she unfortunately lost. Ever since then Richard had been lost. He had considered suicide but couldn't follow through. And to date he hasn't been himself, floundering around like a fish out of water.

As Richard turned to leave, the new Chief said to him, "Mayor, since I'm the new Chief, I feel my first act must be to close the Billy Bollinger case."

Billy Bollinger was the son of the previous Chief of Police. Billy was being watched closely by state and federal authorities as an integral player in the distribution of drugs in the small town of Ganister. Billy worked on the ambulance crew and would pick up drugs in the ambulance out of town then bring them back to town and sell them. The Chief knew his son was soon to be arrested so he arranged for him to leave town and go to Florida to live with a relative. Richard saw Billy leaving town, followed him, and gave his a car a little tap driving Billy off the road. Billy was eventually found with two bullet holes in his forehead. When Mayor St.Clair was questioned by Chief Bollinger and the state detective, he admitted pushing Billy's car off the road. He also admitted placing a gun to Billy's forehead but not pulling the trigger. Plus he admitted to giving Billy a bloody nose. All this was done because Billy had attempted to manhandle Richard's wife Pamela on a beach in Aruba after dark and stealing her favorite necklace in the process, making a mistake or two and having Richard find out about it. The Chief learning of the events and especially regarding his dead son, knew exactly who he wanted to see put in jail, that being his own boss, Mayor Richard St.Clair. The Chief broke into Richard's home early one morning on the pretense of arresting him and ended up getting himself shot by Detective Brown of the Pennsylvania State Police and federal undercover agent, and best friend to Richard, Bobby Morrow.

So the case of who killed Billy Bollinger has been languishing ever since.

"You probably should," replied Richard.

"Then Mayor, I will need to ask you some questions," Chief Farr responded.

"I have already been questioned. You can read the report."

"But, I really feel I should personally interview you, Mayor."

"And you can. When I get back from the Caribbean," the

Mayor stated as he again turned to leave.

"But,.."

But it was too late as Richard closed the door behind him leaving a dumbstruck new Chief of Police staring after the closed door.

Galen gathered his thoughts after a moment and sat back down at the desk. This time not putting his feet up on the desk as it now was his desk. He opened the drawer, pulled out the manila folder marked, Billy Bollinger, and began to read through each page. First was the interview with Richard St.Clair. All the routine questions were asked and the answers appeared very believable. Just as Galen turned to the next page, he was hit by a thought, "there was never any ballistics test done on the Mayor's gun." He quickly flipped through the papers to the Coroner's report. Two holes to the forehead at very close range as evidenced by the powder burns. Two slugs were removed from the headrest of the vehicle. Both slugs were 38 caliber. Chief Farr had been with Mayor St.Clair on several occasions when the Mayor had his gun with him. He carried a snubnose 38 revolver. And yet, no ballistics test on the gun to rule him in or out. "There's a loose end," Chief Farr said to himself. Going back to the papers right after the interview with Mayor St.Clair, he found an interview with Bobby Morrow. Bobby was the Mayor's best friend, the local part-time dentist, and as everyone now knew, a federal undercover agent. Apparently Bobby Morrow had come along after Billy's car had crashed and he stated that the victim had already been shot. Chief Farr now wondered about two things. One, it's quite a coincidence that the Mayor's best friend comes along, and , two, what kind of gun does he carry? No answers in the report. "Another loose end," Chief Farr says to himself again.Then there is the Coroner's report. No other persons interviewed? The ambulance responded, who called that in? No copy of the 911 report. "Another loose end," Farr said to himself, "this thing has more holes in it than swiss cheese."

Chief Farr began plotting his agenda. He would interview Bobby Morrow. He would get the 911 tapes. He would go to the scene of the crime and see if there could have been any other witnesses. And, yes, as soon as the Mayor gets back, he will re-interview him. "Probably should have never left him leave town," he said to himself, "damn!"

Chapter 2

Bobby Morrow was a very early riser. Not necessarily because he wanted to, but because he had problems sleeping ever since his tour in Vietnam. That was where he and Richard St.Clair became such close friends. They were advance operations personnel trudging through the jungles of Vietnam risking death every minute they were there. Bobby managed to amass quite a few medals for his acts of bravery, but now he paid the price. The sleepless nights. So he was up early letting Duke, his huge hunk of a dog out for his morning ritual when his phone rang. One look at the number glowing on the screen of the cell phone and Bobby understood who would be calling at this early an hour.

"Colonel," he said.

"Bobby, I have a new assignment for you."

"What's up, Colonel?"

"We have a man in Bonaire, in the Netherland Antilles, Clint Armstrong."

"Yes, I know him. He served with Richard and I, and Richard and Pamela used to go each year to Bonaire snorkeling. Then one year my wife and I went with them and we ran into Wildman Armstrong."

"Yes, well, he's dead," the Colonel said with bit of a hiss in his voice.

"I'm sorry to hear that, Colonel."

"So's his wife. I want the bastard that did this. I want you to deliver him to me, dead or alive."

"What sort of operation was Wildman Armstrong running?"

"If you've been to Bonaire then you know that it is a haven for divers and snorkelers. Clint Armstrong's cover was he ran a dive operation but unlike the other ones on the island. The resorts there take divers to many spots around the island but all on the leeward side of the island. Wildman Armstrong took divers to the wild side of the island, where the sharks play. Where it's dangerous. He enjoyed it and even made money at it but most importantly it put him right where we needed him. The drug cartels in South America run drugs by boat up to Curacao and Bonaire then get them onto planes to go into the US. Armstrong was making some real inroads into finding us the source of those drugrunners. Now, suddenly he shows up dead. I don't believe in coincidences. Take care of this Bobby!"

The phone went dead. Bobby stared at the cell in his hand for a moment then pressed the end button. "Guess I better pack my swim suit," he said to himself.

He was about to call out the door to his dog Duke when the phone rang again.

"Yeah," he said into the phone.

"Mr. Morrow, this is Chief Galen Farr of the Ganister Police Department."

"Chief? Galen when did you get promoted?" Bobby asked.

"Just a minute ago. The Mayor came in and swore me in then left me with the Billy Bollinger case to complete," Chief Farr responded.

"Well, Congratulations, Chief," Bobby told him, "what can I do for you?"

"I need to re-interview you as part of the Bollinger case."

"Sure. No problem. I'll call you as soon as I get back into town."

Chief Farr was feeling anxious about the lack of respect he seemed to be getting so far, "I need to talk with you today, Bobby."

"Sorry, government business. I'm heading for the airport."

"But....." Bobby Morrow had already hung up the phone. For the second time this morning Chief Farr was left talking to himself.

Bobby Morrow turned his mind to Wildman Clint Armstrong. They first met right after Bobby and Richard had traversed around the Parrots Beak from Cambodia into Vietnam, where Richard nearly got shot, except Bobby had been keeping an eye on him and was able to shoot the North Vietnamese who had Richard in his sights before the North Vietnamese could pull the trigger. After that they ran into Wildman Armstrong. He was a most impressive person, built like a wedge. A big wedge. He stood probably six foot three with broad square shoulders, a small waist and arms the size of most men's legs. His short buzz cut blond hair and the girly tattoo on his bicep that he liked to make dance as he flexed his muscles. Wildman knew no fear and never lost a fight to anyone, until Bobby came along. Wildman wanted to be sure Bobby and Richard knew their place when they met up with him so he let it be known that he was the man. Bobby, having been fed up with soaking wet clothes, jungle rot growing on his feet, and the lack of a good meal was in no mood to listen to Wildman, so he walked right up to him, stomped on his foot, and when Wildman leaned over to grab his foot, Bobby smacked him on both sides of his head at the same time, with open palms, nearly bursting his ear drums. The bewildered Wildman was left staring blankly at Bobby who grabbed Wildman by the back of the head and rammed that head into his rising knee. Wildman dropped like a sack of potatoes. Bobby sauntered off to find some dry clothes, and Richard just stood there smiling. No one else felt any desire to challenge the Wildman so he continued to rule the roost, but he did respect Bobby from that point on. They became very good friends, and after the war, when the Colonel called Bobby to do some undercover work for the federal government, Bobby recommended Wildman Armstrong also be approached. Richard was approached but he turned the Colonel down as he no longer felt the need for the excitement like Bobby and Wildman.

Chapter 3

Chief Galen Farr grabbed the keys to the squad car and left the office for the 911 station after making the call to the judge's office to arrange for the warrant he would need to get the 911 tapes. After arriving, he had to ring the buzzer and produce his badge to gain entry. The security at the 911 center was at a very high level. Chief Galen Farr then sat with an operator and listened to the tapes from the day that Billy Bollinger was shot.

The first call in was from a man who refused to give his name stating that there was an automobile accident along Route 866 and the ambulance needed to get there quickly. After a few minutes there was a second call in. This time the caller identified himself, "there is a dead man in a car on Route 866 approximately 2 miles west of the Ganister borough line. Sir, can I have your name came the 911 operator's response. Bobby Morrow. Please send the ambulance right away," and the line went dead. Galen now had confirmation that Morrow was at the scene, making him even more of a suspect than before. And who was the first caller. Galen thought he might know the voice but so far no name was popping into his head. "Thank you," Chief Farr said and left the 911 center.

On his drive back to Ganister he stopped by the exact spot where Billy Bollinger's car had been off the road. He slowly turned his body looking outward to see if any homes were within viewing distance that might produce a witness. Just one. Up on the small hill was the home of Mrs. Geuring. She was a widow that had lived there for quite a while and everyone in Ganister knew her.

Galen drove up to her house and knocked on the door.

"Mornin' Mrs. Geuring," Chief Farr said when she answered the door.

"Well Good Morning, Galen," she replied as she smoothed back her gray hair with her right hand, "what brings you out this way?"

"I wanted to see if ...."

Mrs. Geuring interrupted, "Oh pardon me, where are my manners? Please come in, Galen. Would you like a cup of coffee?"

"Well, thank you ma'm, don't mind if I do," Galen said as he entered the house and closed the squeaky screen door and wooden outer door behind himself.

Mrs. Geuring led him straight to the kitchen table and poured him a cup of coffee. Then she topped off her cup and sat down, "please sit!"

Galen sat and unable to resist the aroma coming from the steaming cup, took a long drink.

"Mrs. Geuring....."

Again she interrupted him, "Galen, just call me Grammy like everyone else."

"Yes, Mrs. Geuring, uh, Grammy. Anyway, I'm trying to solve the case of who shot Billy Bollinger right down there on Route 866 just a few months ago."

"Oh, that was terrible. Nothing like that has happened out here before that I can remember."

"Did you happen to see anything Mrs. Ge..,uh, Grammy?"

"Well as it happens, I spend a lot of time sitting in my lazyboy. Here come along. I'll show you."

Grammy led Galen into the living room and next to the extremely clean window was a well worn green leather lazyboy recliner. "This is where I spend most of my time. The light is so good and I like to read," she said.

Galen, standing next to the recliner looked out the window, across the highway and there it was, the exact spot where Billy Bollinger's car had been pushed off the road. "So Mrs. Ge......, Grammy, did you see the accident happen?"

"Well, I don't believe I would call it an accident."

"That nice shiny blue car, it was such a pretty color blue. Anyway that car ran right into that old junk heap of Billy Bollinger's and pushed it right off the highway. Then the blue car pulled in front of the other one and a good-looking man jumped out of the blue car and ran back to the old one. He was yelling, and you could tell he was really mad at that Billy. You know that good-looking guy looked sort of familiar."

"Did you hear any shots, Grammy?" Galen asked.

"No, they just yelled at each other," she said, "then the good looking guy went back to his car, got in, then got back out again. I guess he forgot something. Then it looked like he hit Billy in the face and this time he went back to his car and took off in a hurry. The stones were flying and his tires were squealing when he left. It sure was a pretty blue car. Blue's my favorite color you know," Grammy said as she looked up at Chief Farr.

"Did you see anything after that?" Farr asked.

"Well sure. I hadn't had that much excitement since the kids left home, so I just kept watching."

"Did you call 911 or anything?"

"Oh no, I don't like to get involved, and it just looked like a little disagreement."

"Then what happened, Grammy?"

"Well, let's see. I need to keep these things in order." Grammy rubbed her chin while she looked out the window and appeared to be thinking. "Oh, I remember," she blurted, "that silver car was coming down the road, like from Holidaysburg? And he stopped on the other side of the road. He ran over to Billy's car."

"What happened then, Grammy?"

"Well, I had to go to the bathroom. All that excitement, I guess." Grammy blushed.

"What was the next thing you saw?" Chief Farr asked.

"Well, when I got back from the bathroom, the silver car was gone and I saw an old red pickup truck coming that same way pull off, and he ran over to Billy's car. He looked familiar too! I know I've seen him somewhere, but the old eyes just aren't what they used to be. Anyway, he ran over to Billy's car then it looked like he was talking on one of those new little phones that everyone is getting. The kind that doesn't need to be hooked to a line. I just don't understand how those things work. It's just amazing the new fangled things that people have these days..."

"Mrs. Geuring, did you hear any shots when the guy in the red pickup was there?"

Grammy rubbed her chin again, "No. No, he just talked on his new fangled phone then he was sitting in his truck till the ambulance came along. Would you like some cookies? I baked them fresh just yesterday. I have a bit of a sweet tooth, you know."

"No, thanks, Grammy. But just so I have this right, you didn't hear any shots?"

"No, I don't remember any. Of course it could have happened when I was in the bathroom. With that noisy fan on in there you can't hardly hear yourself think straight. But, then, sometimes you can't stand to be in there without the fan on," she nudged Chief Farr with her bony elbow. "Know what I mean?" she asked with a smile on her face.

"Yes, I know what you mean," Chief Farr replied.

Chapter 4

Bobby Morrow spent his time on the flight to Bonaire just
relaxing, reading and watching the onboard movie, knowing
that once he got on the island there would be no time for those
things. Everyone gaped out the airliner windows as it made
its final approach to Flamingo Airport oohing and aaahing as
the plane came in low over the sea where the locals and
tourists at Windsock were enjoying the water and weather.
The Caribbean Sea was the most brilliant hues of blues and
greens and the expressions on everyone's face was that of
sheer joy and excitement while in the back of their head some
probably wondered if they needed to lift their feet to keep
their toes dry. It looked like they may take the roof off the
small truck passing just beneath them on the highway, and
just on the other side of the highway was the beginning of the
runway. The soft touchdown and short taxi to the terminal
was followed by the wait while they wheeled the stairs to the
door. This was not the normal modern airport where the plane
pulled right up to a gateway. This was Bonaire. When the
door swung open and the heat swept into the plane, Bobby
knew he was here. Carrying his bag down the steps and
across the tarmac to the customs and immigration area, Bobby
began to relax as the sunshine combined with the tropical
breeze filled with lovely smells made him relax. The only
thing missing was his wife and his flowered shirt.
Bobby was able to get through customs and immigration
quickly and step outside the terminal. Across the small
parking lot he saw several small car rental buildings; one story
concrete white buildings each displaying a different car rental
company sign covering all the major companies and then a
couple local companies like Island Rentals and Caribe Rent a
Car. Bobby went to the Budget store and picked up a compact
car making sure to get all the insurance they offered. Just in
case. He had been known to return a car with bullet holes in it.

After a quick drive to the Divi Flamingo resort, he checked in, stowed his bag in his room, and immediately struck out for Wildman Clint Armstrong's place.

Bobby put the windows down in the little compact car and started down J.A.Abraham Boulevard toward downtown Kralendijk. There was no need to run the air conditioning as the tropical breeze felt just perfect. Bobby enjoyed the slow drive and turned onto Kaya Simon Bolivar then onto Kaya Korona looking for the small sidestreet and making a right turn onto Kaya Pappa Comes. There a few houses from the corner was the home of Clint Armstrong. His boat and trailer were parked across the street and his Harley Davidson bike could be seen inside the concrete wall that surrounded each home. Clint's home, like so many others here in Bonaire was a yellow stucco one story building surrounded by a yellow stucco wall with flowering shrubs sticking above the top of the wall. Bobby parked the small rental car and rang the bell at the gate. A smiling Matty came out of the home dressed in her customary flowered, flowing sarong, her long blonde hair blowing in the breeze. Any other man's heart would begin racing but Bobby was the epitome of monogamous. Matty and Bobby hugged and Matty invited him in to her home. The walls were covered with photos of fish and birds of the island as that was Matty's passion. She led Bobby out onto the covered open air patio, offered him a seat and went back into the house for two tall dripping iced teas.

"I'm sorry to hear about Clint," Bobby said.

Matty looked away then turned back with tears in her eyes, "I'm sure going to miss him."

"Can you talk about what happened, or is it too soon?" Bobby asked her.

"All I know is what the police have told me, Bobby. They said he was found on the beach. Shot." The tears were now streaming down Matty's cheeks. Bobby didn't press the issue.

He knew he would get this and more from the Bonairean Police so there was no need to put Matty through anymore heartbreak.

"Is there anything I can do for you Matty?" Bobby asked in his earnest sympathetic voice.

"No, I'll be all right. Clint had some life insurance and for years he and I had talked about me opening a studio downtown so we could sell artwork to the cruise ship people."

"Sounds like a good idea."

"I already found a nice two story studio with large glass windows on the front. I repainted the outside and have it almost ready to go inside," she said, "I've needed to stay busy."

"Well you certainly have the talent."

"Yes, but most of the photos were taken when I accompanied Clint on his diving excursions. We worked really well together. So the studio is also sort of a memorial to him since it shows off a lot of his diving and all the sights he saw." Matty's faced seemed to brighten a little with the memories.

"I'm sure you'll do well Matty. Your underwater photos are spectacular and your paintings of Bonaire and the reef just can't be beat."

"Thank you Bobby. You'll have to stop by before you go back home."

"I will. I promise. In the meantime, I've kept you from your work long enough, I need to go. I just wanted to stop and pay my respects," Bobby said as he rose to leave.

Matty walked Bobby to the door and gave him a hug goodbye.

While Bobby was glad that he made the effort to stop and see Matty it also reminded him that he was a few thousand miles away from his lovely wife Claire. He felt an urgency to getting to the bottom of Clint's death so he could get back home to her, so Bobby got into the dusty little compact and headed into Kralendijk to the Bonaire Police Department just off Kaya

Simone Bolivar.

When he arrived there, he went into the small over air conditioned office and up to the counter. There was a lady in uniform manning the counter that asked what she could do for him.

"Can I speak to the Captain, please?" Bobby asked.

"May I say who is inquiring?" she asked Bobby while watching him intently.

"Bobby Morrow, from the states."

The small dark Bonairean lady went to a closed door behind her, knocked gently, then entered. She came back and opened the half door so Bobby could enter, "follow me please."

Bobby followed her into the same office after she again made a quick quiet knock on the door then led Bobby in. The Captain was also a short Bonairean. Older, wrinkled from the years of exposure to the sun, with short cropped slightly graying hair and neatly dressed in his light blue uniform shirt with dark blue shorts. The shoulder patch on his shirt was the Bonairean flag with its yellow, white and blue diagonal fields, representing the sun and sea, and the compass in the corner with the word Policia under it.

"Mr. Morrow, I'm Captain Craane. How may I be of assistance?" the Captain asked while offering a firm handshake and a friendly but controlled smile.

"First, Captain Craane. I am required to give you this letter of introduction from my employer," Bobby said as he handed the Captain a crisp white envelope with the White House picture and address on the upper left hand corner. The envelope was already neatly typed to the attention of Captain Craane, Bonaire Police Department. The Captain motioned for Bobby to have a seat while he returned to his seat behind his desk, sat down, and opened the envelope. After he studied the letter he looked over at Bobby, "your President would like me to consider it a personal favor to have you look into the death of Clint Armstrong," Captain Craane said slowly while intently studying Bobby.

Bobby just smiled and waited.

"Is there a particular reason that your government would be so interested in the death of a man here on our island?"

"He was a war hero, sir," was all that Bobby said.

"Must have been quite a hero for the most powerful man in the free world to take such an interest."

"Some in our country value the contributions made by our veterans, and in particular one who had received so many awards for his distinguished service as Mr. Armstrong."

"While I can appreciate that," Captain Craane went on, "the President of the United States has sent you," the Captain studied Bobby some more, "and I cannot help but wonder if there is more to his death then just a war hero dying."

Bobby took his time in answering, "not to my knowledge, Captain."

"Did you bring any firearms into our country, Mr. Morrow?"

"No. Captain, I didn't. First of all it would have been too hard to get onto the airplane, and more importantly, my President would not permit my breaking your laws. After all, I am a guest in your country."

"Well Mr. Morrow, you may have my permission to make your inquiries as long as you do not break any of our laws and that I stay completely informed about your progress."

"Thank you Captain Craane. I will be happy to let you know anything that I may find out. I would like to ask one favor of you, if I may?"

"What would that be Mr. Morrow?"

"Could I see a copy of the police report and the autopsy report?" Bobby asked.

"You may look at them here. You may not copy them or remove them. Would that be sufficient?" Captain Craane offered.

"That would be most sufficient Captain. I thank you for your assistance and I know the President thanks you as well."

With that Captain Craane spoke quietly into his phone. Immediately the door to the Captain's office opened and the young lady came back in to escort Bobby to another even smaller office with just a desk and two chairs where he waited patiently for the information while he studied the corners of the room trying to guess where the hidden cameras may be. After a few minutes the door behind Bobby opened and the young lady laid two file folders in front of Bobby, "just come out the door when you are finished, please," she said and immediately withdrew.

Bobby opened the top folder and began reading. Clint had been found around midnight on the beach at the boatramp just of Lac Bay. His body lay on the beach on his back, next to his loaded boat. There was one gunshot to his lower abdomen. No signs of struggle. No weapons found on the deceased. He was found because an employee of the nudist colony next door thought his vehicle had been parked there an exceptionally long time after he had earlier driven by and saw Clint loading the boat. No one saw any other traffic in the area, and, naturally, there were no witnesses. Clint's watch and wallet were still on his body. His expensive diving gear appeared to all be in the boat.

Bobby next picked up the second file and read the coroner's report. Not much new there either. Clint had bled to death following a shot to the abdomen. A .38 slug had been removed that was wedged into his spinal column. No other cuts, bruises or abrasions, and there did not appear to be any self defense items like skin under his fingernails.

Bobby thought about the reports for a minute. Robbery was not a motive, and Clint obviously was not threatened by whomever approached him. But then, Clint was a big, bad dude, on an island where the locals were much smaller people. Bobby did make a mental note to check on the location where Clint's body was found; was this a normal place for Clint to go out diving or fishing. Also, was it normal for Clint to be alone or should he have been accompanied by others. After all, he was doing diving tours of the wild side. This would be the wild side, but did he normally go at night or in the daytime. Bobby knew that night diving was a big event here on the island as different fish and reef creatures came out at night like lobsters, shrimp, tarpon and a host of others. Bobby carefully closed the two reports and left the room. He handed the reports to the young lady, waited for her to confirm that they were all there then left the cool building behind and entered the heat of the day in Bonaire. Bobby's shirt was instantly damp as he fished around for his sunglasses to not only protect his eyes but to allow him to quit squinting against the brightness of the lower latitudes. Unfortunately Bobby was going to have to speak with Matty again about the location of his body and if he should have been there, plus if he should have been alone. Also, Bobby was going to need to check with the Colonel to find out a little more about Clint's undercover work and to know if his being near Lac Bay was related to that or not. So many questions, so little time. For now, Bobby would drive out to the spot below Lac Bay and see if any clues jumped out at him. Plus lunchtime was closing in and there was a fabulous little shack at Lac Bay called Jibe City where ice cold beer and great sandwiches were always available while you watched the windsurfers hone their skills. Richard had taken Bobby and Claire there on numerous occassions as it seemed to be Richard's favorite lunch spot. Of course, Bobby remembered teasing Richard that it was Richard's favorite lunch spot because it was next to the nudist colony and occassionally they wandered out past the high wooden fence strutting their stuff in search of that all over tan with no swimsuit lines. The drive over to Lac Bay was a fairly quick one and it felt good to let the tropical breeze blow through the car while he sped along the narrow highway being careful to look for iguanas sunning on the road or flamingos crossing the highway. The locals really frowned on turning their flamingos into roadkill.

Bobby parked in the dusty gravel parking area and made his way across the sandy patch to the bright colored wooden structure that called itself a lunch spot. The small palm limbed roof offering not only protection from the sun but sucked the tropical breeze through. The entire structure looked like it was made from driftwood and items found on the beach that had been discarded by the sea. Russell, the tall blonde, smiling, former American that owned the shack greeted Bobby with his big toothy smile and immediately asked if he would like a beer.

The story that Richard had related to Bobby was that Russell came to Bonaire with a group to dive and somehow just didn't get around to leaving.

"Sure," Bobby said, "Amstel light."

The scantily clad young girl brought the brown bottle that was dripping wet and cold to the touch.

"Would you like anything to eat?" she asked while she waited with her pencil and the small paper at the ready.

"Yeah, bring me an egg and tomato sandwich please," Bobby said, "and you may as well bring another beer." The sandwich sounded very simple, and it was, but the herbs and melted gouda cheese on the special roll made it spectacular. And being close to the equator somehow made the beer taste better.

Bobby was trying to get all the information he had so far about Wildman Clint Armstrong organized in his head but it was a task as the well built young ladies in skimpy bikinis kept flying past his field of vision showing off their windsurfing skills.

The owner, Russell, brought Bobby's sandwich over so Bobby took the opportunity to ask him if he knew Wildman Clint Armstrong. A large smile crossed Russell's face, "knew him?" he said, "he was a regular here. Everyone here knew him. Right there," Russell said while pointing to his left to an end barstool, "right there was his seat."

"What happened to him, have you heard anything?" Bobby inquired.

"Shot. Obviously by some jealous coward." Russell said, "while he was a large and imposing man, he was also the kindest, gentlest man I had ever met. And, like me, he sure loved his life here in Bonaire. He was on his boat out there every day either fishing or diving. And he would dive where few people had the balls to dive."

"Did he have any enemies?" Bobby asked.

"No. No. He was too giving to anyone he met. That's why I say it had to be jealousy. Someone who was jealous that a person could be that happy and enjoy life that much. Were you a friend of his?"

"Yes, we served in Vietnam together. We saw a lot of bad stuff together," Bobby answered.

"I thought I saw you here before. Have you you been?"

"Yes, my friend, Richard St.Clair and his wife, brought me and my wife here a couple years ago."

"Yes, that's it, Richard St.Clair. That is his license plate adorning our patio over there. Russell pointed to a Pennsylvania Parrothead license plate with Richard's initials on it. He came here every year for a few weeks at a time, but I haven't seen him this year."

"Richard's wife, Pamela died of cancer this past year. So he has been rather down in the dumps. He is over in Aruba now, though, because Pamela stated in her will that she wanted her ashes to be spread in the Caribbean Sea."

Russell appeared to be shocked, "but Richard's wife was so young and beautiful and full of life. How can this happen?"

"It was very sudden and very sad. Richard is taking it very hard."

"He should have brought her ashes here to Bonaire, not Aruba," Russell said, "I liked them both very much. They came here for lunch a lot."

"Maybe I'll see if I can get a call to him in Aruba and see if he can come over," Bobby said.

"Yes, you should do that. It would be good for him. I will fix him one of his favorite sandwiches. You tell him the beer is on me if he comes over," Russell said and was forced to excuse himself as the girl behind the bar was calling for his assistance.

As he was walking away, he turned back to Bobby, "you, a friend of my friends Clint and Richard, you don't pay today. On the house. Thank you for coming!"

Chapter 5

Now here was a first. Richard St.Clair was standing at the check in desk at the Aruba Beach Club depressed. Such a thing should not be possible, but such was Richard's life since Pamela passed away. And especially now that he was here with her ashes to do her bidding. The lovely Aruban check-in girl sensing that something was wrong made quick work of the job at hand and handed Richard the keycard to his normal room, room 219. Richard stood there staring at the keycard for a moment as it sunk in. He was here alone. He was brought back to reality by the clanging of the happy hour bell. What the hell, he thought, may as well start drowning my sorrows. His feet moved him along without his thinking about it to the beachside bar where he climbed onto the high stool and placed his one and only bag at his feet. He again tried not to think of the bag. Sure it held his underwear and swim suits and a few shirts, but it also held Pamela's ashes. Reina, the lovely Peurto Rican girl with the long hair and great body, that managed the bar came over to greet Richard. "Mr. St.Clair, so good to have you back," she said while pulling her long hair back out of her smile, "will your wife be joining you?"

"No, I'm afraid not," was all that Richard could get out, but his face obviously told her more for she did not push the issue.

"What can I get for you Mr. St.Clair?"

"The drink with the 100 proof rum in it," Richard replied knowing he wanted to dull the pain as quickly as possible. "The Aruban Dushi. I get that for you, Mr. St.Clair," Reina replied as she showed her dazzling bright smile and turned to make the drink. She was back in no time at all, "shall I put this on your room tab, Mr.St.Clair?"

"Yes, please," Richard said, "and thank you."

A few drinks later and the bartender had Richard spilling his guts about Pamela and her death. The steel drum player was cranking out the island sounds, the sun was going down, the tropical breeze was blowing around the sweet fragrances of the island and Richard was actually holding a conversation.

The next morning Richard awoke, put on his swim trunks and flowered shirt, took Pamela's ashes, and went to the front desk to catch a taxi. The trip up route 1B didn't take long. But then how could it when the entire island is only 21 miles long. And, had it been for any other reason, it would have been a very pleasant drive. Mornings in Aruba with the sunshine and the brilliant blue sky were extremely enjoyable. It always felt like mother nature came at night with a giant hose and washed the island down leaving it fresh and clean.

The taxi left Richard off at the bus stop at Malmok Beach and Richard slowly meandered down to the water's edge. Richard waded into the brilliant blue water up to about his waist, thought to himself about the wonderful years he was lucky enough to have shared with Pamela, and slowly released her ashes into the current. The Caribbean Sea seemed eager to accept them. The colorful fish gathered and swam right up to Richard as though waiting for Pamela. Bright blue parrot fish, black and gold French Angelfish, numerous striped sargeant majors, bright yellow juvenile tangs, and a large orange starfish lay there marking the spot. Richard could only imagine that Pamela was now part of that gorgeous blue water. His first true love was now joined with his second love. He stood there quite a while before deciding he should wade back to the shore.

Standing on the bank was Reina, the beach bar manager from the Aruba Beach Club. She was dressed in her work outfit and had been watching Richard.

"Reina," Richard asked, "what are you doing here?"

"Pamela was a friend. You told me last night at the bar you would be here and I wanted to pay my respects so I followed you," she said, her voice barely above a whisper, "I hope you don't mind."

"No, I don't mind. Thank you for being here."

Reina reached out and touched Richard's hand, "you know that she would want you to move on. you've so much left to live for."

"I know Reina. It's just hard."

"Of course, it is. But, it will get easier."

The calm of the Caribbean Sea seemed to settle over Richard as she spoke. Reina turned to leave and said, "I will buy you a drink tonight at happy hour."

Richard thought for a moment then said, "I don't think so Reina. Thank you but I've had enough to drink to last me for quite a while. Can I buy you breakfast?"

Reina shyly looked at the ground while she shuffled her feet and replied, "I'm sorry. I have to get back to work. Perhaps another time."

"Let's ride back together then," Richard suggested and he led her up the beach to the bus stop where the bus had just deposited several tourists with their flippers and masks, beach towels and sunscreen. They rode back in silence, sitting next to each other, watching the palm trees and hotel fronts pass by until the bus made the corner at the Alahmbra Casino and deposited them near the Aruba Beach Club.

Richard walked Reina into the hotel then turned towards the steps, "thank you for being there Reina."

She smiled and went on her way to the beach bar.

When Richard got to his room, he gathered his sunscreen, his beach towel, a bottle of cold water and a book and headed for the beach. Finding a lounge chair near the water under a chickee, the palm leafed umbrella they built for shelter from the sun, he spread his towel on the chair, propped it in the semi upright position and deposited himself there. He flipped open the new paperback, "Blue Hole" by some unknown author, and began reading. The sunshine was brilliant, the blue sky fabulous, the sound of the surf was music to his ears, and the smells blowing along with the tradewinds left him know that everything was alright. He was near to dozing off and nearly dropped his paperback when he heard one of the front desk girls calling his name.

"Mr. Richard St.Clair. Mr. Richard St.Clair"

"He looked at the young lady and spoke, "I'm Richard St.Clair."

"You have urgent message at front desk Mr Richard St.Clair."

"Thank you he said. I'll be right up." Richard marked the spot in his book, gathered his towel, sunscreen, and water and followed the young lady to the check-in desk.

The lady that checked him in with the long dark hair looked at Richard and said, "I'm sorry to hear about your wife Mr.

St.Clair" and she handed him the message.
Word travels fast on a small island Richard thought as he
unfolded the message and read; "Richard catch a plane to
Bonaire. I need your assistance. Bobby"
Richard thought for a moment, turned toward the ocean, and
walked over to the beach bar.
"Reina," he said to her back.

She turned to face him, surprised by the sound of his voice.
"Richard," she said.
"I have to leave. When I come back in September, could I
maybe see you?"
"I'll be waiting."

Chapter 6

It was almost titillating to Chief Farr to be legally breaking
into the house, then rummaging through every item in there.
And the best part was, he could leave it a shambles and the
law protected him. What made it especially exciting was the
fact that it was the Mayor's house. Galen had gotten his court
order and was now searching for the weapon, that he was
convinced, killed Billy Bollinger. Once he found it and had it
tested this case would make him a real hero not only in
Ganister, Pennsylvania, but all over the state. He would show
them why he should have been the Chief of Police years ago.
And, ever since the mayor strode into his office looking like a
drunk, swore him in, then totally disregarded his first request
to an interview, Chief Farr knew payback was in order. He
first rummaged through Richard's dresser drawers, then even
pulled them completely out to look at the bottoms. Not
because he thought a gun could actually be there, but because
he was determined to leave no stone unturned. And if it left
things a bit messier, so much the better. Chief Farr flipped
over the mattress and box springs. He emptied everything for

the bedside stand. There were 38 shells there along with an
empty holster. Chief Farr's mind took off when he found that.
The mayor has obviously intentionally hidden the gun if it's
not in the holster. And the only reason to hide it would be
because it was used in the commission of a crime. Another
thought passed through the Chief's mind, "and that SOB acted
holier-than-thou when he gave me time off work and made
me destroy the sawed off shotgun that Chief Bollinger had
given to me out of the old evidence locker. I'll show him."
That gun is here somewhere and I'm going to find it. He also
took time to admire Pamela's taste in underwear, as he
rummaged through her drawers, at one point even taking the
time to smell the cologne left on the worn bra. There were
boxes under the bed that he went through. There was a lock
box that he felt sure must contain the weapon, but after he
busted the lock off all he found were insurance policies nd
other papers. He tossed everything out of Richard's closet
taking the time to go through each and every pocket. Then he
did the same with Pamela's closet. Checking every pocket and
at some points remembering how great she looked in some of
the skimpier clothes. He tossed the couch pillows. Overturned
the couch and chairs. Emptied every drawer in the kitchen,
even emptied the cabinet under the sink. Pamela had some
fine dishware, but not after the Chief was finished going
through the china cupboard. When there was hardly a place
left to walk, he moved on to the garage. He even tore apart
Richard's race car looking for the gun. Another thought
occurred to the Chief, "there's an empty stall here. Where is
the mayor's car?" He patted his chin with his pointer finger
the way he always did when he was thinking, "of course," he
said to himself, "it's at the airport. I need to get another
warrant and go get that vehicle. That's probably where he hid
it so it wouldn't be too far away, yet not in his house just in
case it got searched." The Chief left. The front door lock was

broken to pieces, but, no matter this place is a wreck anyway. Galen made the call, got the warrant, and arranged to have the local flatbed towing service pick up the car. He decided he would wait in his office until the car was delivered to him. And while he waited it wouldn't hurt to have a nice cup of coffee and a few doughnuts. He even propped his feet up on the desk. What would be next for Chief Galen Farr after he cracked this case? Sheriff? State Police Commissioner?

Chapter 7

Bobby was sitting on the small dock outside his room at the Divi Flamingo surrounded by the quiet of the morning as he punched the numbers into his phone. The only activity around him were the couple resort personnel at the dive shop that had just brought the white diving boat into the next pier were taking off used air tanks and replacing them with fresh air tanks to be ready for the load of divers they would be taking out to Klein Bonaire in about an hour. The clanging of the tanks was the only sound to be heard but it traveled quickly across the calm blue sea.
Bobby's phone call was answered, "Yeah?"
"Colonel," Bobby said quietly into the phone, "I need a few more details on Clint's activities here."
"There's not much I can add to our previous conversation. The drugs are coming out of South America into Bonaire and Curacao where the police departments are limited in funds and experience, then continue on to the states. We have not been successful in South America in shutting off the flow, so it seemed more advantageous to concentrate on these in between points. Clint was definitely on to something according to our last conversation but he had not given' me any names or specifics yet."
"Any idea where I can start?" Bobby asked.

"The beginning," the Colonel replied, "I knew this wouldn't be easy which is why you were selected. And most likely when you find his killer, you'll find out what he was on to."
"Can you do me favor, since I am limited on resources?"
"Shoot."
"Check on Matty's finances," Bobby said.
"No problem. I'll have the info sent to you a.s.a.p. Anything else?" the Colonel asked.
"Not unless Wildman Armstrong let you know where he stashed his notes."
"If I knew that you wouldn't be enjoying a Caribbean vacation at my expense." With that the phone went dead. Bobby was used to it, the Colonel was a man of few words, not unlike Bobby himself, so when he was done, he was done.
Bobby pressed the end button, folded his phone, and scanned the horizon. Beautiful, he thought, it's amazing how many hues of blue there can be spread out between the sky and the sea. After a few moments he meandered over to the outdoor patio where the tinkling of dishes could now be heard as they prepared the usual breakfast buffet. Fresh omelets made while you watch with what- ever you wanted in them. Bobby usually had tomatoes, onions, cheese, and occassionaly some green peppers. Then after a leisurely breakfast he would take his dusty little rental car out to the airport to pick up Richard. Bobby hadn't heard from Richard, but Bobby knew when the flights from Aruba came in, and he knew Richard would be on the late morning flight. Call it psychic. Call it intuition. Whatever you call it, it showed how close these two were, so Bobby would go the airport, pick him up, then head out to Jibe City for lunch where he could get Richard up to speed on the situation.

Bobby was a little early heading to the airport, but that was a good thing. Just past the entrance to the airport the highway ran next to the beach and one of the best spots for diving and snorkeling was "Windsock". So named because there actually was a windsock flying there to show the landing planes the direction the wind was blowing. The windsock was at the edge of the beach at the highway since just on the other side of the highway was a fence enclosing the beginning of the runway. Bobby found a large chunk of coral on the beach and perched himself on it sucking up the brilliant sunshine while he scanned the ocean for signs of life and the horizon for the small dots of light that would be the airplane lights on their final approach to the runway. After seeing a few dolphins pass by bobbing in and out of the water, he saw the speck of light. The speck became larger and larger as it got closer and closer. After a few minutes Bobby was staring at the front of the dual propeller plane which didn't take long to pass directly over him. He managed to see the blue writing on the side of the plane that said Tiara Air. That would be Richard's flight so he ambled back to the car and went less than a mile to the airport parking lot and picked out a space. No use in hurrying as Richard would have to de-plane then go through immigration and customs, and when he came through the doors, Bobby would be waiting along with the others,.... well apparently there weren't many on this flight, since there weren't but a couple people waiting. There were more taxi drivers sitting at their small table playing dominoes than there were people waiting for the passengers of the Tiara Air flight. After a few minutes the door opened and a local with a child came through the door, followed by a well dressed man overloaded with gold jewelry, then Richard. His one lone small travel bag in his left hand as he strolled over to Bobby and they shook hands and did their man hug, the old arm around the back and kind of bump pecs. Richard smiled at Bobby and said, "how'd you know I was on that flight? Pretty sure of yourself aren't ya'?"

"I know you like a book. Thanks for coming, buddy."

"So where's my chauffeur?" Richard asked.

"See the dusty old blue compact at the left end of the parking lot?" Bobby asked.

"That the best you could do?"

"It's all we need. Come on. How was your flight?"

"Bit shaky but good. It's actually nice to be on these little jitneys cause you get to see things. A lot of little fishing boats out there, and I got to see all of Curacao when we went over it. The port there had several cruise ships tucked in it and the bridge that swings was just opening when we flew over."

"You hungry?" Bobby asked.

"Well, yeah, I haven't had lunch yet."

"What have you been doing all morning?"

"I took Pamela's ashes to Malmok and spread them in the Sea just like she wanted." The mood changed quickly.

"You okay?" Bobby asked as he observed Richard's smile disappear.

"Yeah. It's been several months now. It's time to get on with things."

"Several. More like almost a year."

"Really? Guess I sort of lost track of time." Richard said.

"Well, welcome back. We got work to do."

"Where we headed?" Richard asked.

"Jibe City. Russell wanted to see you and where else are you going to get a great sandwich and cold beer cheap?"

"Jibe City. Perfect. How's old Russell doing?"

"He's like the island, nothing changes, it just putters along."

"So, what is it that is so important that I have to leave Aruba and come help you with?"

"Wildman Clint Armstrong. He took a bullet to the gut. The Colonel wants to know who and why? Clint was doing a little work for the Colonel."

"So it's probably all related. I see. And it probably means sooner or later someone is going to be shooting at us, right?"

"Well you never know, so here, you may want to keep this stashed in your swim trunks," Bobby said as he handed Richard a small Sig Sauer handgun.

"Very nice, but how do you manage to get things like this here through airport security?" Richard asked.

"Well, I don't. They just get delivered to me after I get to wherever I'm going."

"Sweet!"

"Any idea yet who we're looking for?"

"Nope."

"Any idea what whoever it is we're looking for is into?"

"Yep. The usual, running dope. Clint had his own diving operation here where he took tourists on diving trips. His was a little different though cause he took them to the wild side of the island not the usual calm side dive spots. All we know so far is the two things are related somehow."

"Have you seen Matty?"

"Yes, she seemed okay. A little broken up over losing Clint naturally, but moving on with her life. Unlike someone else I know that thought he should try to drink the world dry."

Bobby shot a glance at Richard, but he wasn't looking back at him, he was looking out the dirty windshield staring into the deep blue sky.

Finally Richard spoke, "well, good for her," was all he said.

The duo pulled into the dusty lot kicking up even more dust, left the windows down on the rental and mozied over to the Jibe City bar where they were warmly greeted by Russell.

"Richard St.Clair and Bobby Morrow," he bellowed, "how are my good friends?" Before they could answer he led them to a table."Here, sit down. I'll get you a couple cold beers."

"Thanks, Russell," they said in unison.

"What I can get you for lunch today?"

Bobby said, "I want that seafood salad thing you make so well."

Richard the tamer one said, "the tomato and egg sandwich, Russell. Thank you."

"Coming right up," the gregarious Russell said as he was striding away.

As soon as they were alone Richard asked Bobby, "how are we going to get started on this thing?"

"Well, standard operating procedure for any op is to keep detailed notes," said Bobby, "so somewhere Dick had a journal or computer or something. We need to find that, then we will know what he had uncovered thus far."

"So where do we start looking for that?"

"When I visited with Matty, I asked if Clint used the computer. She laughed. She said not with the big fingers he had, so I think we're looking for handwritten notes. The question is where would he stash them. If I were him it would not be in my home. That 's the first place anyone would look. I also wouldn't use a safe deposit box because, though it would be secure, it would take too many trips to it and arouse suspicion."

"So, if it's not in his house and not in a safe deposit box, what's left?"

Bobby studied the question for a moment, "well his boat seemed to be his prize possession, that's a good starting place or maybe somewhere right around us. Russell said he was here all the time for lunch."

"Dare we ask Russell?" Richard asked.

"No way. Nice a guy as he is, we just don't know who is involved in this so everyone is a suspect."

"Everyone include Matty?"

"Yes, until we exclude her. I'm working on that right now. The Colonel is pulling her financials. That should eliminate her as a suspect or move her to number one on the hit parade."

The duo hushed as the sandwiches came and were placed in front of them. Bobby smiled at the shrimp and crab leg sandwich and asked the waitress for another ice cold Amstel light. After she left the table Richard said, "so what's first?" "First, I think we ask Matty if we can borrow Clint's boat and truck for a little diving or fishing."

The ice cold beers arrived. The bottles dripping condensation from their introduction to the warm Caribbean heat. Out on the flat water of Lac Bay the windsurfers kept passing by. Some practicing their quick turn-arounds. A few occassionally taking the plunge into the water.

Chapter 8

The door opened like a tornado just came through it. The surprise caused Chief Farr to nearly fall off his chair that he had leaned back on just two legs with his feet planted on the desk.

The tow truck operator that had just come through the door bellowed at him, "where do you want this thing?" "The Mayor's car? Out back. Just pull it into the garage." "Who's paying for this?" the squat man with the slicked back hair asked.

"Just see the borough secretary next door. She'll write you a check," the Chief replied. Now standing and brushing the crumbs off his shirt and pants.

The Chief followed the tow truck operator out the door then headed behind the office to the garage. "Now he had him," the Chief thought to himself, "somewhere in this car has got to be the gun."

The tow truck operator brought the car around, backed it neatly into the garage, dropped it off the hook, and wasted no time leaving for his next run. His two way radio was squawking the whole time with more potential money runs. The Chief threw on a pair of coveralls over his nice clean uniform and started by searching under the seats, in the pockets of the seats and the doors. Then the glove compartment. At least the Mayor's car was neat and there wasn't much junk to work around. Then the Chief popped the trunk and searched in there including the spare tire well. Nothing. The Chief thought for a minute, then bounced and tugged on the rear seat until it finally gave way. Nothing there either. "Where could you possibly hide a gun in here?" he asked himself. Disgusted but figuring he just needed some time to think about it, he took off the coveralls, straightened his uniform, looked in the mirror to check his hair, and decided he would temporarily move on to his next item, searching Bobby Morrow's home for a 38 caliber handgun. Just in case. So he closed the garage door, got into the squad car and headed out to the Morrow house.

When he arrived he was amazed at how quiet it was. The log home sitting in the middle of the large field surrounded by trees on all sides. It was a picture postcard place with the brilliant green field, the log house, and the blue sky with just a couple white puffy clouds. Galen left the car, strode up onto the porch and knocked on the door. Bobby's lovely wife Claire answered the door and immediately invited him in.

"What can I do for you Chief? Bobby's not home right now," she said.

"Well, I'm sorry to have to tell you this but".......

"Bobby didn't get hurt, did he?" she interjected.

"No, Mrs. Morrow. I'm here to search your home. I have a warrant here."

"Search for what?" a confused Claire asked.

"Your husband is still a suspect in the Billy Bollinger shooting. I'm searching for the weapon."

"Well Bobby's gun cabinet is right around the corner," she pointed off to her left, "help yourself."

"Well I may have to search the entire home Mrs. Morrow."

"It won't be like in the movies where you leave a big mess everywhere, will it," she asked with a smile on her face.

"I'm not responsible for the condition afterward, only for searching every nook and cranny," he said.

The smile disappeared from Claire's face and she responded, "in that case Duke can stay with you. And if you make a mess, Duke will see that you clean it up."

"Who's Duke".....the Chief started to ask but the answer came in the form of a low growl from behind him. He turned and was staring at the largest dog he had ever seen with teeth the size of a car grill.

"Mrs. Morrow, I must warn you, if your dog attempts to bite me, I will shoot him."

"Hope you're quicker than the last guy that tried to," she said and sauntered off into the living room where the television was playing. "Watch him Duke," were her last words.

The Chief moved rather slowly around the corner where Claire had pointed and found the gun cabinet. It was not locked. He opened it and began picking up and examining each handgun in there. And there were quite a few. The obvious conclusion was that Bobby Morrow preferred his guns be larger than a 38 caliber. This man was a one man army with all his weapons and ammunition. Duke apparently wanted to be sure the Chief knew he was still there so he got closer to him and sniffed his crotch then growled some more. The Chief became uncomfortable again and started to sweat. Perhaps he was better off with the Mayor as his number one suspect. He carefully closed the gun cabinet door, watching Duke as he did it to be sure the dog didn't make any sudden moves.

"All done in there?" he heard Claire ask from the living room?

"Done in here but I still need to look around the rest of the house," he replied.

Carol picked up her phone and punched in the numbers that Bobby had told her to use in any kind of emergency. The phone only rang once and was answered, "Yeah?"

"This is Claire Morrow."

"Yes, Claire," the Colonel answered, "what can I do for you?"

"I think it is just awful that while my husband is out risking his life, serving his country, that this police Chief is searching our home."

"Whoa," the Colonel said, stopping her, "who is there?"

"Chief Farr of the Ganister Police department."

"Hand him the phone Claire. I'll take care of this."

"Chief Farr, there's a call for you she said as she got up from the couch and went into the dining room where he was standing with Duke at his heels.

"Who's this?" Chief Farr asked when she handed him the phone.

"Chief, this is the Colonel. I work directly for the President of the United States. Mr. Morrow is in our employ. You will cease and desist from your actions or I will start with the Governor of Pennsylvania and call everyone all the way down his chain of command until your immediate supervisor makes you cease and desist. Oh that's right, your immediate supervisor would be Mayor Richard St.Clair who happens to be away tending to his wife's last wishes. I guess I'll stop at the State Attorney General and have him come in there and bust your ass. Are you hearing me Chief?" The Colonel was practically yelling by this point.

"Yes, I hear you. I just question your ability to direct my activities," the Chief said feeling confident.

"Well, I wouldn't want that," the Colonel said his voice again soft and pleasant, "just you stay right where you are and my guess is your phone will be ringing in about 3 minutes, then you won't be so cocky!" the Colonel's escalating voice as he immediately hung up. Even Claire Morrow could hear the end of his last sentence as he yelled it into the phone.

Claire stood with her hand out waiting for the Chief to give her phone back to her. The stunned Chief was moving slowly obviously in deep thought as he handed it back to her.

"Well?" Claire asked.

"I'll wait until your husband comes back and we'll continue this then," he said.

As Claire said, "fine, goodbye," Duke increased his growl and practically pushed the Chief to the door.

"Don't let the door hit you where the Good Lord split you," she said.

As soon as the door closed Duke flopped down on the floor and went back to sleep.

Chapter 9

Bobby and Richard left the waitress at the lunch shack at Jibe City a handsome tip, said farewell to Russell and piled into the dusty subcompact rental to head back to Kralendijk. They went up J.A.Abraham Boulevard, made the left turn onto Kaya Grandi and found themselves in front of the freshly painted Gallery of Matty Armstrong. When they entered the cool air conditioning Matty spied them and immediately hustled over to greet them. First she hugged Bobby, then spying Richard she said, "Richard, I'm so glad you have come. I'm also very sorry to hear about Pamela."

"It was quite a shock," Richard answered.

"We are in the same boat you and I."

"Yes and I'm very sorry about Clint. Hopefully Bobby can help bring some closure for you," Richard said.

"You both are very kind. It is no wonder that Clint spoke so well of you both."

"Your Gallery is lovely, Matty," Bobby said.

"Thank you. It makes me feel better to be here because with all the pictures of Clint's diving and the reef, it still seems like at least a part of him is still here," she said but with sadness in her eyes.

Richard and Bobby were impressed by the beauty that surrounded them on the walls of the Gallery.

"I came to ask a favor," Bobby said.

"Whatever you need. You are my friends."

"Could we borrow Clint's boat for a day or two to do some diving and fishing? We'll be glad to pay you." Bobby said. Clint's boat was a thirty foot custom Zodiac dive boat that he had used to take divers to the "wild side" of Bonaire where the larger waves, steep, rocky shorelines and challenging access led to uncharted shipwrecks, pristine coral and lots of large marine life, including sharks.

"Of course, you can take it. But you cannot pay me. Clint would want you to use it. You will need to take his truck to pull it," she said, "wait here. I'll get you the keys, then you can just take it whenever you like." She disappeared into a small office and came back with the keys jingling in her fingers, "here you go. Have fun."

"Thank you so much," Richard said and Bobby concurred. After leaving the Gallery they turned left onto Kaya L.D.Gerharts and in a couple blocks pulled into the Cultimara food store which is adorned with a colorful mural featuring local residents. They stocked up on water, beer, sandwiches and some ice for the cooler then headed off to pick up the boat.

Clint was obviously a neat freak. Everything was clean and shiny on the boat and the truck.

"Try to remember," Richard said to Bobby, "this isn't your beat up old Chevy. Some people actually take care of their equipment."

"So do I," said Bobby.

"Like what?" Richard asked.

"You ever see one of my guns dirty?"

"Well you got me there. It's just that your vehicles leave a lot to be desired."

"Priorities, Richard. Priorities. Now get the cooler loaded and let's get this show on the road."

The duo pulled out onto Kaya Simon Bolivar and wound around the stadium onto Kaya Internashional which would take them out past the airport, past Windsock and Pink Beach. Past the salt works where the flamingos were busy shifting their heads in the water from side to side searching for food, and at the same time getting the bonus of more pink for their feathers. Around the curve at the southern end of Bonaire and up the other side until just before Lac Bay where they took a small road. If you could actually call it a road as it was more like a trail, directly out to the edge of the ocean at the one spot where the banks were jagged lava and coral but where mother nature had provided a narrow sand sloped bottom and enough water to get in the boat before the waves and the current caught you. Before they unloaded the boat they took the time to casually search through the truck including under the dash looking for Clint's journal or notes. Nothing in the truck so while they still had daylight and no one was around to watch them they began searching the boat. They looked in all the compartments and especially any that were locked. They looked under the dash, under the motor cover, everywhere they could think of. They were close to giving up and sat down on the side benches to think and discuss where might be left to search.

"We've looked everywhere but in these air tanks," Richard said.

"Yeah, but they're full of air. Aren't they?" Bobby asked. The two immediately checked the valve on each bottle of air. Only one was empty, the rest were full.

"How do you hide something in an air tank?" Richard asked.

Bobby didn't know but if it was there he was going to find out. He started twisting, pulling and turning everything he could, then, exasperated he slammed it down. "It's not in there," he said.

Richard placed the bottle back where it originally was and strapped it back into place. The strap kept the bottles from falling when the seas were rough. You sure wouldn't want the gauge to get broken off because the airtank would become a missile then. Most boats just used bungi cords to tie down the tanks, but Clint had a nice black strap with velcro to hold his in place which were fastened right into the boat so they wouldn't get lost like the bunji cords. Richard didn't get the velcro strap tightened properly so when Bobby hit the throttle the empty bottle busted loose and rolled back to the back of the boat. Richard grabbed it before it went overboard and struggled to refasten it as the boat surged out through the line of breakers into the swells of the sea. As Richard worked with the strap he found it had a very fine zipper running along the back. He unzipped it and found Clint's notes.

"When you get to a calm area Bobby, you might want to take a look at this" he said as he held up the notes.

"What do they say?" Bobby asked.

"Beats me. It's some kind of shorthand or something. You'll have to look them over."

"Here, you take the wheel while I look at them before we lose what little light we have."

The sun was rapidly dropping into that little seam where the sky meets the water and where doubt rises as to whether the earth really is flat and that it's the edge of our world.

Richard eased off the throttle and let the boat come to a stop after they had gotten out to a point where the lights of Jibe City and the nudist colony were just barely visible. Bobby was using a small flashlight to look over the notes. After a moment he said to Richard, "where does the GPS say that we are?"

Richard read off the numbers to Bobby.

"Keep going straight out until the last number gets to 15," Bobby said.

"So you found something in Clint's notes?" Richard asked.

"Something, I just don't know what. But whatever it is it's at 12 degrees 10' North 68 degrees 15' West."

With that Richard hit the throttle and the nimble little boat shot forward into the now relatively calm waters of the Caribbean Sea. After just a few minutes Richard brought the boat to a halt again, "We're here. Wherever here is."

"Okay," Bobby said, "suit up, we're going in."

"Excuse me, but, in case you haven't noticed it's dark as hell in there. Not to mention there are sharks in there looking for their nighttime snack."

"Stop complaining and put on the wetsuit. You're a tough guy. You can handle a little shark."

"But I don't even like diving. I'm a snorkeler."

"The only difference is you'll be under the water. Let's go. Oh, by the way, guess what the name of this spot is."

"What, shark city?"

"Believe it or not, it's Blue Hole."

"You're puttin' me on. Like our Blue Hole back home where I learned to swim and stuff?"

"Yeah. Blue Hole. Let's go."

The two pulled on the wetsuits that Clint kept stowed on board, put on their belts, tanks, and flippers, and strapped the big underwater lights onto their wrists then backwards over the side of the boat they went. They swam down to about 100 feet and with the darkness did not notice the shipwreck until they were just a few feet from it. The strong underwater lights providing great light but at a minimum range in the deep black water. Richard was studying the opening along a portion of the side when he felt something near him. With his periferal vision he could see Bobby's light moving back and forth just off to his left. When he swung his light to the right there was the huge eyeball of the monster fish just a couple feet to his right, looking right at him.

Chapter 10

Chief Galen Farr came into his office, threw the car keys on the desk and assumed his position. The cup of steaming hot coffee near his right elbow, his feet crossed on the desktop, and the chair rocked back onto the back two legs. Then, after some scrutiny, he picked a doughnut out of the box, studied it some more, and took a bite. Now it was time to get down to business. The business of the Billy Bollinger murder case. The Mayor is still a great suspect, but finding his gun would be the key. The Mayor was definitely at the scene. The Mayor admits to putting his pistol to Billy's head. And he had motive. Billy had assaulted Richard's wife while they were in Aruba. Plus there was the incident, that Galen did not know all the details about, where the Mayor, former Chief of Police Bollinger and Billy were at the Blue Hole. From what Galen heard then Chief Bollinger had lured the Mayor to the Blue Hole with the aim of drowning him there. Somehow Bobby Morrow and Carmine Rizzo, the local mafia head came to the Mayor's rescue. It was right after that that Chief Bollinger was interrogated for the murder of the pizza man and not much later the Chief was shot after breaking into the Mayor's house with the intent of shooting the Mayor because the Chief was sure the Mayor had shot his son Billy. Ganister was becoming a little Peyton Place. Now, it was up to Chief Farr to get this murder solved and this whole mess behind them so the sleepy little town of Ganister can go back to being a sleepy little town. A place where the Chief can kick back and enjoy his morning doughnuts.

Getting back to his thoughts, Chief Farr went on to his second suspect: Bobby Morrow. Bobby more than likely had a 38 pistol. After all, he owned every other type of gun. Just because the Chief hadn't found it, didn't mean it didn't exist. And Bobby had great motive for shooting Billy Bollinger too, because Galen had worked on that case at the time, where

Billy Bollinger had raped Bobby Morrow's daughter. Even the Mayor, at the time, was worried that Bobby would take matters into his own hands and shoot Billy. Maybe he just waited for a more opportune time. And since the man everyone thought was a nice friendly dentist turned out to be an undercover federal agent, he probably had the skills to easily get rid of the weapon and eliminate any traces of his own involvement. Plus Chief Farr's one eyewitness, which no one knew about yet except Galen, saw both the Mayor and Bobby at the scene of the crime. So, at least they could be placed there. The only question is who shot him.

The only other potential is the silver car that Grammy Geuring saw at the scene. But silver is the most popular color for cars and she did not know a make or model. That was like looking for a needle in a haystack. In Ganister alone there probably were a hundred silver cars.

Galen rooted through the remaining doughnuts. Grabbed the chocolate one with the icing on it and resumed his thoughts. As soon as those two, The Mayor and Bobby Morrow got back to town, he was just going to have to haul them in here and get down to some serious questioning. He could break them. They weren't as bright as they thought they were. And then he'd get the gun that shot Billy and wrap this case up in a nice neat bow.

Hum, that chocolate doughnut was pretty good, Galen reached for the box for another but came up with an empty box. Surprised he lurched just a little and the weight shifted on the back two legs of the chair and down he went. Crash. Galen and the chair were stretched out on the floor. He jumped up as fast as he could and looked around the empty office to be sure no one could have captured his fall.

Chapter 11

Richard worked his flippers as fast as he could to come to a complete stop in the water all the while keeping the light drilled on the huge black eyeball of the humongous gray shape next to him and wishing he could shout out to Bobby to save himself before it was too late. Then it happened, a slap on his left shoulder. *"No he thought, there are more than one. I'm going to be eaten by sharks and will never see the light of day again."* Richard's life began to flash before his eyes. His thought of the Blue Hole that he cherished in Ganister and how ironic it was that his life ended here in the Blue Hole in Bonaire. Again. This time harder, the slap on his left shoulder. He wheeled around with the light determined to go down fighting and strike back at his attacker. He nearly knocked Bobby's mask off his face. Then he gathered himself and saw Bobby motioning to go up. Richard didn't need any more encouragement to swim as fast as he could to save his life, hoping Bobby could keep up to him and save his life also. Richard shot through the surface, took a rapid look around and swam as fast as possible across the top of the water to the waiting boat. As soon as he could touch it he launched himself into the boat before any sharks could take off his legs. But then, there was nothing. *"Where was Bobby?"* he wondered. *"The sharks must have gotten my best friend. I should have stayed with him and helped him fight them off."* Just as he was preparing to put his mask on and go back in he saw Bobby break through the surface and slowly make his way to the boat.
"Hurry up," he yelled at Bobby.
"Why? What's the hurry?" Bobby asked.
"There was a shark next to me."
Bobby started to laugh, "that was a tarpon, you idiot. He was just using your light to find a meal." More laughing. "Is that what made you swim like you were in the Olympics?"
"Just come on. Get your ass on the boat before I leave without you."

Bobby was still laughing when he climbed onboard the boat. He looked at the disgusted Richard and said, "great night for a dive isn't it?"

"Oh kiss my..."

Bobby laughed some more.

"So now that we wasted an evening, let's get back to shore," Richard said.

"We didn't waste anything," Bobby said as he smiled and shook a small container in front of him. "I found Dick's notes. Right where he said they would be."

"You're putting me on."

"Get a flashlight. Let's see what's in here," Bobby said as he began unscrewing the lid on the waterproof container which had been taped to the inside of the wreck.

Richard came with the light. Bobby shook the paper out of the container and they both read it. When they were done they just looked at each other.

"That sounds like science fiction to me," Richard said.

"Sounds to me like the bad guys have been studying our navy."

"So what do we do?" Richard asked.

Bobby looked at his watch, then back at Richard, "we wait."

Chapter 12

Richard and Bobby waited. The boat bobbed in the relatively calm, dark Caribbean Sea while they waited. Bobby watching the waves out toward the horizon. Richard watching the tiny lights at Jibe City wishing he were there sucking down an ice cold Amstel Light and eating a fresh homemade Caribbean sandwich. He turned to check on Bobby and just past Bobby in the water, he saw it.

"Look!" he yelled at Bobby, "Look there! I told you there was a shark down there.

Bobby spied the dorsal fin an just shook his head. Then another showed up. Up and down the water they went. A string of dorsal fins up and down in the water as the column progressed.

"They are dolphins," Bobby finally said to Richard, "And somehow we have to get a good look at them."

Bobby began pulling on his airtanks again along with his mask and flippers. "You wait here, while I check this out," Bobby said to Richard. And off the side of the boat he went. Richard just shook his head. He was convinced that his best friend was going to get eaten by a shark. Richard watched Bobby's light sway back and forth in the water as he swam toward the column of dorsal fins. Richard could tell he was right amongst them when he saw the underwater light turn around and head back to the boat. When the underwater light reached the boat it went out and Bobby reached up and grabbed the side of the boat. He pulled off his mask and said to Richard, "I'm going to follow them."

"What's going on?" Richard asked.

"I'll tell you later, you take the boat into shore, then quietly and without being spied, walk down the beach until I signal you," Bobby replied then pulled on his mask and was back under the water. His underwater light again heading to the column of dorsal fins which he joined and swam along with them toward the shore at an angle from where the boat was sitting. The dolphins had a strap around their neck, similar to a bungi cord with a package at the bottom about the size of a brick. It was an easy swim for Bobby as he grabbed onto the dorsal fin of a passing dolphin and let the dolphin pull him along. When they reached the shore Bobby let go and stood on the top of a large brain coral where he was able to have just his head out of the water. He took off his mask so he could observe. There was a concrete canal that made its way from

the sea into the building. It was just like the canal at the
Sonesta Hotel in Aruba. There the canal went into the Sonesta
Hotel's lobby where they loaded their guests into small boats
to ferry them out to their private island where they could sun
and swim. Here the canal was wide enough for dolphins to
swim in and out at the same time. The walls were concrete
and ended in the center of the building in a circular pool. The
dolphins would swim in to where a man stood in the center of
the pool. He would pull the strap with the package from
around their neck and toss it to another man up on the floor.
The man in the water would then give the dolphin a fish
reward and the dolphin would swim around the circular pool
and back out the canal into the dark Caribbean Sea. Bobby
stood and watched the procession a while before donning his
mask and swimming up the beach a ways.

Richard, knowing Bobby had a plan, did as he was told. He
started the boat and cruised into the beach. Finding the
particular sandy area was a little bit of a challenge in the dark
but after a few minutes he located it. Then he had to gun the
motor to get through the last line of breakers and up onto the
sandy beach where he jumped out quickly with the rope in
one hand and hauled the boat up onto the shore. He pulled it
up out of the water as far as he could then tied it off to the
trailer that was hooked to Wildman's truck. When he was sure
it wouldn't go anywhere, even if the tide came in, he took off
the wetsuit, stashed it in the truck, pulled on a dark
windbreaker, made sure he had his gun and a flashlight and
carefully made his way down the coral beach. Richard was
glad he had his water shoes on as the coral underfoot was
nothing like sand. It was actually part coral, part volcanic lava
all mixed together and forming a pock-marked moon-like
surface that was very hard to walk on. The starlight didn't
provide as much light as Richard would have liked, which
slowed him down, but, given Bobby's instructions, he didn't

want to use the flashlight unless he absolutely had to. So he took his time and silently cursed every time his toe caught in a coral hole. He was along the water's edge and a structure of some sort was just coming into view when he saw the quick flash of Bobby's light from the water. Richard made his way a little further down the beach and met up with Bobby who had just climbed out of the water.

"What is that building?" Bobby asked Richard in a hushed tone.

Richard whispered back, "that would be the old shrimp farm. It's been closed down since right after it opened. Someone thought they could raise shrimp here and become a millionaire. It didn't work out. So what's going on, Bobby?"

"They are using trained dolphins. They strap the bags of drugs on them and the dolphins take them from point A to point B. Point B happens to be here. There is a small canal that runs right into the building. The dolphins swim into the building where they unstrap the packages and send the dolphins back out again."

"Are you serious?"

"Our Navy has been experimenting with this for a longtime, getting dolphins to deliver bombs. Apparently the drug lords have stumbled onto the technology. It's perfect."

"So this is what Dick found out that got him shot?"

"No doubt, but there still is the question of how did someone walk right up to Dick and shoot him without Dick showing any signs of defense?"

"Were you able to make out anyone inside the building?"

"Yes," Bobby said in his hushed tone, "but let's get back up the beach where we can talk without getting shot."

The duo cautiously made their way back to the boat and the truck.

"Let's get the boat loaded and head out of here," Bobby said. They kept the lights off on the truck while they backed it down to the water's edge and as quietly as possible loaded the boat, strapped it down, and headed out to the highway with their headlights off. They took the shortcut back to Kralendijk and managed to find parking on the street at the back entrance to the resort. The resort was quiet at this time of night since the majority of the guests were divers and would be getting up early for their first morning dive. The beach bar was closed so the duo went to their room where they could continue their conversation.

Chapter 13

"Come on man, get the hell out of bed," Bobby was saying to Richard while shaking him, "it's almost lunch time. You're going to sleep the whole day away."
A drowsy Richard rolled over and stared at Bobby, "we were out half the night and yesterday was a long day for me. Not to mention you scared the hell out of me with that night diving. Are you sure that was a tarpon and not a shark?"
"Yes, I'm sure now come on, we got work to do."
"All right. All right. I'll meet you at the pool in a few minutes. I need a quick shower."
Bobby left the room while Richard trudged off to the shower. When Richard left the room he found Bobby at the pool chatting with Bob and Betty, timeshare owners from Pennsylvania that Richard had introduced Bobby to the last time they were here, along with their wives, which caused Richard to flash back in his mind. The good old days.
"It's about time. I was justing asking Bob and Betty if they wanted to join us for lunch at City Cafe," Bobby said to Richard.
"Great, can you join us?" Richard asked.
"Not this time," Betty said, "we just got back from shopping downtown. We're going to be by the pool for a little bit."

"Well we'll talk to you later then," Bobby said as the two of them headed for the back gate of the resort and made their way downtown.

City Cafe was on Kaya Craane just a short walk from the resort and situated across the narrow street from the harbor. It was a great place to sit, eat, and watch the ships come and go. Occassionally you could watch more than that. Once when Richard and Pamela were there they saw a large marlin dancing on his tail out in the water. It turned out that a local fisherman standing on the pier had caught him with his spool of fishing line and was slowly hauling him into shore. It created enough excitement that a large group gathered on the pier, including Richard and Pamela, to watch the spectacle. The Bonairean had nearly gotten the fish to the pier when a large freighter came into the harbor to dock at the pier. The Harbormaster, being one of the spectators, and a friend of the Bonairean fisherman went out on his boat and forced the freighter to stop while the fisherman hauled his catch in. The fisherman proudly held the large fish by the spear while people took photographs. He was a happy Bonairean and the visitors were extremely impressed at the crude fishing technique involving only a spool of fishing line. No rod. No reel. Just bare hands wrapping the sharp line around the spool while the large fish fought to get away.

Richard and Bobby ordered burgers and were drinking cold Amstel Lights when Richard stood up from the table. "Hey Bobby. There's Matty. We should go say Hello to her."

Bobby looked in the direction Richard was looking and yanked him down in his chair, "Shhhh. Pretend you don't see her."

"But, why? What's going on?" Richard quietly asked.

"She's with someone," Bobby quietly answered.

"So?"

"That guy was in the old shrimp plant last night. He was the one standing on the floor that the other guy threw the packages to."

"No kidding?" Richard asked as he snuck another peek.

"Now we have a real problem," Bobby continued whispering quietly to Richard, "is Matty in on this thing? And if this guy knows Matty, did he also know Clint?"

"All good questions," Richard said, "but what we need are answers."

"I already have a call in to the Colonel to have him check on Matty's financial status. I guess I better get that info quick. And we need to find out who this guy is."

"I think I can get a photo with my camera if you hold the newspaper up a little. Then we can email the photo to the Colonel."

"Good idea," said Bobby as he held up the newspaper, "how's this?"

Richard flipped open his phone, pushed a few buttons and said, "Okay, got it."

"Good, let's get out of here before we're spotted," said Bobby.

"But we didn't eat yet," protested Richard.

"Catch the waitress. Tell her to make it to go and wait over at the crowded bar. I'll be outside." Bobby got up leaving no room for discussion and slipped out of the restaurant.

Richard stood at the bar with dozens of other people all waiting for food to go and kept watch on the couple. When the waitress brought his boxes of food, Richard paid and left as inconspicuously as possible.

He found Bobby across the street behind the fruit stand sitting on the wall with his feet dangling over but not able to reach the water.

"Here you go, buddy," Richard said as he handed him a box, "cheeseburger in paradise."

"That it is my friend."

The two ate while looking out across the water. Each lost in thought. Both thinking of women. Bobby thinking of his wife, Claire, and wanting to get back home to her. Richard of his former wife, Pamela, and hoping she would be at peace now that he spread her ashes in the Caribbean Sea just as she wished. When the burgers were gone, they looked at each other, and not needing to say anything got to their feet.

"I think we should call the Colonel, then go over to the police station and see Captain Craane," Bobby said.

"Should we go back for the car?"

"No, the police station is walking distance from here. Let me call the Colonel first." Bobby flipped open his cell phone and hit the speed dial number for the Colonel.

"Yes, Bobby," came the Colonel's quick answer to the phone.

"Richard is going to email you a picture. We need to know who he is, if possible. Also, have you had a chance to check on Matty Armstrong's financial status?"

"Yes, I have. It seems she has come into some money recently."

"Do you think she may be involved?"

"That's what you need to find out. Send me the photo." And, as usual the phone line went dead.

"Send him the photo Richard. He's waiting," Bobby said to Richard, "and our friend Matty has come into some money."

"You mean she may be involved in her husband's death?"

"We have to assume that until we find out differently," Bobby replied.

"That's going to make it hard even talking with her.."

"Yeah, well, that's why we get the big bucks. You cannot let on to her. We have to appear naive about her finances while we check on her possible involvement."

"Oh sure, no problem. I'll just say thanks for the use of Clint's boat while we use it to try and prove you murdered him," Richard said, knowing that that was exactly what they had to do.

"Let's go see Captain Craane," Bobby said.

"Lead the way."

Bobby and Richard walked the few blocks over to the police station. Entered, and asked to see Captain Craane. The young Bonairean lady in the uniform didn't say a word to them just turned and went into the Captain's office. She came back out again followed by the Captain.

"Ah, Mr Morrow. Please, come into my office," the Captain said then opened the half door at the counter and let them enter. Bobby followed by Richard walked into the Captain's office and stood while the Captain went around his desk and sat down.

"Please Mr. Morrow, have a seat. And whom is your friend?'

"Yes, Captain Craane, this is Richard St.Clair, a friend from the states. He is Mayor of the town we live in."

The Captain rose from his seat and held out his hand, "so nice to meet you, Mayor St.Clair." The Captain then sat again and looked to Bobby, "so Mr. Morrow, is there something I can do for you?"

"Actually, Captain, I believe it's my turn to do something for you."

The Captain's eyebrows raised, "Really?"

"We have discovered what Clint Armstrong discovered that probably cost him his life."

"Really?" the Captain asked again.

"We have found a source of drugs entering your lovely island. I will give you all the information very soon. I am checking on an identity that will be of immense help to you and we still need to find out how often this occurs or if there is a particular schedule."

"Can you not tell me anything more now?" the Captain asked.

"Well, I could, but I would prefer that only the three of us know anything at this point. No offense but this is a small island. I don't know who knows who. You understand, I hope?"

"I do. And I appreciate you keeping me in the loop. Have you come any closer to finding out who shot your friend? After all, that is why you are here, correct?"

"Yes sir, that is why we are here. The other thing is just something we have come across, and we will be giving you all the information on that so that you can make the necessary arrests," Bobby said.

With that the Captain rose, letting it be known that the meeting had come to an end. Richard and Bobby rose and headed for the door.

"Oh Captain, one more thing," Bobby said, "is there a private number that we could call you at when we get information?"

"Of course, Mr. Morrow, please feel free to call me at 717-8000."

"Thank you, Captain Craane."

As the duo left the Police station, Richard quietly asked Bobby, "Do you really want the Captain's phone number?"

"Sure. Hold that thought," Bobby said. Bobby opened his cell phone and pressed the speed dial button. When it was picked up he said, "Colonel, after you find out who the person in the picture is, perhaps you'll get his phone records. Then cross reference for any calls to Matty Armstrong and this number, 717-8000."

There was a minute while Bobby listened, then, "thank you Colonel." Bobby closed his phone looked at Richard, "we have got to get this finished. I want to go home and be with Claire, and I'm sure you have something better to do. Right?"

Richard looked at Bobby then replied, "yes, I get to have my Chief of Police interrogate me about a shooting I didn't do."

"Well join the club. The Colonel and Claire both told me he was at my house with a warrant looking for a gun. A 38 special. You know, like the one you tossed in the Blue Hole?"

"Yes, I tossed it in the Blue Hole, but for the last time I'm telling you, I did not shoot him."

"Well he was dead when I got there. So, if you didn't do it, then someone came after you and before me. So, when we get back, we have to find out who that someone was, otherwise one of us is going to be sitting in the pokey."

"Yeah, well, more importantly, you do believe me that I didn't do it?" Richard asked Bobby.

"I believe you. You just do stupid things to make yourself look guilty."

"Like what? Tossing the gun?"

"Yeah, like tossing the gun. For a smart guy you do some dumb stuff."

Bobby looked at Richard and paused before he went on, "I'm sorry I couldn't be with you in Aruba when you spread Pamela's ashes in the Sea."

"I didn't ask because I thought it was something I should do by myself. You know, a little private time between me and Pamela."

"Yeah, I understand."

"I miss her Bobby. But letting go of her ashes seems like she's saying to me, 'get on with your life.' Know what I mean?"

"I do. And she would be right. You have to get on with your life."

"I am," Richard said, "I'm here helping you, then I'm going back to Ganister and get on with my life. I'll miss her and I'll always love her, but I will get on with the rest of my life."

"Good man," Bobby said as he punched Richard in the arm, "now. Let's get this thing over with and catch that big bird back to the states."

 The two had walked nearly back to the resort when Bobby's phone rang. He answered it, "Colonel."

"I see," Bobby said, "thanks." Then he hung up.

"The man in the photo from the old shrimp plant, his name is Cordell Sherrod."

"Name doesn't mean anything to me. Should it?"

"Maybe not. But, he happens to be a Venezuelan drug kingpin."

"Great. And Matty is keeping company with him."

"Not only that, but the money that has flowed into Matty's account recently came from his account."

"Now what?"

"Now, we get the car and pay Matty a visit. Let's roll."

Chapter 14

ROY G. BIV. The acronym that describes the colors of the rainbow (red, orange, yellow, green, blue, indigo, and violet) paled in comparison to the walls in Matty's gallery. As soon as you walked through the doors of the downtown Kralendijk gallery your senses were assaulted by an enormous array of colors filling every inch of wall space depicting Matty's paintings and photos of fish and marine life. The vivid colors that they wear in nature were portrayed in her paintings, from bright blue and green parrot fish to the awesome blues and yellows of the Queen Angelfish, the brilliant pink of the Squirrelfish, and even the brown and white combination of the Drum. Not to mention the tremendous assortment of marine life whose color changes constantly. Then there are the underwater backgrounds of colorful corals, sponges and sea fans.

Standing in the doorway of Matty's gallery, which she named in memory of her recently deceased husband, Wildman Gallery, was like walking into the Sea after Moses parted it. On all sides of you were beautiful fish and marine life. Richard stopped just inside the doorway and took pause. Besides being so full of color, the paintings were so real to life. The fish were exactly as he saw them when he snorkeled. Though the gallery was full of guests, Matty caught Richard's arrival and made her way over to greet him. She was the same vivacious person she had always been and looked simple but ravishing in her light blue sundress with her blonde hair blowing back as she crossed the room. She immediately gave Richard a hug and quick kiss on the cheek.

"Richard, so good to see you again."

"Thank you, Matty. I really wanted to spend some more time in your lovely gallery, and, we do need to talk privately when you can," Richard said.

"We had a cruise ship dock this morning so there are a few visitors at the moment but they will clear out very soon. In the meantime, would you like a cup of tea?"

"Yes, that would be great."

"Come," she told Richard as she led the way to the back corner of the gallery and through a small archway into the work area. The water was already hot so she poured two cups and placed the tea bags in to soak.

"First of all, allow me to again Thank you for the use of Clint's boat," Richard said.

"Has it been helpful?" she asked.

"Yes, very."

Matty's smile faded and she became misty eyed as she asked, "have you found out who shot my husband?"

"Not yet. Bobby is making progress but we don't know yet." The bell on the door rang again so Matty got up from her chair and peeked through the archway.

"Just the guests leaving," she said to Richard and made her way back to sit down again.

"So what did you want to talk to me about, Richard?"

"You realize that every inquiry is not done to find a guilty person. Some inquiries are done to remove any doubt about an innocent person."

"Yes..." she said suspiciously.

"So I have to ask you about this," Richard said as he motioned with his hands the gallery around him, "and in particular where the money came from."

"So because I received money I am a suspect in my own husband's murder?" she asked coolly.

"Well Bobby and I would prefer that you look at it differently. We want to remove any doubt by anyone regarding yourself, so we can narrow the field down and get to the guilty person quicker."

"I see your position as mayor has become ingrained in you. You speak like a politician."

"Hopefully not like a politician with a forked tongue. My friend, Gary always says to me, 'how do you know when a politician is lying? His lips are moving.' But I would like to think that I can be an exception to that."

Matty sat motionless as Richard went on, "Bobby and I think the world of you. And Clint was one of Bobby's best friends, so this is very personal to both of us. We want whoever shot Clint to pay. Dearly. And we won't rest until that is accomplished."

"Well, I will tell you that I am coming into some life insurance money from Clint. But I have not yet received that. And frankly, when I do, I will need it to live on. As you can imagine, we needed both incomes to live. Now there is only mine, and it is up and down like a rollercoaster depending on the cruise ships and the economy and everything else that influences a person's decision to pay for art," Matty paused to collect her thoughts, "I was only able to open the gallery because a Venezuelan businessman offered to back me because he liked my paintings."

"And that would be Mr Sherrod?" Richard asked.

Matty looked at Richard strangely and asked, "yes, how do you know that?"

"How well do you know Mr. Sherrod, Matty?"

"Not very. I only recently met him."

"Did he know Clint?"

Jean thought a moment, "I don't think so. In fact, I believe the first time I met him he was actually looking for Clint. Something about diving on the wild side. Then when he came into our house and saw my paintings and photographs, he said that I should have a gallery."

"So when did you actually get the money from him?" Richard asked.

Matty gave Richard the suspicious look again and said, "very soon after Clint's funeral, but, why do I think you may already know that?"

"You're right. We know the date. And I 'm sorry to have to be so blunt but, the question is how well did you know him prior to Clint's death?"

"You surely don't think that the money had anything to do with Clint's death? Can you?" she asked, standing, hands on hips, glaring at Richard like he had the plague.

"Tell me, straight up Matty. When did you become friends with Mr. Sherrod?"

"Like I told you," her voice rising, "I met him shortly before when he was looking for Clint. Then shortly after Clint's funeral he offered to loan me the money to open the gallery."

"Loan? So you have a written document?" Richard asked.

"Yes!" she said defiantly, "and I will show it to you." She moved around Richard to her desk. Pulled open a drawer, ruffled through a few papers, and held the document out to Richard to inspect.

"Are you happy now?" she asked in her nastiest tone.

"Matty....." Richard was temporarily at a loss for words, "Matty, what do you know about Mr. Sherrod?"

"I know that he is, obviously, a successful businessman in Venezuela. What more do I need to know. My attorney's wrote the document. It is a loan. I pay interest. What are you getting at, Richard? And where is Bobby, anyway?"

"Bobby is out looking for Mr. Sherrod."

The silence was immediate and frightening until Matty finally spoke, "why, Richard?"

"Matty, Mr. Sherrod is a drug kingpin in Venezuela. He may have loaned you money to launder it. And furthermore, he may be involved in Clint's death. There. I've said it. It's out

there. And I'm sorry to drop it on you like this but this is not a
time to speak like a politician." As soon as Richard finished,
he moved towards Matty and hugged her. He held her and
comforted her as he knew it would not take long for the words
to sink in. All the hurt of losing her husband would soon be
rushing right back in. Richard knew this well because it
wasn't that long ago that he lost his beautiful partner and
wife, Pamela. So Richard held her. At first there was no
response then he could feel her arms encircle him and her
chest began to heave with the silent sobs that soon turned into
the flooding tears of a woman in love that had lost her
husband.

It took awhile for Matty to compose herself. When she did she
reached for a tissue. Dried her eyes, blew her nose, and quietly
asked Richard, "do you think Sherrod killed my Wildman?"
"We think he is a good suspect. And now that you have told
me he came to your place looking for Clint, I think he is an
even bigger suspect."

Jean stood quietly for a moment, then said, "please find out
for sure. If he did, I want to know. I will kill that bastard
myself if I find out he shot my Clint."

The preceeding outpouring of emotions had prevented Matty
and Richard from hearing the tinkling of the bell attached to
the door when the patron had entered. But hearing the crying
and the conversation the patron had made his way back to the
doorway and had quietly observed Richard and Matty. The
conversation having died down, the patron joined Richard
and Matty in the small workroom. He cleared his throat to get
their attention.

"Sherrod." Richard said as he turned to face the intruder.
"I seem to be at a disadvantage. You know my name, but I
don't know yours."

"St.Clair. Richard St.Clair. What can we do for you?"

"Oh just checking on my investment."

"Could you please leave." Matty said not any too politely.

"Yes, I think I shall. But I think you two will come with me."

"Don't bet on that," Richard said as he took a step towards Sherrod.

Sherrod smoothly produced a small gun, stepped around Richard, grabbed Matty by the arm and placed the gun against her head, "okay, Richard St.Clair, your move. Would you like to join us or shall I just shoot her here?"

"Shoot her and I'll kill you with my bare hands before you can ever get off a second shot."

"Shall we find out or would you rather lead the way out to my car out front?"

Richard didn't have to think too long. He turned on his heel, and slowly made his way to the front door of the gallery. Opening it he saw the black Lincoln with the driver leaning against the fender waiting. Matty struggled to free her arm to no avail and finally followed Richard. The driver opened the rear door and Richard slid in followed by Matty and Cordell Sherrod. The driver jumped in and with the tires squealing made his way down Kaya Grande street and made a quick right turn onto Kaya Gerharts heading out of downtown towards the airport.

Chapter 15

Bobby Morrow could hardly hear his phone ring with the horns blasting from the cruise ship as it got underway to leave the port in Bonaire.

"Bobby," was all the Colonel on the other end said.

"Yes, Colonel," Bobby answered so he could be just as efficient.

"There does not appear to be any connection between Captain Craane and Cordell Sherrod. You may feel free to clue him in on what you know so far since it is his turf."

"Thank you, Colonel."

"Wrap this up immediately, Bobby!"

"Yes, Sir!" Bobby said but no one heard him except line static. Bobby debated for a minute, should he call or visit the Captain. The beautiful sunny day beckoned so he left the resort, jumped in his compact rental car and headed downtown.

Bobby no sooner entered the Police Station when the same Bonairean lady in uniform, after seeing who just came in, and immediately went to the Captain's office and entered. She came back with the Captain on her heels.

The Captain opened the half door and motioning Bobby in said, "Mr. Morrow, Con ta bai?" which is papiamento, the local language, for how are you, and raised his eyebrows slightly when Bobby responded, "Bon dia. Mi ta bon."

"I see that you are adjusting rather quickly to our little island, Mr. Morrow," the Captain said.

"Well I do enjoy it here and the people are fabulous."

"What can I do for you today, Mr. Morrow?"

"Today, Captain Craane, it is what I can do for you. You are the head of law enforcement on this lovely island, and I am a mere guest. I have, however, discovered the source of drugs coming into your country and wanted to make you aware of him."

"Please, continue," the Captain said.

"There is an elaborate scheme using trained dolphins to bring the drugs onto your island. I do not know where they go after they come here, but I'm sure that you can easily find out, if necessary, or just close down their entry onto your island , whichever you see fit."

"Do you have any facts, Mr. Morrow?"

"Yes, I do. Cordell Sherrod." Bobby couldn't help but notice that the smile left the Captain's face, "is running the operation. The drugs come in from Venezuela via the dolphins to the old shrimp farm out near Lac Bay. I also think he may be the person that shot my friend Clint Armstrong, so I, and

my government would certainly like to see him put away.
Saying that, I appreciate that this is your country with your
laws, and we would not presume to interfere with that.
Whatever manner you choose to handle the situation will be
fine with us."

The Captain studied a moment, "Mr. Morrow, you place me
in a delicate situation."

"I don't understand, I thought you would be pleased that you
can shut down a drug smuggling operation and make an
example of the leader."

"In your country that would work nicely. Here in Bonaire
where our entire island is only 24 miles long, 111 square miles
and just 50 miles off the coast of Venezuela. Our defense
consists of an occassional dutch cruiser which comes in and
out of our port. We have no standing army just a few police
officers. The Venezuelan drug cartels could invade our
country with no problem, and you want me to take their
leader into custody? Do I look like I have a death wish, Mr.
Morrow?"

"I'm sorry, Captain, I thought you would be pleased that we
gathered all the intel but then let you handle the situation."

"It's not that I am not pleased. More that I am helpless against
that type of enemy."

The door to the Captain's office burst open, and the young
Bonairean officer rushed to the Captain's side to whisper in
his ear. He listened attentively then asked, "When?"

She whispered in his ear again, and he replied, "thank you.
You may go."

"Mr. Morrow, I'm afraid you may be too late. Mr. Sherrod was
just seen leaving the Armstrong lady's art gallery in a great
hurry, with Mrs. Armstrong and your friend in tow. This is an
unbelievable problem for us."

"Captain, if I may make a suggestion?" Bobby asked.

"Please, speak," the Captain said.

"If you're getting involved with Sherrod is a problem, may I

suggest that you allow me to handle the problem for you?"
"But we can no more let the American government come into
our country and interfere than we can the Venezuelan
government."
"I was not speaking of our government, Captain. Just me. And
hopefully my dear friend, Richard. If we can capture Sherrod
without your assistance and get him out of your country,
neither the drug cartels nor the Venezuelan government can
hold anything against you. You would quite simply not know
anything about him or his drug smuggling operation."
"And if you fail, then I am left with American bodies on my
island and a lot of interference from your government," the
Captain said in an extremely disgusted tone.
"But, Captain. I'm sure I know where he is heading. I'm also
sure there will only be him and his driver or whatever he is.
At the moment I have the advantage of surprise on my side."
The Captain got up from his desk, clasped his hands behind
his back and paced around his office. Bobby did not interrupt
but did check his watch. After all, the clock was ticking. If
Sherrod had Matty and Richard time would be of the essence.
The Captain kept pacing. Then he stopped and looked straight
into Bobby's eyes.
"Can your government assure me that you are not here? That
there would be no retribution.?"
Bobby flicked open his phone and pushed the speed dial
button.
"Colonel, Bobby, we have a situation." Bobby went on to
explain all that he had just learned about Sherrod making off
with Matty and Richard. Bobby listened and threw in the
occassional, "yes, sir," then handed the phone to the Captain.
The Captain listened, then without saying a word hung up the
phone and handed it back to Bobby.
"Sergeant," the Captain yelled.
The young lady in uniform ran into his office.

"Sergeant, please be so kind as to have an officer on patrol stop by Mrs. Armstrong's Gallery and close her door. She just called and apparently in her rush she may have left it open. Thank you, Sergeant."

As the door to the Captain's office closed, he looked at Bobby, and said, "Mr. Morrow, it has indeed been a pleasure Not knowing you. Te aworo!"

Bobby replied, "Danki," and immediately left the office and the police station.

There were times between true professionals when a small glance or a mere facial expression can speak volumes so words are not necessary. There are also times when deniability is of utmost importance. Not saying something means it can be denied later on providing the perfect explanation if needed.

Bobby drove like a madman to the resort where he hurriedly parked the compact rental car and jumped into Clint's big old pickup truck with the boat in tow. Wasting no time he headed out E.E.G. Boulevard past the airport and turned onto Kaya IR Randolf Statuuis Van Eps, the shortcut over to Lac Bay. Mentally he took inventory of what weapons he had found in Clint's boat and truck and how he could approach the old shrimp farm without being seen. It was, after all, daylight, and in Bonaire that meant only one thing, plenty of sunshine and with the terrain consisting of lava, sand and a few cactus, there was certainly nothing to hide behind.

Chapter 16

Sherrod's big black Lincoln flew past the entrance to the airport and made its way down the island.

"I need to know," Matty said as she turned to face Sherrod, "did you shoot my husband?"

"You're better off without him," Sherrod answered.

"Did you shoot him?" she asked again, her voice getting louder.

"Yes, I shot him. I can't let my help have all the fun. And the old American saying is true - the bigger they are the harder they fall. He practically shook the island when the big tough guy fell over with his belly full of lead."

Matty went crazy. She managed to turn in the tight rear seat quarters and attacked Sherrod with both of her small fists hammering at his head and torso. Sherrod was unable to back away as he was jammed tight up against the door so he slammed his pistol into the side of Matty's head. Matty slumped over and Richard grabbed her and pulled her close to himself. Sherrod aimed the gun at her head but Richard reached out and swatted it away.

"You want to shoot somebody, tough guy, you shoot me!" Richard said with no waiver in his voice.

"I may need you for now," Sherrod told Richard, "But it won't be long until you are expendable. Then, I will take great satisfaction in killing you. You Americans make me sick with your holier-than-thou attitude."

"Yes, well, I don't need a crystal ball to know that you don't have much of a future," Richard spat at the drug kingpin.

"Oh, is your famous Bobby Morrow going to ride in like a white knight and save your ass?"

"I doubt he'll ride in, but when you see him you better hope he is in the mood to cut you a break."

"Yes, well your tough guy Bobby Morrow is outnumbered," Sherrod said.

"That's funny, I only count you and your stupid driver up there."

"That's right. Our two guns against his one."

"Then he has you outnumbered asshole!" Richard spat at him. The back seat passengers all quickly leaned to the left as the Lincoln made a fast right turn onto the dusty, bumpy road leading up to the old shrimp farm. It skidded to a stop kicking up a cloud of dust. The huge driver jumped out and opened the door for his boss. Sherrod, keeping the gun trained on Richard spoke, "get out slowly and take the broad with you. No funny stuff or you won't be alive when your friend Bobby comes."

"You better start soaking in this last little bit of Caribbean sunshine Sherrod cause you won't be enjoying it much longer," Richard told him as he slipped out the door of the Linclon being careful to hold on to Matty who was just starting to come around. As Richard pulled her out of the car she rubbed her head. Feeling the wetness on her fingers she looked at them, and saw the red blood. Her blood. Then she looked at Sherrod, "you bastard!"

"Get her in the building Mr. Richard St.Clair," Sherrod said as he motioned toward the door with his gun. The huge bodyguard was at the door holding it open.

Richard held onto Matty's arm as he guided her through the doorway. As Richard passed the driver, the huge man smacked Richard on the back of the head, then smiled. Richard stopped, glared at the huge man, then turned his head to look back to Matty. When he did he kicked him hard on the side of the knee. The driver fell like a sack of potatoes, grabbing his knee and howling in pain. Richard leaned down to give him some more when he heard the action of Sherrod's gun. Richard looked at Sherrod and smiled, "I was just going to help him up. He seems to have fallen'."

"I'll let you live long enough to help him inside. Any more tricks from you and the next bullet will have your name on it." Richard yanked the oaf to his feet and helped him into the building. He was limping badly which made Richard sport a small smile.

"Okay St. Clair. Park him in that chair then get the duct tape off the shelf," Sherrod barked as he kept the gun pointed at Richard.

Richard deposited the driver then went to the shelf and picked up the duct tape. Then stood there, twirling the duct tape on his finger.

"Want me to tape up the oaf's knee?" Richard asked sarcastically.

"No, but he is going to tape up your hands, so give him the tape then turn around."

Richard did as he was instructed. The driver slowly got to his feet putting all his weight on one leg and as roughly as possible taped Richard's wrists together behind his back, then spun Richard around. The driver had a gleam in his eye but Richard stared him down.

"Touch me you tough guy and I'll wreck your other knee," Richard told him. The gleam left his eye.

"Tape up the girl," Sherrod told his driver. The driver hobbled over and taped her wrists together. Sherrod grabbed her by the arm again and turned her to face him. "Now be a good little girl because you and I have some unfinished business," Sherrod told Matty.

Matty spit in his face. Sherrod laughed as he wiped it on the sleeve of his expensive suit, laughing out loud the whole time. Sherrod was about to say something when he heard the roar.

Chapter 17

The Dodge Ram's huge V-8 motor was screaming as Bobby unleashed all the horsepower it had galloping down the narrow Bonaire blacktop pulling the trailer and Zodiac boat towards the boat ramp at Lac Bay. Several times he shot past locals slowly making their way along the highway and leaving them shaking their heads when the force of the wind from the truck and boat nearly blew them off the highway. Of course, being a small island where nearly everyone knew everyone else, they recognized the truck and boat as that of Wildman Armstrong's and had to be wondering for a moment whether or not he was still alive.

Bobby turned off the highway onto the path leading to the boat ramp and swung a quick arc. Before even coming to a stop, he had the truck shifted into reverse and was backing the boat back towards the ocean as fast as possible. At the water's edge he slammed on the brakes, jumped out of the truck and raced to the boat trailer. He worked at breakneck speed unfastening the boat and shoving it off the trailer into the water. He checked the fuel in the big twin motors, grabbed the spare fuel can from off the boat and threw it into the bed of the pickup. Bobby pushed the Zodiac into the water, jumped on board and fired up the two huge Evinrude 300 motors and slammed the throttle forward standing the zodiac nearly straight up and flying out into the Caribbean Sea. After Bobby had pulled away from the shoreline he made a hard right turn and sped down the coast towards the old shrimp farm. It didn't take long at full throttle until he was upon the old shrimp farm. He manhandled the boat up against the concrete walls of the canal that fed into the old shrimp farm, cut the huge powerful motors off, threw the anchor and everything else he could find into the water and jumped up onto the narrow concrete wall. Bobby stood there in his usual confident manner and yelled, "Sherrod. It's Bobby Morrow. I'll give you one chance to live. You let my friends go unharmed and I'll let you go. I have a boat here that you can take to Venezuela."

"So the tough guy has arrived. Well, Mr. Bobby Morrow, I happen to be the person in charge. What say I shoot your friends then......"

Before Sherrod had a chance to finish his statement Bobby dove into the canal and was swimming underwater up it. The driver looked to Sherrod. Sherrod motioned with his gun for the driver to go to the edge of the canal and check it out. The driver limped over and peered into the dark water. He pulled out his gun and shots rang out then he disappeared over the side of the canal. As the group watched a hand came up over the concrete wall followed by the top of a head of wet hair, followed by a gun aiming the laser sight directly at Sherrod. As the remainder of the head appeared Sherrod pulled Matty in front of himself so he could hide behind her and get the laser sight off his chest. But the steady laser sight merely honed in on his forehead as Bobby climbed over the side of the wall.

"Fat boy might need some help," Bobby said to Sherrod, "he's not much of a shot. I would have thought you could afford better help."

"Yes, well I am a good shot and I can't miss your friend Matty at this range," Sherrod said as he jammed the barrel of the gun into the side of Matty's head.

"So you shoot her, then I shoot you. What does that do for you? You're still dead!"

"Get back from the wall Morrow and go stand by your friend Mr. St.Clair," Sherrod said.

As Bobby moved over next to Richard, Sherrod moved to the canal keeping the gun on Matty and Matty between himself and Bobby.

"Sherrod, you will leave Matty here, or I will kill you," Bobby told him.

Sherrod just kept walking out to the end of the building where he could step around the wall onto the wall of the canal and flee to the boat. As he was about to step onto the canal wall he spoke to Bobby, "By the way, drop your gun."

"Can't do it. Sorry. Years of military training. The only way you get my gun is to pry it from my cold dead hand!"

"Then perhaps I'll shoot her now."

"Then perhaps I'll shoot you before your toes touch the boat," Bobby said then continued, "but if you let her go I give you my word I will not shoot you."

"I've heard that you are a man of your word. Let's find out," Sherrod said as he shoved Matty into the canal while he jumped onto the boat. He fired up the two huge engines and

roared away from the shore heading straight for Venezuela.
"What the hell did you let him go for?" Richard asked Bobby.
"Just help help Matty out of the canal," Bobby answered as he
cut the tape from Richard's wrist with his swiss army knife.
Richard jumped in the water and helped Matty out as she was
struggling with her wrists still taped behind her back.
"Here, cut her loose," Bobby said to Richard as he tossed the
knife his direction. Then Bobby ran over and dove into the
canal. When he got to the end of the canal he disappeared
underwater. Richard and Matty watched and waited for a few
moments then Bobby burst through the water.
"What are you doing?" Richard yelled out to him.
"I'm going after Sherrod," he calmly answered.
"In case you haven't noticed he's in a very fast boat, that you
gave him, I might add, and is heading to Venezuela. Now
how do you intend to catch him?"
"I'm going to swim."
"You're going to swim?" Richard asked shaking his head.
"Yes. I left my diving gear here in the water," Bobby said as he
drug the gear up onto the bank.
"And just how fast do you figure you can swim?" Richard
asked sarcastically.
"Slow and steady wins the race, my friend."
"He is already out of sight," Richard reminded Bobby.
 Bobby turned and looked out toward the Sea while he
strapped on his tanks, "Yes he is."
"And you're going to catch him?"
"In about another two minutes, he's out of gas," Bobby said to
Richard with a smile on his face.
Richard just shook his head then said, "but why did you let
him go in the first place?"
"Captain Craane does not want him on his island and is not
comfortable arresting him, so now he's off the island. And his
driver can attest to that so keep him safe till I get back."
With that said, Bobby waded out into the beautiful blue

Caribbean Sea and disappeared under the water.

Richard turned to Matty, "are you alright?"

"Yes, thank you," she said.

"Excuse me for a moment, I have to get the trash out of the canal."

Richard jumped into the canal and fished out the driver who had been clinging to the canal wall for dear life. Unable to use his one leg to push himself up, Richard had to push him up and over the wall. When Richard climbed out after him, he got the duct tape and duct taped the driver's wrists behind his back.

"There's another use for duct tape," Richard said to the soaking wet driver.

Chapter 18

Diving in the warm Caribbean waters is exhilirating, but would be much more fun on the other side of the island. This was the wild side. The current was stronger, the marine life bigger and the water deeper. Bobby was headed for Blue Hole. He figured that with the small amount of fuel he left in the tank, and with those two big Evinrude 300's sucking it down, that Sherrod wouldn't get much further than that. So Bobby maintained a straight line and a nice consistent pace as he worked his way out to Blue Hole. He nearly collided with the huge Eagle Ray that swam toward him curious about who might be in its hunting grounds. The Eagle Ray was about six feet across it's wingspan with the white dots covering it's gray smooth surface and the head which looks so out of place as it truly resembles the head of an eagle. Once it swam up to Bobby and saw he was not a threat, the Eagle Ray continued his hunt along the bottom for food. Several large barracuda followed Bobby but he knew they were just hoping he would scare out some food for them to catch. The bottom became deeper and the current stiffer but Bobby pressed on. He could see the wreck at Blue Hole in front of him and started looking toward the surface. After a few minutes he spotted the bottom of the rubber Zodiac boat floating on the surface. Figuring that Sherrod would be at the back near the engines, Bobby swam up to the front of the boat and slowly poked his head up out of the water. Bobby knew he had to be careful as Sherrod still had the gun and Bobby did not. All Bobby had was a knife strapped to his leg. Sherrod was slapping the motors, cursing in Spanish because they had sputtered to a stop and not knowing why or what to do. Bobby worked his way around the side of the boat so he could come up behind Sherrod. It would be too dangerous to try to slip over the side as his weight would shift the boat and Sherrod would know so he worked his way slowly back to where the motors and Sherrod was. While Sherrod was slapping the side of the engine, Bobby quickly reached out and grabbed his arm pulling him into the water. Sherrod dropped his gun in the excitement and went tumbling overboard into the deep blue Sea with Bobby pulling him downward. Sherrod kicked Bobby and swung his free hand but all the while Bobby was pulling him deeper. Sherrod managed to wriggle out of Bobby's grasp and swam like a shot to the surface and back onto the boat. He was still looking for his gun when Bobby came over the side of the boat.

"Thought you were a man of your word, that you wouldn't kill me," Sherrod said to Bobby.

"Correction, I said I wouldn't shoot you. And I won't, being a man of my word," Bobby said, "but I am going to feed you to the fish."

"Good luck with that Morrow," Sherrod spat.

Bobby casually pulled off his flippers and dropped the air tanks off his back. Before he had time to think Sherrod got into his martial arts stance and threw a kick at Bobby. Sherrod was a black belt and very adept at the martial arts as he spent most of his free time practicing on his employees. The kick knocked Bobby off balance and nearly off the back of the boat, but he fought to stay on his feet and inside the boat, while fighting to shake off the fierce blow that had just doubled him over.

Chapter 19

The Colonel saw Bobby Morrow's number flash on the screen of his cell phone so he dropped what he was doing and answered it.

"Colonel, it's Bobby."

"What's up?" the Colonel asked.

"I'm on my way to collect Cordell Sherrod. He has taken Matty and Richard as hostage and I'm sure he is heading for the old shrimp farm. I'm in Clint's truck heading out there now."

"What's the plan?"

"Well," Bobby said as he sped along, "there is a fly in the ointment, Captain Craane does not want to be involved and wants Sherrod off his island. So I thought we would do just that, get him off the island."

"What do you have in mind?"

"I can get him out to sea then stick him there for a few minutes, can you get me a team there to extricate him?"

The Colonel thought a second then replied, "I have a team in Curacao, I'll put them in a chopper now and send them over. Where is the meeting point?"

"I thought I would give him just enough fuel in the boat he is going to steal from me to get out to the Blue Hole area. I can't be too exact but that would be along a straight line to Venezuela, which will definitely be where he will run to when I let him escape."

"Blue Hole area, it is," the Colonel said, "what's the E.T.A.?"

"Allowing for me to get to the boat ramp, get the boat in the water, cruise down to the shrimp farm, confront Sherrod, let him motor out there; I would say about 60 minutes."

"The team will be there." The Colonel hung up. He had plans to make.

Chapter 20

Bobby fought to stay in the bobbing boat in the Caribbean Sea with the waves pounding the boat and Sherrod pounding him with kick after kick. Ordinarily Sherrod would have put his victim down by now, Bobby was not an ordinary victim. Bobby Morrow, while normally a laid back, casual person, was a trained killer. He was far too stubborn to give in to having someone kick the crap out of him, and it was only a matter of time until he figured out the pattern. Which was just what happened. Sherrod changed legs each time he kicked. This time the right leg would be coming. This time, when it did, Bobby grabbed the toes of Sherrod's foot with his powerful right hand and the heel of Sherrod's foot with his equally powerful left hand. Bobby pulled downward with his right hand and upward with his left hand with all his might. The cracking noise floated out across the blue Caribbenan Sea. The pain shot up Sherrod's leg like lightning and came out his mouth in a terrifying scream as he crashed to the deck of the boat rolling onto his stomach to attempt to ease the pain. Bobby kept the pain coming then got in a kick of his own, pummeling Sherrod's mid section all the while still twisting the broken foot. Then Bobby threw the foot down to the deck causing another scream from Sherrod.

"Go ahead, finish me off," Sherrod managed between cries of pain.

"You're already finished Sherrod!"

"You'll have to kill me. Cause as soon as I can, I intend to kill you," Sherrod moaned, as he tried to crawl away from Bobby. Sherrod then grabbed the anchor and made a lunge at Bobby with it. Bobby sidestepped the swing but nearly lost his balance and went overboard. He was tempted to kill Sherrod then and there, after all, he was a drug pusher. He hooked little kids on his stuff and tore apart many a good family. The world would be better off without him. But Bobby wanted him punished slower, so he waited for the extrication team and let Sherrod lay on the deck whimpering.

It wasn't long before the helicopter showed up and a Navy Seal came flying down the rope and into the boat.

"Mr. Morrow, sir, the Colonel said you had some garbage you would like us to take off your hands," the Seal said to Bobby. Bobby merely pointed to Sherrod. The Seal wasted no time tying Sherrod's hands with the plastic ties while another Seal joined them on the boat.

"That's not too tight is it?" the Seal asked Sherrod while he smiled.

Sherrod just cried in pain.

"Where does it hurt?" the Seal asked.

Bobby responded, "he twisted his ankle."

Like a good doctor would do the Seal grabbed the misfigured ankle and gave it a little twist of his own, "is that where it hurts?" Sherrod screamed, both Seals smiled and Bobby just shook his head. The Seals then roughly strapped Sherrod into the harness and gave the sign to the chopper and Sherrod disappeared into the sky.

"Could you lower me down a little fuel?" Bobby asked the Seals.

"Yes, sir," the second seal responded and he immediately got on his waterproof phone and contacted the chopper. The rope immediately started down with a plastic can of fuel.

"You guys are better than AAA," Bobby said.

"Thank you, sir, and thank you for the gift," the Seal said as he smartly saluted Bobby.

"You don't need to salute me," Bobby said.

"Don't need to, sir, but want to, sir," The Seal replied as he assisted his teammate in getting in the harness which had come back down and quickly zipped the Seal back up. The rotors of the big sleek chopper had flattened the waves on the Sea around the boat and Bobby was struck by the calmness. The second Seal retrieved the harness as it made its voyage back down again and efficiently got prepared then gave the chopper the thumbs up and he disappeared into the blue sky. The Seal wasn't even completely in the chopper when it dropped its nose and took off like a shot.

"Hi ho silver," Bobby said to himself and blushed with the pride that he felt for his fellow military men.

The calmness quickly disappeared, the waves began bouncing the boat around but Bobby maintained his footing and got the gas caps off the motors and the fuel can and with a little bit of splashing he managed to get the bulk of the fuel into the tank. He tossed the spare can aside. Fired up the two monster Evinrudes and at full throttle stood the Zodiac on its tail and spun it around 180 degrees and headed for shore. He bounced off the tops of the waves and had but one thought in his mind. Getting to the airport and getting home to Ganister, Pennsylvania where he intended to squeeze his wife until she could hardly breathe. The Zodiac crossed the sea at a lightning pace and Bobby flew up onto the shore like marines invading a foreign country. He jumped out of the boat, pulled it clear of the surf, and jumped into Clint's pick-up truck, turned the key, hit the throttle, and spun coral back into the Sea. In just a couple minutes he pulled into the old shrimp farm.

"Richard, you here?" he yelled as he entered the building.

"Where else would I be?" Richard shot back while Matty snickered.

"Where's the driver?" Bobby asked.

"In the car," Richard said. Bobby opened the car door but didn't see anyone. Richard walked to the back of the car and popped the trunk. The driver was taped and stuffed in the trunk. Bobby approached him and yanked him over so he could look into his face. Then Bobby pulled the diver's knife from his leg and went toward the driver. The big man attempted to squirm away but there was no room to move and though his mouth was taped you could hear him scream. "Shut up," Bobby yelled at him, "act like a man."

Bobby then cut the tape off his wrists and ankles. The driver with his huge staring eyes kept close track of the knife in Bobby's hand and Bobby reached over and yanked the duct tape off the driver's mouth.

"Best to do it quick," Bobby said, "like taking off a band aid." The driver just stared at Bobby, speechless, probably wondering when or how he would be killed.

"What are you doing with him?" Richard asked.

Bobby ignored Richard and said to the driver, "get out!"

The driver cautiously hauled his heft out of the trunk and the springs of the black Lincoln sighed as they popped upward. The driver stood there leaning on the trunk watching every move Bobby made.

"Where are the keys?" Bobby asked no one in particular.

"Here," Richard said and he tossed them to Bobby who caught them without even looking in Richard's direction. Bobby then handed the keys to the driver who reluctantly took them. He then looked at Bobby and said, "What now?"

"You're a driver, drive," Bobby said and he took a step back from the driver. The driver looked into each face then slowly moved towards the front of the car. As he opened the door on the driver's side of the car, he looked back at Bobby as if waiting for conformation.

"Get out of here. Your boss is already gone."

The driver wasted no time getting into the car, starting it up and he tore off out the lane toward the paved highway and freedom.

"Now what?" Richard asked Bobby.

"Matty has a gallery to run. You and I have a plane to catch. Let's go."

The trio left the building and squeezed into the cab of the truck while Richard said, "I'll drive! You're a terrible driver." Bobby merely shrugged.

"Just stop at the airport," Bobby said, "then Matty can take her truck and come back for the boat. You don't mind do you Matty?"

"No, I don't mind. That you for everything you've done. It's nice to have some closure on Clint's death," she replied.

"You can get Russell to help you load the boat," Bobby told her.

"Of course, he's always willing to help," Matty said as she looked to Bobby, "but, one question."

"What's that?" Bobby asked.

"What of Sherrod?"

"He will be taking up residence in Guantanamo Bay? The Navy Seals are personally delivering him there."

"No chance he can escape?"

"Not from that crew. They would sure like him to try, but I'm sure he's smarter than that."

Matty sat back in the seat between the two friends and felt comfort for the first time in a long time.

Richard pulled the truck and empty trailer up to the front of the Flamingo Airport and jumped out. Followed by Bobby, then Matty.

"What about our luggage?" Richard asked.

"It will find its way home. Trust me. The Colonel will see to it," Bobby replied as they took turns hugging Matty and stepped inside the open air terminal. Bobby walked over to the Delta desk and said to the young Bonairean girl in uniform, "Morrow and St.Clair, I assume you have tickets for us?"

She looked around her desk and found an envelope with their names on it which she handed to him.

"When does the flight leave?" Bobby asked.

"They have been sitting on the tarmac waiting for you," she said then asked, "Who are you guys? Delta doesn't wait for anyone."

"Just two tourists from Pennsylvania," Bobby said smiling and turned to leave.

"Any luggage?" the girl asked.

"No. Thank you," Richard said as they each gave Matty one more hug and sauntered off to the waiting airplane. They walked through the customs area with no delays, were waved through by the immigration desk, and walked back out unto the warm Caribbean sunshine to cross the tarmac to the waiting airplane. The duo climbed the steps and stepped inside the plane and the air conditioning. The door was immediately closed behind them and the stewardess escorted them to their seats in first class.

As they were buckling their seat belts, Richard looked to Bobby and said, "Damn, I'm going to fly with you more often. First class?"

"Nothing but the best for you buddy." Bobby replied.

Chapter 21

The temperature difference was shocking when the plane landed at Pittsburgh International airport.

"We should have brought coats," Richard said to Bobby as they crossed the terminal, "I have to remember where I parked my car."

"The Colonel will have a car for us waiting," Bobby said.

"But what about my car?"

"We'll check with the driver," which is what they did when they saw the man holding the sign at the luggage carousel with their names on it.

"That's us," Bobby said to the sharply dressed man.

"This way gentleman," he responded and led the way out the doors into the frigid air but immediately opened the rear door of the limousine allowing them to get into the warm car.

"But what about my car?" Richard asked.

"I'm afraid your car is already in Ganister, Mr. St.Clair," the driver said.

"What do you mean by, 'I'm afraid'?" Richard inquired.

"Well the Colonel said that your Police Chief had it towed back to Ganister shortly after you left for the Caribbean."

"That, son-of-a..." Richard started to say but Bobby grabbed his arm.

"I told you not to toss the gun. Farr is determined to close that case and you and I are still both suspects. You especially because of the missing gun," Bobby told him.

"I just got back from the Caribbean and already you want to rain on my parade."

"We'll talk to him. We'll find out what he has and we'll get this thing settled. We both know who didn't shoot Billy Bollinger. We just have to figure out who did."

The two chatted as the driver knocked off the miles from Pittsburgh to Ganister and pulled into Bobby's driveway. Duke was waiting and shook all over with excitement as Bobby got out of the car, then rubbed up against him with his heft and nearly knocked Bobby over.

"Stay here tonight, Richard, and I'll take you home in the morning."

"I guess I could but I don't have any clean underwear."

"Claire will take care of it," Bobby said.

"Thanks for the ride," they both said to the driver, who got back into the car and started to drive off, then the back-up lights went on and he backed up to Richard and Bobby.

"Oh, by the way, gentlemen," the driver said, "I'll be here to pick you up tomorrow afternoon at 3 sharp."

"For what?" Bobby asked.

"Because the Colonel told me to," the driver said as he rolled his window back up and drove off.

"What's that all about?" Richard asked Bobby.

"You got me. Guess we'll find out tomorrow."

Claire was waiting at the door in her housecoat and had already poured a cup of hot coffee for Bobby.

"Your tea is brewing," she said to Richard.

Bobby grabbed her around the waist and hugged her then gave her a long hard kiss.

"Don't mind me," Richard said to their backs, "maybe you two should get a room?"

"Fix your tea and be quiet," Bobby said when he came up for air.

When the couple pulled themselves apart, Claire said to Richard, "oh by the way, I had your blue suit picked up at your house today and brought over for tomorrow."

"What's tomorrow," Bobby asked her.

"All I know is the Colonel is having a small party at the Hite Winery north of Ebensburg and we are to be there," she replied.

"But, Richard, I have some bad news for you," she continued.

"What's that?"

"Your house is trashed."

"What?"

"When I went for your suit, I found it just trashed. Stuff everywhere, so I called the Colonel. He said that your Chief Farr had a warrant and was hunting your guns."

"That son-of-a...."

"That's the second time within a few hours that you have called him that. And you made him Chief! How ironic is that?" Bobby said.

"He's going to get ironic, up alongside his head."

"Well there's nothing you can do tonight so relax. Supper will
be ready in a few minutes then you can get a shower and
wash the salt off of you."
Claire prepared a nice dinner with roast beef, mashed
potatoes, asparagus, and a fine Merlot to go with everything.
The hot food, the quiet of the Morrow log home and the fire
crackling in the fireplace brought sleep upon them all. Well, it
did take a little longer for Claire and Bobby to get to sleep as
they kissed goodnight and one thing led to another.

Duke wakened the household early the next morning as he
defiantly stood in the middle of the driveway with his
massive size barking at the police cruiser that was attempting
to get to the Morrow residence.
"Duke," Bobby yelled at him, "get up here." Bobby waited on
the porch in his jeans and coat but without any shoes on.
The police cruiser continued up the driveway and Chief Farr
crawled out from behind the steering wheel.
"Morning, Chief," Bobby said, "come on in. It's cold out here."
Bobby turned and went inside waiting for Chief Farr.
When the Chief came in and closed the door behind himself,
he took off his hat and said, "I heard you two were home. I
really need to talk to you both."
"Have a seat," Bobby told him, "you want a cup of coffee?"
Duke stood staring at the Chief. The Chief kept glancing over
at Duke to be sure he was a sufficient distance away.
"He won't bother you," Bobby said, "well unless you've done
something to piss him off. You didn't, did you?"
"I hope not," the Chief said, "but I did have to come with a
search warrant and I don't think he likes me."
"You didn't give my wife any grief, did you?" The Chief
looked away for a second. Just then Claire entered the kitchen.
"Morning Chief," she said to Farr.
"Morning Mrs. Morrow," the Chief said back, "I apologize if I

upset you last time I was here."

"You didn't upset me, but I can't speak for Duke. He seems to be staring at you like you're a fresh hunk of meat."

"Anyway," Bobby said, "is there a reason you are here?" Richard mozied into the kitchen and spied the Chief sitting at the table with his cup of coffee.

"You son-of-a...." he started to say but Bobby stopped him.

"Chief Farr," Bobby said, "it appears you have greatly pissed off your boss. Maybe something to do with towing his car from the airport. Or maybe with trashing his house. What do you think?"

"I had legal search warrants and thus far neither of you have been very forthcoming with me," the Chief replied.

"Yeah, well, when I get home, if my house is still trashed, you better be looking for a new job. And my Volvo better be in the same shape it was when I left it. If it isn't, after I fire you, I'll kick your ass!" Richard said very defiantly.

"Everything is fine, now," the Chief said, "the workers were there today after your Colonel got done raising hell with the whole town council. I may not have a job much longer anyway, because of that."

"Richard, sit down," Bobby said, "Chief, where are you in this investigation?"

The Chief responded, "first, I have questions for you two. You are my loose ends."

"We're not your loose ends, Chief," Bobby said, "'cause we didn't shoot Billy Bollinger."

"Then why is the Mayor hiding his guns?" the Chief asked as he looked to Richard.

"He's not hiding the gun. Gun, singular. One gun, but he is not hiding it, and he didn't shoot Billy," Bobby replied before Richard could speak.

"I have a witness. There were three cars that stopped at the scene where Billy's car was wrecked."

"Three?" Bobby asked.

"Yes, three. Richard's Volvo. Your old red truck and a silver car."

"Who's silver car?" Bobby asked as he perked up.

"I don't know," the Chief responded.

"Who is the witness?" Richard asked.

The Chief hesitated then said, "Grammy Guering."

"That makes sense," Bobby said, "she sits by that window and doesn't miss anything."

"She didn't recognize the silver car?" Richard asked the Chief.

"Any other witnesses?" Bobby asked the Chief.

"Not that I've found."

"Excuse me for a minute," Bobby said as he got up form the table and went into the open living room while he flipped his phone open and dialed a number.

"Yeah!" was the response on the other end of the line.

"It's Bobby."

"Yeah."

"Can I ask you a question?"

"Yeah."

"You doing any fishing?"

"Yeah."

"Down at the Juniata River?"

"Yeah."

"The day that Billy Bollinger was shot, were you fishing there?"

"Yeah."

"Can I come over and talk to you?"

"Yeah."

Bobby turned back to the the kitchen, "Chief, let's go."

"What do you mean, 'let's go?' I still have questions for you two."

"Chief, you're asking the wrong people questions, if you want to close this case, let's go," Bobby said, "come on Richard you're coming too."

"But we haven't had breakfast yet," Richard said to Bobby as he looked over to Claire with pleading eyes. Claire just shrugged as she continued drinking her coffee.

"Shit," Richard said and got up to go finish dressing.

As the trio was leaving the house, the chief asked, "Where are we going Bobby?"

"Farmer Terry's," Bobby told him as the trio piled into the police cruiser. Richard glared at Bobby as he slid into the back seat.

"Why do I have to ride in the back?" Richard asked.

"Cause the Chief is driving," Bobby said, "And I'm not riding back there."

It was just a few minutes drive to Farmer Terry's, as he was popularly known. His real name was Terry Lee. He lived in an old farm house behind the Blue Hole, that massive deep blue puddle of water that at one time was a working gravel quarry. Fed by an underground stream the solid rock walled bowl contained forty feet of clear blue water. The narrow gravel road alongside the quarry led up to Terry's house. The road was in poor condition. Full of pot holes. Not because of inattention, but because it discouraged visitors, and Terry didn't like visitors. Terry liked to farm, hunt, fish, and be left alone with his family. The police cruiser bounced it's way up the lane and pulled up in front of the two story, hundred year old farmhouse.

As the Chief was getting out of the car, he was stopped by the sound of a shotgun being pumped.

Farmer Terry stood on the porch with the shotgun aimed at the Chief.

"What do you want?"

Then Bobby and Richard stepped out of the car.

Terry, seeing Bobby lowered the gun.

"Bobby. Richard," Terry said as he nodded his head toward them.

"Hey Terry," Bobby said, "How's it going?"

Terry looked at the Chief, "Not sure."

"I came to ask you that question, but wanted the Chief to hear you answer."

"Yeah. Ask."

"Were you fishing in the Juniata River when Billy Bollinger got shot?" Bobby asked.

"You already asked that question, Bobby," Terry answered.

"Tell the Chief," Bobby encouraged him.

"Yeah."

The Chief asked, "Did you see anyone there?"

Terry ignored him. "What's your question, Bobby?"

"There was a silver car that pulled up before I pulled up. Did that person shoot Billy?"

"Yeah."

"Do you know who it was?"

"Yeah."

"Well why the hell didn't you report that?" the Chief asked in a raised voice.

The shotgun swung back up towards the Chief. "You weren't invited here! Just those two," Terry said.

The Chief shut up and looked to Bobby.

"Terry," Bobby asked, "who was driving the silver car?"

"That guy that runs the ambulance service."

"Shawn Boyer?" Bobby asked.

"Yeah."

"And he shot Billy?" Bobby asked again.

"Yeah. Stopped his car. Ran over to Billy's car. Pulled out a pistol and shot him. Then made a phone call and left."

"I ought to arrest you for withholding information," the Chief told Terry.

"And I ought to shoot you for trespassing," Terry responded.

The Chief looked at Bobby and jumped back into the car.

Richard and Bobby thanked Terry for his hospitality. Before leaving Bobby asked, "Terry, your boy doing okay?"

"Yeah. He's a sniper now in the Army."

"I heard. I've been watching him move up through the ranks," Bobby replied.

"He wants to be just like you, Bobby."

"That's quite a compliment, but he needs to strive to be like his old man. You're a fine man, Terry."

"Stop by again," Terry said. "Don't bring him next time," he said as he motioned with the shotgun toward the Chief.

"He's alright," Bobby said to Terry as he got in the car.

"Let's go Chief," Bobby said as the Chief started the car and headed down the bumpy gravel lane.

"I still should arrest that farmer," the Chief said.

"Chief," Bobby said, "don't mess with Terry. You ever hear the old saying 'Never kick a sleeping dog?' You get in a pissing match with Terry and you'll be way out of your league. Trust me."

"I got a gun, too," the Chief remarked.

"Yes, but Terry won't hesitate to use his. Then he'll toss your body in the quarry."

The Chief decided to change the subject, "what possible motive could Shawn Boyer have to shoot Billy Bollinger?"

"Chief," Bobby said, "I've been investigating a drug ring in the ambulance service. That's why Billy Bollinger was getting out of town. I had evidence on him, I was just waiting for a bigger fish, and it makes sense that it would be his boss. So, take us back to my place then you go arrest Boyer and put this case to rest."

The Chief looked in the rearview mirror to Richard, "I'm sorry Mayor, I thought you shot Billy."

"I told you, I wanted to, but I didn't," Richard said, "you just make sure my car and house are back the way they belong.

"Do you think I'll get to keep my position, if I get this case closed?" the Chief asked Richard?

"You're not going to lose your position, Chief."

"But the way that Colonel raised hell with the council..." the Chief remarked.

"The Colonel will be sure that you don't lose your job, just go get that piece of scum in jail."

Chapter 22

The shiny black limousine pulled up the Morrow driveway while Duke watched from the porch where he was sunning himself. Duke raised his head at the sound of the gravel crunching under the tires, saw who it was, and went back to the chore of soaking up rays.

The driver exited the vehicle and stood by the rear door until the Morrows and Richard came out of the house, then he opened the door for them. The trio was very dapper looking. Bobby in his blue suit with Claire in a matching dark blue dress and heels. Richard had on his black suit and colorful fish necktie.

"Watch the place while we're gone," Bobby said to Duke who lifted his head long enough to get his instructions.

The Lincoln cruised up the mountain to Ebensburg then got on Route 219 for a few miles before turning off the highway into the Hite Winery. The green grass was immaculately trimmed, the landscaping just perfect and the old former barn that was now the Winery was freshly painted. As the driver pulled up to the front entrance, a banner flapped in the light breeze, saying "Welcome, Senator".

Richard got out and assisted Claire as Bobby got out the other side.

"I guess the Senator is joining us," Richard said to Claire.

The trio entered and found a small group of people standing at the bar sampling wines. Upon hearing them enter the Colonel turned around and raised his glass towards them, "Welcome Senator St.Clair!" The group raised their glasses and toasted.

"What the hell are you talking about?" Richard asked the Colonel.

"We have placed your name on the ballot to run for Senator," the Colonel replied.

"But, why?"

"You have to be Senator for the next chapter of your life. For the greater good."

"But I thought I might start a bottled water company at the quarry, Blue Hole Water."

"Who would ever buy bottled water?" the Colonel asked, "all you have to do is turn the faucet and water comes out?" the Colonel dismissed the idea with a flick of his wrist.

"Try the black raspberry-chocolate merlot or the pomegranate zinfandel, they are fabulous," Mrs. Hite told the group.

"Senator, huh?" Richard asked himself.

THE GREATER GOOD

Chapter 1 -BEDFORD COUNTY, PENNSYLVANIA

The whamp, whamp, whamp of the rotor blades on the sleek black helicopter never disrupted the muted sounds of the birds, crickets, and cows on the Klaar farm until it was within sight of the occupants of the old two story white farmhouse. One of many that lined this lush Pennsylvania valley. Lost in time and protected on both sides by the Allegheny Mountains. It was a very normal early autumn day in September with blue sky punctuated by fluffy white clouds. The leaves on the trees were still green but wouldn't be for much longer as the sap would soon stop running and the trees would become a photographer's pallet of rich colors.

Before the sleek black helicopter, with no markings or numbers emblazoned on it ever landed, the group of men in black uniforms, balaclavas, and helmets, loaded to the teeth with guns, jumped from the helicopter and ran to take up positions surrounding the Klaar family's humble farmhouse. There were six of them in all plus the pilot and they moved like a well oiled military machine. They were greatly out of place on this peaceful small farm in the valley where not much happened except for watching the hay grow.

When the men were in position the apparent leader of this band of professionals nodded to the pilot. The pilot's voice came out loud and clear over the intercom system, "Bobby Morrow, come out with your hands on your head. We have you surrounded."

The door to the farmhouse opened. Kurt Klaar walked out onto the porch with his hands in his pockets. Kurt was an older man in his sixties, rather scruffy in appearance and just as scruffy in demeanor. Hardened by a life full of hard work and little reward. Though soft spoken he certainly spoke his mind, and with little education, except from the school of hard-knocks, what usually came out of Kurt's mouth was the most common of common sense. He got along exceptionally well on a farm because he couldn't stand to be around most people.

"Sir, remove your hands from your pockets. Slowly," came the voice over the intercom.

"Hey assholes; you're trespassing on my property. Now take a hike," stated the defiant farmer.

"Sir, remove your hands from your pockets," the intercom repeated.

"You're in Bedford County, Pennsylvania shit-for-brains not Russia or Germany. You got any official pieces of paper or even half a reason to be on my property?" Kurt asked without the need to raise his voice.

"We are here for Bobby Morrow, sir, and we have good reason to believe he is here."

Kurt turned his back to the men in black, looked into the still open door, and said, "see Bobby, I told you Big Brother was always watching and could track those damn cell phones. That's why I don't own one."

Bobby Morrow ambled out the door with a cup of steaming coffee in his hand, "Morning gentlemen. Anyone want coffee? Kurt ain't much of a cook, but he makes a mean cup of coffee. He's also not such a bad guy once you get to know him."

"Mr. Morrow put down the coffee and place your hands on your head," the voice on the intercom announced.

"This is my first cup of coffee for the day and trust me, you don't want me to put it down cause then I'll be in a foul mood the rest of the day."

Chapter 2 -ONE WEEK EARLIER

MALMOK BEACH, ARUBA

North of the high-rise hotel area but south of the California Lighthouse, that inhabits the northernmost tip of the twenty mile long island of Aruba, on the western side of the island is the mostly residential area of Malmok Beach. The actual beach here is not as wide and in one area nonexistent, which is why Malmok is the preferred destination for snorkelers. On any given day you will see numerous boats dropping loads of snorkelers into the breathtakingly beautiful blue water of the Caribbean Sea, in addition to those that drive there to snorkel from the shore. The rocky area is quite a contrast to the six plus miles of alabaster sandy beaches that Aruba is famous for. At Malmok the attraction is not the beach, but the fish. Angel fish, Sergeant Majors, Blue Tang, Starfish of every size and

color, and a few turtles. Sensory overload happens to
all the snorkelers here as the many colors and shapes of
marine life combine with the beautiful blue hues of the
pristine water which gently laps onto the shore.
Smiling happy faces are the norm here at Malmok. All
except for the three persons standing at the water's
edge. Richard St.Clair, his best friend Bobby Morrow,
and Bobby's wife, Claire. Standing, staring down into
the Caribbean Sea, looking extremely somber, just as
they have during their visits here for the past eleven
years on the same day each year, at the same spot. Here
again to pay their respects to Pamela, Richard's
deceased wife who died eleven years ago from cancer,
and who requested her ashes be placed here in the
Caribbean Sea at her and Richard's favorite spot,
following her cremation. The three stood reverently
paying their respects. Each in their own way.
After a while they turned, as one, and walked up the
low rise to a palm roofed chickee where they removed
sunglasses and extra clothing, grabbed their flippers
and masks, and headed for the calm blue sea.   Richard
St. Clair needed to relax in the sea watching the marine
life. It had been another stressful year. Now that he was
a United States Senator and most recently got
appointed to the prestigious Armed Services
Committee, he had no time for himself. Of course, that
was also part of the plan. To stay so busy he didn't
have time to think about not having Pamela around
any longer. When he was floating in the water
observing the colorful fishes he was reminded of the
old days when Pamela would be snorkeling right next
to him, holding his hand, and pointing to the next
interesting sight.
Richard was still in great physical condition and could
snorkel around the sea for hours on end. Just shy of six

foot tall with a narrow waist and broad shoulders plus
what most women would call a baby face. Richard's
looks surely helped his political career as he moved
from mayor of his hometown of Ganister, Pennsylvania
into the Senate seat that he has held now for many
years. By contrast, his best friend Bobby Morrow was a
couple inches shorter with rugged good looks and not
an ounce of fat. He generally sported a beard each
winter and was clean shaven in the summers. Bobby
and Richard have been best friends since they served
together in Vietnam. In 1970 they had parachuted into
Cambodia to hike through the jungles and the rice
paddies to stop the North Vietnamese from pushing
southward toward Rocket City, which was to become
the US base of operations. Of course, according to the
politicians, there were no US soldiers in Cambodia. The
objective was to hike through the jungles and rice
paddies into the "Parrot's Beak", that point where
Cambodia and Laos meet Vietnam. Richard ended up
daydreaming and hiking right into the barrel of a North
Vietnamese soldier. Fortunately for Richard, the soldier
was slow on the trigger and Bobby was nearby and
paying close attention. Before the North Vietnamese
pulled the trigger to send Richard home in a flag
draped coffin, Bobby, being a top notch sniper, placed
two extra holes in the North Vietnamese's forehead.
They have been best friends ever since.
Richard was studying a large stonefish hiding amongst
the coral when he caught a glimpse of something in his
peripheral vision. Richard snapped his head to his left
to be sure he wasn't seeing things. When he did he was
staring straight at a beautiful smiling face. Short dark
hair and dangling down in the clear water, two
luscious breasts with very erect nipples. Scarcely able
to believe his eyes he looked to his right to find Bobby

or Claire to confirm his discovery. Unable to locate them, and needing another glimpse Richard turned back to his left. Nothing. The vision was gone.

Dinner that evening was another tradition. Richard, Bobby, and Claire would venture up to LaTrattoria, the Italian restaurant that sits at the base of the California Lighthouse. LaTrattoria sits on a knoll overlooking the western side of Aruba and perfectly situated to catch the breathtaking sunsets. That along with the fine cuisine, the outdoor patio ambience and the meticulous staff of waiters made this one of the most desirable places to be for dinner. More so if you were with your favorite partner.

As the Aruban waiter showed the trio to their table, they noticed some familiar faces and stopped to chat tableside.

"Senator St.Clair, how good to see you again," said the well tanned tall gentleman at the head of the table with his lovely wife in her sundress and another couple.

"Well if it isn't the Sines from Virginia," Richard replied, "isn't this where we ran into each other last year? And, please, on vacation it's just Richard. You remember my friends Bobby and Claire?"

"Of course. You all look tanned and rested," said Mrs. Sine, "and these are our friends from Richmond, the Leuschens."

Richard immediately offered his hand, "so nice to meet you. Hope you're enjoying the island."

"We sure are. It's beautiful here," replied Mr. Leuschen.

His wife spoke up and said, "but we miss our son and will be glad to get back to him tomorrow."

"What's your son's name?" Claire asked.

"George, he's just eighteen months and so precious."
After handshakes and hugs all around Bobby spoke up,
speaking directly to Mr. Leuschen, "whatever you do,
don't let Mr. Sine there order your dinner for you."
Mr. Sine smiled and started to object but Bobby went
on, "last year he ordered the Linguine something or
other, what was that called Richard?"

"Linguine Della Scogliera," Richard answered in his
best imitation of an Italian accent.

"Yea, Linguine Della Scogliera. You should have seen
it. There was an actual baby octopus sitting on top of
the pasta and seafood. You could see the suckers on it's
little legs and everything, and he," pointing to Mr. Sine,
"He actually ate it."

Ellwood Sine smiled, "and I enjoyed it. I might even
have it again this evening." Ellwood and Bobby had
gotten along famously since they met last year as they
both had a military background. Ellwood was a former
Navy man and Bobby a former Army Ranger.

"Well we don't want to hold you back from that," said
Claire as the threesome took their leave and settled into
their own table where the still smiling waiter was
patiently waiting. The Aruban people are nothing if not
patient. They have never accepted the fast pace of
living that the American people seem to endure.

The gentle tradewinds carried the sounds of excited
tourists across the open air patio amidst the flashing of
cameras as everyone vied for the perfect sunset photo
that would make their friends back home jealous.

When the large yellow ball of sun finally dropped into
the inky dark sea the level of conversation picked up as
the sun was replaced by the surrounding torches and
large moon. The red tablecoths, fancy folded white
napkins, crystal wine glasses, and extra forks all helped
establish the atmosphere.

"So, Richard, you've been rather quiet since our snorkel this afternoon, what's up?" asked Bobby.

Richard studied Bobby a minute before responding, "If I told you, you wouldn't believe it."

"Try me."

"Yes, come on Richard," Claire said, "what's going on?"

"Well," followed by a long pause as he looked curiously at both of his friends, "I think I saw a mermaid today."

Bobby immediately launched into a full belly laugh that caused him to spill his water, so Richard buried his head in his menu. The waiter unknowingly came to Richard's rescue. He recited the specials for the evening then looked to Claire to ask if she would care for glass of wine.

"A nice Merlot would be fine," replied Claire.

"And for the gentlemen?"

"Merlot sounds good, you may as well bring us a bottle," Bobby said, then looked to Richard, "that okay with you? Or would you prefer something that would go better with mermaids, I mean seafood?"

"Go ahead, bust my chops. I knew I should have kept my mouth shut, but one minute she was there and the next minute she was gone. And, close your ears Claire. She had fabulous breasts."

Bobby jumped right in, "see, there's the problem. You go a dozen years without getting any and your mind starts to play tricks on you."

"Bobby, stop." Claire insisted. "Change the subject or Richard won't be the only one not getting any."

In the background a faint cry of, "Please help!" came from a table behind them. Bobby jumped up and rushed back to the table occupied by an elderly well dressed couple. The man was leaning over the table.

The lady was trying to pat him on the back. Bobby pulled the man's chair back. By that time, Ellwood Sine had also arrived and pulled the gentleman up from his chair from behind, wrapping his arms around him and performing the Heimlich maneuver. By the time Richard arrived, a projectile was skittering across the patio, and a blue faced gentleman was returning to normal. It was like watching the former Army and the former Navy competing to save a life. The lady was beyond ecstatic and couldn't stop thanking the rescuers.

As everyone returned to their seats, the waiter stopped by to ask if they were ready to order. Claire ordered the Linguine Primevera. Richard ordered the Lasagna Nostrana. While Bobby teased that he wanted the Linguine Della Scogliera with the baby octopus just to get a rise out of Richard, but settled for the Striped Seabass with mixed seafood.

"So, how is Carol doing?" Richard asked Claire.

Carol is the Morrow's only daughter and they were just now beginning to experience the empty nest syndrome as Carol had taken a job out of town.

"We just spent the other weekend moving her into an apartment in Newark."

"New Jersey? Really? There aren't even any white people living there anymore."

"Yes, she got a position with Prudential."

"What will she be doing?"

"Traveling! She'll actually get paid to do what we have to pay to do. She's in charge of arranging their meetings and conventions, so part of the process is for her to fly to the locations to check out the accommodations, food, everything." Claire explained.

"And she gets paid to do it," Bobby said, "can you believe that?"

"Next week," Claire said, "she'll be going to San Fransico to stay at a resort so she can decide if it will be their spring convention location."

The wait staff brought their meals. Piping hot. The steam rising into the bright starry sky, stopping all conversation at the table. The luscious aromas forcing everyone to gather their utensils. The extremely confident and competent waiter smiled a large toothy smile and simply said, "Enjoy!"

After dinner with belts straining and stretching the trio pushed back their wrought iron chairs with the bright red cushions, slowly got to their sandled feet, made their way out of the restaurant and out to the base of the California lighthouse where the subcompact rental car awaited.

They made a slow drive back past the brightly lit high-rise hotels and south along the beach with the car windows down and the tradewinds gently blowing their hair. They cruised past the Alhambra Casino where the large bald man dressed like a genie always stood outside inviting in all who would like to defy the odds at the one arm bandits. There they made the right turn and found a parking space in front of their resort.

As Richard left Bobby and Claire at the lobby he asked, "Where's breakfast tomorrow?"

"How can you possibly think of breakfast right now?" Claire asked.

"I'll be hungry in the morning."

"You decide," Bobby said.

"I would suggest either Salt'N Pepper or IggieMoes. Both are good." said Richard.

"Meet us in the lobby here around nine tomorrow. We'll decide then. How's that?"

"Ayo," Richard said and headed to his room.

Ayo is Papiamento for goodbye. Papiamento is the local Aruban language and Richard was attempting to learn more of it.

Bobby and Claire meandered out to the pool to sit and listen to Lionel, the steel drum player. The soothing steel drum sounds combined with the gentle lapping of the sea and the lovely scents riding the tradewinds made the atmosphere nearly seductive and compelled the couple to dance. Barefooted. Slow. Close. Very, very close. Aruba, one happy island!

Chapter 3 -TWO DAYS LATER

GANISTER, PA

It's refreshing to spend time in the Caribbean letting the tradewinds blow away your anxieties and slowing down to a more relaxing pace, but, it's always good to be back home.

And it didn't take long until the telephone was ringing.

"Bobby," Bobby answered as he flicked open his cell phone.

"Bobby, it's me," was the reply from the familiar voice that belonged to the Colonel.

The Colonel was Bobby's handler for his federal undercover work. Bobby had gathered up quite a few medals while in Vietnam and had got the Colonel's attention so that when Bobby returned to civilian life and the Colonel began doing operations for the federal government to squelch the drug traffic, the Colonel naturally enlisted Bobby as an undercover agent. When he wasn't doing that, Bobby had a part time dental practice in Ganister.

"What's up?" Bobby asked.

"Need you to go down to Stoystown tomorrow. Our pilots have spotted a rather large tract in the side of the mountain, just east of town and south of the highway, that's probably a "pot" farm. I need you to check it out before we send the ATF boys in. Make sure there are no booby traps and get an idea of the best way in, plus how protected it might be."

"You think they may be armed up?"

"Well since California has opened medical marijuana facilities it sure is profitable to grow the stuff. And where there's big money, there's someone protecting it. What I don't want is the ATF boys to wander into a situation where they get shot up. And, Bobby, this is just a recon. No heroics. No dead bodies."

The line went dead. Typical of the Colonel. When he was done, he was done. There was no small talk. No thank yous. Not even a kiss my ass. Just dial tone.

Bobby grabbed his normal couple hours of sleep then put his gear together. Bobby hadn't slept through the night since he was in Vietnam, so he loaded up his beat up old red pickup truck and slowly made his way over to Stoystown. He remembered an old logging road that took off route 30 that would make a good place to hide his truck away from the main road. He had come across the road a couple years back when he, Kurt Klaar, and Mike the Mechanic were hunting bear there.

As the sun rose in the east chasing away the shadows in the forest, Bobby, attired in his cammo pants and coat, takes stock of where he is and what direction might yield the best results. Up, up over the rolling hills. That's where Bobby is being lured. Bobby stuck to the logging road for about a mile until he came across a slightly worn trail heading southwest. His gut feeling was to follow this trail as something about it was enticing to him. It was too wide to be a deer trail, and too narrow for four wheelers. After another mile Bobby came across the first sign that he was on the right track. The slight glint of sun striking dew on what at first appeared to be a spiderweb caused Bobby to squat down and examine it more closely. Thin fishing line stretched across the trail, barely visible except to someone that spent years in Vietnam searching for booby traps just to stay alive. This was either a booby trap or a crude early warning system. Bobby's instincts told him it was the latter and sometimes the simpler the better. The line was too thin to actuate a trap but plenty strong enough to ring a simple bell or rattle a can, anything to warn someone of an interloper. Well, this was what Bobby came for. May as well test their resources. He stood up and walked through the line as though he never saw it.

Chapter 4 -THE SITUATION ROOM,

WASHINGTON, DC, SEPTEMBER 11, 2001

Senator Richard St.Clair arrived to a standing room only crowd after passing through all the required security. He didn't need to get up to speed with what was happening as everyone in the United States that wasn't in a coma was glued to their television or radio catching the constantly repeating reports of the two airplanes that crashed into the Twin Towers and the Pentagon.

Senator St.Clair's presence was demanded at the meeting since he was Chairman of the prestigious Senate Armed Services Committee. Also present was everybody in Washington who was anybody. The President of the United States, the Vice President, dressed as though he should be on the golf course, and probably hoping to get there soon. Admirals, Generals, House of Representative committee members, the balance of Richard's committee, and aides coming out the wazoo.

"Mr. President," the General with enough stars on his uniform to be a planetarium, was saying, "we need to act, and we need to act now."

"General," jumped in the Vice President, "act how? Against whom? What we need to do is get FEMA up to New York and start working on finding any possible survivors."

The General persisted, "We've got more problems and we need to address them right now. A third plane is joining the rukkus."

"How can you be so sure, General?" asked Senator Len Snead of Virginia.

The General wasted no time responding, "We have been monitoring all the air traffic since the first plane went off course. Flight 39 left Newark, New Jersey heading for San Francisco. Well, it just made a near U turn at Cleveland, Ohio and is now on a course either for Pittsburgh, Pennsylvania or here."

"How do you know that, General?" asked one of the committee members.

"Because the pilot is no longer responding," answered the General.

"What are our options, General?" asked the President who up to this point, as was his style, had been quietly sitting at the head of the exceptionally long conference table listening to all the attendees and simultaneously watching the television coverage. His fingers forming a tent perched under his lower lip while absorbing all the information.

The General having just got off his cell phone addressed the President, "Mr. President, we are now positive this third plane is another terrorist action. We have had confirmation from the control tower regarding calls to them from the plane. The hijackers were shouting 'Death to the infidels!' The fact that this third plane has made such a radical departure from its intended course makes it more than suspect."

"But what are our alternatives?" the President asked. The Admiral jumped out of his seat to stand next to the General. "Mr. President," he said, "we need to take that plane down!"

"Down? Exactly what are you saying, Admiral?"

"I have scrambled our F14 Tomcats. They can shoot it down someplace where no further citizens will get hurt."

The President couldn't even speak for the uproar. Everyone was on their feet talking at once. The Vice president finally shouted them down so the President could speak.

"You're suggesting we shoot down an American airplane with American citizens onboard?"

The representative from California could not be restrained, "Mr. President that is ludicrous! We have no right to murder American citizens. Surely you are dismissing this entire conversation."

"Mr. President," the General interrupted, "we are obliged to protect the American citizens. We already have probably several thousand dead citizens attributable to these terrorists. Do you think they will stop there? We must look at the larger picture. The greater good,..."

"You better do a lot more explaining General because you are talking about taking American lives."

"I understand Mr. President. It is akin to everytime we send an American soldier into action. We know we will sacrifice many of them to protect the remainder of the citizens of this country. It's for the greater good."

"I will have to take that under advisement, General."

The Representative from California chimed in again, "there is *nothing* for you to consider Mr. President. We cannot order the deaths of American citizens."

"We should sit here and let the terrorists kill them?" Senator Snead asked.

"It would be better they die at the hands of terrorists than by our hand."

The Admiral was back on his feet "with all due respect Mr. President, Flight 39 went off course at Cleveland and is currently already in Pittsburgh airspace. While everyone is sitting around in these comfy chairs drinking hot coffee the terrorists could be getting ready to take out another building, like the US Steel building in Pittsburgh or the PPG building...."

"Mr. President," the Representative from California started but was quickly put aside by the Admiral.

"Flight 39 is traveling at over 420 miles per hour. Pittsburgh to Washington is 240 miles. Somebody better start doing the math. If they are heading here for the White House, which would be a prime target for them, or the Washington Monument or any other target, they are only thirty minutes away. I suggest the Representative from California put his head between his legs and start kissing his ass goodbye, or make the hard decision."

"Admiral," the President responded, "if we were positive this plane was taken by terrorists. And I say 'if', what action would you suggest."

"Mr. President," the Representative from California stated, "please, I beg you, do not even consider this."

"Well, Mr. President," the Admiral answered, "the F14's are cruising around the Washington area as we speak at 45000 feet. You can't see them, but they are up there. They can travel towards the terrorist plane and from twenty miles out deliver an air to air missile with spot on accuracy. Seventy miles east of Pittsburgh is a large expanse of ..."

"Mr. President," shouted the California Representative, "stop this insanity!"

"Kindly let the Admiral finish, we must know our options," the President admonished the Representative. The Representative grudgingly took his seat.

The Admiral continued, "There is a large area consisting of wooded areas and former coal stripping land. We can drop that plane precisely where no other lives will be threatened.

Chapter 5 -LAUREL HIGHLANDS

NEAR STOYSTOWN, PA

Bobby waited for the two armed men to approach him. "So, Sunshine, let me ask you one more time, what are you doing trespassing on our property?" asked a large ridge runner standing a head taller than Bobby and casually holding his rifle in his arms.

"Just taking a hike. I wasn't aware this was anyone's property," Bobby responded.

"Just taking a hike, huh?" the large man with the bearded face asked, "do a lot of hiking do you?'

"Well, I was hoping to scope out a new spot for buck season."

The smaller man circled behind Bobby and left his field of vision. Bobby listened even more intently for his footsteps while keeping an eye on the bigger man. The bigger man was now pointing his rifle in Bobby's direction. Visions of his time in Vietnam crossed through Bobby's mind. Without thinking Bobby merely reacted. He spun backwards on his left foot grabbing the rifle barrel of the shorter man behind him and continuing his motion slid behind the man with his left arm wrapping around his neck. The larger man pulled the trigger on his rifle without bringing it up to his shoulder to aim. His buddy caught the shot in his midsection. Bobby completely took the shorter man's rifle as he was falling to the leaf covered forest floor, took quick aim at the larger man and demanded he drop his gun. The larger man thought for a second while he looked down the barrel pointed directly at his head while his rifle was now pointing downward and he had not cranked in a fresh bullet.. The big man made the prudent decision and dropped his rifle. Bobby smacked him across the face with the butt end of the rifle he had commandeered and waited for the big man to hit the ground.

"Now, I get to ask the questions," Bobby stated, "who are you clowns and what are you up to?"

"We're just out squirrel hunting," the big man said as he lay looking up at Bobby while he wiped the blood from his face with the back of his hand.

Bobby smiled, then he kicked him in the head. "Wrong answer, asshole. You don't hunt squirrels with rifles. Is this your patch of marijuana growing here?"

"No way man," the guy quickly answered, "we just get paid to keep trespassers out. Don't know nothin' about the marijuana business?"

"Who pays you?"

"Don't really know."

"Wrong answer again," Bobby said as he kicked him in the gut.

"That hurts damnit! I told you, I don't know who. Some stranger met us as we were leaving the bar a few months back. He pulled up in his Hummer. Told us how to get here. Gave us cash. Stops by each week with more cash."

The low flying passenger jet caught Bobby's eye, *what the hell?* he thought and turned to watch the airliner as it passed overhead. Bobby heard the big man move on the fresh leaves, swung around, kicked him in the head again with his heavy boots, then spun back around to watch the low flying airliner.

Chapter 6 -SITUATION ROOM

WASHINGTON, DC

"Mr. President," the General was speaking as he was jumping out of his seat, I've just received an update. Seems a couple of the passengers on Flight 39 have just used their cell phones and contacted the 911 center in Greensburg, Pennsylvania.

The Representative from California started to get out of his seat. Senator Snead who was standing behind him, grabbed him by the shoulders, slammed him back down in his seat and through gritted teeth said, "Shut up and listen!"

The General continued, "we have tape of two calls stating that the terrorists have displayed razor knives and have gained access to the cockpit. They said a group of the passengers is going to try to storm the door as they feel they are in imminent danger."

"How can we be sure these calls are legit?"

"Mr. President, we are out of time. We need to act and act now or more dead Americans will be on your hands."

The Representative from California started to speak then turned to see Senator Snead glaring at him and thought better of it.

The General watching the President continue to ponder spoke again, "Mr. President if we act now we can drop that plane on an abandoned coal stripping reclamation area. No other citizens around for miles. No one will see the missile shot. It will appear as though the terrorists set off an explosion or just flew the plane into the ground to kill the passengers. Mr. President, this is for the Greater Good!"

The President looked to Senator St. Clair, "Richard this is all right up your alley. Care to voice your opinion?"

Richard addressed the President, "Sir, I understand the Representative from California's concerns, however, I must agree with the General."

The President finally moved his pyramid of fingers from his lower lip. He slowly stood, "General, if this backfires on me, you'll not only lose the stars on your uniform, you'll never see another star in the sky the rest of your life. For the Greater Good, do it! Mr. Vice President, I want you and all our media people in my office by the time I get there myself. We've got to spin this thing starting now."

The General nodded to the Admiral who flipped open his cell phone, punched a button and gave the order, "It's a Go. Drop the bogie."

Chapter 7 -LAUREL HIGHLANDS

STOYSTOWN, PENNSYLVANIA

Bobby couldn't help but to watch the low flying plane. He was sure it was heading down. Then he saw what to a Vietnam vet was an unmistakable sign. A small vapor trail followed by a flash at the left side of the plane directly in front of the wing. The plane instantly shattered into numerous pieces. Bobby was momentarily shocked, but the vet in him quickly concluded, *someone just shot down our plane!* Bobby scanned the skies. No other planes in sight. The shot couldn't have come from the ground. The wreckage was probably a mile away over the next ridge. Bobby looked behind him. One man on the ground bleeding profusely from his stomach, moaning and near death. The other man with a bloody face afraid to move. *This can wait,* Bobby thought and took off at a trot in the direction of the wreckage. He was no longer concerned about staying quiet or not leaving a trail. Throwing caution to the wind, Bobby hustled down the hill and up the next hill. It took awhile to reach the second summit. When he did he stopped to survey the situation. Pulling out his small field glasses he scanned the valley below him. There was a ditch cut in the open field that started shallow and increased in size as it went At the far end of the ditch Bobby could make out a few pieces of the plane. A wing, part of the tail, several seats, an engine still giving off heat, but no signs of life. Concentrating to find any movement Bobby continued to stare intently. His concentration was shaken by the sound of a helicopter. No, several helicopters. No, lots of helicopters.

Damn, he thought, *the NTSB isn't wasting any time getting to the crash sight.*

As they began to land Bobby could tell these were not NTSB officials. They were military helicopters and as they were landing armed soldiers poured out of them running in both directions to take positions up along the edge of the woods on both sides of the wreckage establishing a perimeter surrounding the wreckage. *Strange,* thought Bobby. *I better get down there and help them.* He no sooner took a few steps when another fleet of helicopters arrived. More soldiers, but these were armed with chainsaws and equipment. They immediately went to work climbing trees at various points along the path of the wreckage cutting the tops off the trees while a ground crew gathered them and began a large bonfire. More and more workers kept arriving and all the efforts were concentrated around removing the tree tops and burning them. Bobby couldn't help but notice that thus far no one made any effort to search the wreckage or look for survivors. Baffled Bobby put away his binoculars and continued down the ridge toward the wreckage. When he was a couple hundred yards from the edge of the woods he noticed the soldier nearest to him looking his direction. The soldier raised his rifle in Bobby's direction. The unimaginable became real as the tree branch next to Bobby's ear shattered. Images of Vietnam flooded Bobby's mind. His reflexes took over as he threw himself to the ground and scrambled for cover. *What the hell is going on here?* he asked himself. Past experience told him to get the hell out of Dodge! And he did. He gathered himself and scrambled back up the hillside using all the tricks his past training told him were necessary to live to fight another day. Bullets whizzed by on both sides of him. Staying low, zig-zagging, going from cover to cover, Bobby worked his way up the hill and over the crest out of the view of the soldiers.

Chapter 8 -OVAL OFFICE

WASHINGTON, DC

The White house spin masters were all assembled in the Oval Office when the President entered. Wasting no time the President shouted questions as he strode quickly from the doorway to his desk, "what the hell are we going to do here, folks?"

"Mr. President, first of all, there is no reason to assume that anyone will ever know that we shot down our own airplane."

"Screw the airplane," the President shouted, "that was forty-four American lives. Thirty-seven passengers and seven crew members. Americans and we killed them."

"Mr. President, the press is already calling it an act of terrorism. Let's just let them go with that."

"Get Senator St. Clair in here," the President interrupted, "we have to make sure the Armed Services Committee is on the same page as we are."

The Presidents aide, Ms. McIntosh, left the room briefly to make the call, then returned.

"Mr. President," the Press Secretary said, "what if we play up the 'passengers as heroes' angle. We have tapes to the 911 center from them stating the terrorists were in the cockpit and that they were going to storm it."

"That's good," mumbled the President as he sat back in his chair and assumed his position with his fingers forming a triangle under his lower lip.

"Another angle is the terrorists blew themselves up so they could get their sixty virgins, or whatever the hell it is they think awaits them in heaven. Or that they just crashed the plane into the ground. Maybe this group wasn't capable of flying the plane and the pilot was unable to."

"I like the hero angle," the president said, "we can get some mileage out of that.

"We could have the families of the survivors come to the White House and give them posthumous medals for all the passengers."

"Yeah, and with the terrorists crashing the plane into the Twin Towers we already have enough to start working around this whole privacy thing. We could start monitoring everything like Great Britain does, in the name of fighting terrorism. That would keep these people in line."

Chapter 9 - MORROW RESIDENCE

GANISTER, PENNSYLVANIA

Duke was big, black, beautiful, and at times, mean. He patrolled his seventy-five acres of fields and wooded areas daily. The farm was situated on a knoll overlooking the Conemaugh River a couple miles outside of Ganister. Duke's job, as he saw it, was to keep trespassers off his land and protect the inhabitants of the modern loghome at the center of the open field. Few would dare to cross the fence when Duke was on duty. Duke was the Morrow's beloved Rottweiler. He protected the hands that fed him.

Claire Morrow was in the process of getting ready to go in town to Bobby's office to rearrange some appointments, take care of the bookkeeping, and probably run the vacuum cleaner in the waiting area. She left Duke in the house and got herself a cup of coffee. As was Claire's normal routine the television was blaring so she could hear it as she wandered from room to room puttering around the house. The living area was one large open room with log steps going to the upstairs. Claire walked from the kitchen into the living area with her cup of coffee on her way into the bedroom to put on her earrings.

The sounds and images coming from the television stopped her in her tracks. She joined every other American that was awake and had a pulse, glued to the television watching and re-watching the plane strike the Twin Towers causing the massive cloud of smoke. How could this be possible? Terrorists would actually strike the United States? On our own soil? Has the world gone mad? Then the next shoe dropped. The Pentagon was attacked. The same awful pictures just kept crossing the television screen as an audience froze in front of their televisions all across the country. Cell phones rang everywhere, "have you seen the news? We're being attacked!!"

Claire Morrow rushed into the kitchen to replenish her coffee, came back and was standing behind her sofa when the newscaster interrupted with yet another breaking story. Flight 39 was downed by terrorists in Pennsylvania near Stoystown.

My God, Claire thought, *that's where Bobby went this morning.*

The newscaster continued, "Flight 39 originated in Newark heading for San Francisco, when..."

That's when Claire Morrow gasped. The coffee cup in her hand crashed to the hardwood oak floor. Duke rushed to her side, growling at he didn't know what, searching for an intruder to get his teeth into. Claire immediately cried a death curddeling scream, "Carol. Oh my God, Carol, please don't be on that flight!" But, in the back of her mind, she knew. Mother's have a connection to their children. They can sense danger.

She had just spoken with Carol last night and Carol had told her about her big trip to San Francisco this morning to check out a new resort for the company. The newscaster continued, "The plane made an erratic turn over Cleveland and changed course towards Pittsburgh. Officials report the terrorists had stormed the cockpit taking control of the plane and were heading for Washington, DC. The heroic passengers..." Claire Morrow hadn't heard a word, she was clinging to the back of the sofa crying uncontrollably. *This could not be happening.*

Duke, confused, growled at the newscaster. Hair standing up on his back, ready to attack whoever had hurt Claire but not knowing who or where to strike. His drool mixed with the spilled coffee on the hardwood floor.

Chapter 10 -LAUREL HIGHLANDS

STOYSTOWN, PENNSYLVANIA

Bobby kept up the pace till he reached his beat up, old pick-up truck. *Damn,* he thought, *why didn't I bring my cell phone? I need to call the Colonel.* Bobby never took his cell phone when he went on assignment. It could ring at an inopportune time and ruin his cover.

Bobby scrambled into the truck. Started the motor and tore off without worrying about fastening his seat belt or anything else. If he hustled he could be home in an hour. Driving like a madman up route 30 he was approaching the entrance ramp to route 219 but it was blocked by police cars, their red lights flashing. Bobby stopped at the bottom of the ramp. The State Trooper approached the driver's side of Bobby's pickup as Bobby had finished rolling down the window.

"What's wrong Trooper?" Bobby asked.

"The interstate's closed," the Trooper replied.
"What's going on?"
"Where have you been? We've been attacked by terrorists."
"But I've got to get home. Quick. I need to get on the interstate."
"Not happening, sir. Find another way home." The Trooper turned and walked away.
Bobby thought about showing his federal ID then realized he couldn't, even if he wanted to, because, as always, it was at home with his cell phone.
Bobby rolled up the window and tore off back up route 30. The backroads would take longer but he needed to get home.
Bobby thought to himself, *What the hell do they need to close the highway for? And since when do terrorists attack us on our own soil? Is that what happened to the plane?*

Chapter 11 -SITUATION ROOM

WHITE HOUSE, WASHINGTON, DC

Following the President's hasty departure from the Situation Room, the room started to empty. Senator St.Clair asked the General and the Admiral if he could speak with them.
"Gentleman," Richard said, "The President is going to want more details from me, so if you don't mind, there are some things I still need to know."
"Of course, Senator St.Clair," the General responded, "how can I be of assistance."
"First, I guess, I would like confirmation it's done, correct?"

The Admiral spoke up, "Yes, Richard. It's done. Within minutes from making the call an air to air missile was sent from an F14 striking the target and it dropped on a reclaimed strip mine in western Pennsylvania near the town of Stoystown."

"Were there any survivors?" Richard asked.

"No chance."

"What do we need to do now?"

"It's already begun. We have contingency plans already in place which were activated. We immediately sent in troops by helicopter to guard the crash site, plus troops began cutting tree tops off within the crash zone," the Admiral said.

"Why do you cut tree tops off?" Richard asked.

"Well, if a plane crashes, it hits the ground and debris flies outward and upward so it would be collected in the under parts of the trees. But, when a plane or any object is exploded in the sky, the debris falls downward and is collected in the tree tops. We cannot have pieces of airplane and bodies left in the tree tops, so we will cut them all off and burn them, then haul off all the ashes to a separate secure sight."

"Then what happens?" asked Senator St.Clair.

"Then we allow the NTSB in to do their accident investigation and we will let them know that for national security the results of the investigation will be what we want them to be. After all, they work for the President also," the General answered.

"And can you guarantee the President," Richard asked, "that no word of this will leak into the press?"

The Admiral and General looked at each other like, that's a stupid question. But then it was coming from a politician.

"Yes, we can guarantee there will be no leaks to the press," the General said, "all the people involved are military people. They do as they are ordered to do. The punishment for not obeying orders is life in Leavenworth. Nobody wants to go there."

"And the pilot will also be removed from duty while we send him through some psychological testing just to be sure," the Admiral noted.

"Thank you gentlemen," Senator St.Clair said, "I'm sure the President will be pleased."

"I'm sure he will too," the General replied, "he can sleep good tonight knowing a plane is not going to crash into his bedroom now."

Chapter 12 -MORROW RESIDENCE

GANISTER, PENNSYLVANIA

Bobby managed to get home via the maze of backroads and pulled into his long gravel driveway wondering where Duke was. Duke was always there to meet him. It was like he could hear Bobby's truck coming from miles away. Claire's car was still in the driveway also. Bobby jumped out of his truck after hastily parking it and ran up onto the long porch that circled three sides of his home. At the kitchen door, the door he used most often, he hesitated as he heard Claire crying uncontrollably and Duke growling. Not sure what may be happening or if someone else had gained entry, Bobby, quietly backed off the porch and went down the side of the house, around the corner, to the basement door. He unlocked the basement door as quietly as he could, took off his boots so he wouldn't make any noise and made his way up the stairs to the basement door that exited into the kitchen. Slowly and quietly he turned the doorknob. Opened the door a crack, checked for intruders and scooted through the door, staying low until he could get a fix on where Claire was. He peeked over the kitchen counter and saw her leaning over the couch, crying. Duke, by her side, growling. Bobby surveyed as much of the room as he could see but couldn't see anyone else in the room. Claire's crying was too much for him so he decided to throw caution to the wind and just go to her to find out what was wrong. Claire was not the type to break into tears like a lot of women. She was a strong person.

Bobby quickly went to her, wrapped his arms around her, and began to comfort her, "Claire, I'm here. What's wrong dear?"

"Bobby," she managed between sobs, "thank God you're okay. I was so worried about you when the terrorists bombed the plane in Stoystown." Then Claire started crying again.

"What else is it Claire?"

"It's our Carol."

"What about Carol?" Bobby asked and immediately felt weak in the knees.

"She.." Claire was having a problem finishing a sentence, "she was probably on that plane."

Bobby freaked. Bobby was the most in control person you would ever know. He had seen it all in his life. Plenty of dangerous situations. Been shot at. Been interrogated. Seen everything, but he was always in control. Until now. Bobby while hugging Claire, bawled.

Duke had stopped growling once Bobby arrived but now he was upset again. Never had he seen his master cry. Duke paced. His head bobbed up and down in complete confusion, but he never left their sides.

Bobby got control of himself, and gently whispered into Claire's ear, "Sweetie, I'm going to take you into the bedroom and you need to take a pill so you can sleep."

Claire did not object. As soon as Bobby had her lying quietly he stole back into the living area and retrieved his cell phone.

"Colonel, what the hell is going on?" he asked as soon as the phone was answered.

"Bobby, we've been struck by terrorists."

"I'm mostly concerned about the plane in Pennsylvania."

"I don't have all the details on that. You need to talk to your buddy Richard. He was in all the meetings this morning with the decision makers."

"Thanks. Bye" Bobby wasted no time hanging up on the Colonel and immediately called Richard's number. It got forwarded to his office where an aide answered it.

"Where's Bobby?"

"I'm afraid he is in meetings at the White House and can't be disturbed." she replied.

"Listen, this is Bobby Morrow.."

"Oh, hello, Mr. Morrow. I know that you're the Senators best friend. He's always talking about you. In fact he has a picture of the two of you in his office from Vietnam."

"Yeah, yeah, listen to me. You write this word on a slip of paper. He spelled the word for her, T-E-M-P-L-A-R, you find him, wherever he is, and you stick this note under his nose. You do not give it to anyone but Richard. This is extremely important. Got that?"

"Yes, sir" she timidly replied.

"Bye." Bobby said and hung up.

Chapter 13 - OVAL OFFICE

WHITE HOUSE

Senator St.Clair was ushered into the Oval Office after they collected him from the Situation Room at the President's request.

The President got up from his seat behind his large desk and shook Richard's hand then asked him to have a seat. He motioned for the others to leave them. They wasted no time heading for the door.

"Senator St.Clair," the President said, "glad you could meet with me."

"Well, I assumed, Mr. President that we would need to get together regarding the tragedies of this morning. In fact, I just left the General and the Admiral after a good conversation with them."

"You're exactly right. Since you are the Chairman of the Armed Services Committee," the President went on, "I think it's extremely important that we are on the same page."

"Quite right, Mr. President, how can I assist you?"

"Well I'm concerned about public opinion from this fiasco."

"We all should be Mr. President. I was assured by the General and the Admiral that everyone involved thus far is military personnel and that we would have no leaks to the press."

"That's a relief. What about the accident scene in Pennsylvania? That one scares me," the President asked.

"It appears the General has everything under control. They have troops there already guarding the scene and even cutting the tree tops off and burning them."

"What?" the President asked confusedly.

"That's what I asked, Mr. President, then the General explained to me about debris falling downward after the explosion and sticking in the tree tops as opposed to the debris flying upward and outward when a plane actually crashes into the ground. He also had the interstate highway shut down to prevent any eyewitnesses and in case they misjudged the moment of impact. Wouldn't want airplane debris dropping on top of Joe Citizen on his way to work. Air National Guard jets were also scrambled out of the Johnstown airport to form a perimeter in case the hijacked airliner attempted to change course again. "

"Sounds like the General does have everything under control there," the President said with a satisfied grin on his face, "my staff and I have decided that the American people will probably be very fearful from this act. After all, no one has ever attacked us on our own soil before. In fact, following World War II the Japanese general was quoted as saying that he wouldn't think of attacking us here which is why they attacked Pearl Harbor."

"Yes, I know, Mr. President, but he also said it was because all the citizens had guns and that was too big an army to fight against." Richard calmly stated knowing it would irritate a President that was getting flack from the liberals to pass gun control legislation.

"Well, be that as it may," the President said, "we must restore the people's confidence. Confidence in us and in the airline industry, and even in being able to live and work in a tall building without it coming down around their ears."

"I understand, Mr. President," Senator St. Clair said. "So, we have decided that the public will be told that the terrorists blew up the plane when the heroic passengers attempted to get back control of the airplane. We think that is best for everyone, and we intend to seal the records on this incident. The Twin Towers and the Pentagon need no further explanation. They were without a doubt caused by the terrorists."

The President's aide quietly entered the office and stuck a note under his nose.

"Senator St. Clair," the President said to Richard, "it appears your aide is outside with an important message for you. Shall I have her come in?"

"Yes, please. Thank you, Mr. President."

Senator St.Clair's aide sheepishly entered the office and handed the note to Richard. "So sorry, Mr. President," she quietly said with her head bowed down looking at the Presidential Seal on the carpet.

"Thank you for coming my dear. I'm sure the Senator appreciates it."

The aide practically stumbled out the door which was still being held open by the President's aide, but quickly closed after their departure.

"Anything wrong?" the President asked Richard.

Richard glanced at the note which contained just one word, TEMPLAR. Richard and Bobby had used that word as a secret code since their time together in Vietnam. It meant that the other was in danger and needed immediate assistance. Even now, while Richard was in the Oval Office with the President, he would not let his friend down, after all, he owed him his life.

"Possibly, Mr. President, I need to make a call. May I be excused?'

"Senator, by all means, stay here, make a call. If you leave they'll just bring in someone else. This way I can have a moments peace," the President said.

Richard immediately called Bobby.

"Bobby," he said when Bobby answered, "what's up?"

"I need some information?"

"Can it wait? I'm with the President."

"No it can't wait. I need to know what went on with the plane that was shot down in Stoystown," Bobby said. Several minutes of silence followed.

"What do you mean shot down?" Richard asked quietly while he snuck a peak at the President to be sure he wasn't hearing the conversation.

"I was there. I saw it get shot down. Who did it?" Bobby insisted.

"We did. For the Greater Good. This is not public knowledge."

There was a brief silence then Bobby said, "we, who?"

"We, us, so it wouldn't take out another building and cost a few thousand more lives," Richard said.

Bobby calmly asked, "Who, specifically gave the order?"

"Oh come on Bobby. It was the General's recommendation. The President gave the order. I really need to go, I'm with the President."

"And you were there? After all, you're the Chairman of the Armed Forces Committee."

"Of course I was there, why?"

"Well, Senator.." Richard had never heard Bobby call him Senator before. They were too close of friends for that. Bobby continued, "before you leave the President's office, you get a dictionary and you look up the word Retribution...."

Richard interrupted, "Bobby what's going on?"

"My daughter was on that plane!" the line went dead. Senator St.Clair's face drained of all color.

"Senator," the President asked, "are you all right? You don't look good."

Richard slowly faced the President and said, "None of us are alright Mr. President."

"What do you mean?"

"We took forty-four American lives. It's possible there was a witness. My advice to you Mr. President. Be careful. Be very careful. Wear the best damn body armor you can find if you leave this building."

"Senator, if you know something you need to inform the Secret Service."

"I don't know anything Mr. President other than as for myself, I'm getting a bullet proof vest. Real soon." Senator St.Clair exited the White House and strode down the stairs into a waiting black Lincoln limo. The driver was waiting with the rear door open and closed it after the Senator got in. The driver jumped in, put on his seat belt, and headed down the driveway toward Pennsylvania Avenue. He stopped briefly at the small white guard shack, got the thumbs up from the guards, and slowly pulled out onto the street. Normally the sidewalk would be teeming with people. Harried executives in suits and ties carrying brief cases, tourists taking photos of each other in front of the fence surrounding the most famous government building in the world. Today the sidewalk was void of people except for one lone person standing at the black wrought iron fence staring at the White House. She turned and looked toward the shiny black limo waiting to turn onto the street. Inside the limo, Richard was lost in thought reviewing his visit with the President and the strange conversation with Bobby. He was absentmindedly looking out the window to his left when he saw her. The same face. The same hair. His mermaid. She had been leaning on the black wrought iron fence and had turned to look into the blackened windows of the black limo that had just pulled through the guard shack. Their eyes met for a moment. He was about to ask the driver to stop when the driver hit the accelerator and the limo sped away. Richard turned to look out the rear window but he couldn't find the face.

Chapter 14 - MORROW RESIDENCE

GANISTER, PENNSYLVANIA

Bobby's next call was to Claire's sister.

"Can you come over and stay with Claire for awhile? I just gave her a sedative and I need to go out of town until later tomorrow."

"Bobby, what's wrong with Claire?" unable to hide the worry in her voice.

"I'll tell you when you get here. I have to make a few more quick calls. Thank you." Bobby wasted no time getting off the phone.

After Bobby quickly hung up, he dialed his friend Kurt Klaar's number. Kurt was a farmer. Kurt was also a sawyer, a gunsmith, and basically a jack of all trades. Of course to hear Kurt say it, he was a jack of all trades, master of none.

Kurt wouldn't do work for just anybody, you had to be someone he could get along with, and that certainly narrowed the number of possibilities. Kurt had been doing special gun and ammo work for Bobby since Bobby's days as a sniper in Vietnam. Bobby always had problems getting ammo with the proper grain shells for the long range shots he needed to make.

"Yeah, who's this?" Kurt asked in his normal gruffy manner.

"Kurt, it's Bobby. Need a fast favor."

"What do you need, buddy?"

"Couple of cartridges for the M24 for about a 1500 yard shot."

"When do you need them?"

"I'll be by in about an hour. I also need a really special bullet." Bobby went on to explain to Kurt exactly what he needed.

The M24 was the military's favorite sniper rifle. It was a version of the Remington 700 and weighed only twelve pounds. When a Leupold Ultra scope was added it could be very precise at ranges up to 1600 hundred yards.

After speaking with Kurt, Bobby called Mike. Or as everyone referred to him, Mike the Mechanic and Mike deserved the name. He had a specialty auto repair business where he worked on hot rods, Corvettes, and a few Ferraris, coincidentally the same types of vehicles that he also drove.

"Classic Auto," Mike said as he picked up the phone.

"Mike, it's Bobby."

"Morrow, you old son of a bitch, what's up?"

"Need a favor."

"Finally ready to get rid of that piece of shit truck that you drive?"

"It gets me where I need to go."

"It is so dead around here since the news of the plane hitting the towers, I figured I may as well close up for the rest of the week, so what do you need?"

"This is confidential"

"Mum's the word, buddy. What can I do for you?"

"I need to make a fast trip to DC but I also need a driver. Someone that can act as a diversion."

"I'm your man. Want to take the Ferrari or the pick-up truck? Want to be seen or anonymous?"

"Let's take the Ferrari that will be a great diversion all by itself."

"When are we leaving?" Mike asked.

"Meet me at Kurt Klaar's house in an hour."
Bobby hung up. Mike jumped out of his rickety old desk chair, clamped his hands, and said, "Hot damn. This is gonna' be good."
First the planes and the terrorists, Mike thought to himself, *now Bobby Morrow is on a mission. And I get to tag along. I wouldn't miss this for anything.*
Mike raced out of his garage and into the house to pack his bag.

Chapter 15 - JEFFERSON HOTEL,

WASHINGTON, DC

Washington was dead. Probably for the first time since the Revolutionary days there was no one on the streets of DC. The Washington Monument, Jefferson Memorial, the White House, and all the other tourist traps were brightly lit but there weren't any people gawking. The events of yesterday caused an entire country to go home and stay home. Those that could get home, that is. With the airplanes grounded there were a lot of people stranded, wishing they were home with their loved ones, but even they were huddling indoors somewhere.
With no traffic on the streets the bright red Ferrari zoomed down the street and whipped into the circular drive in front of the stately Jefferson Hotel, with it's tires squealing. The bored front desk employees and concierge all ran to the door not knowing what was happening now. They were nearly ecstatic to see a customer coming to break up the boredom.

Prior to his obnoxiously noticeable arrival, Mike had dropped Bobby off in the alley behind the hotel. Bobby jumped out of the bright red Ferrari, threw his odd shaped bag over his shoulder, and watched Mike streak away. He stood for a moment looking both directions in the alley. Convinced no one was watching he eyed up the building. Placing his bag on the ground, he unzipped a pocket on the front of the bag and withdrew a rope with a hook on the end. He swung the rope several circles before letting it fly up to the bottom rung of the fire escape. The hook caught with a slight clang. Bobby again looked around. Not seeing anyone he gathered up his bag and placed it on his shoulder again. He pulled the metal ladder down within reach, jumped up to grab the lower rung and swung himself up on to it. He then climbed up to the first landing. He continued up several more landings on the shaky iron fire escape. The last landing was below roof level and ended at a large window. Bobby pulled a small flat bar from his shoulder bag and was able to jimmy the window. Opening it slowly then cautiously climbing inside after waiting to check for voices coming from within, he entered the building, then closed the window. He slowly and quietly made his way down the corridor until he found a door without a room number on it. He opened the door, stuck his head in and took a look around. Seeing stairs leading upward he made his way up them. They ended at a rooftop exit. The door was not locked. That was maybe not a good sign as it could have meant the employees came up here regularly for smoke breaks or something along those lines. He exited anyway and stopped to survey the rooftop, then the cityscape around him. At the south end of the building he found a weathered brick parapet approximately three feet high which afforded

some degree of cover and which offered a perfect line
of sight to the lawn behind the high wrought iron fence
in front of the most famous government building in the
world.

Mike strutted to the check in desk like a rockstar. An
old rockstar, but a rockstar none the less. But these days
all the rockstars were old and still out on tour. Squeaky
voices and all.
Mike barked orders at the concierge who was carrying
his one small bag while he banged on the bell on the
marble topped desk even though the desk clerk had
already asked if she could help him.
"Hey babe," Mike said in his best sexy voice, even
though it wasn't working, while taking off his shades,
"what's your name, sweetheart?"
"Can I help you sir?" the red-faced young desk clerk
asked.
"You sure can! Need a room. Maybe you'll join me in
the jaccuzi with a little wine. I'll let you wash my back."
"We certainly have a room for you, sir, but I'm afraid
it's against company policy for me to visit your room."
"I won't tell if you don't"
The desk clerk began fidgeting and looking for the
concierge.
"Where the hell is the concierge?" Mike asked as he
turned around and came face to face with him.
"What do you need sir?"
Mike moved closer to him with his lips next to the
concierge's ear and whispered, "Dirty sheets. You get
my meaning? Can you fix me up?"
The concierge glanced at the desk clerk and responded,
"I'm not sure what you mean sir, but, may I take your
bag to your room for you?"
"Sure thing." Mike grabbed the plastic key the clerk

had laid on the granite counter and headed for the elevator with the concierge nipping at his heels.

As the elevator doors the concierge handed Mike a business card, and said, "I believe this is what you want sir. Her name's Bambi. Tell her Denny at the Jefferson told you to call."

"Thanks partner," Mike said as he stuck the card in his jeans pocket.

Mike didn't waste any time getting rid of the concierge after he got to the room. But then after he handed him a fifty dollar bill it would have been hard to keep the concierge from breaking into a sprint out the door.

Mike dialed Bobby's cell phone.

Bobby answered, "Yeah."

"Room 312." was all Mike said and hung up.

Bobby showed up a few minutes later. Mike ordered room service. The two ate and chatted. Mike was about to bust a gut wanting to ask Bobby to spill all the details, but he knew better than to broach the subject.

Bobby's cell phone buzzed. He looked to see who was calling. The name on the screen was Richard. Bobby hit the end button.

Early the next morning Bobby gave Mike instructions, "I want you to go down for breakfast at 7 am. Make sure everybody possible sees you. At 8 o'clock be checked out and pick me up in the alley where you left me off. Be ready to leave this town in a hurry!"

Chapter 16 -WEDNESDAY, SEPTEMBER 12TH

WHITE HOUSE, WASHINGTON, DC

There were always three identical helicopters that landed on the lush green lawn at the White House when the President wanted to go somewhere. The object was to have two act as decoys so no one was sure exactly which one carried the President and where it was headed.

This Wednesday morning, prior to the helicopters arriving the President held a special meeting in the Oval Office with his staff, the head of the Secret Service, the chairman of the Armed Services Committee, Senator St. Clair, plus his friend Senator Snead. The reason for the meeting regarded the President's schedule. Should he keep his appointment to address Congress this morning, or with the previous day's events should he remain secluded at the White House.

"Mr. President," Senator Snead was saying, "the Congress is planning on gathering on the steps of the Capitol Building today to show the citizens we will not be intimidated by terrorists."

The President's aide jumped in, "but Mr. President we have no way of knowing if the attacks are over. Or if you are a target?"

"Senator St.Clair," the President said as he looked his direction, "what is your committee's best guess? Are the attacks over? Am I a target?"

"We think for now the attacks are over, Mr. President, however our intel says there could possibly be a West Coast attack very soon to keep us off guard. As for you, Mr. President, the most powerful man in the world is always a target."

"Regardless, Mr. President," the aide stated, "we think it would be more prudent for you to stay out of the public view for a while."

"I am more inclined to lead by example. To continue my normal meetings and not let the American citizens see me as a coward. And for the terrorists not to think that they can scare me into hiding."

"I would have to agree with your aide, Mr. President," said Senator St.Clair, "now is not the time to place yourself in harm's way. You are of no value to the United States if you are lying in a morgue."

Senator Snead spoke up, "but we cannot afford to let the terrorists think that they have won. That they have chased us all into hiding. That is exactly why the congress will be on the Capitol steps today. To send that message."

"With all due respect, Senator Snead, the majority of those same Congresspersons were the first ones to go into hiding in a secure bunker when the first plane struck the towers. And then demand that there employees continue working," Senator St.Clair stated through clenched teeth.

"I need to speak to Congress," the President said. "I will keep my previous appointment. The helicopters will be here momentarily. I'll be on it. If you senators would like a ride, you are welcome to join me on the chopper."

Senators St.Clair and Snead both agreed that, yes, if the President was taking the chopper and offering them a ride, they would accept.

The President chased his aides out of the Oval Office, then he and the two senators surrounded by the Secret Service, as soon as they left the Oval Office door, made their way down to the lawn exit.

The three helicopters arrived precisely as the President and his contingent were exiting the White House.

Chapter 17 - JEFFERSON HOTEL

WASHINGTON, DC

Bobby had assumed his position on the Jefferson Hotel roof early in the morning, crouched behind the parapet with his binoculars carefully observing the White House. It had been quite a few years now since he used to do this sort of thing regularly, in Vietnam. The waiting without getting tense was difficult to learn but apparently it stayed with you. Bobby's concentration was broken by the sound of the three identical helicopters arriving at the White House. They each hit their marks perfectly as they landed on the lush green lawn in unison. Marines jumped out and assumed their positions while they waited for the president to cross the lawn and climb aboard.

Bobby carefully removed his trusty old M24 sniper rifle, which he kept immaculately cleaned, from his shoulder bag and dialed in the Leupold scope until he had a perfect vision of the President and his contingent. Naturally the President was huddled in the middle of the group of Secret Service men, but Bobby was still able to make out his head and part of his chest. The other two gentlemen followed behind the huddle of Secret Service. That was plenty for any sniper. Bobby placed the crosshairs on his targets bright blue necktie. Slowly he exhaled while thinking, Retribution! His breathing perfect, his gunbarrel not wavering even slightly, he calmly and gently squeezed the trigger. The 173 grains of powder sent the projectile out the silenced barrel and crossed the fifteen hundred yards in the blink of an eye. Bobby watched through his scope as the red appeared on the blue necktie and spread to the white shirt of the target rocketing the recipient backward, knocking him flat on his ass on the lush green lawn.

Bobby confidently and casually gathered his expended cartridge and placed it, and his rifle, in his shoulder bag. He kept low until he reached the rooftop doorway then made his departure. He walked down the steps, out the next door, down the hallway, out the window onto the fire escape, down the fire escape, dropping off the final section and leaned against the building while he waited for his ride.

Chapter 18 - WHITE HOUSE LAWN

The Secret Servicemen flew into action. They surrounded the President even tighter, grabbed him under the arms lifting him off the ground, and carried him back into the secure White House. Their radios began squawking and the contingent on the roof of the White House went into hyper alert scanning every nook and cranny of the DC area in search of something, anything, any bit of movement or a person acting suspiciously.

The Marines from the helicopters assumed their positions, drew their weapons and scanned the buildings looking for a glint of light reflecting off a scope or smoke remaining from a rifle barrel, anything that would give them a location of whoever fired the shot that no one heard. They only knew a shot was fired by the body they saw lying on the ground covered in red.

Senator Snead knelt down on the lawn unconcerned about the grass stains on his pants or the fact that a bullet could also be heading his way with his name on it. He reached for Senator St.Clair, lying on his back, not moving, the front of his shirt covered in red. The sounds of sirens immediately filled the background as he waited, holding Richard's arm and repeating, "Lie still, Richard. Help is on the way."

Oblivious to any danger that he may have been in, he remained by Richard's side until the paramedics arrived with their stretcher and bags. They lifted Richard onto the gurney and nearly ran with him into the back of the waiting ambulance. They wasted no time leaving the White House lawn heading for the nearest hospital with sirens wailing.

The usual gathering of newspeople that were watching the White House also went into action. Reports went out over television and radio. A shooting at the White house. Could it be another terrorist attack? Was the President shot? Who was the man lying on the lawn and taken away by ambulance? A million questions, but at the moment not a single answer.

Chapter 19 - JEFFERSON HOTEL

The bright red Ferrari had just turned the corner into the alley and was making its way toward Bobby. As it slid to a stop directly next to him, Bobby opened the door, tossed his bag into the back, and jumped in. The radio was blasting a Jimmy Buffet song and Mike the Mechanic was singing along, "wasting away in Margaritaville. Searching for my lost.."

Bobby buckled his seat belt, gave the singer an unpleasant look, leaned his head back into the headrest and closed his eyes.

The Ferrari flew up the alley out onto the streets of DC and made its way onto the Beltway heading west chased by the early morning sun. The car flew up I270 and onto I70 at great speed under the control of the extremely capable hands of Mike the Mechanic. A red blur heading west trying to outrun the sun.

The only words Bobby spoke were, "to Kurt's house." Then almost as an afterthought, "And thanks for being here, Mike."

Mike nodded and kept on singing like he actually was a rockstar in concert, "I made enough money to buy Miami, but I pissed it away so fast. Never meant to last. Never meant to last."

The highways had few cars on them, the bulk of people still in shock from the previous day's events and all staying home close to family and friends including most of the police. Mike enjoyed having the road to himself and let the Ferrari run.

Chapter 20 - SEPTEMBER 13, 2001, KLAAR FARM

BEDFORD COUNTY, PENNSYLVANIA

The whamp, whamp, whamp of the rotor blades on the sleek black helicopter never disrupted the muted sounds of the birds, crickets, and cows on the Klaar farm until it was within sight of the occupants of the old two story white farmhouse. One of many that lined this lush Pennsylvania valley. Lost in time and protected on both sides by the Allegheny Mountains. September 13th was a normal early autumn day with a bright blue sky punctuated by fluffy white clouds. The leaves on the trees were still green but wouldn't be for much longer as the sap would soon stop running and the trees would become a photographer's pallet of rich colors.

Before the sleek black helicopter, with no markings or numbers emlazoned on it ever landed, the group of men in black uniforms, balaclavas, and helmets, loaded to the teeth with guns, jumped from the helicopter and ran to take up positions surrounding the Klaar family's farmhouse. There were six of them plus the pilot and they moved like a well oiled military machine. They were greatly out of place on this peaceful small farm in the valley where not much happened except for watching the hay grow.

When the men were in position and each had spoke into the microphone attached to their helmet, the pilot's voice came out loud and clear over an intercom system, "Bobby Morrow, come out with your hands on your head. We have you surrounded."

The door to the farmhouse opened. Kurt Klaar walked out onto the porch with his hands in his pockets.

"Sir, remove your hands from your pockets. Slowly." came the voice over the intercom.

"Hey assholes, you're trespassing on my property. Now take a hike." stated the defiant Kurt.

"Sir, remove your hands from your pockets," the intercom repeated.

"You're in Bedford County, Pennsylvania shit-for-brains not Russia or Germany. You got any official pieces of paper or even half a reason to be on my property?" Kurt asked without the desire to raise his voice.

"We are here for Bobby Morrow, sir, and we have good reason to believe he is here."

Kurt turned his back to the men in black, looked into the still open door, and said, see Bobby, I told you Big Brother was always watching and could track those damn cell phones. That's why I don't own one."

Bobby Morrow ambled out the door with a cup of steaming coffee in his hand, "Morning gentleman. Anyone want coffee? Kurt ain't much of a cook, but he makes a mean cup of coffee. He's also not such a bad guy once you get to know him."

"Mr. Morrow put down the coffee and place your hands on your head," the voice on the intercom announced, louder this time.

"This is my first cup of coffee for the day and trust me, you don't want me to put it down cause then I'll be in a foul mood the rest of the day."

"Last warning, Mr. Morrow. Put down the coffee. Place your hands on your head, and walk into the yard."

"Exactly who are you and what are you accusing me of?" Bobby asked.

"Secret Service. And you are under arrest."

Kurt looked at Bobby and asked him, "Damn boy what did you do to insult the President?"

"Apparently he got offended that someone might get pissed off about having his daughter murdered?"

Bobby became very serious and threw his coffee and the cup into the yard.

"Now look what the hell you've done," Kurt said to the voice on the intercom, "you had to piss him off didn't ya'?" Before the voice could reply, Kurt went on, "I just got him calmed down, now I won't be responsible."

"Mr. Morrow, you have to the count of three, then we are taking you in. Walking or in a body bag, it matters not to us."

The lane up to the farmhouse brewed with what could have been mistaken for a tornado funnel, and it kept growing and growing and coming closer and closer. Bobby watched it intently and ignored the voice.

Finally he looked directly at the leader of the six man squad, "I'm not coming with you. That being said, you now have to decide, what price are you willing to pay to follow an order that you may or may not even agree with?"

"We intend to follow out our orders."

The dust cloud was now close to the farmhouse, out of it rolled pick-up truck after pick-up truck of locals. Each truck had its windows down with rifle barrels plainly sticking out them. The beds of the trucks had hunters, farmers, ridge runners, and every other species of crazy person in them. Like a wagon train they circled the helicopter and the six man squad of Secret Service dressed in their costly black uniforms. Several of the men walked right up and past the men in black uniforms and right up onto the porch.

"Morning Kurt. Morning Bobby. Good morning for a little shootin'" said Mike the Mechanic.

"Is there any limit, today?" Terry the farmer asked as he jabbed his son the former Army Ranger in the side with his elbow. His son stood tall and just smiled and said, "kinda' reminds me of a coupla' years back. "Cept it was the women over there that were all dressed in black with their heads covered."

Someone from one of the trucks shouted, "this ain't fair, hell, there ain't even enough to go around! We're gonna' have to share."

Another shouted, "Kurt you better warm up the skidsteer and get a hole dug so we can bury this shit afterwards. You don't want it stinkin' up the farm!"

And the trucks just kept coming. It was almost as though the entire county was showing up for an auction.

The formerly stoic men in black started spending more and more time looking around. Trying to get a count on how many of them there were, and where all were they. Ridge runners with rifles. Men that were raised to shoot. And shoot to kill. After all hunting here wasn't just a sport but a meal ticket. The tide seemed to have shifted.

Bobby said to the voice on the intercom, "you guys give up?"

Laughter grew louder and louder from the mass of men dressed in their torn jeans, camo coats, wore out ball caps, some with "Git 'er done" sewn on the front.

The laughter was just subsiding when a dusty black limo pulled in and out jumped Senator Richard St.Clair. He slowly made his way up onto the porch. He walked directly up to Bobby, looked him right in the eye, and with his hand out said, "Bobby I am so sorry about Carol. I hope that someday you can forgive me. Had I known she was on that plane, I don't know what I would have done, but it would have been something far different. I would gladly trade places with her."

The intercom voice interrupted, "Excuse me. I hate to break up this love fest, but we still have a job to do."

Richard turned to face the voice and held up his index finger while he pulled out his cell phone and began punching numbers. "Mr. President," he said into the phone, "you need to get your Secret Service people out of here or you're going to be attending seven more funerals." Then to the voice he hollered, "Come here. It's for you. It's your boss."

The voice exited the helicopter rushed up to Richard and took the phone. He held it to his ear and listened. After a few minutes he said, "Yes, sir." and handed the phone back to Richard.

He faced his men in black made a circular sign above his head with his forefinger and headed for the chopper. The six men in black ran after him and piled in behind him. The rotor blades began the slow whirring and eventually picked up speed.

On the porch, farmer Terry looked at the Senator with the rumpled suit and the formerly white shirt and blue tie that was covered in red and asked, "what the hell happened to you, Senator?"

Richard looked at farmer Terry. "Your friend there, and my best friend, Bobby, shot me."

"What?" Terry asked with and amazed look on his face while he casually left his rifle swing to the porch.

"It's true. He shot me and I deserved it. That's all I can tell you."

"Well, pardon me for being skeptical, but I've known Bobby for quite a while and it's been my experience that when Bobby shoots something it usually stays dead."

Mike the Mechanic grinned at Bobby as he said to him, "you must be losing your touch, dude."

Bobby wasn't smiling. Richard said to him, "we need to talk, Bobby."

Inside, Richard looked directly at Bobby and said The pair went into the house. Kurt looked at the mass of armed men in his yard and on his porch and said, "Well, we either go hunting or just sit here and drink beer. What'll it be?" When the noise faded, Kurt yelled in to his son, "Percy, better bring out some beer. And you might as well haul your ass into town and buy some more. It might be a long day."

again, "I'm very sorry. I understand why you shot me. I don't know how you did it and let me live, though, and why you didn't shoot the President."

"Well," Bobby started. "I couldn't shoot the President, though I really wanted to, cause he's my commander in chief. Somebody had to get it, so it was you. I figured you'd wear a vest. If you hadn't we wouldn't be having this conversation."

"But how'd you get all this red on me, and whatever it was, it still hurt like hell. It knocked me on my ass and completely took my breath away. I thought I was shot until the paramedics told me it was the damndest thing they ever saw."

"I had Kurt make me a couple special cartridges with a plastic tip with paintball paint in them. As mad as I am at the world right now, I still couldn't shoot my best friend. But there are principles."

"Bobby there is no way anyone wanted to harm your daughter. Or anyone. But the decision did have to be made to sacrifice the fewer number of people for the good of the greater number of people. It's just like when soldiers like you and me got sent into battle. There is no way every soldier will return, some will be sacrificed."

"I understand that Richard, but this was my daughter. Her and Claire are my life. Now what? Now what, Richard? You know what I'm saying. I'm sure you still miss Pamela and she has been gone for quite a while now."

"I can only somewhat understand how you must feel. I'm sure it is much worse to lose a daughter than when I lost Pamela, and I am very serious when I tell you, I wish I could have traded places with Carol."

"Well you're not through the worst of it yet, Richard," Bobby said with teary eyes, "You're taking me home, and you are going to have to face Claire. You are going to have to tell her why her one and only daughter is no longer with us. You might want to have those Secret Service boys and a few thousand Marines with you when try to explain it to her, but, one way or another you are gonna' man up and tell her. Face to face. Cause if you don't I will shoot you. I'll double tap you at point blank range and don't for one second think I'm not serious. Come on, you're taking me home."

Chapter 21 - OVAL OFFICE

WASHINGTON, DC

The President paced in front of the solid oak desk staring down at the Presidential Seal in the carpet. His aide, sat, watching him pace, barely breathing. The President stopped, looked at his aide, and bellowed, "you get the head of the Secret Service in here. Now!" The President's face was beet red as he continued pacing as though he could wear a hole through the Presidential Seal. The aide jumped and practically ran from the office.

It was no time at all until the aide was back with another gentleman dressed in a conservative dark gray suit with red power tie.

"Mr. President," the head of the Secret Service began, "I still think we should pick up that Morrow character and cool his heels in a cell."

"Why, Scott, because he made you look bad?" the President asked. "You've got bigger problems than Bobby Morrow."

"But, sir, we can't let him get away with this. It sets a bad example. We really need to arrest him."

The President's face reddened as he tried to remain calm, "Arrest him? For what? Painting a Senator? If he had been aiming for me, he would have got me. He was sending a message and I have great respect for that."

"But, sir...."

"But, my ass, Scott. You better ask yourself why was it a sniper had the opportunity to make that shot. And then get all the way back to Pennsylvania. You guys still wouldn't have a clue if Senator St.Clair wouldn't have told you exactly who it was and where to find him. You guys would still be standing around with stupid looks on your faces apologizing."

"You're right, Mr. President, I'll submit my resignation this afternoon."

"I don't want your resignation Scott. I want the Secret Service to be better and smarter than an old Army sniper."

"Yes, Mr. President."

"Instead of wanting to arrest Bobby Morrow, you guys better start wining and dining him while you pick his brain to find out how this can happen. Then you better come up with an even better defense."

"Yes, Mr. President."

"Scott, believe me you're getting off easy. You could be having this conversation with my widow."

"Sorry, sir."

"Get out of here and start puckering up cause you're gonna' need to kiss Morrow's butt."

Chapter 22 - MORROW RESIDENCE

GANISTER, PA

Duke jumped straight up from his favorite old rug by the fireplace. He bared his teeth, growled, and the hair on his back stood on end.

The sudden growling woke both Claire and her sister from their nap on the couch. Both of them jumped and looked at each other. Claire's sister ran to the window. "There's a black limo coming up the driveway," she said to Claire.

Duke was already jumping up at the door trying to scratch his way through it. The rear door of the black limo opened and Bobby stepped out. The instant Duke saw him he immediately stopped growling and assumed his position with his massive front paws on the door, staring out the door window, his tail wagging so fast it gave off a breeze.

Bobby entered the kitchen door and was immediately given a tongue washing by Duke while Richard and the tall chauffeur dressed in the black suit with white shirt, black tie, and black hat just stared in wonder.

Bobby pushed Duke aside and ran to Claire. He squeezed her, ran his fingers through her already disheveled hair, kissed her on the lips, and asked her how she was feeling.

"Miserable," she said and started to tear up.

Richard spoke to Claire from the kitchen, "how you doing Claire?"

"Hi Richard. I'm sorry I'm such a mess," Claire said as she tightened the flannel nightgown around herself, "please, you and your friend, come in and have a seat. Do you want some coffee?"

"We can't stay, Claire," Richard said as he made his way over to her. The tall chauffeur stood motionless at the door with his hands behind his back.

Richard gave Claire a hug and spoke into her ear, "I just want to let you know how sorry I am about Carol."

"I know Richard ," Claire said near tears, "Thank you for coming."

"I just feel so incredibly bad that..." Richard started to say but got distracted and turned to look at Claire's sister who had picked up Claire's ringing cell phone.

"What?" Claire's sister yelled. "Who are you? Is this some kind of sick joke?"

Chapter 23 - GENERAL HOSPITAL

NEWARK, NJ

Movement. The nurse's peripheral vision detected movement as she was checking the rate of drip from the IV. The young lady the IV was attached to had been unconscious since the ambulance brought her in two days ago. The police stopped by every few hours, and had left a standing order to be called when the young lady regained consciousness. The nurse stood by the bed and closely observed the patient. There it is, the eyelids, a slight movement. The nurse became optimistic and started to talk to the patient.
"Come on, Jane Doe. Wake up. You can do it."
It was as though the patient had heard the nurse's plea. Her eyes slowly opened. She looked around the room. She tried to touch the bandages wrapped around her head but she couldn't reach them because all the tubes coming out of her arms and hands limited the amount of movement.
The nurse rang the buzzer, then stepped into the hall and excitedly hollered down to the nurse's station, "she's awake. Jane Doe is awake."
The sound of several pairs of white sneakers pounded down the hallway toward the room. Before long the bed of Jane Doe was surrounded.
"I've called the police department," the head nurse said to the others.
"Hello, Honey," the first nurse said to the now awake patient. How do you feel?"
"My head hurts. And my mouth is dry," Jane Doe said, "But , where am I?"
"You're at General Hospital.
"How did I get here?"

"You just rest easy. The police officer will be here very soon and he can help you fill in the gaps."

"Police? What happened? I don't really remember anything."

Just then a plain clothes Newark police officer entered the room. He held his badge out for the patient to see while he asked the nurse, "can I ask her a few questions?"

"A few but try not to upset her or we will have to ask you to leave."

"Thank you," the officer replied then looked to the patient, "do you remember anything about Tuesday?"

"Tuesday? Tuesday? What day is today?"

"Today's Thursday. You've been unconscious for two days."

"Unconscious?"

"Let me ask you this, do you remember your name?"

"My name? Well yes, it's....it's Carol."

"Carol, what?"

"Carol Morrow."

"Wonderful. Do you remember what happened on Tuesday?"

"No. How did I get here? And what happened to my head.?"

"We think you were mugged. You were found on the sidewalk early Tuesday morning."

"Tuesday? I remember I was going to the airport Tuesday. I was supposed to go to San Francisco. Do my parents know that I'm here?"

"You were found without a purse. You had no ID on you so we didn't know your name or who to contact."

""I need to call my mother. Right away. She'll be worried."

"If you were taking the plane from Newark to San

Francisco your mother will be more than worried and you will be the luckiest victim ever."

"Do I look lucky to you with all these tubes and bandages?" she asked.

"Can you give me your parent's phone number so I can call them for you?"

Carol gave the officer the phone number. As he was flipping open his cell phone the nurse said, "Sorry, sir. No cell phones in the hospital."

"Police emergency," he said then turned back to Carol and said, "Yes, Ms. Morrow, I do think you are lucky. Very lucky. You have no idea how lucky it was that you got mugged and missed your plane."

Chapter 24 - MORROW RESIDENCE

GANISTER, PA

Bobby rushed to Claire's sister and jerked the cell phone from her hand.

"Who the hell is this?" he demanded.

"This is Sgt. Randall Pennington, Newark Police department. I need to speak to the parents of Carol Morrow."

"Yeah, well now's not a good time Sergeant. We just lost our daughter and are still coming to grips with it."

"Is this Mr. Morrow?" Sgt. Pennington pressed.

"Yes, Bobby Morrow, Carol's father." Bobby said near tears.

"Mr. Morrow, again, my name is Sgt. Randall Pennington and I'm about to make you the happiest man in the world. I'm standing bedside at General Hospital where your daughter has just regained consciousness."

"What?" Bobby asked in disbelief.

"It appears your daughter was mugged on Tuesday morning and was later found unconscious.

"You better be serious. If this is some kind of sick joke, I'll hunt you down like a dog."

"Listen, Mr. Morrow, here's my badge number," and he gave it to him, "you call information for the phone number of the Newark Police Department, then call and check on me. And as soon as you're done doing that, you get your ass to Newark to see your daughter." Richard approached him and asked, "Bobby what's going on?"

Bobby turned to face Richard, "it's a Newark cop. Carol's alive!"

"Oh my God," Claire screamed and ran to Bobby, "are you sure."

"Give me his name, Bobby," Richard said, "I'll have this checked out in no time."

"Senator St. Clair called his Washington office, who made official inquiries while Richard waited. After a couple minutes Richard said to Bobby and Claire, barely able to contain himself, "He's a cop. It must be Carol!"

Bobby was still on the phone with Sgt. Pennington, "Thank you so much for this call Sgt.. Believe me we'll be there as soon as we can."

After Bobby got off the phone he said, "Shit. All the airlines are grounded thanks to those damn terrorists. It will take us eight hours to drive there."

"Maybe not." Richard said as he flipped his cell phone open again. The Senator called in favors all the way up to the White House. A helicopter will pick up Carol and bring her home to Ganister Hospital.

Senator St.Clair's driver was still standing in front of the kitchen door when he heard someone knock on it. He turned to look out the window of the door to find a

Sheriff in a brown uniform holding up his ID. The driver opened the door and let the Sheriff in.

Bobby, Richard, Claire, and her sister were still hugging and dancing in circles just ecstatic about the news. Eventually they turned and caught sight of the Sheriff. The Sheriff wasn't a small man, he just appeared short next to the extremely tall chauffeur. He was an older man with the years of experience etched on his face with crow's feet and gray beard stubble. His stance exuded no small amount of confidence.

"Sheriff what can I do for you?" Bobby asked as he walked over to meet him.

"Well you can turn around and put your hands behind your back," the Sheriff answered with a straight face.

Bobby smiled, "seriously Sheriff, what's up?"

The Sheriff was still very stone faced, "I have a warrant for your arrest Mr. Morrow."

Richard's ears never seemed to miss anything. "What's going on?" he asked the Sheriff.

"I'm sorry you had to be here Senator, but I have a warrant to take Mr. Morrow in for questioning."

"What's the charge?" Richard asked.

"Murder."

"Let me see that warrant," Richard demanded.

Not really knowing what he was looking at Senator St.Clair did what any good politician would do, he got on his phone. Again, he called his office, who then called the County Sheriff's office, and Richard had an answer before he hung up.

"Who did Bobby allegedly murder?" Richard asked the Sheriff.

"A body was found in the Laurel Highlands near Stoystown,"

Richard looked to Bobby.

"That's bullshit," Bobby said, "I didn't kill anyone."
Bobby leaned over and whispered into Richard's ear,
"A man got shot in the Laurel Highlands on Tuesday
when I saw the plane shot down, but I didn't shoot
him. His partner did."

"Why didn't you report it?" Richard whispered back to
Bobby.

"I was a little busy trying to get home to my cell phone,
to call the Colonel, to find out why an airliner was shot
out of the sky," Bobby said very matter of factly.

Richard's face drained of color, "Sheriff we have a
matter of national security here. I'm afraid you're going
to have to wait while I call the President."

The Sheriff nearly smiled, "I've heard some good ones,
but this beats all; you're gonna' call the President?"

Richard was already dialing his cell phone. "Senator
St.Clair here. I urgently need to speak with the
President."

This time the Sheriff's face drained of all color.

"Mr. President," Richard spoke quietly while he turned
away from the others, "I have a situation. Seems there
is a county sheriff here at Bobby Morrow's home to
arrest him for killing another man on the day he
witnessed the ..ah...accident."

The President allowed the sentence to sink in. He still
wasn't seeing the entire picture. It was all clear as mud.
"I knew we couldn't keep a lid on this," the President
said, took a moment to think, then continued, "Did he
really kill someone?"

"No he was on a mission for the Colonel. The other
guy's partner shot him."

"So why are you calling me?" the President asked.

"Do you want Bobby explaining why he was there, and
more importantly, what he saw? Plus the other man
may have seen the same thing Bobby did."

The complete picture became suddenly became quite clear and it was the President's turn to have the color drain from his face.

"I told the Sheriff he cannot take Bobby in as it's a matter of national security," Richard said to the President.

"Yes, that's it. You make this Sheriff stay right there. I'll get someone there as soon as possible." The President hung up and left Richard with just dial tone buzzing in his ears.

The Sheriff spoke as soon as Richard put done his phone, "so what did you're President say?" A bit of sarcasm and disbelief attached to the words.

"He agrees with me that his is, in fact, a matter of national security and you cannot arrest Mr. Morrow." The Sheriff started to steam, "We'll see," he said as he jumped on his cell phone and shouted into it, "I'm at the Morrow residence with a warrant. Get me some back-up here. Now! Lots of it!"

Richard's driver backed up to cover the kitchen door as Richard spoke, "well, Sheriff, while you wait for your guys, and we wait for our guy, would you like a cup of coffee?"

"You won't be in such a good mood when my deputies get here," the Sheriff said, "Yeah I could use a cup of coffee."

"You can't dampen our mood today Sheriff. We're celebrating Bobby's daughter being found after we thought she was a victim in the plane crash Tuesday. And as soon as the man from Washington gets here your warrant won't be worth the paper it's printed on," Richard told him.

"I'm glad to hear about you daughter Mr. Morrow, but I do have a warrant, and it is my job to execute it."

The driver cleared his throat. The Sheriff turned to face

him and looked down the barrel of a very large handgun. "Please be kind enough to place your weapon on the counter Sheriff and make yourself comfortable in the chair over there. Drink your coffee," the driver said.

"Do you have any idea what you are doing?" the Sheriff asked the chauffeur.

"Yes, sir, I do," the driver responded as he displayed his Secret Service badge, "we're all waiting for the man from Washington to straighten this all out."

"When my deputies get here...."

"When you're deputies get here Sheriff," the driver interrupted, "they will be welcome to have a cup of coffee also while we wait."

The Sheriff threw up his arms, "could I get some sugar for my coffee?" he asked and settled in.

Wait, they did.

Several county sheriff cars pulled in. A half dozen deputies stood on the porch scratching their heads while the driver displayed his ID through the door window. The driver invited anyone that wanted coffee to come on in while they waited for the man from Washington.

So they waited.

And waited.

Chapter 25 - DISTRIC ATTORNEY'S OFFICE

HOLIDAYSBURG, PA

Everyone jumped out of their desk chairs and ran to the windows facing Allegheny Street to see what was happening. People were still very jumpy, after all the terrorist attacks were just two days ago and still playing constantly on the television, and now there is a helicopter landing on the street which was hastily blocked off by the local and state police. There were police cars parked every which way at both ends of the block and dust and paper swirling as the helicopter sat down on the street.

Two gentlemen with shiny leather briefcases stooped low as they made their way off the helicopter, under the still turning rotor blades, and headed for the building with the windows full of staring eyes.

The gentlemen entered the building nad announced, We're from the Attorney General's Office in Washington. Looking for the District Attorney."

Having just hung up his phone, the District Attorney hustled over to greet the men. "I'm the District Attorney," he said as he stuck out his hand. He was dressed in suit pants but without his jacket and he attempted to straighten his tie as he came over to meet them.

"We need to speak with you sir," one of the gentlemen said. And as he looked around the crowded room full of gawking people he added, "In private, please."

"Yes, of course," the District Attorney said as he led the gentlemen back to his office, "Get back to work people." His voice now exuding a new level of importance since the men from Washington came in a helicopter, blocking off the street, and were here to see him.

The men wasted no time with small talk or even sitting in the chairs offered them, they merely showed the District Attorney their identification and proceeded, "you're Sheriff is attempting to execute a warrant against a Mr. Bobby Morrow, at his residence, as we speak."

The District Attorney was dumbfounded, "how would you know this?" he asked.

"Senator St.Clair called the President, who called us," the gentleman said very calmly.

"What's this all about?" the District Attorney asked.

"Now, it's about national security." the other gentleman said, "But we'll ask the questions. How did these charges come about?"

"Let me pull the file up on the computer. Please have a seat, gentlemen."

They continued standing. The District Attorney got the message and punched the keys a little faster.

"No time. The President is waiting. The facts, please."

"The State Police pulled over a Jeep on Route 30 near Stoystown because the driver was driving very erratic. This was right after the plane crashed there. Well, when they pulled this guy over he had blood all over his face and clothes so the Trooper took him in for questioning. He said he and his friend were attacked in the woods and his friend was killed. He was able to write down the license number of an old red pickup that was parked in the bushes off the highway. The pickup was licensed to one Bobby Morrow so the State Police issued a warrant and the Sheriff was sent to pick him up."

"Who is the man that was first picked up?"

"Let's see here. I'll write down his name and address for you."

"You do that, and you also have him picked up and bring him here as we'll be taking him back to Washington with us."

"Of course," the District Attorney said and he got on the telephone to pass on the orders.

The two gentlemen quietly conferred then one said, "better yet, bring him to the Morrow residence. We are going to fly out there and diffuse this situation with the Sheriff."

Timidly the District Attorney asked, "might I see your warrant first?"

"Of course," the gentleman said as he laid his briefcase on the District Attorneys desk, clicked open the locks, and handed the District Attorney a document.

"Looks to be in order. Do you need assistance getting to the Morrow residence?"

"No thanks. GPS. It's a wonderful thing," the gentleman said, "plus I doubt we could miss it with all the Sheriff cars and a Senator's limo taking up space."

"You have a point there," the District Attorney said. With a hearty high ho silver, the shiny helicopter took off leaving dust and debris blowing in its wake.

Chapter 26 - MORROW RESIDENCE

GANISTER, PA

It's a good thing Bobby Morrow lives on a seventy-five acre gentleman's farm with his beautiful modern log cabin sitting in the middle of a field, otherwise there wouldn't room for all these quests. There were Bobby's cars, his sister in laws car, the Senators limousine, half a dozen Brown Sheriff's cars, and now a shiny silver helicopter looking for an open patch of grass to claim it's resting spot. All eyes were on the bird as it made a gentle touch down and the two gentlemen again made their stooped over escape from under the wash of the rotor blades. Several of the deputies were still on the porch, sitting on the sturdy log railings having a cigarette and wondering what was really going on. The remainder were inside having coffee with all the guns piled on the kitchen counter and the hulking black suited chauffeur overseeing everything.

The driver opened the door for the two gentlemen and

as soon as Bobby and Richard saw them their jaws dropped. They looked at each other in complete disbelief. Claire on the other hand made her way across the kitchen floor and hugged the first gentleman saying, "Ellwood Sine, I never knew you worked for the government. I knew you were from Virginia but had no idea what you did except enjoyed Aruba the same time of year as we did. Please, come in. Would you like a cup of coffee? Bobby don't just stand there with your teeth in your mouth," Claire said as she turned to look at Bobby, "get Mr. Sine a cup of coffee. Oh, and who is your associate? Would you like a cup of coffee?"

Ellwood spoke up, "thank you so much for your hospitality Claire but we do need to take care of business first as the President is waiting to hear back from us. This," Ellwood said, pointing to his associate, "is the deputy Attorney General." The gentleman smiled and nodded his head.

"Then I guess that makes you the Attorney General," Richard said as he came across the room to shake Ellwood's hand. "It's a pleasure to see you again, Ellwood."

"Thank you Senator. Next time we are all in Aruba, we'll have to have dinner together."

The Sheriff prominently cleared his throat, "gentlemen, I appreciate you all wanting to have a reunion, but I have a lot of men standing around doing nothing. Could we get to the matter at hand?"

"Of course, Sheriff," Ellwood said, "You and you're men are free to go. Mr. Morrow is now in the custody of the federal government as an eyewitness. Here is a copy of the subpeona which your District Attorney has just examined a few minutes ago. Do you have any questions Sheriff?"

"Just one, Mrs. Morrow that's some fine coffee, could I
have a cup for the road? And I'm very glad to hear that
your daughter is well." Claire fixed the Sheriff a cup of
coffee and handed it to him. He tipped his cap to her
and looked up at the driver and said, "you don't mind
if I take my gun now, do you big fella?"

"Of course not Sheriff," the driver said with a huge
smile on his face, "in fact if you ever need assistance
when I'm around, I'll have your back." The two
bumped fists and the Sheriff headed for the open doors,
"come on boys. Our job here is done." Just then his
radio squawked. "Sheriff, are you still at the Morrow
place?"

The sheriff pushed the button to answer, "Yes."

"Could you stay put? One of the deputies is bringing
another person out to return to Washington with the
Attorney General. The DA would like you to be sure
the hand-off goes smoothly."

"10-4," the Sheriff responded, then looked at his band
of deputies, "you guys may as well go, I'll take care of
this."

The contingent of sheriff's cars left just in time to make
room for the medical helicopter that was nearing the
Morrow residence and preparing to set down next to
the other helicopter. The farm was starting to resemble
an airport.

Bobby and Claire rushed from the house as they saw
the second helicopter setting down. Claire, still in her
flannel nightgown, pulled it tighter around herself to
fend off the breeze made by the helicopter blades and
they both waited on the porch until they saw the
gurney exiting the helicopter then they ran across the
field to greet their daughter. They held her hands and
spoke to her while the medics wheeled her across the
field, onto the porch, and into the house.

Inside, Ellwood and Richard were sitting at the kitchen table discussing things.

"So, Ellwood, what will happen now?" Richard asked.

"Well, we're going to take this other guy in and go over his story. My gut tells me he will eventually admit to an accident and clear Bobby. The bigger problem is what might he have seen while he was there with Bobby. He may have seen and know enough that we will have to give him a sweet deal just to keep his mouth shut. Either way, it will all get taken care of?"

"Will Bobby have to go with you now?" Richard asked.

"No, we know where he is if we want to talk to him. He needs to be here to take care of Claire and his daughter."

The kitchen door opened and in came the gurney with Carol, and the medics and Bobby and Claire. The room took on a completely different atmosphere. More like a reunion that chased away all the sadness that previously had filled the room. Duke barked and wagged his tail, and now that they were inside the medics took the straps off Carol and helped her off the gurney. "She needs plenty of bed rest for couple more days," the medic said, "but other than that she is good to go."

"Ellwood, would you and your friend like to stay for dinner?" Claire asked, "It won't be any fancy pasta with an octopus on top, but it will be edible."

"Thank you Claire, for your hospitality but we must get back to Washington. I see the sheriff's car coming up the lane now, so our other passenger is probably here. But next time we're in Aruba, we'll all have Linguine Della Scogliera, and for the faint of heart, Pasta E Fagioli!"

Attorney General Sine's pilot came to the door and asked Ellwood, "excuse me, sir, do you think I could use the restroom before we start back?"

Richard turned to answer the pilot for Ellwood, "Please feel free to...." Richard stammered. The politician was at a loss for words. He openly stared at the pilot, a beautiful woman with short dark hair, a fabulous figure, and haunting eyes that he had seen somewhere else. Finally he spoke, "it's you! My mermaid!"

No One Noticed

Chapter 1

The dog days of August came early this year with terrific heat and humidity starting early each morning and growing throughout the day. Such was the case again this morning in Washington, DC as Senator Richard St.Clair made his way from his Volvo to his office, perspiration immediately dampening his crisp white shirt under the impressive gray suit topped off with a bright multi-colored power tie. The Senator, a tall and handsome man, was in excellent physical condition, and one of Washington's most sought after bachelors. As he entered his office he was met by his perky secretary, Bryonna.

"Good morning Senator," Bryonna said as she stood behind her desk holding a handful of pink phone message slips.

"Morning, Bryonna," Richard replied, "What do we have going on today?"

"First you have your Armed Forces Sub-Committee meeting, then lunch with one of your constituents, a Mr. Carmine Rizzo, then…"

At the mention of Carmine Rizzo's name, Richard immediately looked up from the pink slips Bryonna had handed him and stared intently at Bryonna. Staring intensely but saying nothing, making Bryonna nervous, begging for more information without saying a word.

Bryonna quickly composed herself and replied, "Mr. Rizzo stated he was not only a constituent, and a large campaign donor, but also a friend of the family."

Richard continued staring showing no emotions and saying nothing.

"He is," Bryonna asked hesitantly, "isn't he?"

"He is, "Richard finally said softly.

"Did I make a mistake Senator?" Bryonna asked sheepishly.

"No," Richard said and hesitated, then asked, "So Carmine is in Washington?"

"He must be Senator. He made the appointment last week, and specifically wanted to meet with you over lunch."

"Have you made a reservation yet?"

"I was under the impression that Mr. Rizzo was making the reservation. An Italian place near here, I believe."

Richard smirked, "of course an Italian restaurant. No other food would dare cross the lips of Carmine Rizzo." Then gathering his composure he asked, "Anything in the afternoon?"

Bryonna, while being an extremely efficient secretary, was also an extremely beautiful secretary. Long blonde hair, bright blue eyes and a smile that could charm even the hardest of hearts. She just hadn't found the right mate yet and was not rushing into any relationships.

"This afternoon, Senator," Bryonna answered, "you have a meeting with Senator Snead of Virginia."

"Thank you, Bryonna. I guess I'll head over to the Senate Building for my Committee meeting."

Senator Richard St.Clair began his political career in his small hometown of Ganister, Pennsylvania. As a successful insurance agent, he wanted more challenges, so he ran for Mayor of his borough. His tenure as Mayor was certainly more exciting than his previous career. Richard exposed the corrupt Chief of Police who protected several cat burglars, naturally for a percentage of the take. The Chief's son was using his position with the local ambulance service to distribute drugs which eventually got him a bullet hole in the forehead. The Chief had accused Richard of shooting his son, and after having broken into Richard's home early one morning with revenge on his mind, ended up getting shot himself by Richard's best friend Bobby Morrow, and the County detective who had been tailing the Chief to put the finishing touches to his charges against the Chief. At the same time, Richard had lost his beautiful wife Pamela to the death grip of cancer. Richard was devastated after her death and immersed himself into his career which, along with his strong moral fiber, is what got the attention of others and led to his becoming a young Senator. His popularity has waned in recent years owing to his conservative philosophy and being surrounded by a majority of more liberal minded fellow politicians hell-bent on becoming what they broke free from two hundred years prior. The large influx of immigrants from socialist countries, that came to the United States for more opportunity, somehow feel compelled to change their new home to one resembling their old home.

The gavel cracked loudly against the solid oak block as Richard called his Committee to order. The Committee always met in their special room. Completely sound proof. Doors locked, and with no one present but the Committee members. The conference table was filled with uniforms representing every branch of the military and sporting enough medals and ribbons to open a trophy store, plus a contingent of other Senators in their impressive suits and power ties.

"Good morning, gentleman," Richard said after the buzz of voices subsided.

There was a collective return greeting, then Richard asked, "any old business issues before we move on to new business?" Several generals and admirals asked about updates to their requests for funding of various projects. The suits around the table responding with the usual political answers deflecting any real commitment to a future date.

"Okay, gentlemen," Richard said, "any new business?"

An angry Army General who had just been put off again regarding his funding request responded quickly, "yes, I have some new business."

General Bruce Ross was a formidable presence. A huge man with strong facial features, short gray hair always precisely trimmed in the military tradition, gold buttons shining like small halogen lights, shoes so brilliant you had to shade your eyes, and enough ribbons on his chest to open a fabric store. Waiting until he had everyone's attention he asked, "in March, the Department of Homeland Security purchased four hundred fifty million rounds of ammunition. How do they get their requests granted so quickly?"

"That's a damn good question," barked Navy Admiral Joseph Snare. Like General Ross, the Admiral's bright white uniform was crisp as a new dollar bill with creases so sharp you could cut yourself on them.

Richard looked to the other Senators at the conference table, "Anyone care to respond?"

The heads attached to the other suits dropped and stared at the beautiful oak table as if they suddenly had an interest in fine woodwork.

"Well, okay," Richard said, "I guess I'll try to answer that. I saw the item, probably at the same time that you did, and when I asked the question in the Senate I was told that the purchase was necessary for training purposes."

General Ross laughed but with no pleasure in his voice, then turning instantly serious stated, "Training purposes. Training Purposes! They purchased forty caliber hollow point bullets that are designed to expand upon entry and cause maximum organ damage....... for training purposes."

"You have my attention, General," Richard said.

"The fact of the matter is, you don't buy those bullets for training. You buy those bullets to kill people. Who do they plan on killing, and why do they need so many rounds? I was under the impression that the military did the fighting for this country not Homeland Security."

A gray haired Navy Admiral spoke up, his voice dripping with sarcasm, "But General, I have an even better question, why does the Social Security Administration need one hundred, seventy-four thousand rounds of hollow point bullets? And why are they being shipped to forty-one Social Security offices throughout the country? Is there a new "retirement" program being started that I have not heard about?"

Admiral Snare chimed in full of sarcasm, "I'm sure the Social Security Administration has need of all those rounds, especially since they are .357 Sig 125 grain bonded jacketed hollow point pistol ammo. They are either afraid for their lives because they will have to soon tell people there is no more Social Security money available or they intend to take thousands of people off the Social Security roles. This is ridiculous Senator, we ask for funds to defend our country and we can't get them, yet these items are being approved every day by you suits sitting in the rotunda."

The tension was building around the table as men in uniforms began shaking their heads up and down while perspiration began forming on the foreheads of the men in suits. All except Senator Richard St.Clair.

"Gentleman," Richard said, then cracked the gavel again to get attention, "Gentleman. I completely understand your position. And not only do I completely agree with your position, frankly I am appalled at the direction the current administration has gone."

"So, what do you intend to do about it?" asked the not so shy General Ross.

"As a mere cog in the Congressional wheel the only thing I can do is shout it from the rooftops and hope it doesn't fall on deaf ears," Richard replied.

"Congress and the current President keep cutting our budget, but not to save money. They are just reallocating it somewhere else. Mainly Homeland Security and their stupid pet pork barrel projects. Do they not realize that we still have enemies?" Admiral Snare asked.

Another disgruntled Admiral cut him off and chimed in, "the United States is not the most loved country in the world. North Korea, the radical Muslims, China, and everyone competing to get more oil. It won't be long till the Samolian pirates have a larger Navy than we do."

Richard held up his arm to get control of the meeting again and said, "Gentleman, make no mistake, I am on your side. I agree with your assessments and will do my best to make your case on Capitol Hill. What I need from you is factual information so that I can increase your budgets."

The conversation continued for hours, back and forth, like a tennis match with the military brass questioning Congress' rationale and the suits unable to return any serves.

The other Senators were able to relax and stop sweating.

"We expect you to relay our concerns to Congress, Senator," said Admiral Snare.

After assuring Admiral Snare and the other men around the conference table that he would pass their concerns on to Congress, Richard asked, "may I have a motion to adjourn this meeting?"

"Motion to adjourn," came immediately from the far end of the conference table.

"Second," roared another voice.

Richard cracked the gavel and the room emptied.

Richard was lost in thought rehashing the meeting as he slowly made his way back to his office. He was nearing the entrance when the large black limousine pulled up to the curb. The rear window on the driver's side of the car went down and the raspy voice called out, "Senator St. Clair. Ready for our lunch appointment?"

Richard looked toward the voice and stared blankly at Carmine Rizzo. After a few seconds he replied, "Carmine. What brings you to Washington?"

"We'll discuss it over linguine," Carmine replied, "climb in Senator."

The driver jumped out as if on cue, and opened the rear door for Richard. Richard made a quick glance around then stepped inside the limo. The door shut immediately behind him, and the driver jumped in and sped away.

A few minutes of silence passed till Richard finally said, "You're looking well Carmine."

"Thanks," Carmine said with his heavy Italian accent making it sound more like 'Tanks'.

The limo pulled up in front of a small gray brick building with a white awning with a small jester printed on it and the name, Al Tiramisu. The driver again jumped out and opened the rear door. Carmine motioned for Richard to go ahead and get out, then he followed. The two of them walked to the front door of the restaurant which swung open and a smiling maitre d' in a black suit, holding a large wine menu in his arm looked at them and said, "Mr. Rizzo, so good of you to grace us with your presence."

Carmine merely nodded his head and casually strode inside. After Richard had passed the maitre d' scurried around in front of them and again addressed Carmine, "This way Mr. Rizzo. Your usual table is waiting."

He led them to the back of the restaurant in a secluded area and placed Carmine with his back to the wall. After Carmine was seated the maitre d' handed him the leather bound menu and wine list.

"What may I get you to drink, Mr. Rizzo?"

"The usual," he answered.

"Yes, sir," the maitre d' said, "right away sir," then he looked toward Richard, "and for you sir?"

"Just water. Thank you," Richard replied.

The maitre d' scurried off and Richard again asked Carmine, "So, Carmine, what are we doing here?"

"We gonna' eat some pasta," Carmine said, "what you no hungry?"

"You know what I mean Carmine," Richard said, "what is on your mind?"

"I don't talka' business on an empty stomach," Carmine said.

A waiter came to Carmine's side and placed a crystal glass in front of him, then poured a small amount of the bright purple liquid into the glass and stood back alongside Carmine as though he were in the army and at attention.

Carmine picked up the glass. Twirled the liquid around. Smelled the bouquet then gulped it down.

"That's a fine," Carmine said, "leave the bottle."

The waiter quickly sat the bottle by Carmine's arm and left the table.

"You remember when I saved your ass from being thrown into the Blue Hole?" Carmine asked Richard.

The Blue Hole was a large limestone quarry outside Richard's hometown of Ganister, Pennsylvania that contains forty feet of the most brilliant blue water you've ever seen any where north of the Caribbean. When Richard was Mayor of Ganister and was making progress on exposing the Chief of Police's criminal activities, the Chief and his son lured Richard to the quarry one night on the pretense that they discovered a body in the quarry and that Richard would be interested. Their intention was to give Richard the so called "Cement shoes". Tie a cement block to his feet and throw him into the quarry. What the Chief hadn't counted on was that farmer Terry Lee lived just above the Blue Hole, and Terry kept a close eye on the Blue Hole because in actuality it belonged to Carmine Rizzo. When Terry called Carmine to tell him there was something strange going on at the Blue Hole, Carmine and his main man, the muscular son-in-law Gino showed up along with Richard's best friend Bobby Morrow the former military sharpshooter. Needless to say, Mayor Richard St.Clair did not get wet that night, but the Chief and his son were chased off with their tails between their legs, and the groundwork was laid to indict the Chief.

"So," Richard said to Carmine, "you here to call in your marker?"

"No," said Carmine, "just reminiscing."

"So you drove from Ganister to Washington DC to take me to lunch to reminisce?"

"Always right to the point with you, huh St.Clair?"

Richard sat back and looked at Carmine.

"You probably neva' knew how much I donated to your campaign when you run for Senator, did ya?" Carmine asked.

"I'm still waiting for the other shoe to drop Carmine."

"Thatsa' no way to treat a friend of da family."

"That's another thing Carmine. I know my father may have worked for you in the past, but what does that have to do with me?"

All talk stopped as the waiter appeared and handed out the menus. Carmine merely handed his back and said, "I'm a gonna have the Ravioli Ripeni. You should try it St.Clair. You're a gonna like it."

Richard folded his menu and handed it back to the waiter and said, "Sure. Why not?"

The waiter left and Richard absently brushed both hands across the red and white checked cotton table cloth to smooth out an invisible crease.

"Your old man was something," Carmine said and nearly chuckled as he poured himself another huge glass of wine.

"You should try this St.Clair. This is good stuff."

"No thanks, Carmine."

"Nip and Tuck," Carmine said as Richard stared at him, "That's a what they called your old man and his older brother. Nip and Tuck."

Richard sat quietly acting as disinterested as he could.

"Nip and Tuck," Carmine repeated, "They were something. Your dad's brother was older and bigger. He started boxing in the Navy. Then when he came home from the Navy he used to do some work for me. And since your dad was always following him around everyone called them Nip and Tuck." Carmine stopped for another large drink of wine.

"That was back in the good old days. They were big and strong so when I needed to collect some money due me or other odd jobs, they would always taka' care of it for me."

"So you're here to blackmail me with my father's past?" Richard asked.

"Justa reminiscing St.Clair," Carmine reminded him.

Two huge plates of steaming round ravioli stuffed with spinach and ricotta showed up and was placed in front of each of them.

"You gonna like this St.Clair," Carmine said as he picked up his fork and dug in.

Richard sat watching Carmine. Still waiting for the other shoe to drop.

"So anyway, St.Clair. I gotta small problem and I thought sinca' you was my Senator and all that maybe you coulda go to bat for me and get it straightened out."

"Just spit it out Carmine," Richard said, "what's your problem."

"Well youra' IRS has stolen my money."

Richard could barely keep himself from laughing. Smiling for the first time since seeing Carmine, Richard asked, "the IRS has stolen money from you?"

Carmine looked at him as serious as possible, "Yea. They taka' my money!"

"You care to elaborate on that Carmine?"

"Okay. Here a goes. I inherited some gold coins..."

"From who?" Richard interrupted to ask.

"From my wife's father."

"What kind of coins?" Richard asked.

"They were 1933 Saint-Gaudens double eagles twenty dollar gold pieces."

"You're serious!" Richard exclaimed.

Carmine stared intently at Richard, "Your damned right I'm serious."

"So what happened?"

"I wanna know what they worth, so I asked around. My accountant he says we should ask the Phildelphia Mint to have them authenticate them, then I should take them to Sotheby's auction in New York and sell them. So I sends them down to da mint in Philly."

"Then what happened?"

""I never getta them back, so I calls Philly and says where da hell is a my coins?"

Richard was now interested and hanging on every word.

"So da man says da IRS came in when they heard the coins wuz there and confiscates them."

"Why?" was all Richard could think to ask.

"They says I can't prove how I gotta hold of them and that they was stolen from the mint," Carmine said between mouthfuls of Ravioli.

Richard started to eat now that he was engrossed in Carmine's story and asked, "so have you contacted the IRS?"

"Well notta' me, but my overpriced attorneys did."

"And what did IRS say?"

"They says justta what I tell you. But they was legitimately my wife's father's coins. He bought them when they was minted and saved them all those years. Nobody except hissa wife ever knowed he had them tilla he die, then we open da safe and there they be."

"So what do you think I can do?" Richard asked.

"You worka for da government, you tell them a jackasses they either give my money back or I gonna sue them for the seven and a half million dollars that they worth."

Richard scratched his head, "I don't even know anyone in the IRS."

"You my Senator. You getta my money," Carmine said with a mouthful of ravioli.

"I'll make some inquiries," Richard said, "but under two conditions."

Carmine nearly dropped his fork as he looked toward Richard, "you gotta conditions?"

Carmine glanced around the room then back to Richard, "who da hell you think you talkin' to?"

"I know exactly who I'm talking to Carmine. The guy who wants to hold things over my head and have me jump through hoops."

Carmine stopped chewing. After a few seconds he said, "I neva' gonna' hold anything over your head. You don't wanna do this for me thatsa okay. No problem. I go back to Ganister and you neva' hear from me again."

Richard sensed the old mafia boss was actually telling the truth but waited.

"So whatsa' your conditions?" Carmine asked.

"First, that you never bring up the Blue Hole incident again."

"No problem, I justa' thought it was a funny story. What else?"

"I want to know exactly what my father did for you?"

Now it was Carmine's turn to stare at Richard. Carmine put down his fork, leaned over the table, as much as his large stomach would allow and quietly said to Richard, "No. You don't wanna' know. Plus, I promisa' your old man that I never tella you."

"But you'll continue to hold it over my head?"

"No," Carmine said as he wiped marinara sauce from his lips, "I hava' too much respect for Nip and Tuck. They was great guys."

Richard stood up from the table. "Thanks for lunch Carmine," he said, "I'll ask around about your coins."

"You wanna ride back to your office?" a surprised Carmine asked.

"No thanks," Richard said, "I'll catch a cab."

"By the way St.Clair, I gotta beautiful single niece about your age. You should come see her."

Senator Richard St.Clair, after shaking his head, strode out of the dim restaurant into the bright sunshine and heavy humidity and hailed a cab.

Chapter 2

Overlooking the East River in the Turtle Bay neighborhood of Manhattan in New York stands a thirty-nine story concrete and glass structure that was built in 1952. The representatives gathered in the United Nations building from all over the world on this day were listening to a speech from the United States Secretary of State.

"I am here on behalf of the President of the United States," she said and continued, "to pledge my country's support for the United Nations Programme Against Small Arms."

The gathered representatives, hearing the translation into each of their own languages, applauded. The United Nations Programme Against Small Arms wanted to enact global gun registering followed by confiscation to eliminate individuals possessing firearms.

The ruggedly handsome Bobby Morrow was spending a leisurely day hunting. Well, probably not so much hunting as taking his rifle for a walk through the quiet woods enjoying nature and the wooded areas of his seventy five acre farm situated just outside of the borough of Ganister. After returning from the jungles of Vietnam with a chest full of medals for bravery, and finishing up college with his degree in dentistry, Bobby purchased the seventy five acres and he and his lovely wife built a modern log cabin where they could comfortably raise their daughter. It didn't take Bobby long to get bored with poking around in people's mouths filling cavities and yanking out rotted teeth. It just wasn't the same as quietly hiking through the jungle looking for booby traps and North Vietnamese behind every bush. The heat, followed by the torrential downpours while carrying the heavy pack and gun all the while nursing foot fungus and lack of sleep. That's when he and Richard St.Clair became the best of friends. Richard wanted to be somewhere else. Anywhere else. And because of that he neglected to be a real soldier. Boredom caused Richard to get lax which is what allowed the anxious North Vietnamese soldier to wait while Richard strolled right up to him without noticing. That's when the North Vietnamese soldier stuck the barrel of his gun just inches away from Richard's chest, smiling as he prepared to pull the trigger. And he would have pulled the trigger with absolutely no compunction had the bullet not tore through his forehead dropping him instantly to the ground. Richard was still trying to analyze what happened and why he was not dead on the ground when Bobby Morrow made his way quietly over to Richard to inspect his most recent kill. Bobby was a sniper, and a serious soldier. He operated on instincts. He didn't debate whether he should pull the trigger. If you were in the enemies uniform there was no hesitation. That's what kept him alive. And also what kept Richard St.Clair alive. Not his own instincts, but the fact that Bobby always watched Richard's back.

Bobby was daydreaming about those days in Vietnam with Richard when the white tailed buck quietly slipped onto the trail in front of him a mere hundred yards. An easy shot for Bobby and though his instincts immediately brought the barrel of the gun up and the stock to his shoulder with the sights perfectly positioned on the buck's heart just behind the top of the animal's front leg. Bobby's finger twitched. He smiled and said to no one but himself, "I'm going to let you get a little fatter." He lowered his gun and watched the dashing deer waive his white tail as he ran through the woods leaping over logs and bushes and dodging trees. Bobby's euphoria was whisked away by the ringing of his cell phone. Looking at the caller i.d., Bobby flipped the phone open and answered, "Yeah."

"Bobby," came the reply, "It's the Colonel."

"I know. What's up?"

The Colonel and Bobby had a long past. At one time the Colonel was Bobby's commanding officer in Vietnam. Then the Colonel kept moving up through the ranks while Bobby kept saving lives, shooting the enemy, and earning more medals. The Colonel always kept in touch, and when he found out that Bobby was bored with his career as a dentist, the Colonel made him an offer he couldn't refuse. Bobby became the Colonel's right-hand man when the Colonel became the President's right-hand man. An undercover agent both in the United States and any other country when the Colonel either needed to have someone silenced or information gathered. With Bobby's abilities as a sniper and his ability to escape detection in nearly any environment, he was a natural.

"Have you been watching television?"

A smile crossed Bobby's face as he looked around and replied, "not exactly. Why?"

"You're going to want to check out the Secretary of State's speech today at the UN."

"Why?" Bobby asked in a hushed voice as he was still trying not to spook the woodland creatures.

"The Secretary of State is supporting the United Nations Programme Against Small Arms."

"And I should care, because?" Bobby asked.

"Well, you should care for two reasons," the always intent Colonel replied, "number one because it is an attempt to skirt around the Second Amendment and remove guns from every American citizens hands."

"They'll never get that passed in this country."

"Exactly why they are trying to get world opinion on their side and force it upon us."

"You said two reasons."

"Yeah. The second reason is because the new President just fired me. I'm no longer his advisor."

"You're putting me on."

"There's more, Bobby. Since I don't have a job, you don't have a job."

It took a moment for the words to sink into Bobby's mind."You fired me last year, remember?"

"Yeah, but then I needed you to train Sarge to take your place since you got older on me and lost a step, and because Sarge was young and eager just like you used to be. But this time it's for keeps."

"Why doesn't the new President want you as an advisor?"

"It's the new gentler age. They are now hiring young geeks fresh out of college that are good with computers and playing computer games. They sit in an office at the Pentagon, and with their computer and a few satellites and drones armed with cameras, weapons and even biological warfare options they can spy on anyone or eliminate anyone they want with the push of a button. They don't even get their hands dirty."

"This sucks!"

"Yeah, well you better brush up on drilling teeth cause it looks like you're on your way back into the office."

"This really sucks!" Bobby said as he hung up the phone and made his way back to his house. The mood to enjoy nature just evaporated.

Chapter 3

Senator Richard St.Clair was downcast as he entered his office. His secretary Bryonna immediately jumped from her chair.

"Senator," Bryonna said, "Senator Snead is waiting in your office."

Richard automatically looked at his wristwatch.

"Has he been waiting long?" Richard asked.

"Probably twenty minutes Senator."

Richard merely shook his head and quickened his pace as he reached for the doorknob of his inner office. Before entering Richard stopped and turned back to face Bryonna.

"By the way," Richard said to his secretary, "Will you give Attorney General Ellwood Sine a call and see if you can set up a meeting?"

"Of course, Senator."

"Thank you," Richard said then he burst through the door and addressed the waiting Senator Snead.

"I am so sorry Leonard. I got tied up in a meeting with a constituent."

The two men shook hands and Richard sat in the empty chair next to Senator Snead.

"No problem," Senator Snead said, "I hope your meeting went well."

"I've had better," Richard said, "but what can I do for you Senator Snead?"

Senator Snead considered his words carefully before he spoke, "you and I have quickly become dinosaurs, Richard."

Richard listened intently and waited for what would follow.

Leonard continued, "I remember when I came to Washington. I was going to change the world. I was going to actually bring the concerns of my voters here and force these old farts to listen."

"Aaah, yes," Richard said, "the good old days."

"But how did we reach the point where we actually pass a new law that changes our way of life without even reading it?"

"Well, Senator, that new health care law is twenty-seven hundred pages long. Did you have time to read it?"

"I didn't then, so, like you, I voted against it. But I have taken the time to read it now."

"And?" Richard asked.

"And, it scares the hell out of me. The pendulum has swung from one side to the other," Leonard said.

Richard waited for him to continue.

"Remember when the Wall got torn down, and Communist Russia just fell apart?"

"That was a monumental time," Richard said, "President Reagan won the war against Communism without firing a shot." "Well that's when the pendulum started swinging," Senator Snead said, "and now Russia is a capitalistic society. But look where we are heading."

"Socializing medical care. Intentionally bankrupting an automobile manufacturer so you can redistribute the stock to the union members to buy their votes. Handing out free cell phones to people that already pay for them, at tax payer expense to buy a few more votes. Giving foreign governments

grants to drill off shore for oil while you place an emabargo on American companies drilling in the gulf. Need I go on?"

"But what can we do?" Richard asked, "We seem to be in the minority."

"We need to fight fire with fire. It doesn't matter what a person stands for anymore. It only matters how well the commercials on TV are received. We need to get better commercials. It's all marketing."

Richard was shocked to hear Senator Snead speak so freely so he attempted to change the subject, "was there something else on your mind Leonard that you wanted to see me about?"

"Oh, yes. I nearly forgot," the Senator said, "I have been invited to Camp David for a meeting with the President and he asked me to bring you along."

Richard was shocked. "The new President wants to meet with you and me? His two biggest opponents? At Camp David? Are you sure?"

"Positive," Senator Snead replied, "I have to assume he wants to make us a deal we can't refuse to swing to his side."

"I like being an American," Richard proclaimed, "If I wanted to be Socialist, I'd move to Europe. He may as well not waste his breath trying to swing my votes that direction."

"Yeah, well you've been in Washington long enough to know how the game is played. You scratch my back, I'll scratch yours."

"So when is this big event?" Richard asked.

"First thing Monday morning. The President's helicopter will pick us up at the White House and take us there."

"Great," Richard said his tongue dripping with sarcasm.

"It's not like you have a date. Speaking of which, I know a beautiful woman that wants to go out with you."

"Why is everyone always trying to fix me up?"

"Maybe you need fixed up," Leonard said with a huge smile on his face.

Chapter 4

Bobby Morrow walked slowly back to the log house in the middle of the emerald green field. He crossed the porch that encircled the house and opened the door into the cozy kitchen. His beautiful wife, Claire, was standing at the kitchen counter occasionally looking out the window while she chopped vegetables on the wood block chopping board.

"You're back early," she said.

"I was interrupted by a phone call from the Colonel."

"Oooh?" Claire said trying not to pry.

"We're out a job."

"Who is out of a job?"

"Me. The Colonel. Sarge. All of us. The new administration is going a different direction."

"What do you mean going a new direction?" Claire asked.

"High tech. Drones in the sky operated by geeks on computers. They don't feel the need to have feet on the ground anymore."

"Well," Claire said, "I'm actually glad. I want us to spend more time together."

Bobby's muscular arm reached out and pulled her close to him. They kissed. They held each other close.

Bobby's phone rang.

"Shit!"

"Ignore it," Claire said but Bobby had already looked at the caller i.d.

"It's Terry Lee. I have to take this call," Richard told Claire as he backed away from her then spoke into the phone, "Terry, what's up buddy?"

Terry Lee was like Bobby in at least one way. He was a man of few words also.

"Sarge got a phone call," Terry Lee said.

Sarge was Terry Lee's son and Bobby's trainee.

Terry continued, "he lit out of here like his ass was on fire. I was just concerned and wondered if you knew what was going on."

"I have a good idea," Bobby said, "do you have any idea where I can find him?"

"Probably that bar at the edge of town. The Broken Nose."

"I'll go see if he's there. Don't worry Terry, I'll take care of him."

Bobby turned to Claire.

"I heard," she said, "I'll hold dinner. You go ahead and go."

Bobby kissed her lightly on the cheek and grabbed the keys to his old red dented truck.

He didn't have to go far because Terry was right. Sarge's truck was parked at the Broken Nose bar. Bobby was still dressed in his old hunting clothes when he entered the dark smoky bar. He waved his hand in front of his face to try to move the cloud of smoke away from himself to no avail. He stopped inside the door to allow his eyes to adjust to the dim light then scanned the room for Sarge. Sarge was always hard to miss. He was about the same height as Bobby but was extremely broad across the shoulders with muscular arms and practically no neck. Bobby spied Sarge sitting at the end of the bar, by himself, hunched over a drink.

Bobby approached him and said, "I take it the Colonel called you."

Sarge slowly turned his head to look at Bobby and answered, "Yeah."

"Sucks, I know."

"What'll you have?" the bartender hollered down to Bobby above the noise of the other patrons.

The Broken Nose was an old bar with the typical large dark wooden bar lined with stools covered in cracked black leather and a brass foot rail that hadn't received any polish in many a year. Behind the bar was a full length mirror tainted by years of nicotine. There were a half a dozen booths lined up along the other side of the narrow room each with a low hung light fixture that was a remnant of the 50's. The bartender was big with greasy hair and an unshaven face. If he ever smiled his face would probably break. He stood behind the bar next to the ashtray where his cigarette lay when he was forced to draw a draft. His tee shirt at one time was white, now it was off white with faded colors of a picture of an old rock band.

"Beer," Bobby said then turned back to Sarge, "You okay?"

"I liked what I did. What *we* did. "

"Yeah. I know Sarge."

"What am I gonna' do now?"

"I don't know but some………..

A disruption and loud voices arose from the doorway. Bobby snuck a quick peak in the mirror behind the bar. A large black man with a red dew rag tied over his head and waving a pistol was shouting towards the bartender. The room fell silent.

"..as I was saying," Bobby continued keeping one eye on the mirror, "Something will come up. Things will change."

The bartender had backed over to the large silver cash register and was opening the drawer pulling out money. The big black guy wandered over behind Bobby and Sarge.

"Yo. Ladies," he said to their backs, "How's about you hand over your wallets?"

Bobby and Sarge ignored him while still each keeping an eye on the mirror.

The black man raised his voice, "hey assholes, I'm talking to you."

Without turning around Bobby said, "go away this is a private conversation."

The robber was furious. He drew back the hand with the gun in it to smash Bobby in the head. As the gun and the arm came down Bobby turned slightly to his left. His muscular elbow ripping into the face of the big black man. Blood spurting from his nose. Bobby followed through on the turn and with his right hand grabbed the gun and with a quick forward motion snapped it out of the beefy black hand. Making a full circle Bobby spun around and with his right foot slammed it into the side of the man's left knee. The man fell to the floor. Groaning. Not knowing which to hold first, his broken nose or his painful knee.

Bobby sat back on the barstool and motioned for the bartender to bring him another beer. The bartender didn't move but eyed the doorway nervously.

Now three guns in the hands of three similar dressed black men appeared out of the darkness.

"Who hurt my bro'?" the lead man asked with ghetto slang. No one answered but all eyes went to Bobby. The man yelled towards Bobby, "Hey asshole, what'd you do to my bro'?" Bobby slowly spun his stool around to face the angry black man.

"Look, we're trying to have a private conversation. Go away."

"Well excuse me," the black man said looking at his compatriots for laughter, then he continued, "get your ass off that stool, hand me your wallet, and help my friend up."

"No thanks," Bobby said and turned his back to the man.

The black man chambered a shell. The room fell deathly silent. Bobby slowly turned on his stool again. With a slow exaggerated movement he pulled back his open hunting shirt to reveal the pistol at his waist then said to the black man in an even, calm voice, "do you really want to get into a pissing match?"

Sarge, who had been quiet up to this point started to laugh. The black man pointed to Sarge, "you, you big oaf, what are you laughing at?"

"You," Sarge said and then pointed to the other two black men with guns and nervous looks on their faces, "and them."

"Yeah, well what's so funny, Oaf?"

"You're outnumbered."

"What the hell do you mean we'se out numbered?"

"Well there are only three of you, not counting the big

bleeding pile of crap on the floor, against Bobby. You're outnumbered." Sarge picked up his beer and took a large gulp.

"I'll shoot your ass man. We'll see who's outnumbered."

Sarge responded, "People have been shooting at him since Vietnam. He's still here. In fact, I think he likes it."

Bobby slowly got off the stool and took a slow step toward the man while staring intently into his eyes.

"Let me ask you something," Bobby said to the tough guy holding the gun while he continued to nonchalantly approach him, "If the Unites States goes along with the United Nations Small Arms Treaty and it becomes unlawful to carry a gun, are you and your boys going to turn your guns into the government?"

The dazed and confused gunman looked first at his cohorts then back to Bobby and said, "What the hell are you talking about? Why the hell would we turn our guns in to the government. What is wrong with you man?"

"Never mind, I was just taking a little survey. Okay, shoot me tough guy," Bobby said as he took another step closer.

A bead of sweat appeared from the black man's dew rag. Then the incredibly quick devastating right foot of Bobby Morrow knocked the dew rag completely off his head as he fell backward into his accomplice's arms. Sirens could faintly be heard in the background. Getting louder and closer with each tick of the clock. One of the men turned around at the sound of the sirens and ran out the door. The man who grabbed the falling gunman ,who now had a bloody face, started to drag him out the door backwards keeping a wary eye on Bobby who had turned around and resumed his position at the bar.

Sarge nudged the groaning man on the floor with his foot and said to him, "you lay around here any longer the cops are gonna' haul you off to jail."

The man painfully got up on one knee then pulled himself up

onto one leg and clumsily made his way to the doorway dragging the twisted left leg.

Sarge shook his head and motioned to the bartender for another beer.

The bartender brought it with a smile on his face and said to Sarge and Bobby, "the beer's on the house. Thanks, guys."

Chapter 5

The President was a tall intimidating man with a deep voice. When he sat behind the highly polished wooden desk in the oval office with the Presidential Seal woven into the carpet separating him from his visitors he became even more intimidating.

The Secretary of State sat in one of the upholstered chairs facing the President quietly waiting for the President to end his phone call. As soon as the President hung up the phone he was buzzed by his secretary, Matty.

Matty had been secretary for three Presidents now. She kept her position while politicians came and went for two reasons. Number one she was efficient. She knew what needed to be done before any of her bosses ever did. And number two because she knew stuff. Every succeeding president hoped to tap her knowledge of the preceeding President but Matty could keep secrets better than the Secret Service.

"Your next appointment is here Mr. President," Matty said through the intercom.

"Tell him to have a seat. The Secretary of State and I are not done."

The President finally looked over to the Secretary of State and said, "You gave a nice speech at the United Nations."

"It was exactly as your speech writers wrote it, Mr. President."

Arrogance showed on the President's face.

"They are good, aren't they? I owe my election to those speech writers."

"They are good Mr. President," the Secretary of State concurred.

"But, you are still not completely onboard with our program are you Mr. Secretary?"

The Secretary of State lowered his eyes and spoke, "not exactly Mr. President."

"Look, we need the guns out of the hands of the populace. Do you realize the number of murders committed in this country every day?"

"I do Mr. President, but I also know that the numbers are even larger in countries that have taken the guns. It is the possibility that another person has a weapon and can fight back that keeps the murder rate low Mr. President."

"I want the guns!"

"And I gave the speech for you Mr. President. Just like you ordered."

"Asked. I asked Mr. Secretary. And you got what you wanted in return. You get to be Secretary of State and fly all over the country in Air Force One."

The Secretary of State again looked downward.

"Now Mr. Secretary, I have another job for you. "

"Yes, Mr. President."

"I want you along at Camp David when I meet with those two Senators from the other side of the aisle. They need to get with the program. They are not helping our cause with all their rhetoric."

"It's called Free Speech, Mr. President."

"Yes, well not when it goes against this President. So you have the FBI bring me some dirt on these two so we can get them in line."

The President shooed him with a flick of his hand and said, "go ahead. We're done."

The President put on his charming deep voice and said on the intercom to Matty, "The Secretary of State is leaving, you can bring in my next appointment."

The door opened and Matty let the tall, slender, handsome dark haired gentleman in the black suit enter the Oval office then she closed the door and went back to her desk.

"Mr. President," the gentleman said as he stood before the President's desk.

The President had risen from his seat and shook hands with him, "Alex, how have you been my friend?"

"I've been well, Mr. President. Thank you for asking."

"To business, Alex. How is our fund raising coming?"

"Quite well Mr. President. We just increased our coffers significantly with our latest acquisition."

"So you got the coins from the old man?" the President asked.

"Of course. He put up a little fuss, but nothing we can't handle."

"What sort of fuss?" the President inquired as he rubbed his chin in thought. The President was a control freak that needed to know every little detail.

"He said he was going to speak to his Senator about us "stealing" his coins. He'll come around."

The President stared at Alex, carefully watching his eyes, and asked, "Did he say what Senator?"

"St.Clair."

"Damn," said the President as he sank back into his seat.

"Is there a problem Mr. President?"

"St.Clair's the problem. Everytime I turn around there he is. He's a pain in my ass. We need to neuter that dog," the president thought for a moment then continued, "I have the FBI looking for dirt on him, but we need something more immediate. "

Chapter 6

"Get up in the morning, look in the mirror, I'm worn as the toothbrush hanging in the stand, My face ain't looking any younger, Now I can see love's taken her toll on me, She's goooooone ...." Richard was singing along with Daryl Hall and John Oates as they vibrated the windows of Richard's Volvo as he crossed D.C. in the afternoon traffic on his way to Attorney General Ellwood Sine's office. Unfortunately Richard knew the words to this particular song all too well. One might say it has been his theme song since his lovely wife Pamela died from cancer many years ago. Pamela had been Richard's high school sweetheart and they married as soon as Richard returned home from the Vietnam war. Fortunately Bobby Morrow was with Richard so that he was able to come home other than in a black body bag with a flag draped over it.

Richard's mind now went back to those years with Pamela. After all these years without her she has been put on a pedestal and Richard can no longer even remember any flaws that she may have had. Probably why he was still single. No other woman was able to stack up to his memories of Pamela. Of course, just last year there was C.J.. Richard was starting to like her a lot. He actually dated her more than once, but then the blush sort of left the rose when Richard thought that she was the assassin that shot at him while he was racing at Watkins Glen, New York, in the formula car race that nearly killed him. Fortunately it turned out that it wasn't C.J. that had shot his tire out on the race track but was a hired gun from the political action committee that Richard had been giving such a hard time. It made Richard sad that C.J. was killed. Shot in his own bed, in fact. Perhaps Richard was not meant to have a mate. First Pamela dying of cancer, then C.J. shot to death.

Richard tried to put his thoughts out of his head as he arrived at the federal office building where Attorney General Ellwood Sine's office was. Richard stopped the Volvo at the armed gate, showed his ID to the guard and told him he had an appointment with Attorney General Sine. The guard checked his records then lifted the gate and motioned Richard through. Richard still maintained some of his old habits and just naturally drove to the back of the lot to park his now old Volvo all by itself so that no one would dent it with their doors. Plus it gave Richard some exercise. After all, he spent most of the day sitting on his duff. The brisk walk across the parking lot and into the federal building would be good for him.

When he arrived at the Attorney General's office he was shown right in.

Ellwood came around the desk and shook hands with him. A nice firm handshake. Always a good sign to Richard. You just couldn't trust someone with a weak handshake.

Ellwood was a very fit man. About six feet tall. Handsome with dark black hair when most men would be graying and well dressed in his pinstripe suit, white shirt, and blue tie. Shoes immaculately shined, probably a habit of his from his old days in the Navy.

"Senator St.Clair," Ellwood said as he shook his hand, "please have a seat."

"Please, just Richard."

"Okay, Richard then just Ellwood."

"Deal," Richard said as he took a seat.

"How is everything with you Richard. We haven't gotten together in a little while."

"Just staying busy. You know how it goes."

"What about your friend Bobby Morrow, he doing okay?"

"Well he was, but he just got his walking papers. Seems the President has left the Colonel and everyone associated with him go."

"Wow. That's surprising. The Colonel has been the right-hand man to the last couple Presidents. And I know he saved their butts on numerous occasions."

"I think it was a big surprise to Bobby too."

"Well tell him I asked about him. And I'll do some checking around. There must be a position somewhere for a man with his talents."

"That would be nice of you Ellwood," Richard said as he brushed fuzz from his pants leg.

"So what can I do for you, Richard?"

"I debated whether or not to even ask you about this, but it just seemed like I should expend a little effort on it."

"Well toss it out there. We'll see if I can do anything for you."

"I have an old constituent; and to be honest, a friend of the family. Anyway, he came into possession of some rare golden coins. 1933 Saint-Gaudens double eagle coins. Well he had the Treasury authenticate and value them for him. These coins are extremely rare and worth about eight million dollars.."

Ellwood whistled.

"Yeah, the problem is the Treasury won't return them. He has been told that his ownership is questionable and that they actually belong to the federal government."

"You know I heard about a similar case to that a few years back where the proceeds were split between the government and the family that had the coins after the coins were sold at auction. But you're saying now that the government wants the coins completely?"

"That's what I am told."

"And you would like me to officially look into this?"

Richard him-hawed then finally said, "only if you are comfortable doing so. The owner is Carmine Rizzo from Ganister, Pennsylvania. In the olden days he was the local mafia chief. I'm sure that he has no connections or power these days but you may not want to be associating with him due to his past, and I can certainly understand that."

"Let me do some checking, then I'll let you know if I feel there is something to investigate."

"That would be perfectly acceptable Ellwood. I would never ask you to do anything that made you uncomfortable. I have too much respect for you to do that," Richard said earnestly.

"Likewise, if you think this is important then I will look into it if possible."

"Well thank you for that for me Ellwood," Richard said as he stood to leave.

Ellwood rose from his seat and came around his desk again to shake Richard's hand once more. As he shook it he said to Richard, "this Rizzo guy, if I go see him, should I take a body guard?"

"I don't think that's necessary, just tell him you're a friend of Bobby's. He thinks the world of Bobby and I can guarantee no harm would come to you when Carmine knows that."

"Good to know," Ellwood said as Richard left his office, "Good to know."

Richard strolled lazily across the parking lot to his Volvo as he thought about the lost loves in his life. He got in his car, buckled his seat belt and put in an Adele CD, then started singing along with Adele, "hold me closer one more time…"

Chapter 7

The four rugged looking guys in the dark booth in the far corner of the bar nodded at each other then got up and followed Bobby and Sarge from The Broken Nose bar. Outside in the crisp clear night Sarge and Bobby strolled over to their trucks which were parked side by side. They stopped at the first truck and were saying their goodbyes when the group approached them from behind.

Bobby's instincts started ringing bells and whistles and he became very alert to the sound of the crunching gravel behind him. He guessed by the number of footfalls that there was at least three of them and possibly more. As he shook Sarge's hand he squeezed it a little extra hard to send a quiet signal and motioned with his eyes. Sarge casually turned to look at the group of approaching men. Sarge said to the men, "What's up guys?"

The four were all dressed in camo and the bulges of guns were easy to make out under their long shirts. They looked at each other then the tallest one spoke, "we were just wondering if we could talk with you guys?'

"What about?" Sarge asked.

"We saw how you handled those black guys in there this evening so we thought maybe you'd like to stop by and maybe join our group."

"What kind of group?" Bobby asked.

"Penn Patriots," the leader said with pride as he stuck out his chest.

Sarge looked at Bobby. Bobby looked at Sarge, then in unison they asked, "Penn Patriots, is that a militia?"

The guy in the back of the group replied, "We're this country's last line of defense."

"Against what?" Bobby asked.

"Those damn towel heads trying to take over our country," he answered slightly amazed that he even had to explain.

Bobby was obviously no longer interested and just stood listening. Sarge pressed on and asked, "So where do you guys meet?"

"If you're interested we'll just meet you in Ganister and take you out there," the leader of the group said to Sarge.

Sarge turned and opened the door to his truck, "Naah. You let me know where it is, and if I'm interested in the morning, I'll be there." Sarge got in his truck and pulled the door shut. His window was down and he folded his muscular arm out the window the way he always did when driving.

The leader looked to his other compatriots then faced Sarge and said in a hushed tone, "Out Clover Creek road towards the base of the mountain, the old Claycomb farm. Do you know where it is?"

"Of course I know where it is. My old man's a farmer too," Sarge said as he started his truck then continued, "I may see you there." Sarge looked at Bobby and said, "See you buddy." Bobby just nodded his head and walked off towards his old beat up red truck, casually got in, started it up and drove off. The group of guys were still watching them both leave as they exited the parking lot.

"Last line of defense," Bobby thought to himself, "where the hell were they when I was on the first line of defense in 'Nam? They're drinking beer at night and shootin' guns all day long at targets that don't shoot back. We had jungle rot, torrential rain, rotten rations to eat and every bush seemed to be shooting back at you." Bobby shook his head, "Last line of defense. Humpf. We're in deep shit if they're the last line of defense."

Chapter 8

Richard absent mindedly had wound his way through the bumper to bumper DC traffic and ended up on Interstate 270 heading for Interstate 70 and home. Perhaps it was the thoughts of his non-existent love life that was pulling him back to Ganister, Pennsylvania. As he set the cruise control to sixty-five his cell phone rang.

"Senator," the always cheerful Bryonna said, "will you be coming back to the office?"

"No Bryonna. I'm heading back to Ganister for the weekend."

"I have a couple messages for you if you would like them now."

"May as well. What have you got?"

"Well Senator Snead, just wanted to remind you that next week is the meeting with the President at Camp David, and he wanted to know if you wanted to drive to the White House together?'

"Call the Senator's office and let him know that sounds like a good idea. I'll call him Monday and we can make arrangements where to meet."

"Admiral Snare wants to speak to you. He has more info regarding your last meeting."

"I'll call him from the road. Anything else?"

"Yes," Bryonna said hesitantly, "a lady has called three times asking for you."

"Did she leave a name or number?"

"No, she said it wasn't anything important, she just wanted to catch up with you."

Richard was curious, "did it sound like anyone that had called before?"

"No," Bryonna said, "but she sounded like she was not from here. She sounded exotic and sexy."

"Exotic and sexy? Why didn't you get me a phone number?" Richard asked with raised eyebrows.

"I asked but she didn't want to leave one. She said it wasn't urgent."

"Well if she calls back be sure to give her my cell number."

On the other end of the conversation Bryonna was smiling. Beaming, actually. Her boss finally had a little excitement in his voice and Bryonna knew he needed a little excitement in his life.

Richard was lost in thought and pushed the end button on his cell phone not really sure if Bryonna had anymore messages for him or not. But, not really caring as his mind went over the same two words, Exotic and Sexy. Who could that be?

Bobby awoke the next morning to the smell of fresh brewed coffee and the smell of breakfast. He rolled out of bed and quickly threw on some clothes then ambled down the stairs toward the source of the culinary scents.

"Hey, Babe," Claire said to him as he wandered into the kitchen "I thought you were going to sleep all day."

Bobby made his way to Claire's side sweeping her into his powerful arms and giving her a long slow kiss. Afterward she asked, "So is that because you smelled breakfast or because you did something last night that you shouldn't have?"

"Well I didn't do anything last night but have a couple beers with Sarge," Bobby replied.

"So then it is breakfast," Claire said.

"Nope. Not breakfast."

Claire smiled then said, "I love you too."

"I've been thinking," Bobby started but Claire interrupted. "Does it hurt?"

Bobby shot her a glance then continued, "Let's go sit on the swing for a minute while I tell you my idea. Now that I have time off, we should go somewhere. Remember how we used to go surfing?"

"You mean how you went surfing with your buds and I was along for the ride," Claire said while a smile played across her face.

"Yeah, like that," Bobby responded, "maybe we should dig the longboard out of the basement, strap it to the car and head for the beach. Remember the time we caught those big waves in Virginia Beach?"

"Well, as I remember it," Claire said, "we drove into a hurricane so that you and your friends could be surfing as soon as the hurricane passed by. That was a horrible trip driving through that torrential rain and the wind nearly whipping us off the highway."

"But we made it. And the waves were incredible. I remember eight and twelve foot waves that day. I was crouched on my board gliding along that one big sucker while it was curling over top of me, the fingers of my right hand just barely caressing the wave, and getting out of the tube before it crashed down. What a ride that was. Then there was that monster wave that I was riding the curl of. Man that was the best surfing we ever did," Bobby smiled and stared off into space his mind recalling the good times.

"And yet what I remember was taking you to the hospital to get fifteen stitches after your longboard smacked you in the head," Claire interjected snapping Bobby back to reality.

"But that wasn't my fault. I had just had a good run when that backwash came out of nowhere and tossed the front of my board straight up in the air."

"Yeah, well, you caught it with your head, Mr. Hardhead," Claire said "and do you think those old knees can still……"

Claire nearly fell off the swing when Bobby turned so quickly while at the same time pulling the gun from the back of his waistband and aiming at the corner of the porch where the leg of a person stepped into view. Actually four persons stepped into view. All dressed in dark suits. All tall with short dark hair and dark glasses on. All wearing the same narrow bright neckties. All wearing the same shiny black shoes. And all coming to an immediate stop midstride as they looked down the barrel of the Glock in Bobby's steady hand accurately aimed at the leader's forehead. The forehead that immediately began bubbling with perspiration.

"Mr. Morrow," the leader said as he slowly raised his hands to chest level showing he had no intention of attempting to get to the gun that was showing under his suit coat, "I heard that you were good."

Bobby just stared at him while the intruder sweated some more. Bobby's gun perfectly still and never wavering the slightest bit.

"I was told to bring you to DC, sir."

"By whom?" Bobby asked the gun in his hand still not wavering.

"The Colonel, sir."

"The same Colonel that just fired me?" Bobby asked.

"Yes, sir."

"And he expects I should just drop everything and run to DC because he beckoned?"

"Yes, sir."

"And what did the Colonel say to do if I told you to go screw yourself?"

"To be honest, sir, that's why he sent four of us. He said you may not want to come."

"And then what?"

"Then he said we were not to come back without you?"

"And he is of the opinion that the four of you can change my mind?"

"To be honest again, sir, no. He also has the State Police Swat team standing by because he was not sure that we four could bring you in, sir."

"I appreciate your honesty," Bobby said as he lowered his weapon and stuck it back in his waistband, "Have a seat. Care for a drink? Claire makes the world's best sweet iced tea?"

The four in unison moved down the porch closer to Bobby and leaned against the sturdy oak railing.

"Nothing for me, sir, but thank you," the leader said. The others merely shook their heads negatively.

"So what does the Colonel want?"

"I'm afraid I do not know sir. I don't believe I have a high enough security clearance to know."

"Well call him. Ask him."

The leader did as he was told. He pulled the cell phone from his pocket, punched in a few numbers and spoke, "Colonel, Mr. Morrow is insisting that I call to find out why you want him in Washington, sir."

Bobby watched his eyes as they glanced towards Bobby and finally he handed his phone to Bobby, "the Colonel would like to speak with you, sir."

"This better be good!" Bobby said into the phone.

"Well you're still fired," said the Colonel right off the bat.

"Then what the hell are these guys doing here nearly getting theirselves shot?"

"I need to speak with you here Bobby. It is of the utmost importance. A matter of national security."

"And yet, I'm still fired?"

"Yes, the President fired all of us."

"Then what gives?"

"Trust me Bobby. The United States and I need you. I can't explain over the telephone."

"One question, do you really have the State Police Swat team standing by?"

"No, I just needed to emphasize the point to those boys. They are supposed to be the top of their class, but I really didn't think they could convince you and especially didn't think they could force you if you did not want to come with them. What I was counting on was your love of your country."

Bobby smiled and said to the Colonel, "here Colonel, ask Claire if I can go to Washington. If she says yes, I'll come, If she says no, I'm going to throw these young bucks off my porch."

Bobby handed the phone to a stern faced Claire, "Colonel."

"Claire," the Colonel said in his most pleasant voice, "how are you doing my dear?"

"You know how I'm doing, Colonel? I'm living with a man who is acting like a wild bear bit him in the ass!"

"I apologize for that Claire, and, believe me it was not my idea. That came from the very top."

"And yet you need him now?"

"Of course. This is a matter of national security and we can't take a chance on these young people they have now. You just saw how far they got with Bobby. Imagine them going up against an entire unit."

"So would my husband be in danger?"

"I won't lie to you Claire. Of course. But more likely it will be the opposition that is in danger from Bobby."

"Well, he's a big boy Colonel. If he wants to go play, he can," Claire said and handed the telephone back to Bobby.

"One question Colonel."

"What is it, Bobby?"

"Who all will be on this assignment?"

"I was hoping that you would bring Sarge," that should be enough, "that will put the odds at about a dozen to one." Bobby smiled, "sounds fair."

Richard's Volvo was cruising steadily along Interstate 70, the stereo blasting, and Richard taking in the tree lined ridges while the sun headed toward the West. His cell phone rang, not a telephone number he was familiar with but he took the call.

"Hello."

"Senator St.Clair," the all business military voice stated, "Admiral Snare here. Do you have a minute?"

"Of course, Admiral. What can I do for you?"

"I'm sure you've heard about this attack on our embassy in Libya?"

"Yes, Admiral," Richard said, "It's tragic."

"Well it should certainly prove my point from our last meeting of the Armed Services Committee that we must increase our defense budgets not be decreasing them. Those Americans lost their lives for no reason whatsoever. And when those incidents happen we have to have enough of a budget to have a prepared Navy. The present Commander in Chief is more concerned with putting our ships in mothballs and making them tourist attractions than having ships on the seas that could actually go to battle."

"I completely agree with you Admiral," Richard said, "but I am fighting an uphill battle."

"You think you are fighting an uphill battle. You better hope that we don't get called into real battle. It will be more than uphill'" Admiral Snare responded.

"Anything else, Admiral?"

"Are you aware that when the budget for the security forces that was protecting the embassy in Libya got cut, that just four days later the State Department spent over $100,000.00 to purchase a new electrical charging station for the Vienna embassy so we could be considered "green"? Apparently it is more important that we pretend to be doing something about global warming than it is to protect American citizens, including our Ambassadors."

"I'm meeting with the President at Camp David in just a few days and believe me Admiral your concerns will be brought to his attention," Richard stated in his most emphatic voice, especially since he had already made these items his number one priority and was determined to get someone's attention. The Admiral said goodbye and left Richard cruising along mentally preparing his speech for the President. His thoughts were interrupted by the ringing of his cell phone.

Another telephone number that he didn't recognize.

"Hello," Richard said in a semi-distracted voice.

"Richard? Is that you?" asked the sweet sexy voice on the other end of the phone.

Richard snapped to attention. He thought he recognized the voice but couldn't put a name to it.

"Yes, this is Richard St.Clair," he slowly said, "I'm sorry, who is this?"

"Richard, it's Nanita...."

Richard's eyes rapidly flashed to his rear view mirror. No cars on his bumper. He slammed on the brakes and whipped the Volvo towards the berm, sliding to a stop as the traffic zipped by him, the air from their vehicles rocking the little Volvo like it was sitting in a tornado.

"Nanita?" Richard exclaimed and stuttered while he thought what to say, coming up with merely, "It's nice to hear from you!"

"I was afraid that you did not want to hear from me," Nanita said shyly.

Nanita was originally from the Phillipines but Richard knew her for many years as the vivacious and beautiful manager of his favorite restaurant in Aruba. She was short, extremely well built and had long lustrous brown hair and a smile as wide as the island of Aruba itself. She was one of a small group of people that actually helped console Richard when his lovely wife Pamela had passed away. In fact, Nanita was at the beach in Malmok when Richard spread Pamela's ashes in the Caribbean per Pamela's last will and testament. Richard did not think much about Nanita at the time but lately she occasionally poked her smiling face into his thoughts. And now, here she was, calling him.

"Nanita, how could you think that I would not like to hear from you?"

"Because you have never called me," she replied honestly.

"In my defense, I didn't think you would want to hear from me."

"Did I not say to you before you left Aruba to stay in touch?"

"Yes, but I thought you were just being your typical polite self."

"The truth is I was hoping that you would be able to get Pamela out of your mind and give me a call," Nanita said in her shy sweet voice.

"I promise you," Richard said after thinking a moment, "as soon as I can get to the Caribbean I will look you up."

"You don't need to," she replied and Richard could practically hear smile through the phone, "I'm in the states."

"Really?" Richard asked excitedly, "Where?"

"In Richmond, Virginia. I thought perhaps I could travel up to Washington DC and see you since you work there."

"How long will you be in the states?" Richard asked.

"Only a few more days, the beginning of the week I have to be back to Aruba for work."

"I left Washington and was headed for Pennsylvania."

Nanita was obviously saddened by the news, "I was really hoping to see you."

Richard's mind raced. He had to meet Senator Snead Monday morning and head to Camp David to meet the President. He didn't really need to go to Ganister, he had just needed a break from DC. Then the lightbulb went off in his head.

"Can I see you this evening?" he asked.

"I don't think I can get to Pennsylvania or Washington this evening," she replied.

"No. No. I'm coming to you. Where in Richmond are you?"

"I'm staying at the Marriott on Broad Street."

"I know where it is," Richard said, "I can be there in three hours. I'll catch Interstate 81 just west of here and head for Richmond. Would that be alright with you?"

"That would be lovely Richard."

"Great. We can go to Tripps for dinner and catch up on everything that has happened in the past year."

After a little more small talk Nanita said goodbye. Richard put the Volvo in gear, smashed the accelerator and spun the tires back out onto the highway. The engine roared as he flew up the Interstate anxiously looking for the junction that would lead him South to Richmond and Nanita.

Farmer Terry Lee had been enjoying a beer when he saw the signs. First it was a covey of birds taking flight from the trees, then the dust rising from the trees above his road. Then his shotgun came up as he waited to hear and see the vehicle. Eventually it came into view. The stereotypical shiny black SUV racing up his dirt lane towards the farmhouse. Had to be government folks was Terry Lee's first thought but that didn't stop him from taking a bead on the vehicle with the trusty twelve gauge shotgun. As the vehicle slid to a stop and the door opened Terry Lee racked a shell into the chamber. It wasn't until he saw Bobby Morrow's smiling face step out the rear door that he lowered the gun.

"Bobby," Terry Lee said, the sly little grin spreading across his face.

"Terry Lee," Bobby said simply in return.

Terry Lee pointed with the barrel of the gun to the men in suits standing near the now dusty vehicle.

"Yeah," Bobby said, "government men."

"Thought so," replied the always articulate Terry Lee, "what's up?"

"Sarge here?"

"Nope."

"Know where he is?"

"Yep."

"Can you tell me?"

"He in trouble?"

"Nope. Government is. They need him."

"You going with him?"

"Yep," Bobby said, "They need both of us."

"Not surprised," Terry Lee said, "he went over to that militia place this morning. Said you guys met up with them last night."

"Yeah. We did. Surprised he went over."

"He was bored."

Bobby looked around at the group of men in suits and dark glasses standing close to the doors of the black SUV and then said to Terry Lee, "probably shouldn't go there with this bunch."

Terry Lee actually smiled showing his dimples at each end of the blonde mustache, "It might be funny though."

"Bet it would at that. Black government SUV showing up at a militia rally. Real good way to get shot," Bobby said as he snickered while shaking his head and looking down at his boots scratching the dirt in front of him.

"Might be funny," Terry Lee said again.

The men in suits just looked at each other. No smiles on their faces, just concern.

"Think maybe you could have him meet me at the Colonel's sometime tomorrow?"

"Yep."

"Thanks Terry Lee."

Terry Lee nodded at Bobby then sat back on the green metal lawn chair, stood the shotgun against the porch banister, picked up his beer and took a long swig, wiping his lips with his shirt sleeve

Early the next morning Terry Lee and his pickup truck that begged for a bath slowly made its way to the old Claycomb farm.

A young guy dressed in camo jumped out of the bushes when Terry Lee stopped at the rusty metal cattle gate that blocked the road and aimed his gun at Terry Lee. Terry Lee wound down his window and with surprising quickness grabbed the barrel of the gun and wrenched it from the young guys hands. Terry Lee then removed the shells from the gun and threw it at the kid making him duck to keep from getting hit in the head.

"Hey, asshole," Terry Lee said, "Go tell Sarge I want to see him."

"Go tell him yourself, old man."

"Okay," Terry Lee said as he put the old pickup in gear and proceeded to ram the gate breaking it off the hinges and falling to the ground before he ran over top of it. Terry Lee watched the youngster in his rearview mirror jumping up and down, and smiled to himself.

When Terry Lee pulled up to the main barn he parked next to the dozens of other pickup trucks, got out, slammed his squeaky door that begged for grease, and headed towards the field where he heard an army of guns being shot.

There in the field were dozens of men. All dressed in camo or military clothes. Some shooting at targets. Some practicing hand to hand combat, and a small group all gathered around one person who was sitting at a shooting bench aiming a long barreled rifle. That was Sarge. Ever since he arrived the group was enthralled by how well he could shoot. They kept moving the target back until now they had to communicate with radios because now they were so far away from each other. Sarge was a sniper in the Airborne and, like Bobby Morrow, had accumulated quite a cache of medals and ribbons. He was able to routinely make shots at a distance of a mile or more. Which is what he was doing here this morning showing the wanna-a-be militia boys how real soldiers got it done.

Sarge's second sense gripped him and he laid the gun down and looked around. It was one of those feelings that true soldiers get telling him something feels different.

Spying his dad he sauntered up the hill and over to Terry Lee. "Dad," he asked, "everything okay?"

"Bobby needs you," Terry Lee said in his normal short and to the point manner.

"When?" Sarge asked.

"Now."

"Where?"

"Washington."

"Guess we better get goin'," Sarge said.

He turned to the group of men at his heels and said, "see you later guys. Got to go."

"Stop back again Sarge. You're always welcome here."

"Thanks guys."

Sarge and Terry Lee jumped in the beat up truck and slammed the doors. As they made the dust fly going down the

lane, Sarge asked, "How'd the headlights get broke, dad?"
"Oh that," Terry said motioning towards the broken glass,
"Had a little problem with the gate."

The morning sunshine poured into the room through the
partially open curtains warming Richard's face and forcing his
sleepy eyes to open and take in the beauty and glory of a new
day. His body as snug as a bug in a rug in the four hundred
thread count cotton cocoon of high quality sheets. His sleepy
eyed gaze moved to his still sleeping numb left arm. The arm
was tucked under the mound of lustrous brown hair and
Richard's body again became aroused by the closeness of the
smooth skin the color of light brown sugar that was spooned
around his own body. Richard ran his hand over the soft
curves and his olfactory senses again smelled the sweet fruity
fragrance of the Island Kiss perfume. Richard's senses were all
vying for attention as he felt, smelled, and gazed upon the
beautiful Nanita. Being extremely quiet and not moving even
the slightest amount to make the moment stretch on as long as
possible. Steven Tyler's voice filled Richard's head with,
…."lying close to you feeling your heart beating, and I'm
wondering what you're dreaming, wondering if it's me you're
seeing, then I kiss your eyes, and thank God we're together, I
just want to stay with you in this moment forever"…….

The same morning sunshine that awakened Richard shined on
Bobby as he made his way to the Colonel's office in suburban
Washington, D.C. Bobby's mind, however, was mulling over
completely different thoughts from that of Richard. As soon as
he entered the office he was shown into the Colonel's inner
office. The dark mahogany paneling, the bookshelves
overflowing with volumes of written word, the solid wood
flooring beneath his feet that led him to the black leather sofa
in front of the Colonel's desk as the Colonel motioned with
one hand for Bobby to sit as he finished up his telephone

conversation. He no sooner placed the telephone on his desk when he began, "Thank you for coming Bobby."

"You look concerned Colonel," Bobby replied.

"I am Bobby," the Colonel started than paused and flipped the intercom switch and said to his secretary, "make sure we are not disturbed."

Bobby waited knowing the Colonel would continue at his own pace and in his own time.

"Bobby, for years we have been fighting against all sorts of threats to our country from outside our borders. We've fought off the Nazis, we've protected the Koreans, the Vietnamese, we've attempted to control the radical Islamists and their jihads. We've recently had terrorism come into our own country." The Colonel paused and glanced out his window then looked back to Bobby and continued, "We've done as well as could be expected and have been able to maintain our democratic way of life for over two hundred years. Longer than any other democracy has been able to withstand threats from outside. But the tide may be changing Bobby."

"But what are we to do Colonel. We were all fired, remember?"

"Oh, I know full well that we were left go," the Colonel immediately responded, "I don't have to be reminded how our commander in chief has betrayed us. And yet, we still have a duty to our country. Perhaps a bigger obligation than ever before, Bobby."

"But how can we act on anything when we are no longer a part of or endorsed by the government."

"Therein lies the problem Bobby. Do we set on the sidelines and watch our country be consumed, or as patriots and concerned citizens do we grab the bull by the horns and do something?"

"What sort of enemy are we talking about?"

"Let me tell you what I know Bobby," said the Colonel and he sat back in his chair and began. "Your friend and mine,

Senator Richard St.Clair has stumbled onto one piece of this puzzle. It seems that he was approached by a Carmine Rizzo, and I believe that you are very familiar with Carmine?"
Bobby shook his head yes and continued to listen.
"Well, Carmine asked Richard to check on the IRS swooping in confiscating some rare and valuable coins that he inherited."
"Richard told me about that, yes."
"Well Richard contacted Ellwood Sine, The Attorney General on the legality of the confiscation. Ellwood made some inquiries then he contacted me. It seems the IRS while it has in the past demanded taxes from these types of situations and even once before did confiscate some rare coins, was not the agency that ended up with Mr. Rizzo's coins."
"Really?" Bobby asked.
"The IRS was intending to speak with Mr. Rizzo but they were beat to the punch by someone portraying an IRS agent."
"And do you know who that someone is?"
"I do, and I'll get back to that in a minute. Now, you remember the Watergate scandal of the Nixon years, well I was recently approached by a sort of Deep Throat of my own. I started to receive calls giving me bits and pieces of information. I have never been able to trace any of the conversation as they were all made from a pre-paid cellular phone that cannot be traced, and each time a different pre-paid cellular plus the voice was disguised so I was not sure of the validity of the information. I have been working day and night with all the contacts that I could trust to try to confirm the validity of the accusations."
"And have you been able to do that Colonel?" Bobby asked.
The Colonel made a tent with his long fingers and parked his chin on them while he considered his answer before saying, "I'm ninety-nine percent sure."
"Sounds close enough for government work," Bobby responded.

"Ordinarily I would agree with you, however, this could ruin our entire country. This could collapse our government as we know it."

"If it is that big Colonel, how could it have happened?"

"No one noticed, " the Colonel replied, "No one noticed. There was no reason for anyone to notice and so no one did."

"What now Colonel?"

"We have to get the final one percent of information. We have to be one hundred percent sure of this before we make a move because without being absolutely positively certain is for us to be accused of treason."

"I'm not very fond of the idea of being accused of treason and spending the rest of my life in Leavenworth Prison, Colonel. I have a beautiful wife and daughter back home. You better be darn sure before I head down this path," the concern extremely evident in Bobby's voice.

"Bobby, you know that I think the world of you and would never ask you to put yourself in that situation if I thought for a minute that we could not be successful in this endeavor. Which is also why I want this to be a small operation. No possibility of leaks. No possibility of anyone turning back. And no possibility of failure. I will run the operation from here where all communications are secure. Seems the government forgot to take their equipment back when they fired us. You and Sarge will be on the ground."

"So what do we have to do, Colonel?"

"You have to break in to Camp David while the President is having his meeting with Richard and Senator Snead."

Bobby jumped up off the leather couch and strode past the Colonel's desk to look out the window. After a minute he turned back to face the Colonel with a huge smile on his face, " Sarge and I are going to break into Camp David while the President is there protected by dozens of Secret Service agents and every hi tech device known to man?" Bobby started to chuckle, "are you serious?"

The Colonel stared back at Bobby with no hint of humor on his face.

"It was nice visiting with you Colonel but this guy has to go back to good old Ganister, Pennsylvania where good old common sense rules and people don't even consider such hair-brain ideas."

"Bobby, please, if you and Sarge do not do this your good old Ganister, Pennsylvania may never be the same."

"Colonel, let's go back to this source of yours. How do you know this source can be trusted?"

"Because I now know who the source is."

"So you've met with the source?"

"No, the source doesn't know that I know the source's identity."

"But you are positive?"

I'm positive. After a few calls the source got sloppy with disguising their voice and at one point it dawned on me, "I know that voice', and I do. And believe me we can trust this person. But everything here needs to remain on a need-to-know basis so I cannot tell you who the person is. All I can do is ask you to trust me."

Bobby returned to the soft black leather couch and paid close attention to every detail of the plan laid out by the Colonel.

Richard and Nanita spent every minute of each day of the weekend together. By Sunday evening they began to face reality. Come Monday morning, Richard had to meet up with Senator Snead and leave for his meeting with the President at Camp David. Nanita would be catching her flight back to Aruba and her life there.

"Can I see you again, Nanita?" Richard asked.

"I sure hope so," the smiling Nanita replied.

"Do you think we can make a long distance relationship

work?"

"I think if we want it to, we can."

"I'll tell you what, you go back to Aruba and give it some thought. I'll have my meeting with the President then on Friday, I'll catch a flight to Aruba and we can discuss it further. How does that sound?"

The answer Richard received was not verbal but in the form of a long warm kiss.

Chapter 9

The Oval Office was filled with all the president's advisers when he arrived Sunday afternoon. He was casually dressed while the others in the room were in their power suits all with their leather bound pads and fancy pens at the ready.

"Good afternoon ladies and gentleman," the President said as he sauntered to his desk chair, "okay here's what is happening. Tomorrow I am meeting with Senator Snead and Senator St.Clair at Camp David. And before anyone gets any ideas this is going to be a closed meeting."

"So only a few of us will be going with you, Mr. President?" inquired his campaign manager.

"Actually no one is going except Mr. Alex."

Heads turned all through the room with looks of incredulity and glares in the direction of the smiling Mr. Alex.

"But. Mr. President...."

"No butts," the President firmly stated, "we are having this meeting so you can all get me up to speed on all the points we need to present to these two to swing them over to our point of view. I want everything from you today! Got it?"

There was a collective, "Yes, Mr. President."

"I want to know what makes these guys tick. I want to know what pushes their buttons. I may need to use every pressure point possible with these two so I want to know everything. I expect to leave Camp David with those two in my back pocket."

"Mr. President both Senator Snead and Senator St.Clair are opposed to nearly every idea that you champion."

"I understand that, but this is politics. It's give and take. Now it's your job to enlighten me on what buttons to push on those guys to have them start giving so I can start taking. I want to know every dirty little secret they have. I want to know about their home and love lives. I want to know every bill they have voted for and against. We are putting the full court press on the guys and I want them either voting the way we want or destroyed. Quite frankly it doesn't matter which of those paths we take as long as we come back from Camp David with those two firmly in our camp. So take ten minutes, call your spouses or whomever and tell them you won't be home 'till late tonight."

Bobby left the Colonel's office and returned to his hotel. Sitting in the lobby was Sarge.

"Sarge, glad you could make it," Bobby said as they shook hands and hugged each other.

"I told you Bobby. You ever need me just call."

"Did you drive down, Sarge?"

"Sure."

"Good let's go for a short ride so we can talk privately."

"Gotcha'. Walls have ears."

"They sure do, Sarge."

The duo left the hotel and went into the parking garage where Sarge's pickup was parked. They left the parking garage and made a few turns carefully watching that they wouldn't be followed before either one of them spoke.

"Sarge, I have to be honest with you," Bobby started, "this is *not* a government sanctioned job."

"What do you mean Bobby?"

"I mean that it could go all wrong and we could end up in prison for a long, long time."

"But you think we should do this?"

"I've met with the Colonel all morning, and I don't see how we can't do it. Someone has to."

"What exactly are we going to being doing?"

"Well we're going to break into Camp David while the President is meeting there with Richard and Senator Snead."

"Oh. Is that all? I thought it was going to be something difficult," Sarge said his voice dripping with sarcasm, "and why would we want to do that?"

"We need to gather the final one percent of information necessary for the Colonel to be one hundred percent sure that he is on the right track."

"So we have to break in to find out if we should break in?"

"Something like that. It's a Catch-22 I know. You know the old I have flies in my eyes but I can't see them because they are in my eyes."

"Sounds like the story of my life Bobby. Question is, are you convinced we should do this?" Sarge asked seriously.

Bobby hesitated a few seconds before responding, "Yes. We have to. I don't want to, but we have to."

"Yeah though I walk through the valley of the shadow of death, I will fear no evil, because Bobby Morrow is by my side," Sarge quoted.

"Hope you're more serious tomorrow."

"I'm serious now, Bobby. I assume you and the Colonel have a plan?"

"We have most of a plan."

"Most of a plan?"Sarge asked as he turned to face Bobby.

"We figure the way to penetrate the most high tech secure facility in the world is with good old low technology. So what we need first of all, and which we haven't completely figured out yet, is we need a really good distraction. Something that will send most of the Secret Service people running, and

distract the geeks watching the monitors. Have any ideas?"
"Well, I'm not the idea man of the group, but since you rudely took me away from a weekend of guns and booze, I have one idea."
"Spit it out Sarge."
"I'll bet we could get that gung-ho militia group I just left to do almost anything."
Bobby considered the suggestion for a few minutes, "you know that just might work Sarge."
"Do you think you could get them down there?"
"Well it's only about a three hour trip for them. They seem to idolize me already, and they are sure chomping at the bit to prove they are true blue Americans."
"Do you have a way to contact them?"
"Not exactly but dad can always run by and rally the troops."
"Okay. Let's have Terry Lee go see them. Now here is what we need. We need them not go off half-cocked. They need to act like a professional military unit. They will need to come in force to Camp David. We want them there at exactly four hundred hours on Tuesday morning. They need to ram and infiltrate the gate. Now this will be the tricky part. The Secret Service are going to be shooting back, so we do not want them to get shot, and at the same time we do not want them to shoot to kill any Secret Service. They need to be heavy on the body armor, and use something non lethal to put down the Secret Service, maybe syringe shells like you would use to put down an animal temporarily. Do you think they can get hold of that kind of ammo?"
"Old Kurt Klaar can get his hands on anything."
"That's right," Bobby said, "I'll give Kurt a call and place an order. I'm sure he can deliver the stuff then all we need them to do is enter the gate. Subdue as many Secret Service as possible then leave before any of them get shot. That should give us the few minutes we need to get to where we need to go. Oh yeah, and I can have Mike the Mechanic get us the

perfect vehicle for ramming a gate. I'll call him too."

Kurt Klaar was a farmer, a sawyer, and a genious when it came to guns. Bobby and Kurt had been friends forever and, in fact, Kurt had personally built Bobby's sniper rifle and loaded every shell Bobby used to take out his targets. Mike the Mechanic was another friend of Bobby and Richard and true to his name he was a mechanic. But not your average mechanic. Mike could make an engine sing and squeeze more horsepower out of it than others thought possible. He owned his own repair garage and was particular on what he worked on and who he worked for. For that he was well paid and his toys included several Corvettes, a classic hot rod and even a new Ferrari. Plus Mike could do more than just make them run, he could drive almost as well as he could walk.

"So I assume we are going in a different way?" Sarge asked. "Over the river and through the woods to the President's house we'll go," sang Bobby. Sarge held his ears to try to block out Bobby's singing.

Camp David is nestled in the low wooded hills in Frederick County, Maryland. Lush hardwood and pine trees surround the simple wood and stone structure that has been the retreat to every President since Franklin D. Roosevelt. It is not open to the general public and in fact is not even noted on any maps of the area, other than that it is within the Catoctin Mountain Park. The main lodge sports a curved swimming pool filled with pristine blue water and surrounded by many species of oak, cherry, and poplar trees. It's rich history includes Roosevelt meeting with Winston Churchill.

John F. Kennedy took his family there for horseback riding, Lyndon B. Johnson hosted Australian Prime Minister Harold Holt, Gerald Ford rode snowmobiles at the compound, Ronald Reagan met with Prime Minister of the United Kingdom, Margaret Thatcher, and George Bush met with

Vladimir Putin, the President of Russia. The facility was built in 1935 by the Works Progress Administration which employed millions of workers to complete public works projects following the Great Depression. Nearly every community had a park, bridge, or school constructed by the WPA. The compound is now controlled and staffed by the U.S. Navy and U.S. Marine Corps. The wooded area is full of paths for exercising and relaxation. Bobby Morrow was fortunate enough to have met with a President and the Colonel there several years prior. While there Bobby took advantage of the hiking paths and trails and learned his way around the facility. He will now have to draw upon that experience and discreetly enter the premises without detection by high tech security systems and an army of Secret Service, naval and marine forces.

Chapter 10

The shiny black limousine with the President's flag flying on the fender followed by a small army of shiny black SUV's pulled up to the gate and was met by the crisp salute of a naval Officer and several Secret Service agents. The driver's side front window went down and the chauffeur announced the arrival of Senators St.Clair and Snead. Their helicopter flight from Washington to Camp David was changed at the last minute and instead the duo was ushered into the limousine.
Several Naval officers looked under the vehicle with mirrored staffs while the identification of the Senators was scrutinized even though they were expected. The trees were green and reflected off the black fenders of the car as the sun warmed the interior while the blackened windows were down for the inspection. The two Senators had enjoyed the sixty-two mile drive over from Washington with the fully stocked bar in the car and no worries about traffic or tolls. A second smart salute from the Naval officer and the limousine rolled past the small

guard post, through the gates and began winding its way up the long tree lined drive. On several occasions they were entertained by deer and other wildlife along the side of the road raising their heads as if to acknowledge their arrival. Birds sang and squirrels rustled through the trees as the vehicle pulled up in front of the main lodge and the chauffeur jumped out to open the door for the Senators. A small contingent of naval personnel gathered their bags from the trunk and followed them inside. The building was not that large but was a well built wooden and stone structure fitting the area that it occupied. The hardwood floors shone and spoke with each step that the two made. They were each led to a separate room and advised that they would be meeting with the President in just a short time followed by dinner in the main dining room. They could use the free time to enjoy the outdoors or just rest up for later.

Richard took to the walking paths and got his heart rate up while speed walking and thinking of the past weekend with Nanita, which by itself increased his heart rate. Senator Snead sat on the open porch area and returned phone calls with his office in preparation for his upcoming meeting while the sun warmed him.

"Senators, welcome," the President announced as he met them with a firm handshake. The Presidents booming voice and rugged good looks were a large part of his being elected three and a half years ago. His well prepared speeches and the ability to properly emphasize his points made him very likable to the masses. Richard and Senator Snead were not as impressed as the majority of voters. The Senators were extremely concerned by the burgeoning debt the President had taken on and they wanted to get back to some sort of fiscal saneness. Good looks and nice speeches did not excite the Senators as they too were both good looking and capable of motivating voters with their own words of wisdom.

"Mr. President," they each said in turn as they shook hands. "What would you like to drink gentlemen?" the President asked and waiters immediately scurried to fill the orders. The President then led them over to a casual but extremely comfortable sitting area.

"I do hope, gentlemen, that we can break down some of the barriers that exist between us over the next few days," the President began, "we really need to bring the two parties together during my next term so that we can accomplish more in the next term than we did this term."

Senator Snead needed no more encouragement as he jumped into the conversation, "that sounds good for the voters, Mr. President but we have some serious differences."

"You're absolutely right Senator. May I call you Leonard?"

"Yes, you may Mr. President."

"Good, Leonard, we are a bit apart on several issues but I strongly believe there is some middle ground for us somewhere. For instance, the debt. You want to chop budgets. I'm not totally against that, we just need to put our heads together to decide what is best to chop."

"But Mr. President you want to increase taxes for everyone."

"Yes, but as I've said many times, I want the rich to pay more."

"But they pay considerably more in dollars. You just want to compare percentages and you are not comparing apples to apples."

"Okay, we'll come back to that, but I'm sure we can work something out. What do you say we go have a lovely dinner?"

The group strolled into the main dining room and was seated and waited on by the very proficient naval staff. Mr. Alex had joined them at this time and before sitting down approached the President.

"Everything arranged?" the President asked Mr. Alex.

"Yes, sir, Mr. President. Following dinner and an after dinner drink, you should excuse yourself, perhaps to attend to some matters of state, then a couple of lovely and competent wenchs will entertain the two Senators."

"Excellent, Mr. Alex," whispered the President, "perhaps by morning we will have these two exactly where we want them."

"Senators, please eat, drink and be merry. Tomorrow we will work out our differences for the good of the country," the President announced and the food was served.

The crisp fresh salads were followed by a choice of fresh pheasant, salmon, or venison, along with succulent well prepared vegetables and copious amounts of wine.

After a while Senator Snead pushed his chair back from the table and rubbed his stomach, "excellent dinner, Mr. President. That is the finest meal that I think I have ever had."

"Well, I'm glad you enjoyed it. What say we move into the library and have a cigar or a bit of brandy?"

"Sounds good, Mr. President," Senator Snead said.

Richard while enjoying his dinner had been rather quiet thus far with Senator Snead doing most of the talking.

The four gentlemen strolled down the short corridor to the library and were met by more staff members holding out a humidor of fine cigars and glasses of bourbon. After the President finished his glass of bourbon, one of the staff whispered in his ear. He then turned to the Senators, "Please excuse me gentleman. I t seems I have an urgent phone call that I must take. Please stay here and enjoy yourselves."

Senator Snead raised his glass in a farewell gesture as the President turned to leave. No sooner had he left then several beautiful young ladies entered the room, their low cut tight blouses a big change from the previous wait staff.

"Is there anything I can get you Senator?" the vivacious blonde asked Richard as she approached him and made a point of brushing her ample but firm breast against his arm.

"No thank you. I'm good," Richard said.

Senator Snead looked at Richard and winked. Richard ambled over and whispered in his ear, "This is too convenient Leonard."

"I like convenient. Check out the blonde."

"Frankly, I smell a set-up."

Senator Snead sobered quickly, "do you think they would stoop to that?"

Richard just smiled and rolled his eyes.

Chapter 11

Normally the brilliant twinkling stars would light up the rural Maryland sky like a frozen fireworks show. Tonight the clouds covered the glowing orbs and it was dark. So dark you couldn't see your hand in front of your face. Bobby Morrow and Sarge Lee had spent the last hour hiking through the Catoctin Mountain Park to get to their current position outside the electrified fencing that surrounded the Camp David compound. Because the compound had been around since 1935 and with the budget cuts of recent years it was only a matter of time until they found what they needed, and here it was. A large oak tree that had not been pruned in a couple years. The limbs growing toward the sun in the south grew over the fence. Bobby and Sarge were huddled at the base of the tree diligently checking the time. At 3:55 am they climbed quietly and dropped to the ground on the other side of the electric fence. They were both dressed completely in black looking like a pair of ninjas. Their faces had been blacked out also as this entire operation would be done under the cover of darkness. The two slowly and quietly made their way through the woods toward the south. The going was very slow with all the twigs and leaves underfoot announcing every move they made so they crept along like two Indians in the night so as not to get the attention of any Secret Service or Navy personnel. After all, there were plenty of them there guarding the President. They were within sight of the compound when Bobby's watch struck 4:00am.

Mike the Mechanic threw the tarp off the old Dodge Ram that sat behind his garage and was rarely used. It was already painted black and the motor, like the motors in all of Mike's vehicles, purred to life immediately and announced the abundance of horsepower that was waiting to be unleashed. Kurt Klaar appeared driving his eighteen wheeler with boxes of body armor and ammunition of all sorts to Mike's garage followed shortly by a contingent of black camo clad angry white men sporting tattoos, beards and the occasional piercing. They loaded the pickup, the body armor, the ammunition and all the men into the eighteen wheeler and Kurt Klaar with Mike the Mechanic riding shotgun pulled out from the Klassy Kar garage heading for Bedford and Interstate 70 towards Maryland.

The contingent got to their destination around 3:30 am and began unloading then reloading the Dodge Ram pickup. They tore down the road and turned onto the driveway toward the security entrance of Camp David with no headlights on. They were on top of the guards before the guards knew what was going on. The Naval Officer at first stood in front of the gate with his hand held up to stop the oncoming vehicle but when he saw that it was not slowing down he pulled his pistol from it's holster. He was not quite quick enough as the dart struck him in the neck and he slumped over onto the ground. The commotion brought another guard and several Secret Service men running to the gate with their weapons drawn. They fired at the rapidly approaching black object but were unable to get a good shot at anyone. They also received darts in various parts of their anatomy. Mike rammed the gate as planned. The flashing lights and alarms went off and a small army of Naval personnel and Secret Service agents, some not even fully clothed ran toward the gate. The Dodge Ram slid to a screeching halt, spun the tires in reverse and backed out over the downed gate. As soon as they were out of sight of the gate, the black four wheel drive whipped around so it could travel forwards away from the scene and before they got to the main road, they went off road and cut through the national park. When they came out on the primary road they went west for several miles and waiting along the road was Kurt Klaar and the tractor trailer with the gate down. The Dodge ran up the ramp, came to a stop, and the jubilant militia jumped out of the vehicle, hastily changed out of their black fatigues into jeans and shirts and the tractor trailer set off down the highway before the sun had a chance to rise on their backs.

Two Secret Service men were watching the back entrance that Bobby and Sarge had approached. Bobby motioned to Sarge with hand signals to prepare his crossbow and which agent to shoot at. Both men let the darts fly from their crossbows at the same time. One agent grabbed his neck as he was struck and the other his chest. Both agents collapsed onto the sidewalk. Bobby and Sarge ran across the lawn. Bobby picked the lock on the door and they entered the compound in a low crouched position.
"Remember," Bobby said to Sarge in a whisper, "get in the room, but stay hidden until the Secret Service comes to check on them. After the Secret Service leave give him the shot." Bobby knew from his previous meeting there which room the President always slept in. He headed there and Sarge headed for the next room which should be Mr. Alex's room. Each man quietly entered the room and confirmed that the sleeping figure was who they thought it would be. Bobby ducked out of sight and waited.

It was only a few minutes till the knock on the door came and two Secret Service men entered.

"Mr. President," the lead man asked the President as he tried to clear the sleep from his head, "are you alright, sir?"

"Yes, I'm alright. What the devil are you doing waking me at…." the President looked at the alarm clock, "at four fifteen in the morning? What's going on?"

"We had an attempted breach Mr. President," answered the lead agent.

"They were turned away at the gate, Mr. President, " said the second agent, "we just wanted to be sure that you were okay, sir."

"I'm losing sleep you fools!"

"Sorry Mr. President. Goodnight, sir," the two said in unison and took their leave.

The door closed, Bobby waited a few minutes for the President to settle in then quietly slid from his hiding area and injected the President.

The pinch jolted the President upright again.

"What the…" the President said, then, "what are you doing here? Who are you?"

Bobby covered the President's mouth with a handkerchief and said to him as sternly as possible, "no noise Mr. President. If you make any attempt to shout I will give you a different shot."

Bobby held up his 45 Glock and let the image of the black pistol sink in, "Do you understand Mr. President?"

The President shook his head positively, and cautiously asked, "what did you inject me with?"

"That was Sodium Pentothal, Truth Serum, Mr. President"

"But, why?"

"I need to ask you a few questions, Mr. President and I need honest answers. I don't have much time so we are going to cut through all the bullshit and get right down to brass tacks."

Bobby pulled out the list that the Colonel had prepared and

began.

"What is your name?"

"President Barry Obannon," the President responded.

"Is that the name you were born with?"

"No."

"What name were you born with?"

"Andrei. Andrei Pankin."

"Where were you born?"

"I was born in Leningrad."

"Are you a member of the Communist Party?"

"Of course. Long live Mother Russia!"

Bobby pulled out his cell phone and immediately called the Colonel. As soon as the Colonel answered, Bobby said, "Got it!"

Bobby could hear the Colonel speaking to someone else in the background, then a different voice came on the phone,

"Bobby, this is Ellwood Sine."

"Yes, Ellwood."

"Are you absolutely positive that he is Not an American citizen?"

"I have given him the Sodium Pentothal. He is babbling like an old woman. Says his name is Andrei Pankin and was born in Leningrad."

"Alright, get as much as you can while we send in the reinforcements."

Bobby hung up the phone and went back to questioning the President.

"Who is Mr. Alex?"

"That is my dear friend Alexi Rostov."

"And is he a member of the Communist Party?"

"Of course."

"What is your mission Andrei?"

"To reclaim what was ours. You have stolen our Mother Russia from us," Andrei spit out vehemently, "you and your President Reagan. Well we will have our pound of flesh. We

will use your own democratic system against you. You people
are so smug and think the world revolves around you."
Bobby interrupted the tirade, "who is the lady that raised you
in Hawaii?"
"Katherine Obannon, she was recruited by the Party."
"How did you get an Hawaiin birth certificate?"
"What you think your CIA are the only people that can fake
documents? I'm sure somewhere in Hawaii there was a male
born on the day that I was selected to be born that is
attempting to clear up the fact that his birth certificate is
missing."
"Then what happened?"
"It is quite simple in your country. You get a birth certificate,
they give you a social security number so they can keep track
of you since you are considered the governments chattel. They
gave me my social security number and I became one of you.
No one noticed. No one cares. I'm a legitimate American.,"
Andrei laughed then continued, "and your President."
"But not for long!"
"Not for long is right, as soon as I win my next term, I am
changing the title from President to Czar. It will be just like
being back in Mother Russia. Czar. Has a nice ring to it
doesn't it?"
"How do you propose to pull that off?" Bobby asked.
"First, we have the guns taken out of the hands of these so
called citizens, let the socialized medical laws get enacted,
have all the financial institutions reporting to the Presidency
and not Congress, and with our campaign chest overflowing
with money our next term shall come easily. Armed men can
revolt and have power. Unarmed men can merely throw
stones and bottles. Then I shall be Czar, after all they have
been using the title here for many years now. In fact your
beloved Franklin Roosevelt started the use of the Czar title
with eleven different Czars, and now this country is up to
thirty-eight Czars. Czar of Foreign Aid, Car Czar, Aids Czar,

Border Czar, Birth Control Czar, and on and on, so it will be a small step to make me the Czar over the other Czars." A smile crossed his lips as he continued, "Goodbye Presidency, hello Czar."

Bobby couldn't help but cringe as he whispered under his breath, "and no one noticed."

Andrei continued to babble on about the new country. Bobby used a zip tie to secure his arm to the bed then went next door to check on Sarge.

Sarge had been given a list of questions to ask also.

"How you doing Sarge?"

"This guy is singing like a canary, but is this stuff all true? Is this guy and the President actually communist plants?"

"It appears so Sarge. What else did he have to say?"

"Well listen to him."

"What did you say Alexi?" Bobby asked.

"I said the immigration of extremist Muslims is troubling. They are coming here, getting citizenship, and multiplying like rabbits. I don't like those people. The extremists and their Sharia laws. They could get enough votes to cause us problems. I say we get rid of them before they build any more of their stupid mosques."

"Who do you think will be running the United States?" Sarge asked.

"Andrei will get re-elected. Those stupid Americans they believe everything they see on the television. You could tell them that black is white and they would believe it. We have spent much money with your so called advertising agencies to twist your own minds into believing what we want you to believe. Promise them medical care for all and they are ecstatic. And now we have already switched the citizens from voting with paper ballots to using computers. You've gotta love computers. They will spit out whatever was programmed in. And no paper trail. It works well for us."

"Listen to this Bobby," Sarge said, then asked Alexi, "and after

Andrei gets re-elected, then what?"

"You mean after Czar Rostov gets re-elected? Then I will follow in his footsteps for two terms after that. We have sixteen years to socialize this country. One entitlement at a time. It is a wonderful system that you have. We give the poor people money so they do not have to work and they must vote for us to keep their paltry check coming in. We give the middle class either union jobs that we control or more government jobs so they think they are secure and they must continue to vote for us to keep their checks coming in. Let me tell you a story; when Stalin was asked how he could continue to lead Russia, he said this: 'Bring me a chicken and a piece of bread. When the chicken and the piece of bread arrived, he said, pluck the chicken of all its feathers.' After the chicken was plucked they dropped it to the floor. Stalin dropped the piece of bread beside his leg. The chicken came, pecked at the bread and rubbed his body close to Stalin's pant leg. And the chicken stayed right there by Stalin's side. Stalin said, 'so it is; keep them fed and warm and they will do as I wish.' The rich, there are not so many of them so they just get to pay more and more. As long as they have their yachts and private jets and golf club memberships they do not care what we do. I love this country. The new Mother Russia."

"What is your position at the moment, Alexi?" Bobby asked.

"I am the Presidents campaign manager."

"And as campaign manager, what are your duties?"

"Mostly I raise money?"

"How?"

"Anyway I can," he said with a twinkle in his eye, "twist arms, steal, whatever it takes?"

"And how are you doing?"

"We are amassing a fortune. But, the best is yet to come."

"What is that Alexi?"

"We have been intentionally letting the economy freefall."

"What about the stimulus items that have been put in place?"

Alexi laughed, "Fools! They are the same stimulus items they have tried in Europe. They do not work. T he Europeans proved that. But the public, they eat that stuff up."

"So why are you letting the economy freefall?"

"When the stock market reaches bottom, we shall buy up as much stock as possible with the funds we have raised. Then when the economy rebounds, we will be rich! We actually copied that idea from the 9-11 terrorists. They did quite well."

"I've heard enough," Bobby said, "I don't know about you."

"Time to gag this bum until the serum wears off," Sarge said.

"And you did record everything, right?"

"Got it right here, Bobby," Sarge said as he showed him the small recorder.

"Good."

"So, Bobby, I do have a couple questions," Sarge said.

"Shoot."

"You do have a plan to get us out of here, right?"

"Not exactly, but hopefully the Colonel will show up."

"Also, I found these syringes in his nightstand. Any idea what they are?"

Sarge handed the syringes to Bobby who read the name, "Succinylcholine. Yes I know what it is, I've used it before. It is a muscle relaxant. It keeps the muscles from contracting which causes paralysis of the muscles used to breathe. When you stop breathing, you stop living. No fuss, no muss."

Bobby looked at Alexi and asked him, "what did you plan on doing with these Alexi?"

Alexi smiled, "those two dimwit senators. They will cooperate. Or else."

Thinking how close his best friend Richard had come to getting killed caused Bobby to react. He pulled the 45 Glock out of his waist and pressed it hard into Alexi's temple then whispered in his ear, "For five cents I'd blow your ass away."

The sharp eared Sarge said, "I have a nickel."

"He's just not worth it," Bobby said and put his gun away.

"What is going to happen to our government? Our country?"
"People smarter than us have to figure that out Sarge. Our job
was to get the final one percent. Let's go check on Richard and
Senator Snead."

Chapter 12

"Colonel, as Attorney General we must follow the proper
protocol here," Ellwood Sine stated.
"And what will that be, Ellwood?"
"First I must call the Vice president and the Chiefs of Staff."
"There's the phone," the Colonel said motioning to the
telephone on his desk.
Ellwood pulled out his cellular and punched in a phone
number. When it was answered he said, "Mr. Vice president,
this is Attorney General Ellwood Sine. We have an emergency
sir. I suggest we gather in the situation room as soon as
possible."
"Have you contacted the President?" the Vice president asked.
Ellwood stammered just a bit then replied, "He won't be
joining us sir."
"I see," the Vice President said in a drawl, "I'll meet you there
in ten minutes."
Ellwood's next calls were to General Ross and Admiral Snare
then he quickly departed for the White House situation room.
As he was leaving he said to the Colonel, "you will have the
tapes, right?"
"I'll have them, Ellwood."
"Thank you Colonel. Your country thanks you."
"Yeah, well good luck straightening this mess out."

In the situation room, the Vice President, The Speaker of the
House, the Joint Chiefs of Staff, the leading Senators, and
anyone who was anyone were gathered around the huge oak

table listening to the Attorney General give his report., "I have a team checking the birth certificate situation in Hawaii. The President has been interrogated while under the control of truth serum and he has admitted his birth in Leningrad, Russia, and his commitment to the Communist Party. I have another team interrogating the woman that raised him, while a third team is being dispatched to check on Alexi's true history. As it stands now, we have a President that is illegally holding office. The president of the United States must be born a U.S. citizen. The full ramifications have yet to be known but what is most urgent is the situation needs to be corrected immediately."

The Vice President asked, "But what are we going to do? We can't tell the American public they were deceived, they will never trust voting again. And we certainly cannot let them continue to take over our country."

"If I may be so bold, Mr. Vice President?" Ellwood asked.

"Please Mr. Attorney General, you brought this to us, what do you have in mind?" the Vice President said.

"Well, I think for starters that you Mr. Vice President should voluntarily submit to a lie detector test."

"I'm not a damn communist," the Vice President snorted.

"We must now be extremely cautious, Mr. Vice President. I don't think you are a communist either, but imagine if this got out. You would certainly be labeled one since the President handpicked you."

"Well, you're right about that. I will gladly take a lie detector test."

"Good," Ellwood said, then the only thing we need to happen is to have a plausible explanation why the President must step down now."

"Why can't he just get shot by an unknown intruder?" someone suggested.

"Because it still reflects very badly on us. Why couldn't we protect our President?"

"Well we can certainly throw this Alexi guy to the wolves. Perhaps we can tie it all together?"

"How about another terrorist attack?"

Ellwood chimed in, "Gentlemen, we cannot deceive the American people. Our duty is to protect them for the greater good. Alexi should be arrested for treason and sent to Leavenworth. The challenge is the President, but since he was already given a shot, he will need to be rushed to the hospital. We'll make the transfer of power and we will let him fade off into the sunset, after all it is only several months until elections, he will have to withdraw and the Vice President or another candidate can run in his place," Ellwood paused, "As long as the Vice President passes the lie detector."

The debate continued as Attorney General Ellwood Sine excused himself, "I must go to Camp David."

Bobby and Sarge located the rooms that Richard and Senator Snead occupied.

Bobby shook Richard awake, "Hey buddy, you gonna' sleep all day?"

"Bobby," Richard said as he rubbed the sleep from his eyes, "what are you doing here? And what's with the black face and clothes?"

"Long story buddy. But anyway, your meeting with the President today is cancelled."

"What do you mean?"

"The President is taking a leave of absence or something. I'm not sure what they'll do with Andrei."

"Who's Andrei?"

"Andrei is the guy you've been calling Mr. President."

"I'm extremely confused. Could we get some breakfast and you can enlighten me? And can you wash that silly black stuff off your face?"

Bobby went into to Richard's bathroom and cleaned off his face while Richard got dressed. They met Sarge and Senator

Snead in the living room and all went off to breakfast. A secret
Service agent came into the dining room to refill his coffee and
looked over the group as they entered.

"Intruder," he shouted and took aim at Bobby dressed in his
black fatigues.

Seeing the gun being pointed at Bobby, thoughts raced
through Richard's mind beginning with Bobby saving his life
in that hot humid jungle in Vietnam.

"No!" Richard shouted and as the gunshot echoed through the
dining room Richard had already leapt in front of Bobby.

Sarge pulled his weapon and demanded in his no nonsense
military voice, while he steadily took aim at the Secret Service
man, "you will drop your weapon, or I will drop you. That
man is an undercover federal agent."

The Secret Service agent immediately dropped his weapon
and was standing there staring at Richard and Bobby while he
tried to get words to come out of his mouth.

"Get on your phone," Sarge demanded and call your superior,
"Tell them that Bobby Morrow has instructed you to stand
down."

The Secret Service man hesitated.

"Now!" Sarge yelled loud enough to sway the chandeliers and
the man fumbled with his cell phone making the call.

When he hung up he looked at Senator St.Clair and said, "I'm
so sorry!"

"Get an ambulance," Bobby shouted as he knelt down over
Richard.

A pool of blood began spreading across the highly polished
oak floor as Bobby held Richard.

"Sarge," Bobby said while still holding Richard, "you better
check on Alexi."

Sarge left and returned rather quickly.

"Bobby," Sarge said, "I didn't zip tie him well enough."

"Is he still here?" Bobby asked.

"Sort of," Sarge replied, "it appears he got hold of his syringes. He injected himself. He's just laying there staring." Bobby just shrugged his shoulders while he thought of the stages the Succinylcholine would go through ending with not enough muscle action to allow the traitor to breathe and starving his brain and body of oxygen, "couldn't happen to a nicer guy."

Bobby returned his attention to Richard and asked him, "What the hell did you do that for?"

Gasping for breath and in obvious pain Richard replied, "I owed you one."

"Yeah, well you could have just bought me dinner or something. Sarge and I have on body armor. Who do you think you are Superman?"

Richard attempted a smile.

Bobby continued, "well you're supposed to get in a phone booth and put on your cape before you attempt stopping bullets," as he sat on the floor holding Richard in his arms.

Chapter 13

The modest tractor trailer chugged westward up Interstate 270 carefully obeying the speed limits and attracting no attention as the sun rose and shone in their rearview mirrors. Inside the cab Kurt and Mike listened to Toby Keith belt out "Ohh justice will be served, and the battle will rage. This big dog will fight when you rattle his cage, and you'll be sorry that you messed with the U.S. of A 'cause we'll put a boot in your ass..." while they second guessed each other with what Bobby Morrow and Sarge were really doing at Camp David. In the back of the truck, the militia men were delirious with their first successful mission and no casualties, as they passed around the beer and reveled in their moment anxious to get back to good old Pennsylvania and tell lies to their friends about how they bested the best.

Meanwhile the gates of Camp David were coming under siege for the second time in the same day. Overhead the heavy whomping sound of the huge sixty five foot Sikorsky helicopter commonly known as Marine One shattered the calm and serenity of Camp David while at the same time the gates were being charged by a convoy of black SUV's with flashing blue lights in their grills and several ambulances taking up the rear. The guards were prepared this time and immediately raised the gates and stood at attention while the processional sped through the gates and up the long curving driveway to the main lodge. The Secret Service men gathered on the porch of the main building to meet their reinforcements. The lead SUV had not come to a complete stop when the dashing Attorney General Sine jumped from the rear driver's side door and ran up the steps onto the porch followed closely by the head of the Secret Service. The two men, followed by the entire contingent did not take time to ring the doorbell, they merely swung the door open and entered as quickly as they could.

Bobby was still on the shiny wood floor holding his friend Richard St.Clair and keeping pressure on the bullet wound to his torso. Ellwood stopped when he approached Bobby, turned around and yelled for the EMT's, "Where the hell are those guys. Get them in here on the double." The group of well dressed Secret Service men parted and the medics ran in pushing their gurney and carrying their equipment up to the men on the floor. As the second group of EMT's entered, Ellwood asked Sarge where the President was and Sarge led the group with their gurney and equipment into his bedroom. Attorney General Sine then leaned down to help Bobby off the floor as the medics took control of Richard and began peeling off his clothes and preparing bandages and IV's. Richard was loaded onto the stretcher while Ellwood said to Bobby, "how is he doing Bobby?"

Bobby looked Ellwood straight in the eye and replied, "He's breathing but very shallow. He's lost a lot of blood."

"How about the President?" Ellwood asked Bobby.

Bobby waved his hand as though it wasn't important and said, "He's alright. He's just has diarrhea of the mouth. Just keeps babbling on and on."

The EMT's came out with the President on the gurney and Ellwood stopped them to give them orders, "take him to Marine One and get him to the hospital ASAP; and no one speaks of this affair. It is on a need to know basis."

The head of the Secret Service ran to the gurney's side and began ordering agents to accompany the gurney and the President to Marine One and the hospital then instructed the other agents how to secure Camp David.

Ellwood, Bobby and Sarge went with the gurney that was now carrying Senator Richard St.Clair and followed it to the ambulance. On their way the head of the Secret Service came running back to Attorney General Sine and asked, "what about the other one?"

"Take him in the ambulance for now and have him checked over, then await further instructions, the Vice President's counsel will handle all the publicity on this entire affair. You and your men are to say nothing to anyone."

"Understood Ellwood," said the head of the world's premier protection agency.

People scrambled. Doors slammed shut. Sirens started to scream and the convoy of black SUV's and ambulances sped back out of Camp David leaving the wildlife hiding amongst the trees and bushes wondering just what these strange humans were up to.

The telephone on the desk of the President's secretary rang only once before the ever efficient Matty answered it, "the President's office, may I help you?"

"Matty, this is the Colonel." Everyone knew the Colonel by his former military rank. Few really knew his real name.

"Yes, Colonel, what may I do for you? I'm afraid the President is not in at the moment."

"Actually, it was you that I wanted to speak to."

"Really, Colonel, what can I do for you?"

"I just wanted to thank you on behalf of a grateful country for buying so many pre-paid cellular phones and keeping me informed."

"But, Colonel,......."

"Matty, don't worry this will stay between the two of us. How were you able to get the information?"

There were several minutes of quiet before Matty finally spoke, "the President has a bad habit of calling me on the intercom then not turning it off. When he and Mr. Alex met they usually had vodka and began rambling on about all sorts of things."

"Well you did your country a great service, Matty. Thank you."

He hung up.

The evening news anchor made the announcement, "Shocking news from the White House this evening. President Obannon has been rushed from Camp David to the hospital. No details on the President's illness are available. The Vice President has been sworn in by Attorney General Ellwood Sine and has assumed the President's duties. We will keep you informed as we learn more."

Richard could feel the straps anchoring him to the gurney so tight it felt like he could hardly breathe as the ambulance flew down the highway. Through the throbbing pain Richard could still sense that Bobby was there. He could feel his hand resting on his shoulder while other figures continued to poke at him and stick more needles into his already aching body. Richard could feel his breathing getting slower and the pain more intense. And the bright light. Richard wanted to shade his eyes with his hands but they were held down too tightly by the gurney straps. Slowly the intense light began to fade and was replaced by the vision of a blue sky. Blue sky with just a wisp of a cloud surrounding the solid gray stone walls of the 'Blue Hole'. The Blue Hole is the abandoned limestone quarry on the outskirts of Ganister that figured so prominently in his life. Filled with forty feet of brilliant blue water this was where Richard learned a lot about life. His father taught him to swim there. His family spent many hours there swimming, picnicking and just enjoying the sun and water. Richard first made out with Pamela there. Aah yes, Pamela that lovely long legged, perky breasted, red haired girl that became Richard's first love and later his wife after his years at college and his tour in Vietnam. God how Richard hated that place. The hot humid jungle with the torrential downpours. And then that one day when Richard walked up to the small dirty North Vietnamese soldier with his beat up rifle just inches from Richard's chest. The grin on his sweaty face letting Richard know that the end was near. Richard could almost feel the enemy squeezing the trigger, and yet there was nothing Richard could do except wait for the pain since Richard's rifle was lazily pointed at the ground. Richard waited expecting the bullet to tear through his body when the two bright red spots appeared on the North Vietnamese soldier's forehead, his smile faded and he dropped backwards crashing onto the thick underbrush of the jungle floor. Richard remembered still being in a daze as Bobby approached him silently from behind and put his hand on his shoulder. In much the same way as his hand rested on Richard's shoulder now. A new wave of pain shot through Richard and his vision changed from the jungle to the funeral service for his lovely wife Pamela. Still beautiful. The red hair shimmering. Her perfect smooth skin waiting to be touched, but her eyes, her green eyes, no longer bright. They were cold. She was dead, and Richard remembered thinking his life may as well be over also. Richard remembered the booze. Then the Chief of Police entering Richard's home early that morning and waking Richard from his drunken sleep with his pistol pointed at Richard's face. He had a grin on his face also. Not unlike the North Vietnamese soldier. This time was different though. Richard was ready to welcome death this time. After all, Pamela was gone, what did he have to live for? Being Mayor of Ganister? Big deal. Without Pamela everything was different so Richard taunted the Chief, "go ahead. Shoot you big sack of shit! I didn't shoot your son Chief, but if it will make you feel better then squeeze the trigger cause I just don't care." The Chief's son had been shot in the forehead after being stopped along the road by Richard. Richard knew that the Chief's son had accosted Pamela in Aruba and was in fact wearing the Brazilian Rial coin around his neck that he had taken from Pamela as she was making her escape. But Richard swore the Chief's son was still alive when he left and the actual murderer was caught later, but at this point in time the Chief still thought Richard was to blame. And again, like in the jungle of Vietnam, the Chief fell over following the gun blast. And again, Bobby was there along with the county detective who had been following the Chief to arrest him for harboring criminals. Now he could also arrest him for rudely waking up the Mayor. If he lived that is. Richard remembered Bobby grabbing his shoulder. The same way he could feel the strong grip on his shoulder now. Richard's vision changed again. There was the sleepy little town of Ganister. No stoplights, just the stop sign in a barrel full of concrete sitting in the middle of the street where First Street and High Street met. The little gray barbershop with the red striped pole. The big spring at the end of High Street with large trout swimming around without a care in the world. Richard's home. The big two story house with the peeling paint. The same house that Richard's mother was raised in. His mother, petite, dark hair, smiling. Smiling even after a long day at work on her feet then coming home to a house full of kids bickering, asking when supper would be ready. Richard remembered his youth being perfect and it made him smile. The intense light was back. The pain shot through Richard as they roughly drug the gurney out of the ambulance. The sky was no longer blue.

Chapter 14

The room was full. On one side of the room, Carmine Rizzo was pumping the hand of Attorney General Ellwood Sine, while his beautiful wife stood next to him, with Carmine saying, "Thank you for getting my coins returned to me. You ever in the neighborhood you be sure to stop by my place and I get you the best Italian dinner you ever had."
On the other side of the room, Mike the Mechanic and Kurt Klaar were discussing cars and motors. Next to them stood Senator Snead speaking to a beautiful island girl, Nanita. Bobby Morrow and his lovely wife Claire were there along with Richard's mother. Farmer Terry Lee and Sarge stood off to the side of the room watching the other guests. The impeccably dressed gentleman in the black suit cleared his throat to get the attention of the large crowd and announced, "Ladies and gentlemen, if you will be so kind as to take a seat in the chapel we will say our final farewells to Senator Richard St.Clair."

Old Dog, New Trick

Chapter 1

The high peaked ceiling with the lustrous dark wood accented the off-white walls. On both sides the walls were filled with tall bright colored stained glass windows depicting various scenes from the Bible. The front of the church was the same glistening rich dark wood that covered the ceiling and was accented by the large gold cross hanging at the center, flanked by two tall gold posts topped with white candles sporting a flickering flame. The altar again constructed from the dark mahogany wood displayed a green satiny banner with gold embroidery of three crosses. The pews were filled with men and women dressed in expensive suits and fine dresses in the first few rows then giving way to packed pews of hardworking men and women far more casually dressed. The aisles were crowded with men that all appeared to use the same tailor. All dark blue suits with white shirts and plain blue ties. And each of these men also wore the same dark sunglasses and earwigs. Everyone knows a Secret Service agent when they see him. These men were lined around the small Lutheran Church in Ganister, Pennsylvania for the first time in its over hundred year existence, and probably the last time, because the President of the United States felt compelled to make an appearance at the funeral of Senator Richard St. Clair. What the other guests would only be able to guess at was whether the President was there to honor the deceased Senator or to gloat that his biggest nemesis was lying in a coffin while he was still in power. Numerous other Senators were in attendance and filled part of one side of the church including Richard's friend Senator Snead from Virginia, plus other high ranking officials like Attorney General Ellwood Sine. On the other side of the church Richard's mother sat in the first pew flanked by close relatives and friends including former undercover agent Bobby Morrow, his protégé Sarge, the former military sniper and Sarge's father, Terry, the farmer. Terry was seated next to his lovely wife Mickey. Behind them sat as many of the citizens of Ganister as the church could hold. Richard's mother was on the small side, just a few inches over five feet tall, and yet her sons all grew to the six foot tall range, apparently getting those genes from the father's side since he was a mountain of a man. Others were standing outside the church hoping to catch a glimpse and admiring the fleet of black shiny government cars including the black limo with the Presidential Seal.

The closest the small Borough of Ganister had ever before been to any famous persons since this former hunting ground of the Lenape and Shawnee Indians was settled was when Amelia Earhart arrived for the funeral of Wilmer Stultz a Ganister native who piloted Amelia across the Atlantic before she became the first woman to make the flight. That was in 1929, quite a while back in time. Since then Ganister has been a sleepy little town filled with twelve hundred hardworking average Americans. And like in 1929 it took a funeral to get the rich and famous to visit.

The pews overflowing, the ceiling fans desperately trying to move any resemblance to cool air, Pastor Tyme in his white clergy robe, beads of sweat forming on his brow, made his way to the altar. After saying his usual quick, silent prayer to himself, he looked out over the congregation raising his arms in a signal for the masses to stand. Pastor Tyme was short in stature with a full head of gray hair that was rapidly receding at the temples, but his deep voice was full of authority and he did not need the microphone on the altar to gain everyone's immediate attention.

The pastor opened with a prayer, read a few scriptures, and began speaking about the life of Richard St.Clair.

"When I was first assigned this church," the Pastor said, "Richard was one of the first people in Ganister to welcome me and we became very good friends from the beginning. We would spend hours reviewing recent sermons and debating whether or not they struck home with the members of the church. Of course we also spent a lot of time discussing hunting and cars. As you know, Richard and I hunted deer together." The pastor paused for a moment looking down at the altar then back to the congregation and continued, "of course he probably told this story a little differently but there was one time when we were hunting in the hills behind the quarry when we walked up to the tree stand where his brother had been patiently watching for a big buck to come along. I began talking with Richard's brother and he offered me something to eat. Seems he had brought enough food to feed a small army, so as I was partaking and speaking with his brother, Richard turned to me quickly and said, Pastor, there's a buck for you. I looked but I couldn't see it through the brush, so I asked him where. He pointed and says 'hurry, he's gonna' get away', but I still couldn't find him. Richard then pulls up his rifle, aims, pulls the trigger, and says to me, he's down there, just walk straight ahead until you trip over him. I got the impression he thought I should do less talking and more hunting."

The pastor smiled, the congregation let out a respectful laugh and the Pastor continued, "Richard was a very giving man and did a tremendous amount for our fine town. I would like you," he said as he motioned to the congregation, "to say a few words about our dearly departed Senator Richard St.Clair. Please come up and speak. Do not be shy."
The Pastor took a seat behind the altar.
Pastor Tyme had no sooner got seated when a tall woman sitting next to Richard's mother stood and made her way to the aisle and up the few steps to the altar. She was dressed in a long black dress and a small black veil covered her well-coiffed black hair with a few streaks of gray showing through. She carried a Bible in her right hand held rigid against her body as though protecting it from muggers. Tears welled in her eyes as she began to speak, "Richard was my nephew, and my dear sister's son. He always called me Auntie M. and was such a cheerful and positive person up until his young wife Pamela passed away from that terrible breast cancer. Richard wasn't quite the same after that but fortunately he got his act together and completely immersed himself into being a fine Mayor of our quaint little town, then went on to work just as hard as our Senator. It's a shame that he was killed when he had so much to live for. We will really miss…". The tears overtook her and she struggled to pick her Bible up off the altar, stick it back close to her side and make her way back down to the first pew.
The Chief of Police in the borough of Ganister was Galen Farr. He stood from his seat at the end of the pew next to the aisle; straightened his gun belt, ran his right hand under his belt to be sure his shirt was neatly tucked in and strode with authority to the front of the church and up to the altar. It was one of the rare occasions when he did not have his "smoky the bear hat" covering his receding and graying hair. Chief Farr adjusted the microphone, though it wasn't necessary with his husky voice. "Richard St. Clair was a friend of mine. He

promoted me to Chief of Police here in Ganister and I owe him for that. We had our disagreements, and I nearly arrested him for the death of our old Chief's son, which would have been a grave error. Mayor St. Clair showed how honest and sincere he was when proving his innocence and after that I had nothing but admiration and respect for him. He will be remembered as one of the finest Mayor's our town has ever had."

Sarge gave Bobby a quick poke in the ribs and asked him, "Why did Farr almost arrest Richard? That must have been when I was quite young."

Bobby spoke in a hushed voice without turning his head, "Richard had proof that the old Chief's son, Billy Bollinger, was bringing in drugs via the ambulance service that he worked on and selling them in town. When the Chief and his son found out that the Richard knew all about it, the Chief sent his son out of town to go live with a relative. Richard saw Billy leaving town with his car stuffed full of clothes and followed him out of town and managed to stop him. Anyway, long story short, Richard smashed Billy in the face with the butt end of his revolver that he always carried. Unfortunately, after Richard left Billy sitting there along the side of the road, Billy's accomplice came along and shot him in the head. Naturally Chief Bollinger thought Richard did it so Chief Bollinger went to Richard's house early one morning to arrest or kill him, not sure which. The County detective and I happened to be tailing Chief Bollinger because we had the goods on him for having a burglary ring consisting of criminals from other areas. Richard hit the Chief. The Chief pulled a gun on Richard, and I shot the Chief."

"Damn," Sarge said, then immediately covered his mouth and said, "Sorry, forgot where I was. Is that when Farr became Chief?"

"There was a vacancy and he was next in line," Bobby said.

Chief Farr strutted back down the aisle and took his end seat in the pew as a minor gasp went up from the crowd. All eyes turned to the back of the church as Carmine Rizzo waddled down the aisle. Carmine in his later years was showing his girth resulting from all the spaghetti he consumed. Carmine was widely viewed as the leader of the local mafia in and around Ganister, and not a person that anyone ever crossed. Standing at the back of the church along with the President's Secret Service agents were Carmine's two "associates". They were both large men dressed in matching black suits, white shirts and no ties. Their collars were open a few buttons down revealing large gold chains around their necks. Their suit coats were bulged out under their right arms which caused the Secret Service agents to immediately talk into their sleeves and begin to move toward the men.

Carmine reached the altar and pulled the microphone down some so he could speak into it, made the sign of the cross over his chest and spoke.

"I liked Richard St. Clair. His old man did a little work for me from time to time, but Richard didn't let anything influence him. He was a straight shooter," the mafia boss smiled, "and honest, too," Carmine smiled a little bigger at his own joke, "but he sure earned my respect and this town and this state will miss him. I remember the time that crooked IRS tried to take away some coins that I inherited. Richard didn't give me any preferential treatment but he had that Attorney General look into things, and I got my coins back from them bums." Carmine then spotted Attorney General Ellwood Sine sitting in the back of the church and gave him a quick wave saying, hey, Mr. Attorney General, it's a good to see you again. You come over to my restaurant after this service and get you some pasta. On the house. Mrs. St. Clair," Carmine said addressing Richard's mother, "Richard and his father were both good men. You need anything, you call me." Carmine made his way to the back of the church. The President watched his every move with a red face as he wondered how the Attorney General rated a mention and the leader of the most powerful country on earth got snubbed by a local thug then Carmine stopped dead in his tracks when he was at the aisle the President was sitting in. He glanced at the President of the United States, causing the Secret Service men to come to a sharper attention and lower their hands to the butt of their respective revolvers. Carmine spoke to the President in a low voice that only those nearby could hear, "One of your men killed my friend Richard. Either you put that rabid dog down, or I will. Good day, Mr. President." The President now was beet red with embarrassment and wondering how the hell he could be treated so rudely by these country bumpkins. Did these people not realize that he was the President of the United States of America? The most powerful leader in the entire world!

The church crowd was still watching as Carmine made his exit, followed by his beefy bodyguards, when a beautiful, petite woman in a stunning short black dress entered the church after Carmine's men held the door for her. She was holding the hand of a small boy. She looked around for an empty seat but there was none. Two men in the back row stood and motioned for her and the boy to take their seats which she did. The eyes of the other parishioners stayed glued to the young woman and child as they were definitely not from Ganister, and judging by the light cinnamon tone of her skin, not from this country.

Sarge again bumped Bobby with his elbow, "whoa," he said, "who's that?"

"Nanita," Bobby replied.

"Nanita who," Sarge asked with a curious expression on his face, "and how do you know her?"

"I met her in Aruba with Richard."

"She came all this way for a funeral service?"

"Apparently."

"They must have been more than friends," Sarge replied, then as an afterthought, "is that her kid?"

"Don't know that," Bobby answered as he turned to face the front of the church.

Sarge was still staring and said under his breath, "she sure is pretty."

The President of the United States was anything but shy and was feeling the need to show these common folks who was in charge.

"Ladies and gentlemen, we all mourn the loss of Senator Richard St.Clair," he said putting on his most somber face. "Richard and I did not always agree on things but I had tremendous respect for his opinions. The Senator will be sorely missed, not only by the fine citizens here in Ganister and central Pennsylvania but by everyone in Washington, DC as well. Some of my more extreme colleagues might say he was a bit of an instigator, but I liked to think that he kept everyone on their toes. I remember..."

Bobby Morrow received a sharp blow to his rib cage delivered from the hard elbow of Sarge. Bobby glanced over at Sarge. Sarge leaned in and whispered in Bobby's ear, "isn't that the Secret Service guy that shot Richard back in the rear corner of the church?"

Bobby immediately shot a casual glance in that direction. Being a person who never forgets a face the muscles in Bobby's neck and cheek area began to tighten. Bobby then whispered in Sarge's ear, "Just keep an eye on him. I still need to talk with that guy."

"You're not going to kill him here, are you?"

Bobby just glanced at Sarge. The kind of unspoken signal that meant Sarge should not ask any more questions, so Sarge did as Bobby suggested and kept a casual eye on the agent in the dark blue suit.

The President, finally done rambling on with lies of how close a liberal President was to a conservative Senator, and feeling he got all the sound bites that could possibly make the evening news, he, with great pomp and circumstance stepped from behind the altar, waved at the masses, and strutted down the aisle and out the door where the citizens of Ganister that were outside pointed and gasped while men in suits scrambled to open car doors and speak on hidden microphones.

Bobby, followed by Sarge, exited out the side door and came up behind the Secret Service agent that Sarge had previously pointed out. Bobby came up behind him as quietly as a deadly snake and grabbed the unsuspecting Secret Service Agent by his elbow with fingers that closely resembled a vise. The agent stopped in his tracks and turned to face Bobby.

"You and I never have had that conversation we were supposed to have," Bobby whispered to the agent.

"I have my orders. And at the moment the President is waiting for me."

"Let him wait," Bobby whispered harshly, "you're gonna' answer a question first."

"I don't take orders from *former* undercover agents. Let go!"

"You had orders to shoot me and the Senator didn't you? You weren't surprised that we were at Camp David, were you?"

The agent merely stared at Bobby. Not saying a word he jerked his elbow out of Bobby's grasp and quickly made his escape. Sarge came from behind Bobby to catch him. Bobby reached out and stopped Sarge.

The look in the Secret Service agent's eyes told Bobby everything he needed to know.

"Let him go," Bobby said to Sarge.

"But he shot Richard."

"Just following orders the same way that you and I have on many occasions."

"But we can't just let him get away with it."

"There's a time and place. This isn't it."

Then Bobby said to Sarge, "go back in and look after Richard's mother. I'll be back in just a minute."

Sarge did as instructed. Bobby stayed put and watched the Secret Service agent hustle over to the President's motorcade. When he reached the side of the President's car, he turned his head in Bobby's direction and gave Bobby a sinister smile and a small salute of the hand. Bobby turned and went back into the church

A second later the left side of the Secret Service agent's head blew off. Blood and tissue splattering on the side of the President's formerly immaculately clean black limousine. The silencer did its job to perfection and no one ever heard the bullet leaving the rifle and slicing through the air, penetrating the Secret Service agent's skull, flattening out, and causing fatal damage.

Chapter 2

The death of Senator Richard St.Clair came several days ago after the President invited Richard and Senator Snead to Camp David for a meeting under the pretense of getting the conservative Senators to think a little more liberally so the President could get his agenda passed. The President knew that without their support his grandiose plans would wither on the vine because the bottom line was the costs were far too exorbitant. Richard wasn't very anxious to go but agreed to appease his friend Senator Snead.

The shiny black limousine with the President's flag flying on the fender followed by a small army of shiny black SUV's carried Richard and Senator Snead from Washington to Camp David where they were met by a crisp salute of a naval officer and several Secret Service agents. The driver's side front window went down and the chauffer announced the arrival of Senators St. Clair and Snead. Several Naval officers looked under the vehicle with mirrored staffs while the identification of the Senators was scrutinized even though they were expected. A second smart salute from the Naval officer and the limousine rolled past the small guard post, through the gates, and began winding its way up the long tree lined drive, coming to a stop in front of the well built wood and stone lodge with a rich history of entertaining leaders from all over the world. The Senators met with the President. Enjoyed a fine dinner and drinks and spent the night in the historic Camp David.

The Colonel, former head of security for the former President had received information that the President was not exactly who he appeared to be, and in fact, was a Russian plant from childhood raised to infiltrate our government to destroy it from within, so the Colonel dispatched Bobby and Sarge to clandestinely enter Camp David during the late night hours. Bobby and Sarge hiked the long way through the wooded park surrounding Camp David and waited in the early morning dark until their prearranged diversion took effect. The diversion consisted of Bobby and Richard's friends Mike the Mechanic, Kurt Klaar and others attempting to run through the guard post with Mike's old black evil Dodge Ram. They shot the guards with dart guns to put them to sleep for a few minutes instead of shooting anyone. It was not their intent to hurt any of the guards, their only objective was to distract the guards away from the back of the building in order that Bobby and Sarge could enter.

Bobby and Sarge had made a successful entry and while the President was asleep managed to inject him with sodium pentothal, more widely known as "truth serum". The pinch of the needle jolted the President awake.

"What the...." the President started to say, then "what are you doing here? Who the hell are you?"

Bobby covered the President's mouth with a handkerchief and said to him as sternly as possible, "no noise Mr. President. If you make any attempt to shout I will give you a different shot."

Bobby held up his 45 Glock and let the image of the intimidating black pistol sink in, then said in a near whisper, "do you understand Mr. President?"

The President shook his head affirmatively and cautiously asked, "what did you inject me with?"

"Sodium Pentothal, Mr. President."

"But, why?"

"I need to ask you a few questions Mr. President and I don't have time for bullshit or political non-answers. I expect the truth, and I expect it right now."

The President started to protest. Bobby waved the gun in his face again and the President shut up.

"What is your name?" Bobby asked.

"I'm President Barry Obannon," the President responded.

"Is that the name you were born with?"

The President hesitated then said, "no."

"What name were you born with?"

"Andrei. Andrei Pankin."

"Where were you born?"

"I was born in Leningrad."

"Are you a member of the Communist Party?"

"Of course. Long live Mother Russia!"

Bobby pulled out his cell phone and immediately called the Colonel.

"You were right," was all that Bobby said then he hung up his phone.

In the meantime Sarge was in the next room questioning the President's number two man, Mr. Alexi, and getting the same responses. After going through the questions supplied by the Colonel and the President and his number two falling back to sleep, Bobby and Sarge located Richard's room and informed him of what was going on. They all met in the dining room to get coffee and a bite to eat when it happened.

A Secret Service Agent wandered into the dining room to refill his coffee, and observed the group entering the dining room. "Intruder," the Secret Service agent shouted and took aim at Bobby dressed in his black fatigues.

Seeing the gun being pointed at Bobby, thoughts raced through Richard's mind beginning with the time Bobby saved Richard's life in the jungles of Vietnam.

"No!" Richard shouted and before the gunshot echoed through the dining room Richard had leapt in front of Bobby to take the bullet.

Chapter 3

Pastor Tyme immediately returned to the altar that was vacated by the president as he made his grand exit.

"Who would like to be next?" the Pastor asked.

The church was so quiet you could have heard a pin drop followed by a large gasp as everyone turned in unison. Terry Lee, the farmer, had risen from his seat and was working his way to the front of the church. The good people of Ganister, Pennsylvania were unaccustomed to seeing farmer Terry dressed in anything other than his jeans, flannel shirt, mud encrusted work boots, and weathered baseball hat. The farmer Terry that was on his way to the altar was clean shaven except for the blonde mustache, hair immaculately combed, and attired in a light gray suit that fit like it was tailored specifically for him. He looked like a cross between Pierce Brosnan and country singer Alan Jackson. The congregation was also surprised to see Terry approaching the altar because he was normally very shy. No one had ever heard Terry speak in public, or for that matter to more than one person at a time.

As Terry worked his way behind the altar the crowd again quieted, Terry tilted the microphone up as it had been lowered for the much shorter Pastor and the President. "Forgive me," Terry said quietly, "I'm not a speaker. I just want to say a few words about my dear friend, Richard St.Clair. I guess I should say Senator St.Clair, it's just that I remember him before he was a Senator. I was a couple years younger than Richard yet he and Bobby Morrow included me in most everything as we were growing up. We spent a lot of time at the Blue Hole," Terry paused and looked up at the packed pews then started again, "For those of you that aren't from around here, the Blue Hole is the abandoned limestone quarry that we all swam in. While large enough to place a football field inside it, the forty feet deep water is a brilliant blue that rivals the Caribbean." Terry stopped, and a small smile crossed his lips, "At least from the pictures that I've seen of the Caribbean." The folks in the congregation that knew Terry chuckled at that as they knew that Terry had never been out of the country, and probably if the truth was known, never out of the county.

Terry continued, "I was around when Richard and Pamela, his wife, first met and spent quite a bit of time at the quarry, mostly fogging up the windows of Richard's dad's car. Then when Richard and Bobby went away to college followed by Vietnam, I purchased the farm that overlooks the quarry. I was lucky enough to be able to help Richard when that crooked Police Chief that we used to have lured Richard to the Blue Hole in an attempt to kill him."

The heads of the locals were all nodding positively as they remembered the event. Richard had been Mayor of Ganister at the time. The Chief of Police who had been in power for many years had been offering protection to a ring of burglars in exchange for a percentage of their take. The ring began to unravel when one of the ring members was taken to jail for a domestic disturbance. That was when the county found he had an outstanding warrant in California. Eventually the whole story came out. Terry was making his way back to his pew when the commotion outside the church stopped the service. Sirens were blaring, vehicles were screeching to a halt and it sounded like an army was outside the church taking over the street.

Sarge looked around for Bobby. He was not yet back, so Sarge ran out the side door to check on the commotion. The President's entourage of limousines was gone and in it's place were State Police cars, black government SUV's, even the Ganister Police were there with the bright blue and red lights breaking up the afternoon sun. Sarge ran down to the street and saw the body. The body of the Secret Service Agent that he and Bobby had just had words with. Sarge could only think of one thing as he stood there turning in circles trying to observe every inch around him, "where was Bobby?"

Pastor Tyme ruled his church with a firm hand and an even firmer voice. After all, he reported to only one boss, God, and he took his duties very seriously, therefore the commotion caused by the President and his entourage leaving Pastor Tyme's holy house was of no consequence to him. After all, his boss was a much higher authority than the President of the United States.

The rich bass voice penetrated every square inch of the hundred year old house of God without the aid of a microphone, and immediately the undercurrent buzz of whispering parishioners caused by the curiosity of the happenings outside the hallowed walls came to an abrupt halt. Pastor Tyme extended his arms first to the heavens, while he prayed silently, then to the open casket below the altar that contained the now lifeless body of Richard St.Clair. "Ladies and gentlemen," Pastor Tyme began, "we are here to pay our last respects to our dear departed friend Richard

St.Clair. Who would like to be next to say a few words in remembrance?"

Most of the people seated in this church knew Mike the Mechanic, however, they recognized Mike by his Ferrari red work shirt. Today Mike sported a modern blue Perry Ellis pinstripe portfolio suit which appeared to be exquisitely tailored and topped off with a colorful Jerry Garcia necktie. All eyes watched Mike as he ascended the stairs to the altar. Some were thinking, "I'm paying him too much to fix my car." Others, particularly the women, were thinking, "Damn, that man cleans up real well!"

Mike addressed the stunned crowd, "my fondest memories of Richard naturally involve cars and racing. Watching Richard run so fast and yet so smoothly through the turns at Watkins Glen racetrack was true artistry. And when he took me for a drive in my Ferrari it was an unbelievable thrill. I will truly miss him."

Chapter 4

The long string of cars being led by the shiny black hearse left the Ganister Lutheran Church and slowly made their way to their next destination. The Canoe Creek cemetery was a couple miles outside of the borough. As the convoy drove past the church, they encountered numerous police cars, local, state, and federal with numerous policemen standing guard at an area of the street that was blocked off with yellow police tape, or as the locals referred to it, "dead-man-tape." There were also several official looking men watching the area dressed in dark suits and sporting dark sunglasses. Federal law enforcement of some sort, no doubt. Never before had the local citizens seen so many police cars on one street before. As the processional slowly drove past, every head turned and took in the drying puddle of now blackish red blood, and

everyone thought to themselves the same thought: "Bobby Morrow told us that a Secret Service agent shot Richard. Actually he was trying to shoot Bobby but Richard jumped in front of Bobby to save him. Is it possible that the same Secret Service agent was here today, at Richard's service, and is it possible that he received his just dues. It would be only fitting if he was shot today in Ganister. An eye for an eye. And didn't we see Bobby and Sarge leave the service for a few minutes following those agents. Plus Carmine out and out threatened them right there in the church. It sure is possible that Carmine wasn't threatening, maybe he was making a promise. The old mafia kiss of death. He might already have known who shot Richard and this probably wouldn't be the first person that old Carmine put six feet under."
As the procession passed each head turned back to look forward again but each replaced their previously solemn look with a small smile. Justice. Ganister style justice.

The President's motorcade had followed it's established procedure and after the splattering of the agent's blood and brain matter all over the side of the presidential limousine, the limousine made a hasty departure with several agents piled on top of the President practically smothering him in an effort to protect him from any further flying bullets. A few of the black SUV's filled with other agents immediately began securing the area, removing the body of the dead agent and searching for the gunman and his lair. Calls went out immediately and in no time the area was flooded with state police, county sheriffs and of course more federal police in the form of FBI and Secret Service. A quick study of the probable trajectory of the bullet led to a search of the library just a few buildings down the street. On the flat rooftop they found the gun which was apparently left by the sniper in his rush to leave the area. The gun was immediately placed in an evidence bag and several state police officers were rushing it back to their lab to be checked for fingerprints.

 Photographs were taken from every angle of the crime scene and the sniper's lair. Measurements were made, checked and double checked. This was a serious breach as the area was to have been checked and double checked prior to the President's arrival to prevent this from happening and the only snipers that were to be in position were the Secret Service agents that were protecting the President from various sniper positions. The position used by this sniper was in between several positions that the Secret Service agents were using and yet they had not spotted this sniper. Heads were going to roll over this screw-up so the best possible outcome was to find this murderer and find him fast.

The funeral processional meandered up the gravel driveway at the Canoe Creek Cemetery and came to a stop near a large burgundy tent set over an open hole in the ground with a silver frame set up around the rectangular hole. The back door of the hearse was opened and the pole-bearers began to assemble. Bobby Morrow was the first with Sarge on the opposite side of the fine oak casket, each of them firmly grasping the shiny brass side rails and slowly pulling the casket from the hearse while others joined in. Kurt Klaar and Mike the Mechanic plus Farmer Terry and lastly Senator Snead from Virginia all took the respective positions and made their way to the tent with the casket. They set the casket upon the silver railings and went back to join their friends and families. Pastor Tyme stood behind the casket and addressed the gathering, "dear friends and relatives, we will first allow Richard's Masonic lodge to perform their ceremony."
A large contingent of men dressed mostly in black tuxedos or black suits came single file from the back of the group to the casket. Some of the men were wearing bright blue wide ribbons around their neck with silver shining jewels dangling from the end of the ribbon. All were wearing white leather

aprons and white gloves and each carrying a small sprig of evergreen. The leader of the group began, "Forasmuch as it hath pleased Almighty God in his wise providence to take out of this world the soul of our deceased brother, we have come to the performance of a duty which the dearest ties of friendship and love enjoin, that of laying his body in the dust. As we mourn his departure, let us sadly learn the lesson of our own mortality. How honorably he maintained the cares of life, we can attest; let us, therefore, preserve his memory and dwell on what was good and amiable in his character. That our Brother was faultless cannot be supposed, but as we shall all appear before the Almighty Judge, let our hearts register only our Brother's worth. Farewell my Brother; thou hast gone to meet thy God, and may he approve thee. May we be faithful, and when our end approaches, may our eyes be closed in peace. Farewell, till the Grand Summons comes. Then, Brother, may we rise and greet thee. And now, because our God is the God of hope and consolation, and doth not willingly afflict or grieve the children of men, let us invoke His mercy and His grace. Let us pray."

A prayer followed by another of the group ending with "Glory be to God on high."

All the men then responded, "As it was in the beginning, is now, and ever shall be, world without end. Amen. So mote it be."

Then the leader spoke again, "This scroll, on which is inscribed the name of our departed Brother, I now deposit in his grave." And he dropped the paper into the grave then continued, "He has passed away, nevermore to return. Let us hope that his name is registered in the Book of Life." The leader continued with more pleasing words then the group in single file, beginning with the leader, walked past the grave depositing the sprigs of evergreen into the grave and each saying in his turn, "farewell, my Brother."

The leader made several more invocations followed by responses from the group, then they retired.

Pastor Tyme waited an appropriate second then addressed the gathering, "Let us pray." And he did. Pastor Tyme closed by saying, "We brought nothing into this world, and it is certain we can carry nothing out. The Lord giveth and the Lord taketh away; blessed be the name of the Lord."

A contingent of impeccably dressed military men formed their formation and with orders from their leader fired their rifles into the air. Three volleys of shots fired in honor of the deceased veteran. A lone bugler played taps. Then the flag that had been draped over the coffin of Richard St. Clair was smartly and crisply folded by two of the soldiers and reverently handed off to their leader with smart salutes who then reverently handed the crisply folded flag to Richard's mother while quietly speaking just a few words to her and leaving with another slow salute.

The crowd slowly rose from the chairs they had warmed and one by one made their way to Mrs. St.Clair to offer their condolences to her. Mrs. St.Clair being a very small lady and her sister, Auntie M being a tall woman, it was only natural that Auntie M acted as a sort of gatekeeper and protector. No one came to Mrs. St.Clair, commonly referred to as "Shorty" by Auntie M without her approval. Richard's friends and relatives politely waited in line and one by one were permitted to speak with Shorty. They then trudged across the cemetery to their waiting cars and headed back to the real world that awaited each of them. There was only a small number of people left, Bobby Morrow and his wife, Claire, Sarge, and the beautiful young lady with the child in tow who was approaching Mrs. St.Clair. Auntie M stepped between Shorty and the young lady with her hand out and asked her, "I don't believe we have been introduced? Were you a friend of Richard's?"

Bobby spoke to Auntie M, "this is Nanita. A friend of Richard's from Aruba."

"How nice to meet you," Auntie M said to her, "and is this beautiful child yours?"

"Yes, this is my son."

Being allowed access to Shorty, Nanita took her hand and offered her sincere condolences that she had lost her son.

"Thank you," Mrs. St.Clair replied.

Auntie M then looked from the child to Shorty and said, "Shorty, doesn't he look just like Richard when he was a little boy?"

"He certainly does," answered Mrs. St. Clair then looked to Nanita.

"What is his name?" Richard's mother asked.

"Richie," Nanita replied.

Mrs. St.Clair and Auntie M exchanged glances which Nanita couldn't help but notice so she said, "perhaps sometime soon we could get together and talk."

"Yes, please Nanita, come by anytime you wish."

"Well, I will only be in town for another day."

"Why wait dear, please stop by this evening," Shorty said.

Nanita, with the handsome young child in tow made her way across the cemetery to a waiting car.

Auntie M said to Shorty as they both stared after the couple, "Well, well, well."

Mrs. St.Clair cast her eyes toward Auntie M. No words needed to be exchanged.

Several police cars made their way into the cemetery and the policemen walked down to the ceremony tent and offered their condolences to Mrs. St. Clair. After doing so they immediately pulled Bobby and Sarge aside and said in a hushed tone, "the two of you need to come with us."

Bobby looked at the officer that was attempting to grasp his arm, and said, "I'll take my wife home, then I'll come over to the police station."

"You are not getting my meaning," the police officer said with pursed lips and again attempted to grasp Bobby's arm. Bobby immediately pulled his arm away and whispered into the policeman's ear so no one else could hear, "touch me again and you'll pull back a bloody stump. Now what the hell is going on?"

The policemen shared a glance before he said to Bobby, "you and Sarge are under arrest for the shooting of the Secret Service agent."

Claire spoke up immediately, "how damn dumb can you be? Bobby and Sarge were at the church when that happened."

"They slipped out for a few minutes, ma'am and had words with the man."

Claire looked to Bobby. Bobby said to Claire, "that's true, but we didn't shoot anyone."

Claire knowing Bobby would never lie to her poked the police officer in the chest while saying, "They didn't do it. I'm sure he'll go with you to straighten this all out, but he better be home in time for supper or I'm coming after you buster!"

The policemen pulled a pair of handcuffs off his leather belt. Claire wasted no time in telling him, "How stupid can you possibly be. They are going with you, unless you try that, then these two will probably thump your asses and leave you lying in the hole over there waiting to have dirt put on top of you. But, hey, it's your call, asshole." Claire stomped away leaving several highly confused policeman scratching their heads and looking at each other. They decided that Bobby and Sarge didn't need to be handcuffed and would go along peacefully. Bobby walked by Mrs. St.Clair and stopped to give her a hug and whisper in her ear, "You know, if you need anything, to call me. Please. It's my fault what happened to Richard and I now owe you my life."

"Sweet of you to say, Bobby, but I know that on several occasions you saved Richard's life, and I know that he is now in a better place and feeling proud that finally he could partially repay you. Your slate is clean," she said, "and I love you like a son. Always have. Always will. Make sure you and Claire come around. Often." Mrs. St.Clair was holding back a flood of tears as Bobby and Sarge walked away followed closely by the policemen.

"What's that all about?" Auntie M asked Shorty?

"They probably need Bobby's assistance with whatever went on that caused the scene outside the church," Shorty replied then she walked to Richard's casket. Kissed the casket and the flood of tears came. After she got under control she said to her sister who had been holding closely around the shoulders, "Parents are not supposed to outlive their children. It's just not right."

Pastor Tyme came around the casket, embraced them both, and said to Mrs. Mrs. St.Clair, "our Lord only picks the finest flowers from his garden. He chose Richard. Peace be with you Mrs. St.Clair."

Chapter 5

The small Ganister Police dept was overflowing when the policemen entered with Bobby and Sarge in tow. A path materialized as the two were led to the Chief's desk where the Chief sat staring down at his desk with a dejected look on his face. He glanced up at Bobby and just rolled his hands over in a not-my-call gesture to Bobby. A fit and trim federal officer in the usual dark suit and short hair, slapped Bobby on the chest with a folded piece of paper.

"The warrant for your arrest, Mr. Morrow," he spit out.

"For what?" Bobby asked.

"The murder of a Secret Service agent."

"Yeah well you got the wrong man," Bobby replied.

"One of you did it," he said as he looked past Bobby to Sarge.

"Got any proof?" Bobby asked.

The agent smiled, a huge beaming smile, and said, "Well sure. We didn't just fall off a turnip truck. We actually have a gun. Your rifle. With your fingerprints on it. And we have no doubt that as soon the ballistics are done on it, that it will match the bullet that killed one of our own."

"How convenient," Bobby spat back at him, "too bad I didn't do it. Hate to ruin your not so airtight case."

Bobby then turned to look at Sarge, and asked him, "Sarge, did you shoot this agent of theirs?'

"No, Bobby I didn't. I wanted to, but you wouldn't let me. You said now was not the time. And look, some jerk beat us to it."

Bobby turned back to the agent, "he didn't do anything, let him go."

"So you're saying that you did?"

"No. I know I didn't shoot him, but someone obviously framed me and if I find out it was you then I'm going to kick your ass."

"I think we'll just hold onto both of you for awhile," the agent said with a smug look on his face.

"It's your career that you're flushing down the toilet," Bobby replied then he looked at Chief Galen Farr and said to him, "you better call my wife, Chief, and tell her I won't be home for supper."

Bobby and Sarge were led to a cell and were deposited there where another person already sat contently on a bunk watching the new arrivals.

"Carmine," Bobby said, "what the hell are you doing here?"

"These bozos think because I threatened to kill whoever killed Richard that I shot their man."

"Did you?" Bobby asked.

"No, I was waiting until after the funeral then I was going to find him and have him fitted with cement shoes and dropped into the Blue Hole," Carmine said matter-of-factly.

"He was there today, but I don't know who got shot so I can't tell you if it was the right guy or not," Bobby replied.

"Well, if you didn't do it, and I didn't do it, and I assume Sarge here didn't do it. Who the hell did?"

"Good question," Bobby said.

Sarge joined the conversation, "if it wasn't the right guy, are we still going to get him?"

Bobby gave Sarge the look that said of course.

"Good," Sarge replied.

Carmine looked at his watch then said to Bobby, "I'm getting out of here in just a couple minutes. You want to come with me?"

"How do you know that, Mr. Rizzo?" Sarge asked.

"I got a very good mouthpiece and he knows I don't like to spend too much time here, so he'll be here any minute now," Carmine said in his heavy Italian accent.

The three could hear the commotion in the other room and the door swung open. A tall slim, middle aged man with graying hair pulled back in a tight ponytail and wearing faded jeans and a Hard Rock t-shirt strode into the room and up to the jail cell. He looked at Carmine and said, "Sorry it took me so long to get here Carmine. I was over on the other side of the county. You ready to go?"

Carmine stood and walked to the door. By then a police officer was opening the door so Carmine could leave. Carmine looked to the pony-tailed man and said, "my friends need to come with me."

The smug agent was standing in the doorway and overhearing Carmine said, "That's not going to happen."

Carmine shot a quick glance to his mouthpiece who turned on the agent, "I beg to differ, whoever you are."

"I'm the agent in charge and a member of the Secret Service," whereupon he pulled out his creds and flashed them at the lawyer.

"Damn, I'm impressed," the mouthpiece said dripping sarcasm off his tongue.

"I'll see your badge and raise you a business card."

The mouthpiece pulled out a business card and handed it to the agent. The agent laughed and said, "Wow I'm impressed, so you're Robert Germain!"

The attorney reached back in his pocket and pulled out another card, which he checked before handing it over to the agent.

"Oh, so now you are Ellwood Sine the U.S. Attorney General?" the agent said with a chuckle.

"No, chuckles, I'm Robert Germain. The other card belongs to Ellwood, the U.S. Attorney General and if you look on the back of it, you will see his personal cell phone number that he wrote there. And now, you should call that number before you end up parking cars on the Capitol lawn while some other flunkie takes over your job."

The grin left the agent's face. He deliberated a moment while the attorney bored holes in him with his stare, then he dialed the number figuring this could be a ruse.

"Ellwood Sine," said the voice on the other end of the phone.

"Mr. Sine, the Attorney General?"

"Yes," he replied, "who is this?"

"Agent Carson of the Secret Service."

"Well what do you want, Agent?"

"I have one Bobby Morrow and one Sarge Lee in custody for the shooting of a Secret Service agent who was protecting the President while he was at Senator Richard St.Clair's funeral in Ganister, Pennsylvania."

"Why?" Ellwood asked.

"Mr. Morrow's gun was found at the scene with his finger prints on it."

"Well of course his fingerprints would be on his gun, but how do you know it is his gun?"

"We searched his home, knowing he had a sniper rifle from his former military days, and finding an empty space, but no gun plus the serial number matches."

"And who approved this search warrant agent? No never mind that, just tell me that you legally carried out the search?"

"Well no one was home at the time, but we had a valid search warrant."

"Word to the wise agent, unless you want to forfeit your pension, you better cut those guys lose. But first, how did you get this number?" the Attorney General asked.

"Robert Germain, an attorney for a Mr. Carmine Rizzo, gave it to me and insisted I call."

"Give Carmine my regards."

"But, sir," the agent frantically asked, "how can you be so sure that Morrow did not shoot my agent?"

"Because he was at the funeral service , as was I, and he sure as heck isn't stupid enough to leave his gun at the scene, the U.S. government trained him!" The phone went dead.

Another uproar came from the front door of the police station, "Galen," came the loud shriek, "Where the hell is my husband?" Claire Morrow had entered the building and Chief Farr was trying to hide in the crowd.

"Relax, Claire," Bobby shouted over the din, "I'm coming now."

"What about Sarge?' she asked.

"Yeah, I guess there will be another mouth at the kitchen table for supper."

Claire pointed her long finger at Chief Galen Farr and said in no uncertain terms, "You're lucky!"

"One thing before we leave," Bobby said to Claire then looked to Chief Farr, "Galen, can I see a picture of the deceased?"

"Why?" the agent interrupted.

"I want to know if it was the guy?" Bobby said.

"What guy?" the agent asked.

"The one that shot Richard," Bobby said on the verge of getting mad.

"How would you know?"

"I was there. He was actually trying to shoot me and Richard jumped in front of me."

The agent got quiet. Galen showed Bobby a photo. From the good side of the head where the bullet entered leaving only a small hole Bobby could tell and said just loud enough for Sarge and Carmine to hear, "that's him."

Bobby, Claire and Sarge left the building and jumped in Bobby's old red pickup that was parked directly in front of the police department in a no parking zone. Claire sat in the middle and they headed home.

Claire was the first to break the silence, "I'm glad that's over."

"I'm afraid it's not," Bobby answered.

Claire immediately looked his direction. Bobby answered her glare, "someone tried to frame me. That was my rifle that shot that man. There is more here than meets the eye. We have to find out who and why."

Sarge shook his head, "yep. You're right, but I'm just a grunt. I don't know how to do detective work."

"Well for starters, Sarge, you are not just a grunt, you were a highly decorated sniper during the Iraq war."

"Sure, I can shoot him, but first we have to find him, don't you think? So I guess that will be your job. After all, you were the undercover federal agent."

"True, but I usually knew who I was going after. Right now, we have to find the target, that's not exactly the same thing."

"One thing we know for sure. This was a professional."

"Why do you say that?" Claire asked.

"Because this person was able to set up a sniper's nest in the middle of the Secret Service's protection where they had men on the roofs. Take a shot. And then get away clean," Sarge answered.

"You're right Sarge," Bobby said, "that should narrow down the list considerably."

"Oh yeah," Sarge said, "Now we just have to get a list of professional snipers that wanted that Secret Service agent gone."

"Are you sure whoever it was wasn't aiming for the President?" Claire asked.

"No," said Bobby, "Someone this good would not mistake the two or be that far off the mark. This person got the man he was gunning for."

You could see the lightbulb going off in Sarge's head, "if we were doing this, we would have spent some time beforehand scoping out the area. Especially when you know you have to work around the President's Secret Service detail."

"Exactly!" Bobby responded, "And the Secret Service would normally begin about a month in advance, but they only had a five day window from the time that Richard was killed until his funeral."

"So as soon as the President would have made his decision to attend the funeral, the Secret Service would have come and started their planning," Sarge said.

"That means we only have to go back five days to start checking for this person," Bobby replied.

"You need to call Carmine," Claire said to no one in particular.

Both Bobby and Sarge looked at her.

"Why?" Bobby asked.

"Because if anything or anyone moves in this town, Carmine is the first to know about it. Just about everyone in town is one of his snitches."

"She's right about that," Bobby said to Sarge, "I'll call him after supper."

Chapter 6

The cell phone call originated in Chicago, Illinois, the "Windy City" which is a misnomer as the wind blowing in Chicago is not much different than other cities. Milton, Massachusetts is really the windiest city in the United States. The cell phone transmission flowed through a cell tower in Chicago out into the great abyss and landed at a cell tower in Punxsutawney, Pennsylvania. Originally settled by the Delaware Indians, they gave Punxsutawney it's name which meant "town of mosquitoes", but today is more famous for the weather predicting groundhog, Punxsutawney Phil, that emerges from his hole each February 2nd, Groundhog Day, and determines from his shadow whether or not winter is almost over.

The cell phone in Punxsutawney was quickly answered, "It's me."

The voice on the other end of the call was garbled and not a happy camper, "you failed."

"I did exactly what you asked me to."

"Then why did Morrow and that Sarge person get released from jail already?"

"I used his gun. His are the only prints on it. They'll never find a trace of me."

"The deal was Morrow and Sarge rot in jail then you get your family back."

"Please don't hurt my family," the voice pleaded, "I did what you asked, please let them go."

"Since you have failed me, we may have to move on to plan B."

"Anything just please don't hurt my family."

"If they are not going to rot in jail, then I want them dead. Do you hear me?"

"I hear you."

"I'll be back to you soon with the details."

The line went dead. As he closed his phone the man from Punxsutawney slapped a mosquito that had been sucking blood from his neck.

"Go ahead, take my blood, everyone else is," he said to himself.

Chapter 7

"Carmine," Bobby said, "first of all, thank you for getting us out of jail today."
"No problem, "Carmine said in his thick accent.
"Do I owe your attorney anything?"
"Don't worry about the mouthpiece," Carmine said, "he gets taken care of."
"Carmine, I hate to ask, but I was wondering if you could do me another favor?"
The typical silence followed so Bobby continued, "someone has tried to frame me. They stole my rifle and left it at the scene. The ballistics will show the man was killed with that rifle, and yes, I wanted that man dead, so they may continue to try and pin this on me."
"What kind of favor?"
"Whoever made that shot had to be in Ganister before today to establish a nest to shoot from, plus they had to come to my house at some point to steal my rifle."
"And you want me to find out who this mystery person is, is that right?"
"I figure if anyone knows what's going on in Ganister, it's you."
"Thattsa' right," Carmine replied, "this is my town," Carmine paused, "I like you Morrow, but remember, a favor is a favor. It may need repaid one day."
"I know Carmine," Bobby said, "and you know that I can be trusted to pay my debts."
"Thattsa' why I'm gonna' do you this favor."
Bobby hung up his phone. Claire and Sarge watched him and waited like expectant parents about to find out the sex of their new child.

"So?" Claire finally asked.

"So I'm about to owe Carmine a favor."

"He won't ask you to kill someone will he?" Claire asked meekly.

"No," Bobby said smiling, "he has people for that."

"Oh good," she said with a breath of relief.

"How long do you think it will take him to find out?" Sarge asked.

"Hard to say," Bobby said, "until then we get our stuff together and be ready to move."

"You may as well stay the night Sarge," Claire said, "you can use Carol's room."

Carol is the Morrow's daughter who has grown up and moved from home making Bobby and Claire empty-nesters. Claire takes every opportunity she can to get extra bodies in the house as the shuffling of other feet and extra mouths to feed brings back the good old days.

"Okay, you two get out of my kitchen while I make supper," Claire said.

The two migrated to the living room, which was Bobby's favorite room. Bobby's home was a modern log home and the living room showed the style off better than any other room with the high peaked ceiling made of log trusses and bare wood for the actual ceiling. The west end of the home being nearly all glass except for the huge stone fireplace in the center of the room that stretched all the way through the high peaked ceiling. Raw logs formed the sidewalls. Facing the fireplace was a comfortable, well worn leather couch. Wood floors with an occasional area rug and the brass hanging lights gave the room a warm glow.

"Bobby," Sarge said, "I need to ask you something."

"Shoot," Bobby said snickering then adding, "Figuratively speaking."

"Why do you have two plastic pink flamingoes in your yard?"

Both men laughed and Bobby said, "They were a gift. Maybe a joke from Richard. He spent as much time as he could in the Caribbean, especially Aruba and Bonaire, and Bonaire is one of the few places where flamingoes breed. Anyway, he thought it would be funny to have them guarding the log home."

Bobby stared off for a minute then continued, "before our dog Duke got shot," Bobby said, "he used to lift his leg on those flamingoes every chance he got."

Both men laughed at the image of the huge black dog lifting his leg to spray the pink plastic flamingoes.

"Supper's ready," Claire shouted from the kitchen.

Following supper and some time in the living room watching Gibbs on NCIS solve another mystery the group decided to hit the sack. Claire led Sarge up the split log steps to the second floor and entered the first bedroom on the left, turning on the light as she entered. Sarge stopped in his tracks in the doorway.

"You can sleep here in Carol's room," Claire said to Sarge. Sarge stood in the doorway, not budging, the blood draining from his face.

"Now what's your problem?" Claire asked.

"It's so.....uh...," Sarge was having a problem getting the words out,' "it's so pink and frilly! I can't sleep here."

"Why not, it won't bite you. It won't infect you with some kind of girly genes. It's a very comfortable bed."

"It's all pink and frilly."

"Oh, go to bed you big lug," Claire said with finality as she pushed her way past Sarge leaving him standing in the doorway.

When Claire reached her own bedroom Bobby was already in bed.

"Sarge all settled in?" he asked Claire.

Claire rolled her eyes, "who knows. Remember that old
television show, Monk, about the detective that obsessed
about nearly everything and had to have the cabin in the
woods sanitized before he would stay there?

"Yes," Bobby said with a small laugh.

"Well, your six foot macho man up there," she said pointing
to the upstairs, "Is acting about the same way because Carol's
room is pink and frilly."

Bobby shook his head.

Claire went on, "How can someone that used to kill people for
a living, and looked death in the face every day when he was
in the Iraq war, be afraid of pink and frilly?"

Bobby laughed a little harder now.

"And you," Claire said turning on Bobby, "Before you fall
asleep, you and I are going to have a little chat."

Bobby immediately covered his head with the brown
comforter covered with pictures of Moose, bear and little log
cabins.

"You can't hide from me," Claire continued, "And we ARE
going to talk."

Bobby brought the covers back down from covering his head
knowing that when the wife isn't happy, nobody's happy, and
if she wanted to have a so-called "little chat", she was not
going to be happy until she did.

"What's up?" Bobby asked to get the ball rolling.

"I have always honored your wishes about not asking what
you did for the government when you went away on
missions," Claire began, "even when people with guns came
to our house. Even when they shot our dog Duke. I knew that
you had your reasons for not wanting me to know but we've
just spent the day at Richard's funeral and all I know is that he

got shot taking a bullet that was meant for you. Then you get arrested because someone shot a Secret Service agent and is trying to frame you for doing it. It's time for you to come clean. I need to know what is going on. You no longer work for the federal government so there are not going to be anymore secrets."

Bobby hesitated a minute then began, "Richard and Senator Snead had a meeting with then President, Obannon, at Camp David. The Colonel, who used to be the President's head on intelligence, called me, even though we both had recently been fired, to tell me that there was intelligence pointing to the fact that the President may not be who he claimed to be. That he, in fact, was one of the many Russian plants from during the cold war."

"The President is a Russian plant?"

"Yes, during the cold war the Russian's planted youths in our country that had been pre-programmed to pursue certain activities at some future time."

Claire rolled her eyes.

"I'm serious Claire," Bobby said, "It sounds like fiction but it's true. Several have been caught hiding old nuclear devices that they have sheltered for many years waiting until they received a pre-arranged signal. The problem now is that the Iranians have found out about the program and they are after the moles as much as we are so they can get their hands on nuclear bombs already here on American soil. Anyway, the Colonel received intel that the birth certificate that Obannon provided was fake and in checking that out he found that Obannon was actually of Russian birth and sent to the U.S. as a youth. Then his most trusted adviser came under the microscope, so the Colonel and the others that had their suspicions wanted some final bit of evidence. That's when the Colonel called to see if I could get it for them."

"How do you go about getting that kind of evidence?"

"I figured I would just ask him," Bobby said, "after

administering some truth serum, that is."

"So you drugged the President?"

"I guess you could say that. Not any different from having him take a lie detector test, except it's more accurate and I didn't wait for his permission."

"What did you do just waltz into Camp David and say 'Mr. President I need you to take a truth serum shot?' "

"Not exactly."

"And what do you mean by not exactly?"

"I knew I needed back up, especially since there were two people, the President and his adviser, so I took Sarge with me and we had to break into Camp David."

"You two snuck into a highly secure area where the President was staying while his entire entourage of Secret Service stood guard and gave the President a shot?" Claire asked incredulously, "What would have happened if you two would have been caught?"

"We would have been arrested and taken to Leavenworth then shot as traitors."

"Oh is that all?"

"We didn't get caught, well almost didn't get caught."

"Almost?!"

"We had Mike the Mechanic and the guys cause a disturbance at the front gate while we snuck in the back door, and we were able to give the shots and ask the questions."

"Really, What did they say?"

"They each actually admitted they were Russian born and professed loyalty to Mother Russia. President Obannon actually said their goal was to continue socializing the United States by making us citizens dependent on the government for everything from jobs, to college tuition, to healthcare and more until we actually became the old Russia in every way."

"You can't be serious!"

"I'm very serious."

"So what happened then?"

"To me and Sarge or to Obannon?"

"Well both."

"Sarge and I had made our call to the Colonel who had the Attorney General, the Vice President, and all the top bigwigs in DC at a meeting waiting to hear the final confirmation. When we passed on what we heard from Obannon's mouth, they immediately made plans for Obannon to need to be hospitalized to quietly get him out of the public realm and swore the Vice President into office."

"Then how did Richard get shot?"

"I woke Richard up in his room and we went to the dining room so Richard could get his precious morning cup of tea. That's what we were doing when the Secret Service agent supposedly wandered in and attempted to shoot me since I wasn't supposed to be there. Richard jumped in front of me and took the bullet for me."

Bobby became very morose.

"That's not your fault," Claire said as she rubbed Bobby's cheek.

"All these years, I've been the one protecting him. That's the way it was supposed to be."

"And you saved his life several times in Vietnam and at least once recently. Maybe he really needed to pay you back and wipe the slate clean."

"I really miss him Claire. He was my best friend."

"Tell me honestly Bobby, were you going to shoot the Secret Service agent that shot Richard?"

"Yes."

"But he was doing a job. The same way that you were doing a job."

"Maybe."

"Maybe?"

"I have this hunch that there is more going on. And now that someone else took out the agent and tried to frame me, I'm convinced that there is more going on that we don't yet know about."

"Go to sleep Bobby. Thank you for talking to me."

Claire awoke the next morning at her usual early hour and made her way to the kitchen to start the coffee brewing. The noise in the living room sidetracked her. There, snoring contentedly on the couch with a knitted throw cover bearing a picture of a moose, was Sarge.

Claire shook her head and padded on to the kitchen her fuzzy pink slippers making very little noise on the hardwood floors. The smell of the coffee brewing and the bacon frying stirred the two men and their arrival at the kitchen table was imminent.

Sarge arrived first since he was a bit closer to the kitchen with Bobby right on his heels.

"Hey Sarge, how'd you sleep?" Bobby asked him as he smacked him on his broad shoulders.

Claire interjected, "you should be asking him WHERE he slept."

Bobby shot Sarge a glance and with a smile on his face asked, "Where'd you sleep Sarge?"

"I curled up on the couch."

"How's come big boy?" Claire asked.

"I didn't want to muss Carol's nice clean room."

Claire shook her head and said, "Pink and frilly won't kill you Sarge."

Sarge's face reddened as he reached for the cup of coffee that Claire had sat in front of him.

The trio was nearly done with breakfast when Bobby's cell phone rang.

Bobby answered it. "This is Bobby."

The deep voice on the other end said, "Carmine says you should come by the restaurant."

"What time do you open?" Bobby asked.

"Don't worry about it. Use the back door."

The caller hung up. Bobby was staring at his cell when Claire asked, "Who was that?"

"Carmine wants to see us."

Sarge jumped in, "you mean he found out a name for us already?"

"When Carmine wants someone people jump," Bobby replied.

"Well let's go," Sarge said jumping up from the kitchen table.

"Try to stay out of trouble," Claire said.

The duo made the short drive up the mountain just outside of Ganister to the restaurant owned by Carmine. They parked Bobby's beat up old red pickup truck in the empty lot and made their way to the back door normally used for deliveries.

"Go on in," Bobby said to Sarge.

"You first," Sarge said, "These guys may think we're burglars and shoot first then ask questions later."

Bobby pushed by Sarge saying, "Don't be a sissy, he's waiting for us."

Carmine's bartender and occasional bodyguard was waiting just inside the door. He was a wide thick man whos face had never smiled and who's vocabulary was extremely limited. In fact at the moment he didn't even speak, just motioned with his head to Bobby that he should go into the next room.

Carmine was sitting in a booth upholstered in red naugahyde with a red and white checked cotton tablecloth staring at the flatscreen television hanging behind the bar, immersed in the morning stock market data flowing across the screen. Without even looking at Bobby and Sarge, Carmine motioned with his empty hand for the two to sit opposite him. The duo no sooner got seated when Carmine slapped his open hand down on the table with enough force to rattle his empty dish and silverware.

"Everytime those politicians in Washington open their mouths the stock market in New York drops like a rock. It's getting' damn hard to earn a buck the legitimate way."

Carmine grabbed the remote and turned off the television, then looked at Bobby and said, "you're not gonna' turn girlscout on me are you?"

"Not exactly sure what you mean by that Carmine," Bobby responded.

"I mean I wanted the head of the guy that shot my paisano Richard. Okay somebody beat me to that, but that just tells me there are a few more people involved in Richard's death."

Carmine gave each Bobby and Sarge a cold stare, "So now, I want them all. If you two are not up to taking a life then I'll just pass this info on to my boys. I know they'll get the job done."

"I'll be honest with you Carmine," Bobby said, "my intention is to see whoever went to all the trouble of framing me either dead or in jail for life, but I have to be positive."

"That's what I mean about being a girlscout. They don't want to hurt anybody, but this mess needs cleaned up. Someone needs to get the message that they messed with the wrong person."

"Carmine, please let me handle this," Bobby implored.

"Since Richard chose to give up his life for yours, you get one chance. After that my boys will take care of it," Carmine said as he looked toward his man who, unbeknownst to the others, had slid behind the bar and was paying attention to every word that came out of Carmine's mouth. The man merely gave Carmine a quick, barely noticeable nod of the head confirming that it would indeed be taken care of.

Carmine then slid a small piece of paper across the table to Bobby's fingers and said, "alright, get outta' here."

Bobby took the paper and as he was getting out of the booth said, "How did you..."

Carmine stopped Bobby instantly by placing his forefinger in front of his lips, then motioning them away with the same hand. As the two were leaving the bar area and entering the backroom Carmine said to their backs, "Remember if you girl scouts need help, just whistle." Carmine's bartender picked up a glass out of the sink and started to dry it with a white towel, a small grin spreading across his large face.

After Bobby and Sarge got in the truck, buckled their seat belts and Bobby put the old truck in gear and headed for the highway, Sarge spoke up, "what's it say?"
Bobby had stolen a peak while he was getting in the truck but it was nothing that rang a bell with him.
"Just a name," Bobby replied.
"Okay," Sarge said getting exasperated, "what's the name?"
"Calvin Barnes."
"Calvin Barnes!" Sarge shouted, "are you putting me on?"
Bobby whipped the truck over to the berm, "you know Calvin Barnes?"
"Well I know A Calvin Barnes," Sarge said, "he was a sniper in my unit."
"A sniper?" Bobby asked.
"Yeah. We were in Iraq together and even did a short stint in Afghanistan, of course, officially we were never in Afghanistan."
"Get to the point, Sarge."
"Well he was good, he just wasn't as good as me."
"Where is he now Sarge?"
"Well, hell, I don't know."
"That doesn't help much Sarge."
"I know he was from the Punxsutawney area."
"Okay, now we're getting somewhere."
"We'll pack our stuff for a couple days, head to Punxsy, and see if we can round this guy up." With that Bobby wheeled the old red pickup back out on the highway and headed to Ganister.

Bobby packed up all the equipment he felt they would

possibly need for a day or two and he and Sarge left the fine log home and headed for the old red pickup.

"We're not taking this to Punxsutawney, are we?" Sarge asked.

"Well, yes, why?"

"Look at it. Will this thing even make it to Punxsy?"

"Don't worry about it. It might not look good but Mike the Mechanic makes sure it runs like a top."

"We could stop and pick up my truck and use it," Sarge volunteered.

"That thing that stands about ten feet up off the highway. The big bright shiny chrome wheels, the fancy paint job? Sure we'd be very inconspicuous in that thing," Bobby said, "Get in the truck Sarge, we're going to Punxsy."

"Well, okay, since you put it that way."

Chapter 8

The small winding road that ran between Altoona and Ganister was a pleasure to drive. The road ran down the valley, over a few small hills and all the time both sides of the highway surrounded you with lush green trees and when you got closer to Ganister, the Juniata River ran alongside the highway. What a change from the traffic and congestion of Washington, DC, Nanita thought. Her mind went to poor deceased Richard and how this area must have been such a wonderful area to grow up in. The beauty of the surrounding hills, the feeling of security you get having those hills protect you, and the thrill of actually driving the winding roads. It was no wonder that Richard spent so much time on the race track and no wonder that he had a natural ability to race when he spent so much time driving these roads. Nanita looked in the rearview mirror to check on Richie in the rear of the car safely belted into the child seat. As usual, he was fast asleep. Something about a moving car does that to children.

According to the GPS Nanita was entering Ganister on Canal Street. Richard had told Nanita once that Canal Street was named that because in the old days there were actually canal boats that were pulled up and down the river by teams of horses. A person could actually go all the way from Williamsburg to Holidaysburg on a canal boat. Then the railroads came and the canal boats disappeared.

The GPS beeped again, the manly voice telling Nanita to bear to the left in 30 feet to get onto West First Street. Nanita made the small turn onto West First Street. This street was tree lined and both sides were wall to wall with two story square homes probably built in the late 1800's, some with a small amount of Victorian trim, but otherwise basic homes, all neatly painted and lined up one after the other. The GPS beeped again and Nanita was instructed to turn right onto Plum Street at the next intersection. She did as the little box on the dash told her. As she neared the end of Plum Street she was instructed by the manly voice on the dash to turn left onto Black Street at the next stop sign. Black Street may have been misnamed, surely it was just an alley that for some reason got promoted to Street status. At the end of Black Street the GPS chirped again and Nanita pulled into the parking area of a relatively new small ranch home with cheerful light yellow siding and blue shutters that gave a very warm welcoming look.

Nanita parked the car, got out and opened the back door unbuckling Richie from his child seat while he slowly opened his eyes and stared at his mother while a smile spread across his face. The two walked to the door in the breezeway and rang the bell.

Auntie M answered the door, "well, look who's here, Shorty." Mrs. St.Clair came to the door and said, "Nanita, please come in."

"You said to stop by and since we'll be leaving to go back home in just a day or two, I thought I should come today instead of waiting."

"I'm so glad you did," Mrs. St.Clair said, then turning to
Richie she continued, "And how are you sweetie?"
Richie grabbed his mother's leg and held tight.
"Are you going to be shy?" Shorty asked Richie, then to
Nanita said, "Please come in, sit with us. Would you like a
cup of coffee?"
"No thank you," Nanita replied.
Auntie M spoke up, "I still can't get over how much Richie
looks like Richard did when he was that age."
"That's one of the reasons I wanted to see you before I had to
leave Mrs. St.Clair."
"Nanita, please call me Shorty like all my friends do."
"How are you doing Mrs.....Shorty?" Nanita asked.
"I guess I'll take it one day at a time," she said, "it's just so
hard to have a child predecease you. It should have been this
old body that went before Richard."
"Is there anything I can do for you?"
"No dear, I'll be fine. It will just take some time. Let's not talk
about that. Let's talk about you and Richard. How did you
two meet?" Shorty asked while watching Richie sit patiently
in his mother's lap.
"I actually knew Richard for quite a few years. In fact when he
was married to Pamela. The two of them stayed at the resort
in Aruba where I worked."
"Oh," Auntie M chimed in, "you worked in Aruba. Are you
from Aruba?"
"Not originally. I was born in the Phillipines but my parents
moved to Aruba when I was young."
"So you knew Pamela also?" Mrs. St.Clair asked.
"Yes, she was a lovely lady. She and Richard were inseperable
in Aruba. I used to daydream how wonderful it must be to
have a man pay that much attention to you. Then after Pamela
died Richard would come to Aruba by himself and we would
spend long hours talking."

Auntie M chimed in again while nodding towards Richie, "you must have done more than talk."

Nanita blushed, "No, I can assure you Mrs. St.Clair that Richard was always a gentleman. We never dated or anything in Aruba. It was just recently that I came to the states to see Richard."

Auntie M got up off the sofa and went into the dining room coming back holding a picture of Richard when he was a child and showing it to Nanita, "but Richie looks identical to Richard."

"I would like to explain that........

Nanita was interrupted by a knock on the door. Auntie M went to answer the door.

"Claire, how are you doing?" Auntie M exclaimed when she opened the door, "Please come in, Shorty will be glad to see you."

Claire Morrow came in and immediately went to Shorty and hugged her, "how are you doing Shorty?"

"I'll be alright. How is Bobby doing?"

"Well you know Bobby. He and Richard were the best of friends but Mr. Macho wouldn't dare show any emotions."

"Why didn't he come with you?"

"Bobby is not going to rest until this whole mess of who shot Richard is cleared up. I'm sorry to bring that up, Shorty."

"No I understand dear. And I think it is very considerate of Bobby, but according to the news the Secret Service agent that got shot outside the church was the man who shot Richard."

"Yes, "Claire said, "According to Bobby he was definitely the man."

"Then what is Bobby chasing?"

"Are you sure you want to talk about this?"

Shorty reached over and patted Claire on her hands, "yes dear, I care about Bobby as though he were my son also. I want to know that he will be safe."

"Well Bobby is convinced that since they tried to frame him

for shooting the Secret Service agent that someone else is behind the entire affair, and he is not going to stop until he has the entire thing solved."

"I'm a little embarrassed to say it," Mrs. St.Clair said, "but I was almost hoping that Bobby had shot that son-of-a..."

"Believe me Shorty, Bobby wanted to. And would have, but he did not want anything to happen at Richard's service. I have no doubt he was just waiting for the right time, then he was going to go after him. At least this way Bobby won't end up in jail for shooting that slimeball."

Claire turned to Nanita, "it's nice to see you again Nanita. And how is little Richie doing?"

"He's fine. I think he does want to get back to his home and play in his familiar surroundings, but other than that he's good."

"We were just talking," Auntie M said, "about how much little Richie looks like Richard when he was that age."

"He sure is a little cutie," Claire said as she reached over and squeezed Richie by the cheeks making him giggle.

"So where is Bobby off to?" Nanita asked Claire.

"Punsutawney."

"Where the famous groundhog lives?" Nanita asked.

"Yes, apparently there is another sort of rodent there that Bobby and Sarge think may know what's going on."

"I do hope they will be careful," Nanita said.

"Don't worry, those two don't know I know but they took an arsenal with them. I'm sure they will be fine."

Chapter 9

The two hour drive up Route 36 would normally have been a very pleasant drive as the scenery in this part of Pennsylvania is spectacular. And in just a few weeks the trees would begin changing their leaves to the fascinating fall colors and be a photographers dream. But this day Bobby and Sarge had only one thought on their minds. That of getting answers that would get them just a little closer to solving the mystery of why Bobby was framed and what was really going on.

As the duo entered the little town that everyone thinks they saw in the movie, "Groundhog Day", but was really a different city that they used in the movie, Bobby began grilling Sarge.

"So did Calvin give you any hint as to where he might be living?"

"No," Sarge said, exasperated, "I told you we weren't close. I just knew that he was from Punxsy."

"But why do you know that?"

"Well, " Sarge said, "because he mentioned it."

"And what else did he mention when he mentioned that?"

"Nothing,"

"Think Sarge, he didn't just walk up to you and say, hey Sarge I'm from Punxsy."

"Let's see," Sarge thought, "we were in camp one night out in the hills outside of Tehran. We were sitting around, probably half a dozen of us, and this guy next to Calvin, says to him, hey ridgerunner where you off to tomorrow? So I asks him why the guy called him ridgerunner and he tells me it's because he's from the hills of Pennsylvania. So I said, oh yeah, whereabouts? And he tells me Punxsy, so I tell him I'm from Ganister."

"Then what?"

"Then he said he knew where Ganister was and did I live anywhere near the paper mill 'cause he used to haul chips there from a sawmill to get made into paper. So I tell him that all the bigger Ganister is, everyone lives near the papermill. Then he says about how bad the smell is when you drive into town…'

Bobby interrupted, "Hey Sarge, I want to know about Punxsy not Ganister."

"Oh yeah, so I asked him if he had been to see the groundhog."

Bobby rolled his eyes, "get to the point Sarge."

"I am. That's when he said he didn't go into town much unless he had to, that he lived along the creek outside of town."

"So we know he lived along Stump Creek and not in town, and we know he worked at some point driving truck for a sawmill or a company that trucked from a sawmill." Bobby thought for a moment then said, "Let's take Route 119 north of Punxsy and see what we find. Did Calvin drink beer?"

"Yeah, I remember him saying he couldn't wait to get back to the states to have a good cold brew."

Bobby pulled up to the signal light on Route 36 at the intersection of Route 119, just over the bridge that crossed Stump Creek and put on his right turn signal. When the light changed and traffic began flowing they started up Route 119. A mile or two outside of town Bobby saw a bar on the left side of the road. A dark brown one story building with the word bar in red neon lighting and a small sign hanging from a steel pipe extended from the wall that had a picture of a fish on it and the words, 'Mahoney's Bar'. Bobby looked over at Sarge and said, "looks a good place to stop."

Bobby wheeled into the parking lot and parked in line with the other two pickup trucks and one SUV that were already there.

"You buying buddy?"

"Of course, Sarge. Don't I always?"

"I bought one day last week!"

"Just kidding Sarge, come on, let's go in and get a bite to eat." The dim interior was quite an adjustment from the brightness of day on the outside but their eyes adjusted quickly. The interior was all wood, which made Bobby feel quite at home, and had glass jars hanging on cords as lights over the bar. There were two other patrons seated at the bar and a husky bartender behind the bar.

"Afternoon," the bartender said as they entered.

Bobby and Sarge pulled up two stools at the bar and the bartender mozied over, "What can I get you fellas?"

Sarge piped in and asked, "Do you know Calvin Barnes? We served together in Iraq and I wanted to look him up."

"No offense but the witty conversation and answers to questions only get served after the beer has been."

Bobby jumped in, "we'll take two drafts. Do you have any burgers or anything?"

"I make the best burger this side of Pittsburgh."

"Sarge are you hungry?" Bobby asked.

"Hell yes, I want a burger. Come with fries?"

"Sure, how you want the burgers done?"

"Rare," they both said at once.

"That's good," the bartender said, "That's how we cook them here."

"Can I have onions on mine?" Sarge asked.

"This is a bar not Wendy's, they come the way they come, but yes it comes with onions. You don't like something that's on it, pull it off."

The bartender left and went into the back kitchen to start cooking. Before disappearing he hollered, "Anybody want a drink before I go back here?"

No one answered.

Bobby looked at Sarge and said, "I like this guy. He's just like Kurt Klaar. Tells it the way it is."

"Yeah, but I thought we were here to find out if he knows where Calvin lives?" Sarge asked.

"Patience, Sarge. Drink your beer."

The bartender came back a bit later and placed two big plates in front of Bobby and Sarge.

"Here," he said, "enjoy!"

Bobby bit into his while Sarge was lifting the top of the bun on his to see what all was under it.

"Great burger," Bobby said to the bartender.

"Told you it was," he responded.

"You the owner?" Bobby asked.

The bartender held out his beefy hand to Bobby and they shook hands.

"Ed Mahoney," he says, "you from around here?"

"Ganister, actually," Bobby said, "Sarge here was in the Iraq War with Calvin Barnes and we thought we would look him up."

"I could tell they were in the war together," Mahoney said, "they both dress alike."

Bobby looked at Sarge who was stuffing his mouth with French fries covered in ketchup and said, "He seems to like the look of the cammos."

"So's Calvin," Mahoney said, "I don't think I've seen him wear anything else since he came back."

Bobby glanced around the bar then said to Mahoney, "looks like a nice place you have here."

Mahoney grunted, "Used to be, till that damned half-wit President of ours got in office. Then the economy went to pot and I went with it. Hell I could probably make more money these days staying at home and searching under my sofa pillows for loose change."

Bobby smiled at the comment then asked, "so business could be better?"

"Better," Mahoney said, "It sure as hell can't get any worse." Mahoney motioned with his head towards the other patrons, "these guys, whom I think highly of, will nurse a couple beers all afternoon, which won't make me any money. Thank goodness you two came along. Can I get you another beer?"

"Sure," Sarge interjected with his mouth full.

When Mahoney came back with the tall frosty beers Bobby asked, "So would you be able to tell us how to find Calvin?"

"Probably."

"Would it help if we left a really big tip?" Bobby asked.

"Couldn't hurt. This economy really sucks. And another thing. That clown of a President of ours gets reelected to a second term then suddenly he has some horrible medical problem and can't continue as President. What the hell's that all about? He was just on the television last week pumping sunshine up our butts and a couple days later the big news is out that he has to step down. I'm sorry but I don't buy that crap. Something somewhere is all wrong. What do you think?"

"I think you may be on to something," Bobby said.

Sarge had stopped eating and was paying close attention to the conversation.

"My guess is he pissed off too many people," Mahoney said, "And they got rid of him. But he already ruined the economy and my business. I think he was a socialist plant or something."

From down at the other end of the bar came, "Oh great, now you guys got Mahoney on his soap box. Turn up the TV Ed so we don't have to listen to you and your conspiracy theories for the umpteenth time."

Bobby smiled. Mahoney jerked his thumb towards the man at the end of the bar and said in a voice loud enough for the man to hear, "must be a weenie liberal."

The voice spoke up again, "No, Ed. It's just that I can recite your speech in my sleep."

Everyone in the bar snickered.

"Yeah, well, you'll see. Wait till they write the history books on that guy." Then an idea struck Mahoney and he looked Bobby in the eye, "You're from Ganister?"

"Yes," Bobby said.

"Were you at the big funeral? Did you know Senator St.Clair?"

Sarge spoke up, "He and Richard were best friends."

Bobby said, "Everyone in Ganister was at the funeral."

"He was a good man, Senator St.Clair," Mahoney said, "he was one of the few up in that cesspool called Washington that was actually on our side. Best Senator we've had since Heinz out of Pittsburgh. He died real young too. Humphh. Were you there when that Secret Service agent got popped? Did you see it happen?'

"We were there," Bobby said, "saw it after the fact."

"Rumor is he was the one that shot Senator St.Clair and that someone from Ganister, maybe that mafia dude, decided to settle the score. The paper here called it Ganister Style Justice, no long dragged out court case. No putting somebody up in the hotels they call prison and feeding them three squares a day plus educating them so they become lawyers and file their own appeal to get out of jail. Since you're from Ganister what do you think?"

"I like the way you think, but, it wasn't anyone from Ganister."

"Hell for all I know, it could have been you," Mahoney said pointing to Bobby, "If you and the Senator were best of friends why wouldn't you put that dog down."

Bobby motioned with his finger for Mahoney to come closer then whispered in his ear, "Cause I didn't get the opportunity!"

Mahoney stepped back and assessed Bobby. Bobby stared back with a serious look on his face. Mahoney being a person well versed in reading people said to Bobby, "The drinks are on me."

"Well thank you but that's not necessary," Bobby said, "You're not in business to give away the store."

"I like you," Mahoney said, "oh before I forget. Barnes house, well it's not a house anymore. Since he got back from the war and with this crappy economy he hasn't been able to find work. All the sawmills are shut down, you know. His wife is trying to support them working at the Burger King in town there. Anyway they live in a mobile home just up the road. Go about a mile then turn left onto McCracken Road. It's the first mobilehome on the left. You can't miss it."

"Thank you for the info," Bobby said, "and the burger was great. I'm going to bring my wife up here soon for lunch."

"When you see Calvin, you tell him to stop by for a free beer. I appreciate what our military boys have done for us."

"I'll be sure to tell him. Thank you."

It only took Bobby and Sarge a few minutes to end up in front of the mobilehome that Mahoney had directed them to. The grass needed mowed about a month ago, and parked in front was a beat up old pickup truck that actually made Bobby's truck look good in comparison and a small black Chevy Cavalier that hadn't seen the inside of a car wash in a long time. Bobby and Sarge both got out of the truck and meandered to the small three step wooden porch, carefully ascending while checking windows and their periphery for any signs of movement. Sarge knocked on the door. No response so Sarge knocked again louder this time while saying, "Calvin, you in there?"

The door swung open. There stood Calvin Barnes. Drunk as a skunk, barely able to stand without holding on to the doorknob. His glazed over eyes took in Sarge and after a few beats he actually recognized the face.

"Sarge, you old son-of-a-gun," Calvin said slurring the words.

"We need to talk to you, buddy," Sarge said, "Can we come in?"

"We?" Calvin said attempting to widen his eyes, "Who's with you?"

"Bobby Morrow, a good friend of mine."

Calvin was beginning to sober quickly as he repeated Sarge, "Bobby Morrow. Well come in. I was just thinking about you guys."

The trio went inside and Bobby said, "Look Calvin we need to ask you some serious questions."

"I'll just bet you do," Calvin replied.

"We have proof that you were in Ganister yesterday and a few times before that," Bobby said.

"Ganister?"

"Yes, Ganister where the Secret Service agent was shot with my rifle. Remember that Calvin?"

"I heard something about that on the news."

"How did you get into my house to steal my rifle? And who told you about me?"

Calvin plopped onto the worn out dirty sofa, putted his hands to his face and started to cry.

"The damn calls."

"What calls Calvin?" Bobby asked.

I got a call, "said to go to your address, even said when you wouldn't be there. Said to steal your rifle and where to set up a sniper's nest and which of those Secret Service dudes to shoot."

"But why the hell would you do that?" Sarge asked.

"'Cause they got my wife and daughter, man!"

"They, who?" Bobby asked.

"Hell I don't know. I just get calls."

"When did you get the last call?" Bobby asked.

"Last night when you two got out of jail."

Bobby and Sarge looked at each other.

"What did they say?" Sarge asked.

"Said I failed. I was supposed to kill that dude but also you two were to rot in jail for the murder. And I failed 'cause you two are already out of jail. Now they're gonna' kill my wife and daughter."

"Do you have any idea where they have your wife and daughter, or who is calling?"

"The only thing they said was that I better find you two and put you in the ground fast or my wife and daughter are going to six percent."

Calvin broke through his drunken stupor a bit more, "They must watch me. They know everything." Calvin paused, "Excuse me a minute guys. I need to go to the bathroom." Sarge watched Calvin walk down the hall, past the bathroom and gave Bobby a look of concern. Bobby moved a couple paces away from Sarge, as much as the skinny old mobilehome and the piles of garbage would allow and the two waited. Calvin came back into the living room holding a big old forty-five pistol. Now that Bobby and Sarge were no longer standing next to each other he had to wave the pistol back and forth between them.

"Calvin," Bobby said, "even if you shoot us you won't get your family back. Why not let us help you."

"You think you can get my family back?"

"Calvin, if anyone can do that," Sarge said, "it's Bobby. He used to be an undercover federal agent. He has found all sorts of people that didn't want to be found."

Calvin broke down sobbing again, "I need my wife and daughter back. I would never have done such an awful thing if they hadn't taken them."

"We know," Sarge said as he moved closer to Calvin and wrenched the pistol from his hand.

Bobby immediately got on his cell phone, "Kurt, he said, listen to me I don't have much time, wait...." Looking at Sarge he said, "call your Dad, have him meet Kurt and get up here" then back to Kurt, "Kurt, Sarge and I have a problem, I need you to come up here to Mahoney's Bar with Farmer and also to think of the answer to this riddle, 'what does down to six percent mean?......'"

At the same time Sarge was talking to his dad, Farmer Terry, "dad, Bobby and I need some help. Call Kurt and get up here, they got Calvin's wife and daughter and we have to get them back before they....."

The door slammed open. Four men in black SWAT team

uniforms ran into the room knocking the three men to the floor and grabbing up the cell phones.

"What the hell is going on?" Calvin asked.

"Shut up dirtbag and answer your phone."

Calvin's phone began to vibrate from an incoming call. Calvin raised and lowered his eyebrows trying to focus on the call. They said, "Thanks for Bobby and Sarge. We'll handle it from here."

"What did they say?" Bobby asked him frantically.

"They've been watching."

"Oh shit," Sarge said, "did we just step into a big pile of it." The door flew open. "Shut up!" the uniformed man holding the rifle pointed at him said. Then to accentuate his point he rapidly swung the butt of the rifle around smashing Sarge on the right side of his face and knocking him back to the floor. Bobby jumped off the floor and headed for the attacker only to be smacked in the back of the head by the person holding him at gunpoint.

Chapter 10

Claire was listening to Nanita when her phone rang. She looked at the screen to see who was calling to decide if she would answer or ignore it. It was Kurt Klaar. Odd, she thought, he never calls me.

"Kurt," she answered, "how are you doing?"

"Where's Bobby?"

"He and Sarge are in Punxsutawney, why?"

"I just had a call from him but it got cut off. Sounded like there was a scuffle and I didn't know where he was."

"Did he say anything to you?" Claire asked. The other ladies in the room were now riveted to Claire's conversation.

"He mentioned some six percent bullshit and a Mahoney's Bar but hell I didn't know where Mahoney's Bar was. Oh and he said to meet up with Farmer Terry. There must be something going down. Thanks for the help. I gotta' go and get hold of Farmer." He hung up. Claire stared at her phone for a moment, then got peppered by the same question from all the ladies in the room, "what's wrong?"

"Something must be happening with Bobby and Sarge. I'm sorry ladies, I'm going to have to go," Claire said as she stood and put her cell phone back in her purse.

"Is this about Richard?" Nanita asked.

"Probably about the Secret Service agent that got shot, yes, so ultimately about Richard."

"Then if you're going, I'm going with you," Nanita said as she stood.

"But the baby," Claire said.

Nanita looked at Shorty and Auntie M. Auntie M spoke first, "we'd love to look after him for a while. You go make sure those guys are okay."

The two women rushed from the room out to Claire's waiting bright red Challenger.

Farmer Terry answered his cell phone, "Hello."

"Farmer, it's Kurt."

"Figured you'd be calling. What's up?"

"Don't know much only a riddle and the name of a bar in Punxsy."

"Sarge told me they needed to save some Calvin guy's family."

"Well let's meet at Mike the Mechanic's to get some fast wheels and get up to that bar and get some more information."

"See you in a couple."

Kurt Klaar was one of Bobby's oldest and dearest friends, and in fact almost a second father to him. Kurt was a crude old sawyer who did not have much of a school education but was quite versed in the laws of common sense that he received from the school-of-hard-knocks. Kurt's outspoken demeanor put some people off but mostly people had tremendous respect for the man.

Terry Lee was Sarge's father and most people knew him by either just Farmer or Farmer Terry as he had a small gentleman's farm outside of Ganister behind the old limestone quarry that everyone from this area was very familiar with and referred to it as the Blue Hole. It earned its name from the forty feet deep brilliant blue water held within the straight up and down limestone walls of the former quarry.

Terry was the first to get to Mike the Mechanic's as he was was much closer than Kurt who lived in the Osterburg area. Mike and Terry chatted for a while then Kurt pulled in quickly and jumped from his truck.

"Did you tell him we need to borrow his wheels?" Kurt said as he approached the other two men.

"Didn't get around to it yet," Farmer said.

"What's up Kurt?"

"Bobby and Sarge need us in Punxsutawney. We need some fast wheels so we can get the hell up there quick."

Mike the Mechanic was the local mechanic but not for everyone. Mike was specialized. He worked on Corvettes, hot rods, Ferraris, and the vehicles of certain friends including the former Richard St.Clair and Bobby Morrow. Kurt's news had Mike sprinting off into his garage where he threw the cover off mean-looking black Dodge Ram club cab and started the engine. He pulled the truck out of the garage, wound down the window and said to Kurt and Farmer, "come on. I'm driving."

Kurt and Sarge both grabbed duffels from their vehicles, threw them in the bed of Mike's Ram, and jumped in the cab. Before their seat belts were buckled, Mike had hit the accelerator and the tires were howling as he laid down two big black strips of rubber in his driveway heading off to Punxsutawney.

"Okay," Mike said, "where am I going?"

"A bar called Mahoney's?"

"Any idea where in Punxsy this bar is?"

"Hell no," Farmer answered, "don't you know?"

"No."

"Then why are we letting you drive?" Kurt asked.

"Cause it's my truck and I can get us there faster than anybody."

"Good point," Kurt replied.

"You got a GPS thing?" Farmer asked.

"Oh yeah, in the glove compartment. Get that baby fired up maybe it knows where Mahoney' Bar is. If not we'll stop when we get close to Punxsy, someone will know where it is."

The GPS wasn't much help. Obviously the owner of Mahoney's Bar wasn't one of the new generation that felt compelled to put everything out on the web for the world to see. Mike made quick time up Route 36 passing every car that had the audacity to be in front of him. Near the city limits of Punxsutawney there was a 7-11 store. Mike wheeled into the parking lot.

"Run in there and find out about Mahoney's" Mike said to no one in particular.

Kurt opened the door and strode as fast as he could into the store asking the man behind the counter, "can you tell me where Mahoney's Bar is?"

"Aah, Mayonzee's," the man said shaking his head up and down, "Da be nort along da riber."

"Thanks," Kurt said rushing back out of the store.

"Did you find out?" Mike said as he gunned the truck and flashed back out on the highway.

"Why is it that not one convenience store in this country is owned by an American?" Kurt asked.

"Oh get off your soap box," Mike said, "Foreigners own all the convenience stores, gas stations and hotels. Get used to it. But did you find out where Mahoneys is?"

"I don't know about Mahoney's but I now know where Moyonzee's is."

Mike rolled his eyes.

"Go north."

"Mike pulled up to the same signal light at the intersection of Routes 36 and 119 that Bobby and Sarge had been at just hours before. And like Bobby and Sarge, Mike turned right and headed north although he did it a bit faster than Bobby had. In just a few minutes they were leaving Punxsy and traveling along the river. Farmer was the first to spot it, "there it is on the left."

Mike whipped the Ram to the left and skidded to a stop in the gravel parking lot. The three men piled out of the truck and headed for the door.

They entered squinting in the lower light and were greeted by the proprietor.

"Afternoon, gentlemen," Mahoney said, "boy this must be my lucky day."

Mike took the lead and strode to the bar, "are you Mahoney?"

"Yeah," Mahoney said, "and who might you be?"

"We had an urgent call from our friends and they may be in trouble. All we know is that Calvin's family's lives are at stake and Calvin and our friends may be also."

"You must be friends of that Morrow guy. Nice guy. I liked him."

"Then you won't mind helping us out?" Kurt asked.

"Do what I can. He left me a nice tip. First, you boys need something to drink?"

"Hell yes," Farmer said, "just whatever's on tap. What about you two?"

"Sure," they both said in unison.

While they were waiting for the beers, Kurt asked, "are there any dry kilns around here?"

"Sure," Mahoney said looking over his shoulder while he drew the drafts, "there's a huge operation at the edge of town then there's a smaller one just west on Route 36. 'Course that one's shut down 'cause of this shitty economy that our illustrious leader has got us into."

"Can you give us directions to that closed place and also directions to this Calvin's place."

"Sure," Mahoney said, "I gave your friends directions earlier to Calvin's."

Chapter 11

The men in black behaved like an elite group of well trained military men. After gathering up Sarge and Bobby's cell phones they cuffed their hands behind their backs with heavy duty plastic pull ties. Then they stood each of the two men up, frisked them, and placed black blindfolds over their eyes. Bobby and Sarge were then led out of the mobilehome to waiting SUV's. If they hadn't had blindfolds on they would have noticed the SUV's certainly looked like government issue. Attempting to walk down the steps, Bobby stumbled. One of the men smacked him in the back of his head with the butt of his gun. Bobby swore. Eventually they were placed in the waiting vehicles and quickly driven away. Bobby attempted to keep track of the approximate length of the drive; the order of left and right turns; which direction he could feel the sun on the side of his face, and bumps in the road in a vain attempt to learn where they were being taken. When they reached their destination the men roughly drug Bobby and Sarge out of the vehicle. Bobby stumbled again.

And again one of his kidnappers smacked him in the back of the head with the butt of a gun. When Bobby got to his feet he said to whoever the culprit was, "hit me again and I'll kill you."

The man began laughing and Bobby could tell from the sound of his voice that as he was laughing he turned his back to Bobby to address his companions, "Whoa, the big man is going to...."

Bobby used all his strength to jump straight up in the air tucking his legs and feet under his chin and with dazzling speed bring his cuffed arms from behind his back, under his feet and in front of him. As his legs unfolded and he assumed a standing position again, his arms continued on the same arc they were travelling and with his outstretched thumbs he peeled the blindfold from his face., his hands continuing in the same fluid motion over the head of the cocky military man while he spoke to his companions. As Bobby's cuffed hands reached the man's throat, Bobby yanked back and up, lifting the man completely off the ground where he hung gasping for his last breath. The other military men were dumbfounded for a few precious seconds then they all charged Bobby. The damage was done. As they knocked Bobby to the ground and began pummeling him with their fists and butts of guns, Bobby kept hold of the man he made the promise to. The man breathed his last breath. Bobby let go and attempted to protect himself. While Sarge and Calvin could hear the ruckus, well Sarge could anyway. Calvin was still trying to break through his drunken stupor. Sarge charged with his head down toward the center of all the noise and fell on the pile of men. Eventually the men with complete access to their hands and weapons managed to subdue Bobby and Sarge. The odds had been improved though.

Kurt, Terry, and Mike rushed back out of the bar to Mike's truck. Mike spun gravel and headed for the vacated lumber yard that Mahoney had given him directions to.

"Why aren't we going to that Calvin guy's house to check on whether or not Bobby and Sarge are there? Terry asked.

"Cause if they were there, they would have taken this Calvin fellow and moved on. There is something going on at the lumberyard which is why Bobby asked me about the clue – down to six percent."

"What do you think the clue means Kurt?" Mike asked.

"I been in the lumber business all my life and that phrase has always referred to kiln drying lumber. Wood has a lot of moisture in it. After all, trees are sucking water out of the ground through their roots and out of the atmosphere through their leaves. But after lumber is cut it will warp and not be very good for building or furniture making until it is dried down to the level where only six per cent moisture is left in the wood."

"And from what little Sarge told me," Terry said to the group, "someone has Calvin's family and I'm guessing Bobby and Sarge would want to be getting Calvin's family back."

"Who is this Calvin," Mike asked.

"He's a sniper that was in Iraq with Sarge," Terry said.

"Maybe he's the sniper that took out the Secret Service agent," Mike said.

"Yeah," Kurt said, "and maybe he was coerced. Maybe someone else has his family."

"If that's the case," Terry said, "We need to be careful, these are obviously not your average Punxsutawnians."

"That's why I brought enough guns to supply an army," Kurt said as he looked at the duffel bag sitting in the bed of the truck."

"Got something in there that I can use?" Mike asked Kurt.

"Sure," Kurt replied, "you want a nice little Sig Sauer pistol, a sawed off shot gun, or an AK47?"

"You got all that stuff in there?" Mike asked.

"And more, pal. I learned a long time ago when Bobby asks you to help him, you better be loaded for bear, cause he has this gift for pissing people off and getting his ass into real sticky situations."

"Sounds like our buddy Bobby," Mike said.

"There, up ahead," Farmer Terry shouted, "there's the sign that Mahoney said to look for."

The sign down the road had just come into view and it said - MOE'S CONVENIENCE STORE – 1 mile ahead –If you need it, Moe's got it.

"Turn right," Terry said, "just after the sign on the small paved road."

"I know that," Mike said, "are you being a backseat driver?"

"Just don't want you to miss it. I've ridden with you before, remember? Like that time at Camp David when we had to provide a diversion for Bobby at the gate. And what I remember is that you're nuts and you can get carried away."

Mike smiled, "please don't remind me. We barely got out of there alive and I spent the next two weeks patching bullet holes on this baby."

"That's what started this whole mess. That's when Richard got shot," Terry said, "Makes me wish we would have never gone on that trip."

"Just be glad that Sarge didn't get shot instead of Richard," Mike said.

Then he whipped the Ram onto the paved road without slowing down. The tires howled and Terry and Kurt sloshed around inside the truck like they were on a roller coaster.

"Don't miss the next turn," Terry said, "Mahoney said it comes up on you quick, just after the large oak tree turn right again then you'll go down a hill and we should be there."

"How close do you think we should drive?" Kurt asked, "We may want to walk the last part so the whole world doesn't know we're coming."

With that Mike pulled the Ram off the side of the road and stopped the engine.

"How should we handle this Kurt? You're the best hunter in the group."

"Let's stay about ten to fifteen feet apart and stick to the sides of the road near the trees. We'll just slowly and quietly work our way up to the building. If we don't get shot before we get there, we'll find a way inside. It sure looks from here like no one is there, but you never know."

The three men got quietly out the truck, none of them speaking as they knew what they were going to do. They each stocked up on guns and ammo and when they were ready each nodded in turn to Kurt who immediately took the lead and set off like an Indian in the forest carefully watching each step he made so that he would not be heard.

At the edge of the wooded section they stopped in a group before crossing the open area to the building. Each scanned the building ahead of them paying particular attention to the roof and anywhere else that would make a good place to hide and shoot from. Each confident, they again nodded to Kurt who pointed at each man in turn and pointed out a direction to each without speaking. They took off at a quick but quiet run to the building. No shots were fired. When they reached the side of the building they made their way to Kurt's position which was next to an entry door. Kurt fingered the lock hanging from the door and looked to Mike with inquiring eyes.

Mike nodded his head affirmatively, leaning his rifle carefully against the side of the building, he pulled a small pair of bolt cutters from his pocket. He smiled at the other two then with a bit of strain cut the lock off the door.

Kurt put this forefinger to his lips reminding each man to be quiet then he slowly opened the door while Mike and Terry aimed their rifles into the spreading crack. As soon as the door was open wide enough Mike charged through with Terry right on his heels.

Chapter 12

The bright red Dodge Challenger was breaking every speed limit on Route 36 as it roared up the highway with Claire at the wheel passing every other car in sight. Unlike Bobby who preferred his old beat up pickup truck, Claire preferred the modern version of the old muscle cars. Plus she had the ability to drive it to the breaking point. More than once Claire pulled out to pass someone that was holding her up, with a large log truck heading directly for them, but with her faith in the horsepower under the hood and the horsepower itself straining to the limit she was able to safely tuck back into her lane without becoming a hood ornament on an eighteen wheeler that had no intention of slowing down. Nanita spent most of the trip with eyes as big as saucers and a viselike grip on the armrest like a person taking their first airplane flight. Claire made good time but still had not been able to catch up to Kurt and Terry who she figured would contact Mike to get them there quickly. A few minutes after Mike, Terry, and Kurt left Mahoney's the bright red Challenger slid into the gravel parking lot. Nanita jumped from the car wanting to get down and kiss the earth but not having the energy left to do it. Claire strolled to the door of the Bar, whipped it open and made her grand entrance. Mahoney wasted no time in spreading a huge smile across his face before saying, "well, damn, things are finally looking up."

Claire turned on her thousand watt smile that will melt any man and casually strutted to the bar where Mahoney was standing pretending he was wiping invisible beer from the top of the bar.

"You must be Mr. Mahoney?" Claire asked.

"Yes, I am you pretty little thing," Mahoney replied still smiling, "what can I get you sweetheart?"

"A beer for starters," Claire said, then looked towards Nanita, "what are you drinking Nanita?"

"Something strong," she replied with a look of terror still on her face, "Real strong. How about a shot of Tequila?"

Mahoney was beaming. Not only did he now find himself in the company of two beautiful women but he was ringing the cash register more today than he had in a long time. Maybe the new President made some changes, he thought to himself. Mahoney set the drinks in front of the women and leaned against the bar making no attempt to move away.

From the other end of the bar one of Mahoney's old customers began asking loudly, "Ed, where's my beer?"

"You've had enough Jerry, go home," Mahoney said without taking his eyes off the two women.

"So, Mr. Mahoney," Claire said.

"Please just call me Ed."

"Ed," Claire said demurely, "Have you seen two big guys here earlier? One was wearing jeans and a flannel shirt…"

"The other one was dressed in cammos," Mahoney finished her sentence.

"Yes, that's them," Claire said.

"Bobby something and Sarge," Mahoney continued, the smile fading from his face realizing that he now had zero chance of improving his love life, "yes they were here. Then a bunch of other guys were here looking for them. One of them had on a bright red Ferrari shirt with the name of some garage embroidered on it."

"That would be Mike," Claire replied.

"So do you have any idea where they all are?"

Nanita had quickly finished her shot of Tequila and was now tapping her glass on the bar to get another. Mahoney quickly obliged her and set another shot in front of her which disappeared as soon as his fingers left the glass. The color began reappearing on Nanita's cheeks.

"I feel much better now," Nanita said to no one in particular. Claire and Mahoney both looked at her at the same time.

"What?" Nanita asked the two smiling faces.

Claire turned back to Mahoney and asked, "Did they say where they were heading?"

"Well I gave them both directions to two different places."

"And where would those places be?"

"First I gave them directions to Calvin's house."

"Is that far?"

"No, but I doubt if they are still there."

"Because they also asked directions for a lumberyard that kiln dries wood. So I figure they will grab Calvin then head for the lumberyard."

"And what makes you so sure of that?" Claire asked.

"I'm a professional bartender, lady, I've been reading peoples body language since you were knee high to a grasshopper."

"Then will you give us directions to the lumberyard?"

"I can, but I'd rather show you the way."

Claire looked around the bar that only had three other patrons and said, "But you have a business to run."

"Mahoney glanced around the near empty bar and said to Claire, "Those guys are always here. Hell, they wouldn't even notice if I was gone until they drained their glasses. But you folks just keep coming in and I can't help but wonder about what I'm missing."

"Can you drive?" Nanita said while staring at Claire.

"Sure," Mahoney said, "I'll drive." Mahoney was taking off his apron before anyone could change their mind and started around the bar. He stopped and looked down the bar at his regular customers.

"Hey Jerry," Mahoney shouted, "Can you play bartender for a few minutes?"

Jerry perked right up and with a finger that he meant to point towards himself but which was missing the mark by a large amount replied with slightly slurred speech, "Me? Hell yes!" Getting off his stool and nearly falling, Jerry gathered himself up and asked Mahoney in a straight face, "Do I have to wear the apron?"

"No, Jerry, you don't have to wear the apron."

Jerry beamed and made his way behind the bar holding tightly to the edge of it as he did.

Bobby, Sarge, and Calvin were roughly thrown to a concrete floor. The remaining three black clad military types pulled the blindfolds from Sarge and Calvin's faces. Sarge immediately looked towards Bobby who had quite a few bruises, cuts and Welts on his face. One of his eyes was nearly swollen shut but the other had his steely gaze locked onto his enemies noting every single move they made.

"You alright Bobby?" Sarge asked him.

"Shut up!" one of the military types yelled .

"Shut me up," Sarge yelled back, "I get my hands free and I'm gonna' ring your scrawny little neck."

The three military types laughed.

"Laugh all you want now but it's only a matter of time till I rip off your arm and beat you to death with it," Sarge spat back at them.

One of the military types strolled over to the equipment behind him and pushed the large green button. The headsaw on the sawmill slowly began to whirl around, gaining speed with each turn.

"So," one of the men said to the other two, "should we send the boss their heads or just a hand from each to prove we earned our pay?"

Sarge with his hands still cuffed behind his back began feeling around behind him. He was leaning against a large extra sawblade. Attempting to not show any signs of movement he began running his wrists up and down over the sharp teeth of the huge circular blade. After a couple minutes he had worn through the plastic ties enough that his brute strength busted them. He kept his hands behind his back waiting for an opportunity. Bobby was sitting next to Sarge with his hands still cuffed in front of his body, and Calvin was on the other side of Sarge but looking like he probably wouldn't be of much use. Bobby had his legs pulled up under him while Sarge's legs were sticking straight out from under him.

"Hey asshole," Sarge shouted, "I need to piss."

"Don't worry. It soon won't matter."

Sarge started to push himself up the wall with his hands still firmly planted behind his back.

"Sit your ass back down," one of the military types yelled while starting over towards Sarge with his gun pointed in Sarge's direction. When the man got in front of Bobby and stretched out his arm to push Sarge back down to the floor, Bobby swung his left leg with amazing speed and crushed the outside of the man's knee with his foot. The man fell like a sack of potatoes. As he was falling Sarge jumped up and grabbed the man's rifle which was hanging from a strap over his shoulder. Sarge twisted the strap strangling the man and at the same time shot one of the other military types that was beginning to understand what was happening and had begun moving towards them. Bobby shot off the floor and using his head like a ram knocked the guy back against the table near the whirring saw blade. Bobby used his cuffed fists like a club and began beating the man around his face. The man realizing he had no room to use his rifle pulled his knife and swung towards Bobby's face. Bobby knew the exact moment when to sidestep the slash then smashed the guy with his cuffed fists on the back of his arm after it had passed by Bobby's face. The momentum took the man's hand with the knife into the sawblade. Blood flew everywhere. Bobby grabbed the man and pulled him back before he got sucked further into the vicious sawblade. Bobby threw the guy onto the floor and took away his weapons. Then using the man's knife he cut his cuffs off. With both hands free Bobby took the strap off the man's rifle and wrapped it tightly around the man's foreman to stop the flow of blood before the man bled out and was of no use to them.

The man was looking faint. Bobby slapped him on the cheek
and asked him, "where is Calvin's family?"
The man was groggy already. Bobby asked him again, "where
is Calvin's family? And who hired you?"
The man's lips began to move but Bobby couldn't hear what
he was saying. Bobby placed his ear next to the man's mouth.
The man breathed his last breath.

Calvin finally came around and jumped off the floor. Sarge
took the knife from the dead man's hand and cut Calvin's
cuffs off his hands. Calvin immediately started swinging his
fists at Bobby.
"You killed him. You killed him," Calvin ranted, "How will
we ever find my family? You just signed their death order!"
"Take it easy," Sarge said, "We'll find them."
"How? You just killed the only people that knew where they
were."
 Calvin broke down crying and slumped to the floor.
Bobby stepped down to the green starter button and pressed
the big red stop button. The whirring sawblade began slowing
and after a couple minutes the building was quiet except for
Calvin's sobbing. Sarge put a hand on his shoulder to comfort
him. Calvin sharply shrugged the hand off and grabbed the
pistol in Sarge's leg holster.
"Back off you two," Calvin said, "you bastards just couldn't
leave well enough alone. You just had to meddle in my
affairs."
"Calvin," Bobby said in a soothing tone, "we'll get your
family back. I have an idea where they may be, but we need to
get going. Give Sarge back his gun and let's go."
"I don't think so.," Calvin said, "my family is going to die and
you two are going to pay for it. I'm going to turn you two in
myself then they will let my family go free."
"Turn us in to who?" Bobby asked.
"Whoever calls me. Whoever took them."

"And you think they will just let your family go. No hard feelings. No consequences when you know how to contact them?"

"I have to try," Calvin said in desperation.

"What you have to do," Sarge chimed in, "is give me back my gun before I ram it up your…"

"Calm down Sarge," Bobby said.

"This guy's not playing with a full deck," Sarge said.

"His family is missing," Bobby replied, "imagine how you would be if you were in his shoes."

Calvin momentarily closed his eyes. Bobby grabbed the hand with the gun in and bent it back until the pain caused Calvin to sink to his knees and let go of the weapon.

"Now get up and come on," Bobby said, "we have to find your family."

"This is not a good idea," Sarge said, "Why don't we tie him up and leave him here so he doesn't keep trying this crap."

"Let's go," Bobby said, "We don't know how much time we have."

"Yes, we do," shouted Calvin through his weeping as he looked at his watch, "My forty-eight hours will be up in thirty-five minutes."

"Then don't you think we should get moving? Grab the guns off those guys and make sure you get all the cell phones that they have on them. They should still have our phones also."

Sarge searched all the bodies and recovered numerous phones and several more guns.

The trio climbed into the shiny black SUV that brought them to this place. Sarge got behind the wheel with Bobby riding shotgun and Calvin sitting behind Sarge.

"Which way?" Sarge asked.

"Turn right," Bobby said, "That's the direction we came from. Stay on this road almost to DuBois then take a right onto route 119 south, that will get us back to Calvin's then follow Mahoney's directions to the lumberyard. Right now, I need to call Kurt. Did you find my phone?"

"Yes," Sarge said as he dropped the pile of phones on the seat between them. Bobby rifled through the pile of phones and found his. He immediately started to call Kurt. Nothing happened. Bobby checked the phone. His battery was good. He had enough bars to connect to a tower. He pulled the back off, lifted out the battery. The SIM card was missing.

"Shit," he said as he tossed the phone into the floorboards. "Which one is yours?" he asked Sarge.

Sarge picked his out of the pile and handed it to Bobby. Bobby immediately took the back off and again no SIM card.

"Do you know Kurt's number?" Bobby asked Sarge.

"No. I've become dependent on the phone knowing the numbers."

"How about your dad's? I'll call Terry 'cause he may be with Kurt."

Sarge called out the numbers while Bobby dialed. No answer. "Just get us to the lumberyard that Mahoney gave us directions to," Bobby said exasperated.

Sarge floored the SUV and they sailed down the highway.

"This isn't a stock Chevy," Sarge said to Bobby, "do you feel the power this thing has. It has to be a government vehicle."

"No doubt," Bobby replied, "but why or who in the government would be trying to stop us?"

"Maybe they aren't trying to stop us," Sarge said, "just him." Sarge pointed toward Calvin.

"That makes no sense," Bobby said, "why would the government hire him to shoot a Secret Service agent? No someone else is behind this but they sure must have connections in the government. Come on Sarge, push this thing. Let's get there to see if that's where his family is."

Sarge drove even faster.

Chapter 13

Mike and Terry were inside the building aiming in every direction with their rifles looking for any signs of life. Kurt was ready to follow them in when he heard the roaring of a big engine coming up the lane behind him. He could see the cloud of dust rising through the trees. Whoever it was would be on them in just few seconds. Kurt jumped through the door and slammed the door shut.

"What the hell's going on?" Mike asked in a whisper.

"We've got company," Kurt replied quietly.

"We still don't know if we have company here or not," Terry said.

"Let's fan out and get further into this place," Kurt said.

The group headed off in different directions, all crouched over to be as small of a target as possible and each of them constantly moving the barrel of the rifle to cover every square inch of space as quickly as possible. The only light in the building was a bit of sun coming through a couple rooftop skylights. When they got to the other end of the huge building they came together again.

"It appears to just be full of these microwave kilns," Kurt said, "I don't see any place for anyone else to be hiding. How about you guys?"

Both replied that they didn't see anyone or any place for anyone to be either.

The door at the other end of the building that they had just entered was thrown open making a crashing noise.

"Kurt, Mike, Terry, are you here?" shouted Claire.

The trio looked at each other in amazement, then Mike jumped up and yelled back, "We'll be there in a second."

Mystified the trio made their way back to the beginning of the building. Standing there was not only Claire but the pretty woman from the funeral and Mahoney, the bartender.

"What are you guys doing here?" Kurt asked.

"We know that Bobby and Sarge are in trouble so we came to see if we could help them," Claire said.

"I see you've met Mr. Mahoney," Mike said to Claire.

"Yes, he was nice enough to show us how to get here?"

"Thanks, Mahoney," Kurt said, then asked, "who's minding the bar?"

"Jerry," Mahoney said shrugging his shoulders, "or probably more accurately he's drinking me out of house and home."

"So why are we here?" Nanita asked.

"Because Bobby called me and wanted to know what a phrase meant?" Kurt replied.

"What phrase?" Claire asked.

"It was about going down to six percent moisture. Well being an old sawyer myself I knew that referred to drying lumber. You dry it so that it only has six to ten percent moisture left in it," Kurt replied.

Terry held his arms out and said, "And this is a kiln drying facility."

"But is there anyone here?" Claire asked.

"Not that we've found."

"Then why are we here?"

"All we know," Terry said, "is that is has something to do with saving this Calvin person's family."

"And Bobby is expected to come here?" Claire asked.

"Well we don't know if he meant to come here or some other lumberyard with kilns. We chose this one because Bobby seemed to be asking Mahoney more about this one because it was closed down due to the economy."

"Has anyone seen Bobby?" Claire asked.

"Not since Mahoney saw him earlier today."

Claire looked at Mahoney, "So where did he go?"

"The only other place he asked about was Calvin's, like I told you, and most likely he would go there first."

"That makes sense," Kurt said.

"Hopefully Bobby will end up here also," Mike said, "in the meantime we should do something."

Kurt looked around then said to the group, "Let's check these kilns."

The group turned simultaneously and looked down the large open building filled with two long rows of kilns. They looked like oblong silver caskets except about twice the size.

Since Kurt knew his way around a lumberyard the group followed Kurt as he started down the ranks of microwave kilns. Looking at the front of each kiln as they made their way down the long rows and coming to the end of the line.

Kurt," Mike asked, "what are you looking for?"

"Well none of these are turned on."

"How do you know?"

"The green button on the front of each of them would be lit. None of these are turned on," Kurt repeated, "Are we on a wild goose chase?"

Sarge nearly missed the turn off at the MOE'S sign on route 119 but at the last minute he whipped the wheel. The tires on the big old SUV howled and the vehicle leaned precariously close to flipping over but Sarge hung on and they made the turn. Sarge then immediately went back to full throttle. He slid past the next turn-off then backed up and made the turn. He was barreling down the lane when they both spotted Mike's shiny black Dodge Ram sitting off the side of the road.

"Slow down," Bobby said, "In case they are in trouble, we don't want to alert anybody."

Sarge slowed to a near stop and continued down the lane.

"Stop. Stop. Stop." Bobby yelled.

Sarge stopped the truck, "What is it?"

"That's Claire's car parked up there near the building with the doors hanging open."

Sarge pulled the SUV off the side of the road.

"We better go on foot from here," Bobby said, "Calvin you stay put."

"No way I'm staying here," Calvin said as he scrambled out of the vehicle, "My family could be in there."

Bobby and Sarge were quiet as Indians sneaking up on the building with their weapons at the ready. Calvin was not so quiet. The anxiety that his wife and child may be in the building were too much for him. As they neared the building Calvin took off at a run and burst through the door.

"Shit," Bobby said as he and Sarge took off after Calvin.

The door slammed against the wall and Calvin came to a screeching halt as he stared into the several gun barrels.

"Where's my family?" Calvin blurted out as he kept an eye on the gun barrels.

"Who the hell are you?" Kurt asked.

Calvin was shocked when the gun barrels simply fell away to the floor, not as a result of anything he said, but owing to the appearance of Bobby and Sarge.

"Nice to see you guys," Bobby said.

Sarge pushed his way through the doorway and a smile warmed his face. Claire pushed her way through the group and just stared at Bobby.

"Honey, I'm home," Bobby said with a smile.

"Are you sure that's you. That's not the face I kissed goodbye this morning."

Bobby gingerly rubbed his cheek as he said, "I've been using it to stop punches."

Calvin feeling left out of the reunion shouted, "Where's my family?"

Bobby and Sarge got back to the situation at hand and said to Kurt, Mike and Terry and the others, "Have you found anyone?"

"There isn't anyone here," Terry said.

"Yeah, we've checked the building," said Kurt, "Just a bunch of empty kilns in here."

"Are you sure they are all empty?" Bobby asked.

"Well we didn't open each one and look," said Kurt.

"Then let's get to it."

Kurt and Terry were the first to start down the aisles of kilns lifting the shiny stainless steel lids that opened like the trunk lid on a car except considerably bigger. As they opened them they left them open and went on to the next one. Mike joined the hunt and they eventually got to the end of the line.

Kurt hollered back to Bobby, "Nothing here but empty kilns."

Mike was standing next to the last kiln and said to Kurt and Bobby, "This one won't open."

The group immediately rushed to where Mike was standing. Kurt ran his hand along the seam where the lid met the body. Feeling something he stooped over to take a closer look.

"This one appears to have a small weld spot holding it shut," Kurt explained.

"Well we have to get it open," Bobby said.

"I believe I saw an acetylene torch in the back corner over there," Kurt said, "Somebody go get it. I'll get this thing open."

Mike had wandered around the back of the kiln as most of the group was watching Kurt while Terry and Sarge ran to get the acetylene torch.

"Excuse me gentlemen," Mike said waiting for their attention.

"What?" Kurt asked him.

"You better get a move on it," Mike replied.

"What?" Kurt asked again.

"There is a timer tied into the electric wire on this one. You have 3 minutes and 10 seconds."

"Hurry the hell up Sarge," Kurt yelled.

The acetylene torch tanks which were heavy were mounted to a dolly with heavy rubber wheels. Hearing Kurt shout Sarge began to run dragging the tanks behind him. As soon as he got to Kurt, Kurt took the helmet off the tank and placed it on his head, then grabbed the striker that was hanging from the tanks, turned the knobs on the tanks and struck the end of the torch. The hot blue flame ignited. Kurt adjusted it to the size flame he wanted and made quick work of cutting through the weld. Bobby grabbed the lid and opened it as Kurt shut off the valves on the tanks and removed the helmet. The group pushed forward as the lid went up with Calvin pushing his way to the front. Inside the kiln were two human figures, duct taped together and not moving. Claire pushed her way to the open lid as her former life as a nurse took over.

She felt the neck of the bigger person and said to Bobby, "weak pulse. They are probably being starved for oxygen. Get an ambulance here fast. Help me get this duct tape off them." All hands reached forward and began the process of pulling the tape gently from their mouths and not so gently from around their legs and hands. Calvin was attempting to speak but couldn't.

"Get some blankets or coats or something around them to get them warm," Claire shouted. The men in the group immediately shed as much clothing as they could and Claire wrapped up the lady while Nanita bundled up the child as well as she could then held her close to herself. Bobby and Terry lifted the woman from inside the kiln and laid her gently on top of a pile of shirts and coats. Mike hung up his cell and announced, "the ambulance is on its way."

"Let's get them down near the door," Claire said.

"Kurt, what happens when this timer goes off?" Mike asked.

"Probably nothing as long as the lid stays up. They have a safety switch built in."

"Good," Mike said, "Because you are out of time."

"Nanita looked at Kurt and asked, "What would have happened if you would not have got the lid open on time?"

"Well, it would have been just like putting steak in a microwave. The moisture in the body would start leaving at an alarming rate leaving nothing but dried up skin and bones."

The ambulance slid to a stop at the door where Terry and Mike had motioned for him to come to. The ambulance crew swung into action placing the two on oxygen, placing them on the gurney closely together and piling them high with warm blankets. Before they shut the back doors to the ambulance Calvin climbed in. He stopped, turned around and said to Bobby and Sarge, "Thanks guys. I'm sorry I ...'

"Get out of here," Sarge ordered as he shut the doors then slapped his hand on the rear door as a sign to the driver to take off. And the ambulance did. Siren wailing through the previously peaceful countryside drowning out the chatter from the birds and crickets.

Mahoney had been quietly assisting and watching but now said, "could I get a ride back to the bar? I better check to see what damage Jerry did."

"Just so happens we're going that way," Mike chimed in, "'Because this man needs a drink."

"Me, too," said Kurt. Terry nodded and joined the group as they headed for the big Dodge Ram parked down the lane.

"How did you get here dear?" Claire asked Bobby.

"In a stolen government vehicle."

Claire rolled her eyes and held up her open palm, "Please, forget I asked. I don't want to know anymore."

"So does that mean you'll give us a lift back to Calvin's?" Bobby asked as he turned on his thousand watt smile.

Claire gently patted his bruised and swollen cheek, "We'll make room for Sarge but you're not so cute at the moment." The horsepower came to life instantly when Claire turned the key and the dual exhausts roared. She pulled the gearshift into gear and they flew down the lane back towards the highway.

"Are we going home?" Claire asked.

"You and Nanita are," Bobby answered.

Claire sighed, "And where are you two going?"

"Drop Sarge off at the Punxsy hospital then take me to Calvin's house."

"May I ask why?"

"So far all we have done is save Calvin's wife and daughter. We still don't know who tried to frame me. Oh by the way, let Sarge have your cell phone. Ours sort of got damaged."

Claire pulled the phone from her pocket and gave it to Sarge. Bobby asked Sarge, "Do you still have the cell phones from the military guys?"

"I have two of them."

"Hang onto them, if they still have the SIMS cards in them maybe we can get a phone number to whoever put them on the case."

Claire followed the blue signs with the white H up to the entrance of the hospital. Sarge jumped out.

"Anything in particular you want me to do?" he asked Bobby.

"Be careful. Whoever is behind this may try again on Calvin and his family if they find out they survived. Try not to be noticeable," Bobby instructed.

As a former sniper, Sarge knew exactly how to blend in and become invisible in his environment. He proceeded to the Emergency room desk and found out where Calvin's family would be, then he searched the halls for what he would need. He was able to lay his hands on a set of hospital pants and shirt almost big enough to fit him; he procured a bucket and mop and in general acted like he belonged right there outside of Calvin's family's room.

"You'll have to give me directions To Calvin's," Claire said to Bobby.

"Stay on this road to the red light at the bridge then make a left onto route 36."

"So I'm heading back towards Mahoney's bar?"

"Yes, it's just past Mahoney's."

"Maybe we should stop for a drink first."

"Or maybe you can drop me at Calvin's then you and Nanita can stop for a drink."

"Got ya!"

Claire knew when to pull into Calvin's mobilehome owing to the fact that she saw Bobby's beat up old red pickup truck parked in front of it.

"Please be careful, dear," Claire said to Bobby.

"I will. And when you get home please do me a favor since I am without a phone. Call the Colonel and let him know that there are a few military type bodies here that need to be collected and I also need to know who they are and who might have sent them here."

"Anything else?" Claire asked.

"No, but please be careful. Stay somewhere other than our house. They could still come for me there."

Bobby gave Claire a long kiss and closed her door. The Challenger roared away.

Bobby got in his old pickup and drove up the road a short distance finding a place where he could hide the truck in the brush off the road, then he hiked back to Calvin's mobilehome and with a quick glance around made his way inside. Waiting was always the hard part but during his career as a sniper and then as a federal undercover agent he had done plenty of waiting. Sometimes with good results. Sometimes all he got was a sore butt. He wished he had a way to stay in touch with Sarge but unfortunately they were now working in less than perfect conditions.

Chapter 14

As Mike pulled the black Ram into the parking lot at Mahoney's bar he had to stop and look for a place to park. The bar seemed to be doing a fabulous business based on the full parking lot, which made Mahoney quite anxious.

"I hope that son–of–a–gun isn't giving away all my good booze," Mahoney said as jumped out of the truck and practically sprinted to the door of his establishment.

Mahoney hesitantly entered with Mike, Kurt and Terry on his heels. The place was alive with music pounding out of the jukebox. The game was on the television and several were huddled around the bar there screaming at the television screen. Jerry was behind the bar pouring beers with both hands, and then the sight that made Mahoney relax. Jerry took money from a customer, rang the cash register and placed the bills inside it.

Jerry spied the door opening and looked in that direction. Seeing first Mahoney then the others Jerry said, "Gentlemen come on in the beer's cold and the women are hot. What can I get ya?"

A dumbfounded Mahoney sat on a barstool and mumbled, "My usual."

Jerry quickly sat a shot of tequila in front of him and said, "That'll be two bucks."

Mahoney started to reach for his wallet then it hit him like a ton of bricks. Jerry laughed and walked away asking Mike, Kurt and Terry what they would like to have and with great efficiency placed the ice cold beers in front of them. Mahoney drank his shot then let his eyes wander around the nearly full bar and smiled. He banged his empty glass on the bar and said, "I'll have another!"

"Oh, I almost forget," Jerry said to Ed, "You had a call while you were gone."

Mahoney looked at Jerry with a serious expression waiting for him to relay the message. When Jerry wasn't forthcoming he asked, "Who was it?"

"Wouldn't leave a name. Said you'd know who it is. Had a strange accent."

"Okay. Thanks, Jerry."

Mahoney pushed off the barstool and headed for the peg where he hung his apron.

"Is there a problem, Ed?" Jerry asked noticing the immediate change in mood.

"Same old shit," Ed said under his breath.

The cell phone in Chicago, Illinois shrilled. The owner
answered, "Where the hell have you been?"
"Waiting to get a report from the ground before I called you."
"And?"
"And it appears we have lost our boots on the ground."
"What the hell does that mean?"
"It means I cannot get through to anyone there."
"Oh great, so you screwed this all up?"
"I'm sending in some more people. They'll let me know what
has happened to our guys and what the situation is now."
"If you don't get Morrow and that sidekick of his in the
ground soon, you are going to become a loose end and you
know what happens to loose ends, don't you?"
"Yes, I do. Don't worry I'll handle it."

Sarge was mopping the same clean hallway for the third time
when Claire's cell phone that was now in Sarge's pocket
began to vibrate.
Sarge looked at the screen and it said the caller was unknown.
Sarge answered, "Yeah."
"Where's Morrow?" a strong male voice asked.
"Who wants to know?" Sarge asked.
"Listen up toughguy. Tell Morrow he should have worried
more about protecting his own family and less about
Calvin's."
The call was ended. Sarge stood staring at the phone a minute.
Should he find a way out to Calvin's to tell Bobby? Should he
leave Calvin and his family alone to do it after Bobby
instructed him to stay here?
Sarge stood the mop in the bucket of water and made his way
to the stairwell where he dialed a familiar number.
"Dad," Sarge asked when the phone was answered, "where
are you?"

"We're still at Mahoney's Bar but we're leaving soon. Why?"

"I need to get a message to Bobby."

"Why don't you call him?"

"He doesn't have a phone. Ours were destroyed."

"Where is Bobby?"

"He's at Calvin's house."

"Okay. We'll run out there. What am I to tell him?"

Sarge told Terry about the call he had just received.

Terry rose from the barstool. Threw some money on the bar and said, "Mike, can I borrow your truck for a few minutes?"

Mike noting the seriousness of the request said, "Sure. Need us to go along?"

"No I can handle it. I'll be right back."

Mike passed Terry the keys to the big Ram. Terry looked around the bar for Mahoney and saw him putting on his apron and heading behind the bar. Terry made his way to where Ed was and asked him in a low voice how he could get to Calvin's house as he needed to talk to Bobby. Mahoney took his apron back off and said, "come on. I'll show you." The two got into Mike's truck and Terry started the powerful engine.

"Buckle up," Terry said to Mahoney.

Terry pulled out of the parking lot. No flying gravel. No tires squealing. Mahoney gave him directions and in just a few minutes they were at Calvin's. The mobilehome was dark and there was no sign of Bobby's truck.

"You sure he's here?" Mahoney asked.

"He's here. Just sit tight."

The words were no sooner out of Terry's mouth when the sudden knock on Mahoney's window caused him to jump. Staring at him from outside was Bobby. Mahoney pushed the button to wind down the window.

"You scared the crap out of me," Mahoney said.

"Sorry," Bobby said, "what's up Farmer?"

"Sarge called me. He said you didn't have a phone but I was to let you know that he received a call on the phone that he has. Someone told him that you should be watching out for your own family and not worrying about Calvin's."

"Is that all they said?"

"That's all he told me."

Bobby thought for a long moment.

Terry asked him, "Do you want me and the guys to go back to your house?"

"I'm not sure. It could be a ruse to get us away from Calvin and his family."

"But what if it isn't?"

"Claire is not at the house. I'm not sure if they could find her. Can I use your phone?"

Terry handed Bobby his phone and Bobby dialed a number from his memory.

"Is Claire there?" Bobby asked.

After a minute Claire came on the line and Bobby asked her, "where you at Babe?"

"I'm exactly where you told me to be."

"Good," Bobby said with a sigh of relief, "everything alright?"

"Sure."

"Do you have your gun with you?"

"Several. Should I be worried?"

"Not worried. Just prepared."

"Anything I should know?"

"I expect that somebody's coming for Calvin or me and Sarge. Sarge got a strange phone call on your phone."

"So they at least know my phone number?"

"Sure. But it's listed. They could call information and get it. Just be very careful."

"I will. You be careful. I expect you back in one piece, and stop using your face to stop other people's punches."

"Yes, dear."

Bobby hung up the phone and dialed Claire's number.

Sarge answered, "Yeah."

"Be alert," Bobby said, "Especially between three in the morning and five in the morning. That's always the best time to strike."

"You still think they are coming here?"

"I think the call was to mislead us. Claire's fine."

"Maybe your dad, Mike, and Kurt will hang around a little while yet." Bobby looked at Terry as he said this and Terry nodded affirmatively. Bobby handed the phone back to Terry and thanked him for making the trip out.

"What would you like us to do?" Terry asked.

"If you're still here between three and five in the morning you may want to be at the hospital in case Sarge needs a hand."

"What about you?"

"I'll be fine and if no one shows here I'll be over at the hospital around six."

Terry started the Ram and headed back to Mahoney's bar. Mahoney asked Terry after they pulled out onto the highway, "is this guy some kind of superman or something?"

"No," Terry said, "just a very experienced warrior that is still connected in Washington, D.C."

"I was shocked when you guys found Calvin's wife and daughter in that dry kiln. Would somebody really have killed them?"

Terry gave Ed a serious look and answered, "There are some bad people out there. Fortunately Bobby is one of the good guys and usually wins."

As Terry pulled into Mahoney's parking lot, Ed slapped his forehead with the palm of his hand and let out an audible, "Shit!"

"What's wrong?" Terry asked.

Ed pointed to a black Mercedes parked at the end of the lot with blacked out windows.

"Is that a problem?" Terry asked.

"Not yours," Ed said as he started out of the truck.

Terry came around the front of the truck and placed his hand on Ed's shoulder.

"Ed," Terry asked, "What is it?"

"I'm not going to bother you with my problems. Hell I don't know you well enough for that."

"Pretend you do know me better, what's the problem?"

"Part of the reason my business is so bad is because I've had to raise my prices."

"Can't you just lower them?" Terry asked.

"These guys won't let me."

"But I thought this was your bar?"

"Supposed to be."

"Then what's the problem?"

"These guys demand money from me each week and if I don't pay, they'll burn the place down and maybe my home too."

"So you're paying protection money? Who is it the mafia?"

"Worse," Ed said, "they're Russian."

"And they are here in little old Punxsutawney?"

"They've been spreading out from Pittsburgh. They open marble and tile shops for fronts then they just come in and strong arm people."

"Well if it was me," Terry said, "I'd just tell them to go to hell."

"You haven't seen these guys. They are scary."

"Well let's go meet them."

Mahoney and Terry entered the bar and scanned the interior quickly. At the end of the bar where Ed hangs his apron was three large men wearing suits and sunglasses in the dark interior. One of the men had a strong grip on Jerry's arm.

Ed walked up to the three and demanded, "Let him go!"

The obvious leader of the group acted surprised and said in broken English, "Better let him go boys before Mr. Mahoney gets upset." The three enjoyed a good laugh. Mike sat his glass down on the bar and watched as Terry stood next to

Mahoney. Mike bumped Kurt with his elbow and with a small unnoticeable motion of his finger pointed to the group where Terry was standing. Kurt gave Mike a quick barely noticeable nod and the two got up from their barstools and casually walked over to the group.

"Jerry," Mike said in a loud voice, "We were hoping to get a refill."

Jerry tried to wave them off. One of the men in suits gave Mike a small push on the chest and told him in barely understandable English to "Take a hike."

"Don't touch me," Mike said. Looking back at Kurt, Mike said, "Isn't that what Bobby always says?"

Kurt smiled, "Yes, that's what Bobby always says when someone touches him."

"Then what happens?" Mike asked Kurt.

"Then Bobby usually kicks someone's ass."

The bruiser in the suit was looking between Mike and Kurt and finally said, "Shut up and leave."

"You need to work on your language skills," Kurt said.

"Leave now," the bruiser said, "Or I will kill you!"

"Now you're scaring me," Kurt said with a sneer on his face. The bruiser in the suit reached under his suit coat. Mike grabbed the man's arm before it could come out from under the suit coat and with his other hand squeezed the muscle on top of the man's shoulder next to his neck with as much force as he could muster. The man started to shrink down away from the excruciating pain. The other bruiser in a suit turned and started under his suit coat for his weapon. Terry grabbed him around the throat with his forearm and squeezed him the way he did cattle that he used to wrestle to the ground. The leader of the group seeing his hired muscle in dire straits casually took off his sunglasses and jabbed Mahoney in the chest with them.

"These guys are making problems for you my friend," he said to Ed.

Ed grabbed the man's sunglasses, bent them popping the lenses out. Threw them on the floor and ground them into the oak floor with his shoe. Ed then poked the man in the chest with a very stiff pointer finger and said, "you will never come here again. Understand?"

"Big mistake," came back the reply in a Russian accent.

The man that Terry had in a choke hold head-butted him with the back of his head breaking Terry's nose. Terry threw the man to the floor and as he was holding his bleeding nose Terry kicked him hard in the gut. The man grabbed his gut moaning but was able to pull his gun out and aimed it at Terry. Kurt jumped on the man pinning him to the floor while grabbing the hand he held the gun in. With his other hand Kurt poked him in the eye. The man let go of the gun. Distracted, Mike had loosened his grip on the other man. The man whipped out his gun and pointed it at Mike. Terry still holding his bleeding nose tapped the man hard on the shoulder and said to him, "You shouldn't do that."

Mike grabbed the man's gun with both hands and twisted it back towards the man's gut. The man was forced to let go. He then turned to push his way past Terry who smacked him on his nose with an open palm with enough power to stop the man dead in his tracks. The sound of the breaking bone could be heard throughout the room. The leader pulled his gun and stuck it in Mahoney's chest.

"Stop or I shoot," he shouted.

Mahoney looked the man right in the eye and said, "Shoot and you'll never leave here alive. Any of you. You are all free to go, just don't ever come back. And if my bar burns down we're coming for you. Or if my house burns down, we're coming for you. Oh, and before I forget, I'll take the keys to the Acura parked in my lot. I've paid you enough to buy it, so you clowns can walk back to whatever rock you crawled out from under."

"This is not over," the man spat out.

"It is for you. Go back to Russia where you can push people around."

Terry grabbed one of them by the collar and Kurt grabbed another by the collar and walked them to the door. Mike opened the door and the two were roughly thrown out into the gravel parking lot causing a few more scrapes and cuts. Mahoney then led the leader to the door where he unceremoniously kicked him in the ass and sent him flying into the pile of ripped suits.

Mahoney shut the door and looking at the others said, "you know they'll be back and you guys won't be here to help me. This was a big mistake."

"We know a guy that fixes things like this. We'll ask him if he can help you out," Terry said.

"Well then the drinks are on the house," Mahoney said.

A loud cheer went up and the noise level went back to normal. Mahoney went to Jerry and said, "I'm sorry that happened to you."

"No problem," Jerry said, "I just wish you had told me earlier about them. You shouldn't have been worrying about them by yourself. You think these guys really do know someone that can help if they come back?"

"I hope so!"

Chapter 15

Bobby heard the barely noticeable sound of gravel crunching then quiet then the slight crunching sound again; the sounds registered in Bobby's mind as someone taking careful steps on Calvin's driveway. Bobby checked his watch. Four o'clock in the morning.

"That's about right," he said quietly to himself.

Bobby had assumed they would come in the rear door first then the front door as soon as the person in the back entered so Bobby had stationed himself in the bathroom just off the hall and only inches from the rear door. Bobby was able to view the rear door in the mirror while not exposing his position. He watched as the doorknob slowly turned, then the door slowly and quietly began to open into the mobilehome. A second passed before the intruder made his way through the door. He was dressed in black holding a black rifle high and swinging it as he scanned as much of the hallway as he could while entering. Bobby waited until the intruder turned his back toward him and began slowly making his way into the living room. Bobby took two long quiet strides and reaching around the intruder's neck placed his knife firmly against his throat. The intruder stopped. Bobby held the man firmly with the knife ready to slit his throat if he moved while Bobby leaned further into the man and whispered as softly as he could into the man's ear, "not a sound or the next sound you hear will be your blood gurgling out of your neck." Bobby kept the man frozen while he watched the front door. The knob on the front door began to turn slowly and then another figure clad all in black entered in a crouching position while swinging his weapon from side to side from one side of the room to the other. Bobby said in his soft voice, "Psst."

The second intruder stopped dead in his tracks, turned on a light mounted on the barrel of his gun and aimed it at his partner. Before it could dawn on him that his partner had an extra arm Bobby placed the finger of his free hand on the trigger of his hostage's gun and squeezed the trigger. A short burst of shot erupted from the weapon and the light on the second intruder's gun went out with the sound of breaking glass. The intruder moaned and dropped to the floor.

Bobby again whispered into his hostage's ear, "Are there any more?"

The hostage being afraid to shake his head answered a simple, "no."

Still holding the knife to the man's throat Bobby asked him, "who sent you here?"

"I don't know."

"You don't know who sent you?"

"No. I get a phone call. The money gets wired to an account."

"Why are you here?" Bobby asked.

"To kill you and the soldier dude."

"How many were dispatched?"

"Five."

"So there are three after Sarge?"

"Yes."

"Where are they?"

"At the hospital."

"How did you know he would be there?"

"We were told he was there and you were here."

"So you're no longer after Calvin?"

"Don't know about any Calvin."

"Where's your phone?"

The man started to move his arm.

"Slowly," Bobby said as the knife maintained its presence against the man's throat.

The man slowly moved his arm, dug into his pocket, and pulled out his phone. Bobby took it from him.

"Is this the phone you received your calls on?"

"Yes."

The man swung quickly to his left, raising his elbow to smash Bobby in the face with the elbow.

Bobby had seen this move before. Bobby dropped instantly straight down bending at his knees. As the elbow whisked over his head, Bobby jumped straight back up and as he did he thrust the knife into the man's gut with the upward momentum. The man crashed over backwards wriggling in agony.

"I told you not to move," Bobby said.

Bobby checked the recent phone calls on the other man's phone that he still held in his hand. The last call was a number that he was familiar with. Bobby leaned over, wiped the blood from the knife onto the man's black clothing, stuck the knife back in his waist band and left Calvin's mobilehome through the front door. Sprinting to his truck up the road hidden in the brush. He passed a black SUV that probably was his attackers. "Why do all these people have black SUV's?" he thought to himself.

As Bobby started his truck and headed for the hospital he dialed the number for Claire's phone that Sarge now had in his possession. Sarge did not answer. Bobby pushed the accelerator a lot harder.

The hair on Sarge's arms began to stand on end. That innate sense that a soldier has that the enemy is near. That there is danger just around the next corner. Sarge ducked into the first dark room that he came to and stood quiet as a churchmouse waiting. He heard the soft slow footsteps in the hallway. Someone was trying extra hard to not make any noise. The silent stalker was making his way down the hall and would soon be passing the dark room where Sarge stood. Ready. When the form appeared in front of the doorway Sarge made his move. He grabbed the large male figure around the neck with his right arm covering the man's mouth with his beefy palm while jamming his pistol in the ribcage with enough force to leave no doubt what it was. Sarge pulled the man into the darkened room and whispered into the person's ear, "one word when I take my hand away and I'll pull the trigger. Understand?"

The person made an attempt to shake his head affirmatively. Sarge slowly removed his hand from the man's mouth but he did not remove his arm from around the man's neck.

"What the hell are you doing Sarge?"

Sarge spun the man around, "Mike, what the hell are you doing here?"

"Bobby told us to come over and give you some back up. You know I'm gonna' have a bruise where you shoved that damn cannon into my ribcage!"

"Sorry Mike." Sarge said then instantly clamped his hand over Mike's mouth again.

Sarge removed his hand but instantly put his forefinger in front of his pursed lips giving Mike the sign to be quiet. Sarge pulled Mike back behind him as he again melted in the darkness.

Sarge turned and whispered into Mike's ear, "is anyone else coming behind you?"

Mike shook his head negatively. Sarge assumed his position. This time the stalking figure was on the other side of the hallway away from the darkened room where Sarge and Mike were hiding in the darkness. When the figure appeared in their sight across the hallway Sarge saw that this was not another of his friends but another intruder dressed in black with a short automatic weapon hung from his neck and pointed directly in front of him. When the intruder was a step passed Sarge's doorway, Sarge took two long fast steps ending up behind the intruder grabbing the automatic weapon with his left hand and using his momentum to push the intruder hard against the wall pinning him there while ramming the business end of his pistol into the intruder's neck vertebrae. The intruder immediately but slowly began to raise his hands in the air. Sarge pulled the automatic weapon off the man's neck and tossed it to Mike, then Sarge turned the man flat against the wall and while continuing to hold the pistol in the man's neck, Sarge used his left hand to pull each of the man's arms down behind his back.

"Get a plastic cuff out of my back pocket," Sarge said to Mike, "and cuff this guy."

Mike pulled the plastic tie tight breaking the skin on the man's wrist and causing him to wince.

"I didn't say to cut his wrist off," Sarge said to Mike, "Take him into that room we were just in and put him to bed."

"Put him to bed?" Mike asked.

"Yes," Sarge answered, "Put him on the bed them cuff his feet and cuff his hands and feet to the bed. Then jam a sheet into his mouth so he can't yell."

Mike grabbed the man roughly by the arm and drug him across the hall throwing him roughly onto the bed then doing exactly as he was instructed.

"Stay there with him, "Sarge said to Mike, "I'm going down the hall 'cause the next one will probably come from the other direction."

Sarge was a professional and knew that that was how he would handle this operation if he was on the other team, so he crept slowly down the hall carrying the intruder's automatic weapon, his eyes sweeping every inch of open space in front of him. When he was passed Calvin's room, he looked for an empty room. The first room he turned into he heard soft moaning coming from the bad. He immediately took his leave and continued down the hallway to the next room. The phone in his pocket began to vibrate as he had turned the sound off like any good soldier would do. Sarge ignored it and continued on sweeping the space with his ever moving eyes. He ducked into the next darkened room. Listened for a second. No noise so he melted back into the darkness and waited. Mike had been peering around the corner of the room he was in watching Sarge make his way down the hallway and turn into the room. Mike was just about to pull his head back into the room when he saw another figure creeping down the hallway towards the room that Sarge was in. This intruder was stopping and carefully checking each room with the barrel of his automatic weapon pointed into each of the dark doorways. Mike continued to watch the intruder. When the intruder started to turn into the doorway of the room where Sarge was Mike jumped into the hallway and dashed across the hallway into the room on the other side of the hallway. The intruder noticed the movement and instead of turning into the room that Sarge was in he took another step down the hallway with his weapon pointed down the hallway towards the room where Mike ended up.

Sarge jumped out of the room, smashed the butt end of the automatic weapon that he took from the other intruder into the head of the newest one. The man staggered but swung around with his weapon. Sarge grabbed the barrel of the man's weapon with his free hand and physically forced it up under the chin of the intruder. Pulling the trigger now would be suicide. The intruder let go of the weapon and using both hands grabbed Sarge by the throat. The intruder used his momentum to push Sarge across the hallway and into the wall. Sarge dropped the weapons he had and with both hands flat smacked the intruder on the sides of his head with both hands at the same time. The instant pressure on the intruder's eardrums forced him to instantly let go of Sarge's neck so he could grab his own ears and stop the excruciating pain. When the man covered his ears Sarge drove his knee deep into the man's privates causing him to double over. Following all the years of good training that Sarge had, when the man doubled over, he hammered him on the back of his neck with his big beefy hands entwined together to form a powerful hammer. The intruder dropped to the floor like a sack of potatoes and did not move. Sarge drug him by his feet into the darkened room that he just left. There he put the plastic cuffs on him and cuffed him to the bed. He pulled the pillowcase off the pillow and jammed it into the man's mouth to prevent him from yelling. Mike had stepped back into the hallway to watch Sarge apprehend the intruder and was amazed at the speed with which he did it. He started down the hallway

toward Sarge and Sarge started down the hallway toward
Mike . Sarge motioned for Mike to go into Calvin's room and
Sarge entered immediately after him.

"Very nice," Mike whispered to Sarge.

"It's what I should have done to you," Sarge replied.

"Glad you didn't. What do we do now?"

"Wait."

"For what?"

Sarge merely shrugged his shoulders. Any good soldier will
tell you that the only thing predictable about an enemy is that
they are unpredictable. There could easily be more intruders
on the way but one thing was certain, they wouldn't catch
Sarge with his pants down. Sarge glanced around the room.
Calvin was sleeping in the chair in a position that he was
going to be sorry for when he woke up. Calvin's daughter was
sleeping quietly in one bed and his wife softly snoring away
in the other bed. And Sarge was on duty. Ever vigilant. No
harm would come to any of the inhabitants of this room while
he was on guard. Mike wanted to talk to Sarge more about
what he just saw but the steely determined look in Sarge's eye
gave him fair warning that now was not the time. Sarge was
in the zone and to interrupt him would be akin to taking a
bone away from a hungry dog. Not a good idea.

Mahoney's bar did not open until eleven o'clock in the
morning. Give or take a few minutes either way. Mahoney,
however, was always there bright and early in the morning.
He enjoyed his coffee and morning newspaper without any
disruptions except for the talking heads on the television that
he always had on in the background. When Ed pulled into his
parking lot a black Cadillac was parked there with no
occupants. Ed didn't give it much thought as that happened
quite often. People left their cars there either because they had
a designated driver the night before or they met up with
someone else in the morning and Mahoney had never

bothered anyone's cars. He was not the type to call a tow truck and have them hauled off.

Ed parked and ambled to the door. He stuck his key in the lock like every other morning, and like every other morning, he unlocked the door and entered the still dark bar that was his own private sanctuary. He flipped the light switch and the lights flickered on. The one difference this morning was there was a portly gentleman sitting in a chair facing the doorway.

A startled Mahoney shouted, "Who the hell are you?"

The man was dressed in a black suit, black shiny shoes, a white shirt and a black necktie pulled down away from his thick neck. Without moving from the chair the man said in a low gravelly voice, "I'm Carmine."

Mahoney swung his head around the bar looking for others then settling back on Carmine he said, "How'd you get in here."

"Not important."

"Why are you here?"

"My friend, Terry, said you had a little problem."

"That was last night. The problem is gone."

"Don't kid yourself," Carmine said as he casually took inventory of his fingernails.

"What do you mean?"

"I mean you wounded their pride. They'll be back."

"When?"

"Real soon."

"What am I going to do?"

"You?" Carmine said in his thick Italian accent, "you aren't going to do anything except keep your mouth shut."

"What are you going to do?" Mahoney asked.

"I'm going to handle your problem once and for all."

"Why?"

"Because my friend Terry asked me to," Carmine replied amazed that anyone would ask the question.

"But..."

"But, nothing," Carmine said, "Go do what you always do."
A baffled Mahoney stepped around the back of the bar and stopped dead in his tracks.
"Don't mind them," Carmine said, "They're with me."
Mahoney stepped back along the mirrored wall behind the bar and picked up the television remote and put on his morning show on Fox. The talking heads were again discussing what the new President would do now that he has taken over for the former one who was suddenly committed to a hospital with no explanation to the American people. Each of the talking heads was surmising what kind of medical problem would land a seemingly fit and healthy man in a hospital with no chance of coming back out again. Enough so that the Vice President was appointed to the top slot.
Mahoney looked at Carmine and said, "Mr. ..ahh.."
"Carmine. Just Carmine."
"Carmine," Mahoney said, "Do you believe all this stuff about the President."
Carmine merely shrugged his shoulders, "In my business people disappear all the time."
A shocked Mahoney opened his newspaper and spread it out on the bar in front of himself and began reading with one ear tuned to the television.
After a few minutes a car could be heard pulling into the gravel parking lot. Four doors banged shut. Mahoney began to sweat and his eyes were glued on the door. The door opened and the three Russian men from last night plus a fourth one entered the bar and strode up to the bar.
The lead man snapped his fingers and the other three pulled out guns.
"Excuse me," said Carmine.
The group looked in his direction noticing him for the first

time. Carmine slowly rose from his chair to his full stature of about five foot seven inches, straightening his suit coat and tie with his hand. Then he pointed his stubby fat finger at the lead man and said in his heavy Italian accented voice, "you guys need to get out of here and you will never come back. Capice?"

"Who the hell are you old man?" the leader spat out turning to his companions that laughed on cue.

"I'm the man who's gonna' make you cement shoes if you don't get your ass out of here pronto."

The group laughed again. The leader pointed his gun at Carmine and said, "Make me old man."

Carmine looked at Mahoney and said, "Kids, always thinkin' with their dick."

"Hey old man," the leader said with his fading Russian accent, "Are you ready to die?"

"Better men than you have asked that," Carmine replied, "Those men are no longer with us."

The group laughed. Then the smiles disappeared from their faces. From behind the bar two huge men also dressed in black suits stood with assault rifles pointed at the group which made the tactical error of staying grouped together. Then the door to the restroom area opened and several more huge men in black suits stepped out with their assault rifles aimed at the group.

"I didn't stay alive this long by being stupid," Carmine said as he strode up to the leader. Carmine wrenched the pistol from his hand then backhanded him with his beefy hand and said, "Look, punk, you need to make a quick decision. You can die here and now or you can take your Russian ass back to where it came from and never show your face here again. Capice?"

The group lowered their weapons. One of Carmine's men came from around the bar and gathered up all the guns. The newest addition to the group did not want to let go of his gun. Carmine's man stomped hard on his foot. When the man yelled in pain, Carmine's man smacked him hard in the gut bending him over. Carmine's man then grabbed him by the chin and pulled his face up to his eye level and said to Carmine while sneering at the man, "I think he'll take about a size ten cement loafer, boss." Carmine's man left go of his chin and smacked him on the cheek with his open palm while laughing in his face, "You putz."

"Mahoney," Carmine said, 'call these putzs' a cab."

"There aren't any cabs in Punxsutawney."

"That's okay call one in Pittsburgh, that's where they're heading anyway. And I'm sure these tough guys can afford the cab fare."

The leader summoned up his courage and said, "We'll drive our own car back."

"Oh yeah," Carmine said to Mahoney, "Call the fire department too."

"Why," Mahoney asked. No sooner were the words out of his mouth when they all heard the explosion and the whoosh of fire from the parking lot.

"Cause these guys lost their ride," Carmine said.

As if on cue three police cars screamed into the parking lot and entered the bar with their guns drawn. Carmine's men faded into the background. The lead police officer a state policeman looked around the room. Spying Carmine he asked him, "Is everything okay here?"

"Sure, these guys were just waiting for a cab 'cause their car caught fire."

The state police officer smiled at Carmine and said, "That's a shame."

The police turned to leave when the state police officer turned back to Carmine and said, "If you need anything Mr. Rizzo, just call."

"You bring that pretty wife of yours by the restaurant sometime soon and have a nice pasta dinner on me," Carmine replied.

Chapter 16

The phone in Sarge's pocket vibrated again. This time he answered it.

"Yeah," he said quietly.

"It's Bobby. How are you doing?"

"Okay, got two of them bagged and gagged."

"There's a third. Call your dad or Kurt, let them know. After you get the third one, meet me at Mahoney's bar."

"Sounds good."

Sarge immediately called his dad.

"This is Terry."

"Dad," Sarge said, "You and Kurt okay?"

"Sure."

"We caught two of the guys. Bobby says there's a third and after we catch him we're to meet Bobby at Mahoney's."

"Well then let's get going. I could use some breakfast."

"First we have to catch the third one."

"That'll be easy. We have him in the back of Mike's truck."

Sarge hung up the phone, shook his head and said to Mike, "We need to find a gurney or two to transport our catches downstairs. Dad and Kurt have the last one. We're to meet Bobby at Mahoney's."

Bobby pulled into the parking lot at Mahoney's in time to watch the fire department put out the remaining fire on a vehicle. He went inside the bar.

"Well, I'll be damned. Carmine," Bobby said, "What are you doing here."

"Terry called and asked me to do him a favor so I came over this morning."

"You're a good man Carmine."

"Don't let shit like that get around," Carmine said in his heavy accent with the beginnings of a smile on his face.

"Hang around just a couple minutes, Terry and the others will be over real soon."

"Hey Mahoney," Carmine said, "You got some breakfast here you can cook up? My boys worked up an appetite."

"Sure," Mahoney said and he wrapped his apron around him and went into the kitchen.

"Make plenty Ed.," Said Bobby, "Cause when Sarge, Terry, Kurt and Mike get here, those guys can put away some food."

It was only a few minutes till everyone in Mahoney's bar could hear the roar of the big Dodge Ram pulling into the parking lot throwing gravel from the huge tires. The door opened and the group of men piled in.

Mahoney had just brought out a huge plate of scrambled eggs that he sat on the bar like a buffet with crispy bacon, toast and plenty of coffee. Carmine's men were not shy as they loaded down plates with food and sat at a table to eat. Everyone else followed suit, except for Carmine. One of his men had brought him a plate of food and a cup of coffee and placed it carefully in front of him waiting for his nod of approval. When he slightly nodded his head the man went back to filling a plate for himself.

"So Sarge," Bobby said, "how did it go?"

"All three are out in the back of Mike's truck, gagged and bagged. How about you?"

"Mine weren't so lucky. They didn't choose to come along peacefully, which reminds me, I need to call the Colonel to clean up that mess."

Carmine looked at Bobby and asked, "You got a guy what comes and takes away dead bodies for you?"

"Yeah, the Colonel, he's the head of an agency that I can't tell you about because it doesn't exist."

Carmine looked at his men and said, "That's what we need boys. Someone to come and haul the bodies away."

The men laughed heartily and one of them said, "Yeah, that's the messiest part. I've ruined some good suits doin' that."

The men laughed again. Mahoney shivered and went back into the kitchen coming back out with more coffee.

"So, are we all done here?" Sarge asked Bobby.

"We will be as soon as I make one more phone call," Bobby answered then began dialing a phone.

"Where'd you get the phone?" Sarge asked.

"From one on the guys that tried to kill me a few minutes ago."

"Spoils of war," Carmine said and this time he did actually smile.

Mahoney's phone rang and he answered it, "hello?"

"Hi Ed," Bobby said, "we need to talk!" and he hung up the phone and with his finger motioned for Ed to come over and sit down at the table with him and Carmine.

Carmine was a person that missed nothing. He may have been eating but he caught not only every word that Bobby said, he also caught every bit of body language.

"You want we should leave while you take care of business?" Carmine asked Bobby.

"No Carmine. I got no secrets from you."

Carmine shrugged his shoulders and picked up his coffee cup, waiting and watching.

"Why'd you call me Bobby, when I'm right here?"

"This isn't my phone," Bobby replied as he held up the phone and showed Ed.

"I don't understand."

"I took this phone off the man that just tried to kill me a few minutes ago."

"I still don't understand."

"The last phone call this man received before he decided to come after me, came from you," Bobby said and he stared seriously at Mahoney.

The sweat beaded up on Mahoney's brow. Carmine sat down his coffee cup and said to Mahoney, "I come up here and help you and you do this?"

"Wait, please, you don't understand."

"Obviously," Bobby said.

"It's not what you think."

"I know a man just tried to kill me. And I know you called him right before that happened. What is it that I don't understand?"

Mahoney put both hands to his face and trembled. Finally in a hushed voice he said, "They made me. They took all my life savings. It just vanished from my bank and my IRA overnight."

"Who? Those clowns that Carmine just sent packing?" Bobby asked.

"No. I don't know who. It's just a voice over the phone."

"Well what did this voice say?"

"And make it good," Carmine interjected.

"I was told that I was being recruited to assist my country and when I did all my assets would be returned."

"Was this voice a man or woman? Foreign or local?" Bobby asked.

"I couldn't tell it was like a machine talking."

"And you listened to a machine?" Carmine asked.

"I thought it was a joke then my money disappeared. I even called the bank and the insurance company and they told me the IRS had placed a hold on it."

Carmine looked at his group of men and said, "We need to learn how to do that?"

Bobby asked Mahoney, "Exactly what were you to do?"

"First I was told just to keep track of Calvin and his family. The voice said he was going to be a traitor to his country and that they would take care of him, they just needed someone local to keep track of him."

"What else?"

"When you guys showed up I got another call that said just to keep track of you guys, and every now and then they would call and ask where you were."

"And you told them?" Bobby asked.

"I did. And I'm really sorry. I would never want anything to happen to you guys."

Carmine looked at Bobby, "you want we should make him disappear or are you gonna' call this Colonel fella and let him take care of it for you? I can't believe you got such a sweet deal."

Bobby looked towards Sarge, Terry, Mike and Kurt. They all understood what he was asking without asking. They all gave a small nod.

Bobby answered Carmine, "no, I think he's a victim. I think we'll rehabilitate him."

"What does that mean?" Mahoney asked in a shaky voice.

"Means it's your lucky day, Ed," Bobby replied, "I guess the guys like you. Now what number does this voice call from? Let me see your phone."

Bobby scrolled down through the list of received calls and as he expected the callers either had been assigned names or it said "No number."

Bobby made a call with Ed's phone. When it was answered he said, "Colonel, I need you to trace some calls back from this phone for me."

When Bobby hung up Carmine looked at him and said, "can you hook me up with this Colonel of yours? He could come in real handy."

Bobby smiled but said nothing. After a minute Bobby said, "Let's go home guys."

Then looking towards Mahoney, Bobby said "I'm going to keep your phone and take your calls for the next couple days. If you hear anything from anybody, you call me immediately."

Mahoney nodded his head affirmatively.

Carmine looked at Mahoney and said in his low heavily accented voice, "Don't send anyone else after Bobby, or you'll be dealing with me."

"Bobby," Mike asked, "What am I supposed to do with the crap in the bed of my truck."

"Take them to Calvin's house and drop them with the bodies. The Colonel will take care of them."

"Come on Bobby," Carmine said, "Introduce me to this Colonel guy."

Chapter 17

Bobby Morrow lives in a modern log home just outside of the borough of Ganister on seventy five acres of fields and woodland. The home is situated on the back corner of a former corn field that now requires many hours of mowing to prevent the grass from taking over the gravel driveway. Ten yards from the back of the two story home the maple, oak, and cherry trees take over providing excellent cover for the numerous deer, squirrels, raccoons, turkey, and every type of bird in western Pennsylvania plus the occasional black bear and mountain lion.

Bobby was spending a lazy morning drinking his coffee while gently gliding back and forth on the swing that hangs from the rafters on the expansive side porch. His mind kept going back to Mahoney's cell phone which he was also fidgeting with, in the hand not occupied by the coffee cup. His intense thoughts were abruptly shattered when the cell phone rang. Bobby stared at it for a moment then looked to see who the caller was. It was the unlisted number of the person that had been giving Mahoney his instructions and the false information that Calvin and everyone connected to him were traitors of the United States. Bobby made the decision and casually answered the phone.

"Yes," he said.

"Who's this?" replied the mechanized garbled voice.

"Who's this?"

"Well let me see. You're not Ed Mahoney."

"That's right."

"So you must be the infamous Bobby Morrow."

"You win any prize on the bottom shelf," Bobby said, "Now who are you?"

"Who I am is not important yet."

"Yet?"

"All in due time Mr. Morrow. All in due time."

"Look," Bobby said, "let's cut to the chase. Why are you trying to frame me for shooting a Secret Service agent, and then actually trying to kill me?"

"All in due time."

"Well here's a news flash. If you want to get me, then stop sending amateurs that will just continue to get hurt. In fact, why don't you just come yourself and we'll settle this once and for all. You and me. Mano a mano."

"As I said, all in due time."

"Well there's no fence around me, if you want me, come and get me, "Bobby spat out then hung up the phone.

He immediately called the Colonel on his own new phone and asked if the Colonel had been able to trace the mysterious number back to the owner yet.

"Not yet, Bobby, "the Colonel replied, "And we may not be able to. It just bounces off cell towers and satellites all over not only this country but several other countries."

"Thanks anyway," Bobby said and hung up.

His nice laid back morning shattered, he decided to take his empty coffee cup into the house, grab his favorite rifle and pistol and take a walk around his seventy five acres. That would not only give him time to think but hopefully also bring his blood pressure back down.

Bobby went out the backdoor, across the porch, down the steps, across the lawn and stepped into the woods. His woods. His pace slowed considerably as his eyes shifted all around, and up and down, looking for his neighbors, the woodland creatures that called his woods home. He spied a redtail hawk sitting near the top of a pin oak tree scanning the area for any signs of life that could be converted to breakfast. The hawk looked upward and Bobby's eyes followed where he spied the low but fast moving helicopter that was closing in on the Morrow residence. Bobby looked for marks on the helicopter curious to know if it was from the Altoona hospital on its way to pick up a passenger. There were no marks on the helicopter. It was black with no letters or numbers on it at all. The only other helicopters that Bobby had seen like that ended up being government copters. As it stayed on course for Bobby's farm, Bobby looked lower and saw the two black SUV's turning off the asphalt highway and onto his gravel lane where they immediately kicked up dust clouds. Bobby didn't waste any time, he dialed Claire's cell phone. She answered quickly and he said, "Claire go immediately out the back door and into the woods. I'll meet you there."
Claire started to say something but Bobby had already hung up so Claire did exactly as she was instructed. She ran out the back door and sprinted across the lawn into the tree line. Bobby was waiting and grabbed her around the waist as he immediately set off further into the woods where they would not be spotted but where he could watch whatever was about to happen.
Bobby had excellent instincts and the ability to make immediate decisions which had served him well and kept him from harm's way when he was a soldier in Vietnam, then as a federal undercover agent, and even now as a supposedly retired federal undercover agent. The sight he was watching was an aggressive and deadly maneuver in the making.

The two black SUV's slid to a halt, the doors opened, and men dressed all in black ran from the vehicles to Bobby's house. The helicopter made a fast stop, dropping off a lone figure then taking back off again. The men from the SUV's had surrounded the house and all had their automatic weapons slung from their shoulders and pointed at Bobby's house. Bobby couldn't see the front of the house but he assumed they were entering through that door. His hunch was verified when he saw the soldiers pacing past the windows down stairs, then he noticed a couple upstairs looking back out through the windows.

"Were you able to grab your gun?" Bobby asked Claire.

"No, you sounded like I should hurry."

"And you were right to hurry."

Bobby pulled out his cell phone and was about to call Sarge when he closed the phone again.

"Aren't you going to call someone?" Claire asked.

"Too risky, they may home in on the phone's GPS and come and get us. Do you have your phone?"

"No, I left it in the house."

The group of men began filing back out of the house.

"Come on," Bobby said to Claire, "we better move on. Be very quiet and stay close to me."

Bobby moved deeper into the woods then curved around to the right so that we would end up behind where the SUV's were parked.

Carmine Rizzo was seated in his usual booth in his own restaurant reading the newspaper, watching the financial channel on the television and waiting for one of his men to bring him breakfast. He had just sat his near empty coffee cup down on the red and white checked tablecloth that always adorned his tables when he heard the low flying helicopter buzz over his restaurant.

"What the hell was that?" he asked no one in particular but everyone in general.

"Don't know boss," one of his men answered.

Another went out the back door to see what was going on. One of the features of Carmine's restaurant that everyone that ate there liked was that it was perched on the side of a short mountain. From the back windows or outside you could see the highway below that ran into Ganister along the Juanita River. Carmine's man saw the back of the helicopter which was incredibly low to the ground then he noticed the two fast moving black SUV's down on the highway racing into Ganister. He watched for a minute before reporting back to Carmine.

"Boss," he said to Carmine after going back into the restaurant, "must be the feds up to something."

"Why? What did you see?" Carmine asked.

This new black chopper was way too low, plus down on the Ganister road there were two black SUV's speeding along."

"Did they all go into Ganister?"

"No turned just after the bridge and headed up the hill out towards your friend Bobby's place."

"No shit?" Carmine asked.

"Get Morrow on the phone. Let's see if he knows what's going on. You other guys make some calls. I want to know what's going on in my town."

Everyone dropped what they were doing and began calling people. Loud voices could be heard all through the restaurant and free hands were waving furiously as though it helped them talk faster. The cook brought Carmine's breakfast and he dug in as though he was late for an appointment.

By the time Bobby and Claire had moved quickly and quietly through the woods curving around toward the open lawn where Bobby had a view, the men in black military uniforms were in a line approaching the tree line. The house being empty but obviously just deserted they assumed the woods was the place to find who they were looking for. Bobby raised his rifle and shot the man closest to him. As a former sniper it would only take one shot for each man. Bobby worked the bolt on the rifle ejecting the spent shell and placing a fresh one in the magazine while he put his sights on the second man who was in the process of moving toward the woods line. The crosshairs in Bobby's scope marked the spot, he squeezed the trigger and a second man dropped. The odds were getting better. The sounds of the two quick shots finally registered in the minds of the attackers. They dropped to the ground and looking for the source of the gunshots. Bobby grabbed Claire's arm and they ran while bent over back deeper into the woods. Bobby knew it would only take the attackers a moment to figure out approximately where the shots came from. By then he intended to be somewhere else. After sprinting deeper into the woods for a few yards Bobby slowed his pace considerably and turned back to the left. Back towards where he had just came from. Not very far ahead was what he was looking for as he had been through every inch of his woods many times over the years that he had lived here. He came upon the old wooden tree stand that many years ago hunters used to get their prize winning bucks with ten and twelve point antlers. Bobby told Claire to stay on the ground. He handed Claire his pistol and began climbing the rickety wood stairs nailed to the fat old oak tree. When he got to the platform he scanned the woods through his scope. The men in black would be hard to pick out in the dense woods, but as an experienced hunter Bobby would find them. He caught movement through the gun's scope and moved back to the spot where it occurred. There was one of the men slowly making his way through the high brush. Bobby placed his sights on the man, pulled the trigger and immediately began looking for the next one. Just like in Vietnam. There was no time to spend on the man in the crosshairs after you pulled the

trigger, staying alive meant finding the next predator and
squeezing the trigger again. One man had slipped under
Bobby's field of vision. He was just feet from Claire. Claire not
wanting to give away Bobby's position began to run. The
commotion attracted Bobby's attention. He quickly put the
man in his sights and pulled the trigger. Then he called out to
Claire in a low voice to find out where she had run to.
"Bobby," Claire said in a pained voice, "Help me."
Bobby slid down the tree ignoring the cuts and scrapes he
received on his body after slinging the rifle by the strap across
his back. He ran toward the sound. Claire was lying on the
ground. Bobby pulled his rifle off his back and scanned the
area for attackers. Not seeing any he hustled over to Claire.
"Are you all right?" he asked in a hushed voice.
"I tripped over that branch," she said while pointing behind
her, "I think my ankle is sprained or broken. I can't stand."
Bobby felt her ankle and it had already mushroomed to twice
the size that it should be. Bobby tried to stand her up.
Claire gasped. Bobby looked at her to ask if it hurt. Claire
pointed behind Bobby. Bobby turned. Four automatic
weapons were pointing at him.

Carmine wiped his face with his napkin then yelled out,
"Gino, get the car."
"Yes, boss," came the reply as Gino, who was the size of a
small mountain and had no neck, he was just a massive chest
with a big old head mounted on top, pulled off his white
apron, threw it on the bar and attempted to run out of the
restaurant to get the boss's car. The others immediately
showed up in front of Carmine.
"You guys," Carmine said speaking to the entire group, "Get
some 'tools' and get the other car. Let's go."
"Where we going boss?" one of the braver men asked.
"Morrow's house. My gut tells me something's going on."
The other beefy men ran into the kitchen and came back with

their "tools". The tools of their trade consisted primarily of large intimidating forty-five pistols that could not only put a hole in a person big enough to drive a bus through, but if it was necessary to just put you to sleep, the size of these pistols was akin to smacking someone in the head with a two by four. With the "tools" stuck in their waist bands the men quickly pulled on their suit coats and everyone exited the rear door and into the waiting black Cadillacs. This was friendship. This was helping a friend in need. This was doing it the old way. The Ganister way!

Bobby pulled Claire off the ground and held her tight around the waist with one hand while he took the rifle off his back with the other hand and dropped it to the ground. Claire leaned against Bobby with one foot raised like a flamingo resting, and dropped her pistol next to Bobby's rifle. One of the group spoke into a hand held radio, "we have him." It sounded like a herd of elephants charging through the wooded area and after a few minutes another man in black appeared leading a tall, skinny woman also dressed in black military fatigues.
The women stopped next to the men training their automatic weapons on Bobby. A huge smiled spread across her face.
"Well, well, well," she said, "If it isn't the infamous Bobby Morrow. You said I should, how did you put it? Come and get you? Well here I am! And look at you. Pitiful."
"I should have known," Bobby spat back.
"So you do recognize me?" the woman asked still smiling.
"Sure."
"Bobby, who is this bitch?" Claire asked with pain in her voice.
"Why dear don't you recognize the former First Lady?" Bobby asked.
"Obannon?" Claire asked, "What the hell are you doing?"

"That's right. I'm Melissa Obannon. FORMER First Lady. My husband was the most powerful man in the world and I was the most powerful woman in the world, until this asshole," she said as she pointed to Bobby, "Took it all away. I don't know how you did it. But you did it."

"So you thought you would kill a Secret Service agent," Bobby spat back, "And frame me for it?"

"I thought it would be quite nice if you spent the rest of your life in prison since my husband is locked away somewhere in a "hospital" all because of you."

"Your husband was a traitor. A Russian plant that got elected to office by bleeding heart voters that swallowed his line of bullshit hook, line and sinker."

"I don't care how he got to this country. He was the President and I was the First Lady," she said her voice getting louder and louder until she yelled at Bobby, "Until you took it away from me."

"You're as sick as he is."

"Take the wife," the woman said to her companion. Several of the men with their weapons still trained on Bobby grabbed Claire by the arms and pulled her away from Bobby. Claire screamed out in pain.

"We'll just do this a different way, Bobby Morrow. Since you took away my spouse, I think I'll take yours. Perhaps we can sell her to white slave traders in Columbia."

The woman laughed. A hearty laugh that bounced off the trees in the forest. Bobby dove for his gun.

"Do it and she dies first," one of the men said as he pressed the barrel of his weapon against Claire's head.

Bobby slowly stood back up leaving his rifle lie on the ground.

"Trust me when I say this to you," Bobby said to the woman, "I will find you. I will get my wife back. And I will kill you."

The woman laughed. One of the aggressors smacked Bobby on the side of his head violently. Bobby fell to the ground motionless.

"What shall we do with him?"

"Let him be," the woman said, "I like having this one better."

"Bobby," Claire shouted.

"Shut her up," the woman said.

 The woman and what was left of her marauding group pulled Claire along through the woods and out into the bright green grass towards the waiting black SUV's. Cuffing Claire's hands behind her back and tossing her roughly in the back of one of the SUV's the group started their vehicles and headed down the gravel driveway. Where the driveway meets the asphalt highway a black Cadillac screeched to a halt causing the two black SUV's to slide to a stop. The beefy men jumped out of the Cadillac and aimed their massive pistols at the lead car. The second SUV saw what was happening and the driver put the vehicle into reverse and looked backward. Before he could push the accelerator the driver felt the warmth of the blood and tissue that splattered all over his face from his passenger. The passenger side window was shattered and half of the passenger's head was gone. Before the driver could get his thoughts together there was a knock on his window. A huge pistol was tapping the glass. The man behind the pistol was smiling as he motioned for the driver to get out of the vehicle.

The driver did as he was told. As he got out he placed his hands flat on top of his head.

"No don't do that," the beefy man said with his slurred Italian accent, "make my day! Go for your gun."

"He won't do it," said the man who had shot out the passenger side window and had now come around the back of the vehicle, "He's a putz."

"I knew he wouldn't do it," the beefy man said, "But I always wanted to say that ever since I saw that movie with what's his name in it."

"Clint Eastwood."

"Yeah that's the guy," the man said as a smile crossed his face, "Go ahead, make my day!"

"Let's go see if the boss needs us," the second man said.

"What'll we do with this guy?"

"I don't care. Shoot him if you want."

"But he has his hands on his head like some kind of war prisoner."

"Do whatever you want. Let's go."

The beefy man shrugged his shoulders then smashed the massive forty-five pistol against the man's temple. He dropped like a bag of rocks.

"Don't go away," the beefy man said to the prone body.

The two men walked up to the first vehicle and one of them said, "Hey boss you need any help."

"What the hell for?" Carmine said in his gravelly Italian.

"Just askin', boss."

"Yeah well grab that piece of shit laying there and ask him politely where Bobby is."

The man smiled, reached down and pulled the man completely off the ground with his huge beefy muscular hands. Smiling broadly at the man he said, "I'm supposed to ask you politely where Bobby is."

The man spit in his face. The beefy man looked to Carmine.

"So much for politely," Carmine said.

The huge beefy hand smashed into the other man's face. Blood flew five feet away and splattered all over everyone. The man's nose was twisted to one side.

"Let me ask you again," the beefy man said, "Where's Bobby."

"Screw you!"

The beefy man grabbed the guy's nose and slowly began twisting it. The excruciating pain caused the man to scream and he nearly passed out. Then the beefy man grabbed one of the man's fingers with his free hand and snapped it backward until it laid completely askew to his hand.

"I can do this all day, pal," the beefy man said, "Where's Bobby?"

"In the woods," the man moaned.

The beefy man threw the other man to the ground and turned to Carmine, "He's in the woods, boss."

"A couple of you go find him."

The pair was just getting to the edge of the woods when Bobby stumbled out on the run, his rifle pointed ahead of him. One of Carmine's men grabbed him and said, "Bobby. It's okay. We got your wife."

Bobby looked down the driveway and saw the welcome sight of Carmine, then he took off running to find Claire.

When Bobby arrived he looked at Claire who had been taken out of the car and had the plastic cuffs removed by Carmine's men. Bobby hugged her and gave her a kiss on the cheek.

"Yo Bobby," Carmine said, "I hate to break up this reunion, but what do you want us to do with this skinny bitch?"

"You'll get 'skinny bitch'," the woman began yelling at Carmine.

"Can I shut her up?" Carmine asked Bobby.

"Let's just duct tape her mouth shut for now," Bobby said. Carmine shrugged his shoulders and one of his men went to the trunk of the Cadillac, got a roll of silver duct tape and proceeded to tape her mouth shut. When the woman slapped him, he roughly jerked her arms behind her back and duct taped her hands as well. The woman continued to try to shout but not much could be heard.

Carmine turned to his men and said, "A couple of you guys take Bobby's wife to the doc and get her fixed up."

"Thanks for coming Carmine," Bobby said, "but how did you know?"

"This is my town," Carmine said, "nothing happens here that I don't know about."

Bobby looked around as one of the black Cadillacs drove away with Claire.

"Some mess," Bobby said.

"Yeah, you think maybe you could call that Colonel person to come clean up his mess?" Carmine asked.

"I'll have to," Bobby said.

"Good, then you can introduce me to him."

"The Colonel doesn't actually come, Carmine," Bobby said, "He's got people that do that stuff. The Colonel doesn't get his hands dirty."

"Damn," Carmine said as he snapped his pudgy fingers, "I sure do want to meet him. I like this having someone to clean up the mess."

Chapter 18 – Several days later

Claire, Nanita, and little Richie pulled into the concrete driveway at Mrs. St.Clair's house. Nanita unbuckled little Richie from the child seat and the group walked through the breezeway and knocked on the back door.

As usual, Auntie M answered the door.

"Well, look who's here, Shorty," Auntie M nearly shouted with surprise.

"Come in. Please come in," Auntie M said to the three guests.

As they entered Mrs. St.Clair came up behind Auntie M.

Mrs. St.Clair clasped both hands to her cheeks as she said, "this is such a nice surprise! I thought you had gone back home Nanita?"

"Our last visit got cut short," Nanita said, "and I just couldn't go home without seeing you again to explain."

"I knew it, "Auntie M said loudly, "Little Richie is Richard's boy, right?"

"Please come in the living room" Mrs. St.Clair said, "would either of you like a cup of coffee?"

"I'd love some, Mrs. St.Clair," Claire said, "It's been such a long past few days."

"I heard there was some trouble at your house," Mrs. St.Clair said, "is everyone all right?"

"Of course," Claire said, "I just hate it when Bobby brings his work home with him."

The ladies laughed. Auntie M brought Claire and Nanita coffee and everyone sat in the comfortable living room with the big bay window that let the sunlight pour in. Richie sat quietly on his mother's lap.

"So what do you want to tell us Nanita?" Auntie M asked.

"M," Mrs. St.Clair said to her, "let the poor girl speak."

"Well Mrs. St.Clair," Nanita began.

"First of all," Mrs. St.Clair said, "We're friends, please call me Shorty like all my other friends do."

"Well, Shorty," Nanita said, "I met Richard many years ago when I worked at the resort that he and Pamela always came to each year. We became friends, but Richard was always completely in love with Pamela. He would never think of looking at another woman let alone anything else and I had great respect for that. After Pamela passed away and Richard and his friends came to place Pamela's ashes in the Caribbean Sea as she requested we had an opportunity to talk to each other. Several years later, I actually came to the United States and I called Richard. We went out to dinner and had a very pleasant evening, but it was obvious that Richard was still very much in love with Pamela even though she had been dead for many years. So we had dinner and we were going to meet again for another diner after he got back from his meeting with the President in Camp David."

"And he never came back," Auntie M interjected.

"Anyway, Mrs. St....Shorty, Richard and I had never slept with each other."

"But, he looks exactly like Richard," Auntie M said.

"During one of our conversations in Aruba when Richard was still married to Pamela I remembered him saying that he and Pamela were going to wait a few years before having children, but he wanted to be sure that when the time came they would be able to so he donated sperm at a sperm bank in Pittsburgh. When I wanted to have a child, I wanted him to grow up to be the same type gentleman that Richard was so I contacted the sperm bank. That was why I came to the States to meet with Richard to tell him that he actually had a son, but I never got the chance."

"But those places are supposed to be anonymous," Auntie M said suspiciously.

" Yes," Nanita replied, "they are. But people are people, and they don't pay those people much of a salary so all it took was a small bribe and I was able to have Richard's sperm implanted in me."

"That's such a wonderful story," Shorty said almost in tears, "And I hope you don't mind sharing little Richie so we can still feel like we have a part of our Richard back again."

"I would love for you to be in his life," Nanita said.

"Who knows," Claire said, "Maybe someday little Richie will be a Senator."

"Probably President," said Auntie M, "Because our Richard certainly would have been had he lived long enough."

Carmine was enjoying his breakfast. Looking at the newspaper and commenting on the stupid things that people continue to do while half listening to the financial news that was on the flatscreen TV over the bar facing him. He looked up to watch something that the commentator had just said. A shocked Carmine shouted, "who the hell are you? What the hell are you doing here?" The loud tone of voice was meant to bring his men running from the restaurant kitchen, which it did. In Carmine's line of work when someone mysteriously appeared before you it was usually bad news. Carmine eyed the intruder cautiously. The man was of medium height, medium build, medium everything. Just an average man except his hair was cut extremely short and it was obvious that under the well tailored suit the man did not have an ounce of fat on him. The man stuck out his hand in an attempt to shake Carmine's hand. Several guns instantly appeared in the hands of Carmine's associates. The intruder slowly raised his hands up to shoulder height and made no quick moves.

"I come in peace, Carmine," the man said.

"You sneak into my place," Carmine said, "which should be impossible," he shot a glance at his men, "and you know my name. Just who the hell are you? And again, how the hell did you get in here?"

"Well," Carmine, "please allow me to start with the second question first. I have made my living being unnoticed. I sort of come and go like the wind, or a ghost."

"People don't come and go like the wind here," Carmine replied shooting another mean spirited glare at his men.

"As for my name, Carmine," the man continued, "most people just call me Colonel."

"Colonel! You're Bobby's Colonel?" Carmine said as he jumped out of his favorite booth and put his meaty hand out to shake the Colonel's hand, "I'll be damned. I told Bobby I wanted to meet you!"

"Yes, he told me," the man said, "That's why I'm here."

Carmine turned to look at his men, "It's the Colonel. It's Bobby's Colonel. I'll be…." Carmine slowly turned to address the Colonel again. He was gone. Like the wind. Like a ghost. Just gone.

Chapter 19

Déjà vu. Bobby had his hot cup of coffee and was spending the early morning hour swinging back and forth on the old oak porch swing. The wooded area he was looking at was still full of life. The trees heavy with their green leaves. The birds singing and flying in and out of the wooded area. The smell of the lilacs and gardenias floating up and mingling with the steam from his coffee.

Then the phone rang.

"Yeah," Bobby said not excited by even having to answer the ring.

"Bobby," the voice said, "it's me."

Me was a voice that Bobby immediately recognized as the Colonel.

"I heard you met Carmine," Bobby said.

"Yes, interesting guy."

"Was there a purpose to your visit?"

"You mean other than the fact that you said you would introduce me sometime?"

"Yes, other than that."

"Well," the Colonel said, "Let me ask you a few questions."

"You do realize I was enjoying a beautiful morning on my porch with a cup of coffee and no stress?"

"Whatever. You told me during our debrief that four men were at the scene plus the Obannon woman."

"Boy you talk about hero to zero; just a couple weeks ago she was the First Lady and now you're calling her 'the Obannon woman'."

"Answer the question Bobby before I send a helicopter there to haul you off your porch swing."

"Wow, someone's grumpy today," Bobby said, "Then went on, yes, there were four men and the Obannon woman. One of them smacked me and when I came to they were all gone including Claire."

"And, when you managed to stumble out of the woods, Carmine and his men were at the SUV's and there were three dead men and one unconscious man. Then Carmine took Claire to the hospital."

"Carmine had two of his men take Claire to the hospital."

"Yes, thank you for the clarification."

"Is there a question in here somewhere Colonel?"

"There is Bobby," the Colonel said, "How perceptive of you. Where is the Obannon woman?"

"I assumed she was in one of the SUV's. As soon as I called you, Carmine and his men left, which I thought was a good idea, and I went to the house. I never looked in the SUV's. No offense but I've seen all the blood in the past few years that I care to see. I, naturally, assumed your men took her with them along with the others. She had been in the SUV with her mouth duct-taped shut waiting for the clean-up crew."

"Surprise," the Colonel said, "She was not there when we arrived."

"Could she have gotten away, like after Carmine left?"

"That's one possibility."

"You don't think Carmine took her do you?"

"You know him better than I do. You tell me."

"So your visit to Carmine was really about looking for the Obannon woman?" Bobby asked.

"Your job may be done Bobby but I have to have NO loose ends. Everything in my world has to be explained and accounted for. And yet, I seem to be short a body. Yes, I checked the vehicles for blood at Carmine's, and there was none, except what you would expect to find if someone had smashed their knuckles on another person's face, but, if she was alive when they took her there probably wouldn't be any blood to find."

"Bummer," Bobby said.

"Indeed," the Colonel replied, "Do me a favor. While you are watching the grass grow and listening to the birds sing, see if you can imagine what could have happened to my other person please. You'll do that for me, won't you?"

Bobby started to reply but he was talking to static. He was still staring at the phone when Claire wandered out onto the porch with her cup of coffee.

"Isn't this nice," She said to Bobby.

"It was."

"Why, who called?" Claire asked.

"The Colonel."

"You're not planning on going anywhere are you?" Claire asked as her previously sunny disposition began slipping away.

"It seems we're missing a body."

"Missing a body!" Claire said in astonishment, "How does a body go missing?"

"That witch that was taking you captive, "Bobby said, "She cannot be accounted for."

"Who cares?" Claire said, "Just be glad the old witch is gone."

"The Colonel cares."

"Which means that my husband now has to care," Claire said as she lowered her eyes to her steaming cup of coffee, "You don't have to rush out of here, do you?"

"I have to go see Carmine," Bobby said, "And the sooner the better."

"So you think Carmine took her? What for?"

"Who knows. But the Colonel will want to know if he did take her, was she dead or alive? And if she was alive and he took her, is she still alive?"

"Well frankly, Scarlet," Claire said imitating the Gone With the Wind movie, "I say either way, good riddance."

"But there is another option."

"What's that?"

"No one was watching her and she made a get-a-way," Bobby said.

Claire looked up from her coffee cup, "You mean that sleazy woman could still be out there?"

"And still waiting to put a bullet in me," Bobby said.

"All of a sudden, I don't feel like swinging on the back porch out in the open, do you?"

"Not without a gun."

"And another thing," Claire announced, "We need to get serious about getting another good dog."

"Well I guess I'm driving over to Carmine's," Bobby said. Bobby got up from the comfort of the porch swing, took his coffee cup into the house, put on his shoes and prepared to drive over to Carmine's restaurant.

Bobby was approaching his old truck when Claire came out of the house.

"I'm going with you," she announced.

"Claire, you don't want to go talk to Carmine."

"You're probably right," she snapped back, "But I also don't want to be sitting around here if that woman is still out there somewhere."

Bobby walked around to the passenger side of his old beat up red pickup truck and opened the door for Claire.

"No way," she announced as she opened the driver's side door of her own car, "Get in."

"Claire I can't be getting chauffeured to Carmine's by my wife. The last time I was there with Sarge, Carmine called us girl scouts. Imagine how this will go over."

"Suck it up, tough-guy," Claire said as she settled into the driver's seat and fastened her seatbelt.

"Claire!"

Bobby was lucky to get both feet in the car when the Hemi engine roared to life and Claire started down the gravel lane. When she pulled out onto the asphalt highway, she stomped on the accelerator. Two long black rubber lines marked the highway.

Claire pulled into the gravel parking lot at Carmine's restaurant. Bobby jumped out of the car as soon as it stopped and headed for the back door.

"Why are you going that way?" Claire asked him.

"Because the restaurant is not open yet. If you want to see Carmine, you have to go in the rear entrance."

Bobby started to open the rear door and Claire being used to having the door opened for her, attempted to enter. Bobby elbowed his way in front of her which caused her to stop dead in her tracks and stare holes through the back of Bobby's head. As soon as Bobby entered the door, he stopped dead in his tracks and the now moving Claire ran into him.

"What are you doing?" Claire asked him.

Bobby raised his hands and merely pointed inside where two of Carmine's men stood with guns aimed at the door.

"I just need to talk to Carmine," Bobby said.

The men then saw Claire.

"Sorry Mrs. Morrow," one of the men said, "We didn't know you were coming."

Claire cuffed Bobby on the back of his head, "maybe you should have called, girl scout."

The two large men snickered as they put their guns back into their underarm holsters. The same one that spoke earlier nodded his head in the direction of the bar to tell Bobby to go in.

Claire followed Bobby closely.

Carmine was watching his financial news on the flatscreen television and at the same time reading the newspaper. When Bobby was almost alongside Carmine, he said without looking up, "Morrow, what do you want?"

"I need to ask you a couple questions Carmine."

"I save your ass and now you want to ask me questions?" Carmine noticed Claire, "Oh, Mrs. Morrow, how are you today?"

Carmine then looked back at Bobby and said, "You should have called first Bobby. You could have got this beautiful young lady hurt."

"Sorry Carmine."

"Won't you please sit down Mrs. Morrow?"

Claire slid into the red naugahyde booth opposite Carmine. Bobby slid in next to her.

"So what is so important, Bobby?"

"When you 'saved my ass, as you put it, what happened to the woman that was in the black SUVs?"

"What woman?"

"Carmine, the mouthy one that you had duct taped. I have to inquire for the Colonel as he has to answer to his higher ups."

"Not sure I want to talk to you about this, former undercover agent Morrow."

Come on Carmine," Bobby pleaded, "I thought we were friends."

"We are."

"Then tell me what you did with her."

Carmine studied the newspaper for awhile then said to Bobby, "Mr. Morrow, would you be so kind as to go into the kitchen and ask the boys to bring your lovely wife a cup of coffee?"

Bobby hesitated then got up from the booth and went into the kitchen through the door that said, "Employees only."

"Mrs. Morrow, you really shouldn't be here."

"Carmine, this is exactly where I should be.

"Why is Bobby so concerned about this woman?"

"I'm more concerned than he is. I can't feel comfortable in my own home, wondering if this woman is still out there somewhere and planning how to get at Bobby or me again."

"I like you Claire," Carmine said in his gravelly Italian accent, "So I'm going to tell you something that I will not tell your husband because he still answers to the government and I don't need any problems."

"Thank you Carmine."

Carmine studied her a second then said, "You tell no one that I have said this, but, you can go home and sleep like a baby tonight, because there is no chance that woman is ever coming back to see you."

"Carmine," Claire said in amazement, "Are you saying what I think you're saying?"

"The only thing I'm saying is that you can go home and not have to look over your shoulder for that woman, and you have my word on it."

"Carmine, you didn't do anything that you will get you in trouble, did you?"

"What you think all us old dogs know how to do is fit a person with cement shoes?"

"Well, yes."

"I wouldn't pollute my Blue Hole with slime like that woman, let alone the fact that I'm not stupid enough to put bodies on my own property."

"But these days they test for DNA and all kinds of forensic stuff and I wouldn't want you to get in trouble when you were so nice to help us out of a serious jam."

"Just one more question Carmine."

"No questions, Claire," Carmine assured her, "I gave you my word the woman will not bother you. Ever!"

Bobby came back into the restaurant carrying two cups of coffee.

"So Carmine," Bobby said, "What…

Carmine held up the palm of his hand to stop Bobby.

"No questions," Carmine said.

Bobby nodded.

Carmine asked Bobby, "Did the Colonel come here to meet me? Or was he here for another reason?"

Carmine stared intently at Bobby waiting for the answer.

"The Colonel wanted to meet you," Bobby replied, "But the fact that he came alone means he probably also was looking for signs of the woman."

"Go home, Bobby. Take your lovely wife for a long walk in the woods. Make love. Whatever. Just go home."

Carmine looked at Claire and said, "Thank you for stopping by dear. You come back again, soon."

"Carmine," Claire said, "Thank you for the coffee."
Claire pushed Bobby out of the booth then she stood up to go.
Bobby was dumbfounded.
"So Morrow," Carmine asked, "What are you gonna' tell the
Colonel?"
"I'm going to tell him that you are the most stubborn, tight-
lipped old fart that I have ever known and that I still don't
know if the Obannon woman escaped or was taken away by
you."
"Accounting, schmounting."
"Yes, well the Colonel will not stop digging."
"Sure he will," Carmine said as the beginning of a smile
appeared on his face, "one day the Colonel will find her and
then his bookkeeper will have everyone accounted for and he
can move on to the next problem."

Carmine Rizzo was an old dog. And old school. He had
principles that could not be changed. He believed in Respect,
Trust, and Loyalty to name a few. Carmine demanded that
people respect him, and when others earned it, they were
respected. Richard St.Clair was one of those that Carmine
respected enough to call him a friend. Richard's father had
done some jobs for Carmine and more recently Richard had
called on the Attorney General Ellwood Sine to investigate
when the IRS swooped in and commandeered some rare old
coins that Carmine had inherited. The IRS said that the coins
did not belong to the previous owner legally and thus could
not be passed to Carmine. They had a track record of doing
this on several occasions. On this occasion they picked a fight
with the wrong old dog. Attorney General Sine overturned the
IRS's decision and had the rare coins, worth millions of
dollars, returned to carmine. Carmine would never forget
what Richard did for him.

Carmine was also from the old school that believed in an eye for an eye. He didn't live this long by not being extremely careful in all his dealings and by letting it be known that harming one of Carmine' family or friends could have fatal consequences. Carmine's friends all came under his protective umbrella.

The locals all thought that Carmine only believed in the old cement shoes made famous by the old mafia. But Carmine was much smarter than that. For starters, when Carmine wanted a body to disappear it did just that. It was gone forever. But never on Carmine's property that would be just plain stupid and Carmine was not a stupid man. There were also occasions when Carmine would want a body to resurface, to send a message to an enemy or even to eliminate a potential rival. When these things happened though you could be sure that Carmine would never be implicated. Most people watched the new cop shows and heard about DNA and body fluids and using that to convict people. Carmine watched those same shows, but Carmine also studied more in depth about DNA and the other forensic items as a general business practice so no one in his organization would make such mistakes. Carmine and his men did not leave fingerprints or DNA anywhere. When they packed their guns and other weapons to go on the offensive they took along plastic sheets to wrap bodies in and contain all the bodily fluids. You will never find a speck of blood or other bodily fluids in the trunk of one of Carmine's cars.

Chapter 20 – several months later

Claire Morrow was enjoying her early morning first cup of coffee with her new morning ritual. Claire had become enamored with the intensity which Carmine Rizzo had put into studying the financial news and the newspaper. But the more she thought about it, the more sense it made. In the old days Carmine made most of his money illegally, everyone knew that. But these days, Carmine's business pursuits were legitimate and above board. Carmine had taken those ill gotten gains and used them to create an empire which he now used to do many good things for people.

Claire had reached the point in her life, and especially with the recent downturn in the economy, when she wanted to start building wealth for the future. She began following Carmine's lead and studying the financial news each morning. Claire was watching Becky on Squawk Box when Becky interrupted with a news flash, "we are going to go live now to Punxsutawney, Pennsylvania for a Special report from Joe Kernen. Can you hear me Joe?"

The picture changed from the CNBC studios to Joe Kernen standing inside a huge warehouse type building full of silver objects.

Joe began his report, "This business, Punxsy Lumber was closed down over a year ago due to the downturn in the economy following then President Obannon's many policy changes. Punxsy Lumber is a company the uses microwave dry kilns to dry lumber specifically for the furniture industry. Most dry kilns are large buildings which get filled with long boards stacked with air spaces in between the rows to allow the lumber to dry. For the furniture industry they use a lot of small pieces of wood." Joe held up a block of wood for the camera. "This size wood can be stacked into these much smaller microwave kilns and dried in a considerably shorter time. The large kilns take about a month to dry the lumber. These microwave kilns can do it in a matter of days. The moisture content of wood used in the furniture industry needs to get down to six to ten percent to be able to be used without warping and bending. Then these blocks of wood are sent to furniture manufactures to be lathed into chair parts and other items. With the economy slowly coming back to life since

President Obannon left office, this business called back their employees yesterday and the employees began filling these dry kilns with pallets of wood blocks to be dried and then shipped out to furniture manufacturers. These very same employees were sent home yesterday after only a few hours. The irony of this situation is mindboggling. As you can see to my left," Joe pointed in that direction, "there is police tape around one of the microwave dry kilns. When the employees attempted to fill that dry kiln they discovered a body. The local police were called. The local police then contacted the State Police who in turn contacted the federal authorities. This business has been overrun with Secret Service, FBI, and even Homeland Security. The employees have all been questioned and are right now at home waiting to once again get called back to work. It seems that the body that was discovered in that dry kiln was the body of former First Lady Melissa Obannon. She had eluded her Secret Service detail a few months back, but authorities were convinced that she just wanted to be alone to grieve her husband that is in such poor health that he had to resign as President of the United States. Ironic that her husband's policies caused this business to close and now her shriveled up body is found in a dry kiln. As we learn more details, we will come back to you. Becky, back to you in the studio."

Bobby had wandered into the kitchen but was shushed by Claire when he tried to speak and forced to listen to the live news report.

Becky came back on the television, "we have an update to Joe's story in Punxsutawney, Pennsylvania. The FBI has made an arrest. A picture of a man flashed on the screen. This man was taken into custody just minutes ago by the FBI. His fingerprints were at the scene. The FBI has a witness that saw his vehicle there several weeks ago. The man is a Russian immigrant attempting to extend the grasp of the Russian mafia. He is also being charged with drug dealing,

prostitution and extortion. Let's go live now to Pittsburgh."
The man was being led into the Pittsburgh FBI's building by a
number of federal agents. He was handcuffed but shouting at
the press, "I did not do this! I was lured to that building to
pick up money that I had earned! The body was already there.
This is a set up!"
Unbelievable," Bobby said.
"Not so unbelievable," Claire said as a smile appeared on her
lips, "An old dog can learn new tricks. You know Bobby since
we met with Carmine a few months back, I have been sleeping
like a baby."

Carmine was watching Joe Kernen and Becky on Squawk Box
at the same time as Claire while he ate his morning eggs and
bacon. Carmine had the beginnings of a smile on his face
when he was startled and yelled to his men in the kitchen,
"how the hell does this guy keep getting past you?"
His men came running out of the kitchen their beefy hands
filled with pistols.
The Colonel casually slid into the booth across from Carmine.
"Now what the hell do you want?" Carmine asked.
"Actually," the Colonel said, "I stopped by to thank you and
congratulate you."
"For what?"
"You just watched the news from Punxsutawney."
"Yeah, so what?"
"So, thank you. You saved me a lot of trouble."
"I don't know what you're talking about."
"And I also wanted to congratulate you."
"Still don't know what you're talking about."
"I know," the Colonel went on as he snitched a piece of crispy
bacon off of Carmine's plate, "How hard it is to plan and
implement these things. I've had to clean up messes for years,
most of them created by Bobby, and I can attest that it is not
an easy job. Especially to so neatly lay the blame at someone

else's doorstep. Nicely done Carmine. I'm impressed."

Carmine turned to yell at his men that had disappeared back into the kitchen, "Somebody get this guy something to eat before he eats my breakfast."

Carmine turned back to the Colonel.

"Damn," Carmine shouted, "He did it again."

Carmine's man came out of the kitchen and saw that the Colonel was gone again, "This guy's scary boss. How does he do that? He comes and goes like a ghost."

Captain Cayce

Chapter 1

Gino was more than just a bartender. Gino was Carmine Rizzo's right hand man. He was average in height but broad-chested and with a nose that went every direction but straight owing to his willingness to enforce Carmine's every desire. Gino was not a fighter in the classical sense but he certainly was a brawler. Gino had never backed down from a fight in his life, but had avoided many a fight when the opposition took in his enormous biceps and hands the size of large stones. He normally wore a white shirt with no necktie and traded his black suit coat for a stained white apron when he went behind the bar. This evening Gino has been quite busy making mixed drinks for the diners and cold draft beer for the few people at the bar. The bar was made of fine, highly polished walnut as was the walls of the room. Behind the bar was a huge mirror that allowed Gino to know what was going on even when his back was turned. In fact, Gino and Carmine often secretly gestured to each other through the mirror while Gino had his back to the bar. Subtle little gestures that after years of use meant more than hundreds of words.

This evening Gino gave the mirror an almost imperceptible motion of his head that immediately got Carmine's attention. Carmine glanced in the same direction as the nod, then seeing who Gino was motioning at, he got up from his favorite booth with the red checked tablecloth and meandered over. He pulled his short frame up onto the barstool and reached his beefy hand into the bowl of peanuts setting on the bar. Then Carmine without much effort gave the patron sitting on the next stool a small elbow to the rib cage. The patron slowly turned to face Carmine.

"Carmine, how are you?"

"Probably better than you," Carmine responded, "Is everything okay?"

"Sure."

"And how is your wife?"

"Alright."

"I consider you a friend," Carmine said, "So I'll speak frankly. There is obviously something wrong because it's not like you to sit here and get smashed."

The patron faced Carmine again but said nothing.

"How about I call your wife?"

Again no reply so Carmine made a subtle gesture to Gino who began dialing the phone, then quietly spoke into it. Carmine got up from the barstool and met Gino at the far end of the bar.

Gino whispered in Carmine's ear, "What if he gets unruly?"

"You'll have to do what you always do."

"But, boss, he's a friend."

"Yeah, but you have a job to do."

"The other thing, boss," Gino quietly replied. "They say he can kill a man with just two fingers."

"You're not afraid of him are you?" Carmine asked.

"I'm not afraid of anybody boss. But I'm not anxious to find out if he really can kill someone with two fingers."

Carmine stared at Gino for a minute before saying, "Just keep him happy until his wife gets here. And start watering down his drinks. In fact set a cup of coffee in front of him, maybe he'll drink it."

"Okay boss."

After a few minutes the door to the bar opened, which is separate from the restaurant door even though the two were connected, and the mature but still very pretty woman with the short dark hair entered and strode directly up to the back of the patron still sitting at the bar who was now drinking a cup of steaming hot coffee.

"What are you doing?" she asked.

Without turning to see who was speaking the man said, "Good evening dear. I suppose Carmine called you?"

"No, Gino did."

"Want a drink?"

"No, and neither do you. Get your ass off that barstool and into the car."

"Yes dear," Bobby said as he set the coffee cup down and did as he was told.

A small sigh of relief escaped from Gino as Bobby Morrow wobbled his way out the door leaning heavily on his wife. Carmine approached Gino and asked him, "Any idea what's going on?"

"No boss. I ain't never seen Bobby Morrow get drunk before."

"If he comes back, you better shut him off before someone gets hurt."

Chapter 2

Senator Leonard Snead sat on his butter soft dark brown leather sofa in his richly appointed den staring off into space. The walls in the room were filled with books and photos primarily of the senator shaking hands with famous people or athletes. One photo showed Senator Snead shaking hands with then President Ronald Reagan next to a picture of him standing on the green with Tiger Woods. Row after row of photos, but the senator was just staring out into space, his mind heavy with thoughts of his recently deceased best friend Senator Richard St.Clair of Pennsylvania, and how it could have been him now six feet underground instead of Richard. Both Senator Snead and Senator St.Clair were at a meeting with President Obannon at Camp David when Senator St.Clair was killed by a Secret Service agent who was aiming to kill Bobby Morrow, the former federal undercover agent, when Senator St.Clair jumped in front of Bobby to take the bullet for him. Repayment of a debt carried forward from when Bobby and Richard St.Clair were in the jungles of Vietnam and Bobby saved his life not once but on several occasions. A debt that Richard St.Clair felt compelled to pay. And he did, with his life. The same life that Bobby saved Richard gave up to repay the debt that Bobby did not even consider a debt. To Bobby it had been an honor to do his duty to such a high standard. Competing with those thoughts were questions surrounding Senator Snead's recent meeting with the committee that he chaired, the prestigious Armed Services Committee and the disturbing news he had just received that Iran had indeed acquired not only the ability to make a nuclear bomb but also the materials required. Since Russia had been dismantling their arsenal of weapons per the new treaty with the United States, some radioactive materials have not been accounted for. It was now common knowledge that some unsavory characters in Russia had managed to get their hands on it and it was going to the highest bidder. Such was the new capitalism in Russia. Anything could be had for the right price. The only obstacle that Iran now faced was former President Reagan's "star wars" defense system. The satellites circling the globe that would stop a ground fired missile with a missile of its own to destroy it before it could reach the United States. That still was not much comfort to the Senator as that system had never been tested. What if it didn't operate as it should? What if it was a useless piece of metal circling the globe?

Bobby Morrow had spent the day in the woods hunting. Dressed in his bright orange hunting coat while he took his gun for a walk as his mind wasn't really on the job at hand. Bobby was depressed. His best friend Richard St.Clair was dead. His federal undercover job was gone. Life looked rather bleak for Bobby. He was stumbling through the woods fooling himself into thinking he was hunting when in actuality he was scaring every animal within three hundred feet of where he was.

Bobby was an excellent hunter and normally could make his way through the woods without making a sound. Without so much as stepping on a small twig to have it snap under the weight and spook the forest critters. Silent as an Indian, normally. But not this day. After a while he got bored and stuck his rifle in his old beat up red pickup truck and headed up the mountain to Rizzo's bar and restaurant. He wasn't interested in eating so he went in the door that took him directly into the bar.

When Bobby entered the establishment, Gino was at his usual place behind the bar and looked up as soon as Bobby entered. He immediately shot a glance over to Carmine who was sitting in his normal booth with the newspaper spread out in front of himself. Carmine saw Bobby come in also and when Gino glanced in his direction, Carmine gave him the signal that Gino was not to serve him any alcohol.

"Gino," Bobby said as he pulled himself onto the red leather covered barstool, "Whiskey, please."

Gino said nothing but went and got Bobby a drink which he sat down in front of him.

"This is coffee, Gino."

"Yeah."

Bobby turned to look at Carmine. Carmine met his gaze and was ready to reply.

The door to the bar flung open quickly slamming into the wall. Everyone looked to see what the commotion was. Two men in stocking masks holding pistols in front of themselves stormed into the bar. The first man immediately smashed Bobby in the side of the head and he tumbled off the barstool and lay motionless on the floor. The man then pointed the pistol at Gino who was moving to reach the gun hidden under the bar. Gino was just pulling the sawed off shot gun out from under the bar when the pistol in the man's hand barked and red quickly spread over the front of Gino's shirt. The second man passed the first man and as Carmine was attempting to get his bulky body out of the booth, the second man shot him. Carmine fell back into the booth. The first man ran behind the bar and rang the cash register. He was stuffing all the money into his pockets. The second man stood guard, watching, scanning back and forth looking for any movement, but the others in the bar were frozen in fear. Never had anyone before dared to rob Carmine. Did these half-wits not know who Carmine was? Carmine's other men, hearing the guns go off, ran from the kitchen with their weapons ready. Spying the man at the register Carmine's man shot him. Not once. Not twice. But numerous times because nobody came into Carmine's place causing trouble and left any other way than in a body bag accompanied by the coroner. The second man didn't wait around for his friend when the recruits poured out of the kitchen. He beat feet for the door staying crouched over to be a much smaller target as he now feared for his life. He instantly went from being the hunter to being the hunted. One of Carmine's men stopped beside Carmine to check on him. He was still breathing. The man pulled out his cell phone and called 911. The second of Carmine's men from the kitchen ran out the door and got a couple shots off at the vehicle that was speeding out of the parking lot spraying gravel as it spun from side to side. Glass shattering as some of the bullets reached their destination but the vehicle kept going and Carmine's man went back into the bar to check on Gino. Bobby was just gaining consciousness on the floor of the bar when the sirens screamed outside and police and ambulance arrived.

Chapter 3

"I want to make sure I have this correct in my report," Chief Galen Farr said to Bobby, "A masked bandit came into Carmine's bar and knocked out the former federal undercover agent, and if the truth be known, probably a government paid assassin, and for sure a hunter of enemies of our government? How does that happen to someone in your position? I'm told you are the best. I've even heard rumors that you have the ability to kill a man with just two fingers."
Bobby sat staring straight ahead, sipping his coffee.
"Come on Bobby," the Chief said, "How does someone get the drop on you?"
Bobby slowly turned to face Galen, "Guess you slow down a little in retirement."
"Guess you do. So I assume you can't provide me with any description of the one that got away?"
Bobby started to rise from the barstool, reached into his pocket, pulled out several dollar bills and tossed them on the counter, then looked directly at Chief Galen Farr and said, "Galen, I'm sure once you pull the mask off the guy bleeding all over Carmine's floor, that you'll be able to quickly find out who he is and then find out who he runs with. The problem you have Galen, is getting to the other guy before Carmine's guys do. I seriously doubt that Carmine and his guys are going to let this go unpunished. So instead of throwing barbs at me you might want to get your act together and do your job."

Bobby walked towards the door.

"Who said you could leave?" Galen spat at Bobby's back.

Bobby stopped, turned to look at Galen, smiled and continued on his way.

"Get the mask off that idiot on the floor," Galen yelled at his officers.

"The paramedics aren't done with him yet, Chief."

"He's dead. There isn't anything they are going to do for him. Now who the hell is he?"

One of the officers knelt down next to the body and pulled the mask off his face. The officer gasped and looked at the other officer standing and watching. They both looked to the Chief.

"Well? Do you know him?"

The officers looked at each other and in unison said, "Yeah, we know him."

"Well who the hell is it?"

Bobby turned onto his gravel driveway leading up to the large log house which was majestically perched on the crown in the field surrounded by the lush green grass and bordered by trees on three sides. As Bobby made his way up the driveway he could see Sarge's shiny new pickup parked near the house. Then he noticed Sarge and Claire sitting together on the swing talking and laughing.

Bobby got out of his old red beat up pickup truck and sauntered over to the couple on the swing. He sat on the porch rail.

"What did I miss?" Bobby asked.

"You tell him Sarge," Bobby's wife, Claire said, "It's your news."

Bobby looked at Sarge.

"I'm getting married," Sarge burst out with a huge smile on his face.

"You're what?" Bobby exclaimed.

"You heard me, I'm getting married."

"I didn't even know you were dating," Bobby said.

"For a little while now, but we both decided there was no reason to wait."

"So who is it? Anyone I know?" Bobby asked.

"You know her," Sarge said smiling, "Senator Snead's daughter."

"You two couldn't have been dating very long!"

"Don't start acting like my mother," Sarge said, "we might not have been dating very long, but we've dated long enough to know that we love each other."

"So when is the big day?"

"Actually we are eloping. In two days."

"Eloping? Does the Senator know?"

Sarge looked at his watch and replied, "He probably does by now."

"Where are you running off to?" Bobby asked.

"Going to Aruba."

"That sounds really romantic," Claire said.

"That was her idea. I don't care where we go."

"I know I'm not your father, Sarge, but I have to ask," Bobby said, "You and I just lost our jobs. How are you going to support her."

"I landed a great private security position last week. That was one reason why we decided to go ahead and get married. I'll be making really good money and we are going to move to the D.C. area."

"Wow, you're overloading me with news," Bobby replied.

"So where have you been?" Sarge asked Bobby.

"I was up at Carmine's."

With that Claire got up from the swing and went into the house letting the screen door slam shut behind her.

Sarge glared at Bobby, "Whoa man! You are in some deep shit!"

"Yeah just a little."

"What happened to your head. It looks like it's bruised."

"It should be. It hurts like hell."

"What happened?"

I was sitting at Carmine's, minding my own business, having a cup of coffee." The last part he said loudly so his wife would hear him."Anyway, I'm sitting there drinking coffee. Someone bursts through the door and whacks me in the head knocking me out for a minute and completely off the barstool."

"You mean this just happened?"

"Yeah, Chief Farr just let me go a minute ago."

"What else happened?"

"Apparently two idiots tried to rob Carmine. They shot Carmine and Gino."

"Are they okay?"

"They are going to live. You know those two. They're too stubborn to die."

"And I missed all the excitement. Do they know who it was?"

"Probably by now, but I didn't stick around to find out."

"Carmine will be pissed."

"One of them is dead. Carmine's guys shot one of them. The other one got away."

"He better hope he can run long and hard. Carmine is not going to let this go," Sarge said.

"Yeah, old Carmine is like a junk yard dog when you cross him."

"A junk yard dog with rabies!"

Carmine woke up in the hospital connected to beeping monitors by wires and tubes, and surrounded by doctors, nurses, police, and several of his bodyguards.

"What the hell is going on?" Carmine asked gruffly.

"You've been shot," A doctor said.

"I know that! Don't you think I can feel it. Where's Gino? How is he? Is he alright?"

"For right now Mr. Rizzo, I need you to be calm and get some rest," The Doctor said.

"Doc, shut up. You," Carmine said as he pointed to one of his bodyguards, "Where's Gino?"

"Down the hall, Boss. He's okay. Took a bullet in the shoulder."

"Doc, whoever is in the next bed here, you get them the hell out of here and you get Gino moved into this room."

"I can't..."

"Do it Doc, or else."

"Look Mr. Rizzo. I don't take orders from you."

"Guido, find us an ambulance. Me and Gino are getting the hell out of here."

"But Mr. Rizzo," the doctor pleaded.

"Get Gino in this room or we take an ambulance ride. That's not open to discussion Doc." Carmine looked around the room, "And the rest of you people get the hell out of here. My guys and I need to talk."

"But,..."

"Doc, if I have to tell you one more time, I'm going to have Guido there beat it into your head. Scram!"

The room cleared out including the police officers that apparently figured now was not a good time to question Carmine. Two nurses began unhooking the wires and bags from Carmine's neighbor and pushed his bed out into the hall. In just a few minutes another bed with the big beefy body of Gino was wheeled in next to Carmine.

"Gino," Carmine asked, "How you feeling?"

"I'm okay, how about you, boss?"

"I'm gonna' live, which is too bad for somebody."

"Guido, who were those two jokers?"

"The one full of lead and bleedin' all over your floor was that Stallone kid from Ganister."

"A local kid was dumb enough to try to rob us? What about the other one?" Carmine asked.

"The other one got away in Stallone's truck. I've already put out the word, we'll have him soon."

 "Good," Carmine said, "I want everyone to know you don't live long robbing my place, but at the same time, be sure the cops can't trace it back to us. You understand?"

"I got it boss. Don't worry, I'll handle it."

"You're a good man Guido."

"Gino, how's come you was so slow with the shotgun? You gettin' old?"

"I guess so Boss."

"Yeah, we both are getting' old. This is a young man's game. Maybe we should retire?"

"Whatever you say Boss."

"I'm just messin' with ya'. What the hell else would we do?"

"We could retire to Florida, Boss."

Carmine looked over at Gino, "I don't even want the thought in my head of you walkin' the beach in Florida wearing a Speedo. Damn, now I probably won't be able to eat dinner. Guido, when's dinner?"

"I don't know what time they come around Boss."

"I ain't eatin' this hospital crap. You have the boys make us some good pasta and bring it in here. Don't forget a nice bottle of wine."

"You got it Boss."

Chief of Police Galen Farr left the crime scene in a hurry. The red and blue lights on the roof of his patrol car were flashing as he fishtailed his way out on to the highway with the tires squealing as they fought the losing battle to grip the asphalt. Farr drove back into Ganister and went through every stop sign on the way to his home where he quickly stopped the car without worrying whether it was off the street so other vehicles could get by. He rushed into his home and on the way into the kitchen was yelling for his wife.

She stood from placing a baking sheet in the hot oven and dusted the flour off her hands onto her apron. Her face was white as she feared the worst from having her normally quiet husband yelling as he crashed through the door.

"Galen," she asked in a panic, "What's wrong?"

"Where's Troy?"

Troy was Galen's son. Recently graduated from high school and supposedly looking for that first job while he contemplated if college was the path he should follow.

"He's out with his friends, I assume."

"Is he with that Stallone kid?"

"Well Mick came by here earlier and they left together , why?"

"How many times have I told you to not let him run around with that punk?"

"He seems like a nice boy, Galen."

"Well, then, he *was* a nice boy."

"Galen, what do you mean?"

"I mean he's laying dead in a pool of blood at Rizzo's restaurant."

Galen's wife pulled out a kitchen chair and plopped down on it. Her hand involuntarily covered her mouth as she gasped and asked Galen, "Oh no Galen, what happened?"

"Seems the Stallone kid and someone else tried to rob Rizzo's Restaurant."

"Are you sure?" Galen's wife asked.

"Yes, I'm sure. I saw the body."

"And he's dead?" she asked her breathing becoming labored.

"Dead as a doornail. Lying there in a pool of his own blood."

"How did that happen?"

"You just don't waltz into Carmine's place and expect to rob him without consequences. Everyone around here knows he has mafia connections. What kind of idiot would do that?"

"Galen, where is Troy?"

"That's what I'm asking you?"

"You don't think he had anything to do with a robbery do you?"

"I'm a cop. I suspect everybody. And they were friends, you said yourself they left here together."

"Oh no...." Galen's wife said as she broke down crying. Huge warm tears flowing from between her fingers and dropping onto the freshly mopped kitchen floor.

"I have to go," Galen said as he turned away from his wife, "If Troy comes in you call me immediately."

Galen's wife was still crying.

"Do you hear me?" he asked her again.

She nodded her head without looking up. The dreaded possibility of one of a parent's worst fears working its way into her mind. The tears flowing even harder now.

Chapter 4

Senator Snead was spending the day working from home. Reports from every branch of the military and the alphabet agencies like the FBI, NSA, HSA, and many more scattered across his desk as he attempted to assimilate all the data into precise thoughts and insights necessary for him to do his job and keep the country safe from foreign countries, druglords, crackpots, and terrorists. As the chairman of the Armed Services Committee he had a tremendous need to know about any and all incidents that may be brewing. And when the President asked a question, it would not look good if he were not aware of an incident no matter how large or small. Most recently there was the kidnapping of the freighter captain by pirates off the coast of Somalia. Senator Snead had no sooner read the report when the President had called and asked him for more information even though the President then stalled and did not want to pursue the military approach to capturing the pirates and getting the captain back, that was outlined by Senator Snead and his top military brass. As the Senator studied all the reports the news channel was blaring in the background, and even though the Senator didn't appear to be listening, whenever any comment came up that was useful to the Senator he would stop reading and face the television. Leonard was swearing at the television when the door opened and his daughter, Sadie strolled in. Not checking on whether her father was busy or not, she immediately spoke to the Senator.

"Dad," she said, "We need to talk."

"We'll talk later, honey," the Senator replied without looking up from his work, "I have a lot of work to do first."

"But, Dad," she pleaded with the corners of her mouth turned down, "This is important." Her voice getting higher and higher. Lenny fearing what would come next if he didn't let her have her say forced his to look up from his papers, stared her in the eye, and ask, "Tell me what's wrong, Sadie."

"There's nothing wrong, Dad," she said, "I just need your undivided attention so I can tell you something."

"Sadie, can't you see that I am busy?"

"Too busy for your daughter?"

That line never failed to get immediate results. Guilt was the cattle prod of the younger generation.

Leonard sighed, clasped his hands together and laid them down on top of the many papers he had been studying and looked to his daughter.

Sadie smiled. The Senator's heart melted. And the concerns for the country went to the back burner.

"What can I do for you Sadie?"

"Promise me you'll stay calm when I tell you this."

"Tell me what?"

"First you promise to be calm."

"Calm? How can I be calm when you start a sentence like that?"

"Dad," the pouty face came back. "Dad, you promised to listen."

"I'm listening. I'm listening," he said.

Barely unable to control herself, she blurted it out, "I'm getting married."

The Senator tried to gather his thoughts for a minute then asked, "You're what?"

"I'm getting married."

"To who," he asked with a quizzical look on his face, "You're not even dating anybody."

"Sure, I am."

"Who?"

"I've been dating Sarge for several months now."

"Sarge?" Leonard asked, "You mean the big bodyguard that worked here a short while back?"

"Yes, dad. Sarge."

"How the…, Where's your mother? Have you talked with your mother about this?"

"Of course, dad."

"Well what did your mother say?"

"Pretty much what you just said."

"Sadie, don't you think you're rushing into something?"

"No, dad, I don't. And I'm getting married with or without your blessing. I would just rather have your blessing."

"Go find your mother. Get her in here," the Senator said in a low voice as thoughts of surrender started to fill his head.

Sadie left for the briefest of moments and came back with her mother in tow.

Leonard looked at his wife Karen as she slowly meandered into the room being dragged by the arm by her daughter.

"What is going on here?" Leonard asked his wife.

"You know as much as I do," Karen said.

"Shouldn't you be talking her out of this?"

"I'm tired of beating my head against the wall," Karen said sharply, "You talk her out of it."

"I'm old enough to make my own decisions," Sadie snapped.

"I'm not questioning your age," the Senator said, "I'm questioning your judgment."

"This is not open to debate," a defiant Sadie said as she thrust her hands onto her hips, "The only question is if you want to come to the wedding service or not."

"And I suppose you expect me to pay for some over-the-top wedding?"

"As a matter of fact, I, I mean we, don't."

The Senator's mouth dropped open and Sadie continued.

"We are having a small service with just a couple people then we are leaving for Aruba for our honeymoon."

"Aruba?"

"Yes. Aruba."

"Well, I guess you have everything planned," Leonard said, "So what do you need me for?"

"Because I want you and mom to be at the wedding service."

"Whatever your mother decides," the Senator said, admitting defeat and carrying his suddenly weakened body back to his desk chair where he crashed into the seat.

The Senator had no sooner sat down and his phone rang. He picked up the phone.

"Senator Snead?"

"Yes," a dejected Senator replied, "Who's this?"

"Please hold for the Attorney General."

Bobby always enjoyed the early morning hours at his log home, times just like this when he knew Claire was sleeping deeply as he sat on the swing hung at the corner of the huge porch that went around two sides of his magnificent home. The sun had just come up and Bobby was swinging, drinking his extra large mug of coffee, and watching Mother Nature at work. The bumblebees were trying to bore holes into sturdy wood logs that made up the walls of his home, birds flew past with amazing speed and agility heading to the trees at the edge of his property. The one thing missing was his faithful dog. The big black Rottweiler that had provided him so much companionship. The one those assholes killed when they came to kill Bobby. Bobby mentally tried to change channels. To think of something other than that day. Instead his mind went to Sarge. He was just a big muscular grunt when Bobby took him under his wing. Since then he had grown into an intelligent, sensible man. Or so it seemed until he dropped this recent bombshell about eloping with Senator Snead's daughter. But then, Bobby thought, maybe that was an intelligent move for Sarge also. After all, Bobby himself was a much better man for having Claire beside him all these years. And when they met it was "love at first sight", so maybe it would all work out for Sarge. Bobby hoped so. Bobby raised his mug in the air and did a silent toast to Sarge and Sadie. Bobby's thoughts were interrupted by the ringing of his cell phone. Begrudgingly he answered it.

"What's up," was all that Bobby said when he saw the recognizable phone number.

"Bobby," a desperate female voice said, "It's Amy." She sniffed away tears before continuing, "It's the Colonel. He passed away last night."

Amy was the Colonel's loyal secretary. She probably held as many secrets in her head as the Colonel did. The Colonel was at one time exactly that, a Colonel in the Army. Bobby had met him during his tour in Vietnam when the Colonel came to pin one of Bobby's many medals on him. Several of those were for saving the now deceased Senator Richard St.Clair's life which was practically a full time job for Bobby back then. Bobby remembered when the Colonel pinned on the medal. Bobby sharply saluted the Colonel then immediately unpinned the medal and put it in his pocket where it remained until he got into his bunk area and tossed into the shoebox with all the others. One day he got tired of looking at the shoebox and mailed it home. Medals were not going to keep him out of a bodybag here in the jungles of Vietnam so Bobby had no use for them. After the war, the Colonel contacted Bobby and asked to meet with him. Assuming it was just a friendly gesture Bobby readily agreed and travelled to Washington to meet with the Colonel. The Colonel surprised Bobby with a job offer. The Colonel had become the President's personal intelligence supplier and problem solver. While the president had the FBI, CIA and all the other three letter agencies at his command, the President was wary of how far he could trust them and how accurate the information was so he entrusted that job to the Colonel. When the President had a problem that needed to be solved without attention, he called the Colonel. The Colonel in turn called Bobby. On occasion it even meant using Bobby's sniper skills and taking out a foreign enemy while giving the President deniability. Bobby worked for the Colonel for many years, and for several presidents. Then the republican's lost the White House and the Colonel and Bobby lost their jobs.

"Amy, I'm very sorry to hear that," Bobby said, "Is there anything I can do for you or the Colonel's family?"

"The Colonel had all his arrangements made ahead of time and he wanted you to say a few words at the brief ceremony that will be held at Arlington cemetery."

"You know I'll do anything for the Colonel."

"I'll email you the details," Amy said, "I just wanted to call you in person before you read it in the newspapers."

"Thank you, Amy. What was the cause of death? I know he was diagnosed with a melanoma of some kind."

"He died of a bullet," Amy started sobbing again, "A bullet to the head. They are saying it was suicide."

"What?" Bobby exclaimed.

Between tears Amy said, "The police say it was suicide. You know as well as I do that the Colonel would never do that."

"I'll pack my bags and be in Washington before you know it, Amy. You try to stay strong."

"Thank you, Bobby."

Bobby closed his phone, sat down his coffee mug, and reached his hand up and involuntarily rubbed his chin. He had several days growth of beard. He looked down at himself, his clothes were a mess. He had been spending his time lately drinking and feeling sorry for himself because he no longer was living the exciting federal undercover life. The Colonel would not be impressed. In fact the Colonel would be downright ashamed. Bobby jumped up off the swing and strode into the house and directly into the bathroom.

Chapter 5

Chief Galen Farr scoured every street in the small borough of Ganister and asked everyone he thought might know but he couldn't find his son anywhere. In desperation he decided he better extend his search so he headed for the Blue Hole. The Blue Hole is an abandoned limestone quarry. A huge hole in the ground, big enough to sit several football fields inside it, and full of deep blue water that arrived courtesy of an underground stream. A small stream of water that flowed constantly enough to shut down the quarrying operation and turn it into a favorite spot for locals to swim. Galen turned off of Route 866 shortly after leaving town onto the dirt road that would take him to the Blue Hole. As he rounded the final curve when the Blue Hole came into view he parked at the top of the quarry. He got out of his car and strode the couple feet to the edge of the quarry walls. Looking down into the quarry he immediately spotted his son. Sitting on the limestone edge near the water skimming stones across the flat blue water making circles pop up each time the stone struck the water then glancing back into the air before coming back in contact with the water again forming another circle.

"Troy," Galen yelled at his son, "What the hell are you doing?"

Troy turned his head and looked up at his dad, "Nothing."

"Get yourself up here," Galen said, "I want to talk to you."

Troy tossed one more stone out across the water making three rings. Not a big deal. Anyone could make three rings, it was five or six rings that was hard to do. Troy slowly started up the gravel path that led to the top of the quarry where Galen stood waiting.

Before Troy could cross the top edge, Galen was firing questions at him, "Where have you been?"

Troy spread his arms out to illustrate without saying anything that this is where he had been.

"Don't give me any crap, son," Galen demanded, "I want the truth from you. And I want it now."

"Dad, I've been here."

"You left the house with Stallone."

"Yeah, so what?"

"So were you with him at Rizzo's?"

Troy looked away from his father and back towards the calm blue water.

Galen made his living reading people's body language. He rubbed his forehead and said to Troy, "How could you be so stupid?"

Troy didn't answer.

"Don't you know that Carmine is going to find out you were with Stallone, and he's going to come after you."

"Dad, I didn't know what Mick was up to. He told me it would be blast to pretend we were robbing Carmine just to see what he would do."

"What the hell do you think a mafia kingpin would do when someone enters his business pointing a gun at him? You're an intelligent young man but where the hell is your common sense?"

No response from Troy.

"And Stallone wasn't playing games when he bashed Bobby on the head knocking him off his stool then shooting Gino. I can't believe this. You, the son of the Chief of Police involved in the stupidest thing to ever happen in this town."

"I'm sorry Dad," Troy said as tears sprung from his eyes. Galen grabbed Troy and pulled him close hugging him while tears sprung from Galen's eyes.

"I don't know if I can protect you son."

"But dad, I don't want to go to prison."

"Son, prison is the least of your worries. Stallone is dead. Carmine's people saw to that and they are perfectly within their rights to have killed him. And I guarantee you they are already looking for Stallone's accomplice. They have a reputation. They have to save face. They will hunt you down and they will kill you."

"But dad, I can get away from here and hide from him."

Galen shook his head and stood back from his son, "And yet, here you are, hanging out at the Blue Hole. Skimming stones across Carmine Rizzo's water."

"What?"

"This. Right here, this is Carmine's property."

"Dad, I gotta' get out of here!"

"You can't run from Carmine."

Chapter 6

Pastor Tyme stood in front of the large brick fireplace which covered the one end of Senator's Snead's study, dressed in his simple white frock, holding his worn bible in both hands as he studied the two smiling faces in front of him before saying, "I now pronounce you husband and wife. You may kiss the bride."

Sarge enveloped Sadie in his huge arms giving her a bear-hug while leaning down and kissing her full on the lips. The kiss lasted longer than the people watching expected. When they finally stopped the four persons watching approached them. Senator Snead and his wife Karen, and Terry Lee and his wife Mickey all took turns hugging the bride and shaking hands with the beaming groom.

After congratulations all around, Sarge looked at his watch and said, "Sorry folks, but we have a plane to catch," then he grabbed his new bride in his huge arms and off they went.

"What say we go have a nice meal?" Senator Snead asked Terry.

"Why not."

"I know a nice place not far off. We'll all go in my car."

"Sounds good to me," Mickey said.

"Yes," Karen answered, "And they have a great selection of wine. Which I could sure use."

The couples laughed simultaneously.

From Richmond, the USAir plane with Sarge and Sadie on board flew to Charlotte where the couple changed planes without ever once letting go of each other's hand. Their smiles seemed to be permanently glued to their faces. After a mere four hours in the air from Charlotte, most of which they spent kissing, the plane landed in sunny Aruba. The couple went through Customs, and Immigration and grabbed their suitcases. They walked through the door of the airport into the extremely warm sunshine of Aruba and looked about for the taxis. In front of the doors stood numerous people all holding signs with various names on them to give them special transportation to their hotels. One of the men, a friendly round faced man dressed in what appeared to be a white sailor uniform and sporting a baseball cap with the word "Captain" embroidered on the front of it was holding a sign that said "Sarge & Sadie". Sarge spotted the sign then looked at Sadie and asked her, "Do you think that could be us?"

"Surely there is not another Sarge and Sadie on this small island."

Sarge approached the man and asked, "Are you waiting for us?"

"If you are the Sarge and Sadie that just tied the knot in lovely Richmond, Virginia, then I'm waiting for you," the jovial man said.

"But," Sarge stammered, "How did you know?"

"Connections, son, connections," the man said with a smile on his face. "Tempest fugit!"

"What?" Sarge asked as he grabbed the suitcases plus his new bride and followed the spry older man down the sidewalk to a waiting vehicle where the man opened the trunk and the backdoors to his car.

"I said Time Flies," said the Captain. "Let's get you two to your resort."

As Sarge placed the suitcases into the trunk, the Captain said to him, "You're staying at the Aruba Beach Club, right?"

Sarge eyed him cautiously, "That's right. But how do you know this?"

The jovial man pointed to his own forehead and said, "Kidneys, man, kidneys."

Sarge laughed and got in the backseat of the car beside his beaming new wife while the Captain closed the trunk and got in the driver's seat and started the car. He looked back at the couple in the rearview mirror and said, "You two are going to love Aruba."

"We love it already, the sky is so blue and it's so warm," Sadie said.

"Blue. You haven't seen blue yet Sadie. Wait till you get your first look at the Caribbean Sea. Then you see blue. You'll see so many shades of blue between the Sea and the sky that you'll never forget this lovely island. And you're going to get that first peak in just a minute once we get past the airport."

"You sound American," Sarge said.

"I am. In fact I'm originally from Richmond also," the Captain told him.

"So do you know my father?" Sadie asked.

"Of course I know the Senator."

"So my father arranged for you to pick us up?"

"Not really. He just mentioned that you were coming. I took it upon myself to pick you up. It can be a hassle sometimes getting a taxi. And the way some of those taxi drivers drive these days, you are taking your life in your hands. I wanted to be sure you got to your resort safely."

"Well that's awfully kind of you," Sarge said.

"Well I do have ulterior motives, also," the Captain said as he glanced in the rearview mirror.

"Ohh...."

"I'll show you in a minute. For now, look to your left. There it is. The most beautiful blue water you will ever see in your life. Welcome to Aruba."

The couple gasped as they took in their first sight of the shimmering aqua water of the Caribbean Sea.

"Now this is the downtown area," the Captain said. "And here on the left next to the dutch restaurant is my little office."

"So you have a submarine?" Sarge asked when he spied the sign adorning the front of the small office.

"Yes, that's how I make my living here. I take tourists to the bottom of the Caribbean Sea where you can see all the fish, marine life, sponges, turtles, and if you're lucky even squid and octopus."

"Well Captain," Sadie said, "How can we refuse? We will definitely take your submarine tour."

"Well, thank you. Just a mile up the road here and you will be at your resort. You picked a lovely place to stay. The beach is much wider here than at the high-rise area and you have fewer people to share it with. I don't understand why everyone runs up to the high-rise area."

The couple kept their heads turned to the left all the while watching the Caribbean Sea until they pulled into the driveway of the Aruba Beach Club.

"Well, here you are," the Captain said as he pulled to a stop. The Captain helped Sarge get the luggage then closed his trunk. Sarge attempted to give the Captain a tip, "The rides free young man. I'll take your money when you come to the submarine."

"Well at least tell me what your name is," Sarge asked.

"Captain. Captain Cayce if you want to be formal."

"Well it is a pleasure to meet you Captain," the couple said in unison.

"If you need anything, you just call me. The people at the desk know my number." The Captain tipped his baseball cap, and began singing a little diddy on his way to his car, "Doot, da, de, da, dooty-do…".

Chapter 7

Bobby Morrow was a man of few words which made him an odd choice to deliver the eulogy for his recently departed former boss, the Colonel. Following Bobby's short speech the Marine Corps did a 21 gun salute followed by the playing of Taps and the flag ceremony. The rugged Marines in their neatly creased uniforms crisply folded the American flag that had been draped over the coffin, then, in a tear-jerking ceremony presented it to the Colonel's wife. After the ceremony the guests started to drift away from the burial site and back to their autos. The Colonel's personal assistant, Amy was still drying her tears with a bunched up Kleenex when she caught up to Bobby.

"Are you going to catch the Colonel's killer?" she asked.

Bobby stopped and looked Amy in the eyes, "You know that is not anything I can properly do. Why don't you agree with the police investigators?"

"I've worked closely with the Colonel for many years, Bobby," she said between sobs, "And you know as well as I do that the Colonel would be the last man in the world to ever give up on anything. Suicide would be giving up. The Colonel would fight Melanoma or any other health problem to the very end. Kicking and screaming, that's how he would go. Not quietly sitting at his desk and pulling the trigger on his pistol."

"You're right about that Amy," Bobby said, "It's just that there are lots of more qualified people than me to investigate this."

"Maybe so," Amy said, "But who knew the Colonel better than you?"

"Okay, I'll swing by his office in just a few minutes and take a quick look around," Bobby sighed, "But if nothing jumps out at me then you need to hire a private investigator."

"Thank you for at least taking a look."

"Would you like to ride over with me now?" Bobby asked.

"Sure. I rode here with friends, just let me tell them I'm going with you." Amy scurried away but by the time Bobby reached his car she was only a few steps behind him. Bobby opened the door for her and she slid into the passenger's seat. Bobby walked around the car and gazed out over the green evenly cut grass at the thousands of white crosses that marked the graves. A sense of duty came over him as he got in the car, started it, and pulled out. A duty that he felt he owed all of his fallen military brethren that lie quietly around him.

Bobby pulled into a parking spot at the Colonel's office and they went into the Colonel's office. After a few minutes Bobby sat heavily in the leather chair that faced the Colonel's desk. A chair that Bobby had spent many hours occupying while the Colonel laid out the various details and strategies of the many operations that they undertook. Bobby's eyes kept wandering to the dark blood stain that now spoiled the rich dark oak wood top of the desk. After a minute Bobby looked away taking in every little detail of the office. The desk had sat in an area where the windows formed a partial octagon around the desk. The rich gold curtains to the left of the desk were covered with crimson dots of dry blood. The curtains to the right of the desk were not marked at all. As Bobby absorbed each detail Amy approached him and handed him a set of large photos. Crime scene photos.
"I asked the crime tech if he would give me a set," she told Bobby.
Bobby looked at her then at the photos. It was different when the subject was your colleague. Normally Bobby could study the photos and feel nothing. Today the bile worked its way up his throat. He continued to carefully study each photo. Then he looked through them again. And again. And again, until he could memorize each and every detail. In the back of his head a small thought sprouted that he was unable to clearly bring to the surface. He looked through the photos again.

"Amy," Bobby said, "Who's gun is this?"

"Isn't it the Colonel's?"

"Are you sure?"

"Well, no, I just assumed it was."

"We have to get a look at it," Bobby said, "Do you have any connections at the police department?"

"Don't need any. NCIS will have everything and I'm sure they will be glad to let us have a look."

"Good. Get them on the telephone and make an appointment."

A slight smile crossed Amy's lips, "I knew you would find something."

"We didn't find anything yet, Amy, but I do have a couple questions. Something is not right here."

"I tried to tell you that. The Colonel would not commit suicide."

"We need evidence Amy. Speculation won't do us or the Colonel any good."

Chapter 8

Chief Galen Farr had barely put his foot across the threshold of the hospital room when Gino and Carmine instantly opened their eyes and looked his way.

"Sorry, " Galen said, "I didn't mean to wake you."

"What brings you here, Chief?" Carmine asked looking as though he were part of a plate of pasta with all the monitors and IV's attached to himself.

"I wanted to see how you were doing."

"What else?" Carmine inquired.

"Well, I guess to see if you have gotten any leads on the accomplice," the chief said quietly.

"I thought that was your job," Carmine snapped back.

A flustered chief responded, "Oh, yes, yes, we are making progress with the investigation."

"Really, chief?" Carmine asked, "Then who do you have for suspects?"

Galen's face reddened, "No actual suspects yet, but..."

Carmine interrupted, "Let me tell you a little story." Not waiting for a response he continued, "There was this little boy on an airplane reading a magazine. He noticed that the man next to him was the same man that was featured in the magazine article so he asked the man, 'why should people vote for you to be their Senator?'"

The man looked at the small boy and smiled his big toothy grin and replied, "Well son, because I'm the best man for job."

"Really?"

"Well sure son. I take good care of my constituents and have only their best interests at heart."

"So you must be really smart?"

"Well, yes, I guess you could say that," the man said with a smile.

"But to help people you would have to know about lots of different things?"

"Yes, son, you would. And I do. I'm an educated man," he said. Then he asked the boy, "Would you vote for me?"

"Maybe, but first I would have to ask you a question."

"Well, then, by all means, ask me a question."

"How's come cows and rabbits both eat grass, but cows make great big sloppy patties when they go to the bathroom and yet bunnies just make little round balls?"

"Well I don't really know the answer to that son."

The boy then said, "Well then I wouldn't vote for you."

"Why not?"

"Because you don't know shit."

Carmine then said to the chief, "Get my meaning chief?"

"Your meaning is crystal clear Carmine."

"Another thing chief," Carmine said with a smile, "Don't come sniffing around here thinking we are going to do your job for you. Do your own damn job. Find that other asshole."

A disturbed chief turned to go when he stopped and turned to face Carmine again as he said, "I am doing my job Carmine. You just stay out of my way."

"And if, as some of my friends have mentioned to me, if it's your son that was the accomplice, what then chief?" Carmine asked as he drew out the last word.

Galen turned quickly and stormed out of the room. As he strode down the hall he said under his breath, "Damn that boy!"

The thick colorful curtains could barely keep the intense morning sun out of the room. Sarge woke early because of the sun peeking around the curtains and looked at the pretty face lying next to him to be sure that he wasn't dreaming. Feeling Sarge staring at her, Sadie slowly opened her eyes and returned Sarge's look. He smiled. She giggled. They made love. Again.

After that Sarge jumped from the bed knowing for sure that he was not dreaming and ready to take on the day.

"Let's get on the beach, Sadie," Sarge said as he pulled on his swimsuit and looked around for his flip flops.

"Okay. Give me a minute to comb my hair and stuff."

It was the "and stuff" that made the antsy Sarge resign and flop back down on the bed.

"Sarge," Sadie said as she made her way into the bathroom, "You can go down to the beach and get us a couple chairs and I'll be down in a couple minutes, if you like."

Sarge jumped off the bed, grabbed her and gave her a big hug while twirling her around, then gave her a kiss on the lips and set her back down saying, "Excellent. Bring some bottled water with you. I'll go get us some chairs under a chicki."

"A what?" Sadie asked.

"A chicki, you know those umbrella things made out of a wood pole with a palm roof."

"Oh okay. A chicki."

"Yeah," Sarge said, "A chicki for my chickie!"

Sarge stretched as soon as he left the building as the bright sunshine hit him and he looked directly at the sun as if thanking Mother Nature for the beautiful weather. He strode confidently across the pool area heading towards the clean white sand and the lapping sound of the Caribbean Sea. He stopped under a chicki to survey the area and decide on the perfect spot to spend the day. After making his decision, he picked a chicki closest to the water so nothing and no one would obstruct his view, he hung his towel on the post and drug two lounge chairs over, placing one in the direct sun for Sadie, and the other in the shade of the chicki for himself. Sarge spread out on the lounge chair enjoying the early morning quiet with no sounds except that of the swaying palms and the lapping Sea. He opened the book he brought with him but his eyes would not stay focused on the words, they instantly migrated to the brilliant hues of blue in the water and how the tips of the small waves produced diamond like sparkles in the sunshine. It was as though Mother Nature were holding out her hand and rolling back her fingers in a gesture of "come here". So Sarge did, he went to the water. Cautiously getting close enough so only his toes would get wet when the small waves came into shore, and expecting the water to be quite cold. Miraculously it wasn't cold. It was quite pleasant and refreshing. Sarge threw caution to the wind and bounded into the water a few yards then diving into the calling Sea. He splashed around for a while then saw Sadie walking down the beach towards him dressed in a bright blue bikini top with a light blue flowered sarong that fluttered in the tradewinds showing off her long slim legs. Sarge ran towards her and as he was about to give her another bear hug she moved away.

"You're all wet," she squealed.

"You've got to come in," he said excitedly, "This water is so warm. It's awesome!"

"Let me put these things down and take off my sarong. Which "thingy" is ours?"

"Chicki, Babe, they are called chickis."

"Whatever."

"The one right behind you with the two lounge chairs and my towel on the back of the one chair."

Sadie hooked her towel on the chair, Hung her sarong on a rusty nail on the post of the chicki, and placed her bag with the bottled waters and books on her chair to hold down the towel. Then she slowly made her way back to the Sea that Sarge had again charged back into. She made the same hesitant sampling with her toe that Sarge had, with the same surprising revelation that the water was indeed warm, so she made her way out to the smiling Sarge.

The couple played in the salty sea water splashing each other, holding on to each other, and even taking time for a few salty kisses. Eventually they went back to the chicki to dry off.

As they approached their lounge chairs the lady in the next chicki asked them, "How's the water?"

"Fabulous," Sadie said as she dried her face with her colorful beach towel.

"I guess we'll be neighbors for the day," the lady said.

"That will be nice, " Sadie responded as she made her way over to the lady and asked, "Are you from the States also?"

"Yes, we're from Richmond, Virginia."

"Good. We're from Pennsylvania."

"Oh, whereabouts in Pennsylvania?"

"Near Altoona. A little town called Ganister."

"I've been to Altoona the lady's partner said as he rose from his lounge chair." He approached Sadie with his hand out. Sadie shook his hand as the man said, "I'm Steve. This is my lovely wife Becky."

"It's nice to meet you. I'm Sadie, and this is my husband Sarge."

Sarge meandered over and shook hands with Steve.

"I'm guessing you two are newlyweds," Steve said.

"How did you know?" Sadie asked.

"Just a good guess based on the smile that Sarge here can't seem to keep off his face every time he looks at you and the fact that he can't keep his hands off you."

Sarge's face reddened as he realized he had moved behind Saide and was holding her at her waist.

"We're here on our honeymoon," Sadie said.

"Well you sure picked the perfect place," Becky responded, "This island is seductive. You can't help but be in love here."

"Are you here for the week also?" Sarge asked Steve.

"Actually we come for two weeks. One week just wasn't enough so we started coming for two."

"So you've been here before?"

"Yes, we've been coming for five or more years now."

"Is there any place in particular that we should be sure to visit while we are here?" Sarge asked.

"There are a lot of great restaurants. And if you want to do the tourist thing are all kind s of activities."

"I don't want to spend all my time sightseeing," Sarge said.

"Being newlyweds," Steve answered, "I wouldn't think you would. You'll need some beach time and some romantic walks on the beach at night, and I'm sure you'll spend some time in your room." Steve winked at Sarge.

Sarge smiled.

Becky said to Sadie, "We're going to the Lighthouse tonight for dinner. It's a great Italian restaurant and the perfect place on the island to watch the sunset. If you want to go, you can go with us. We have a rental car."

"That's really sweet of you to offer. We'll talk that over and let you know," Sadie said.

"We'll be right here all day," Steve said, "If you need anything just yell."

"It was really nice meeting you folks," Sarge said as he again shook Steve's hand then he and Sadie walked the couple steps back to their chicki.

Amy had made an appointment so they were met at the door when they arrived at NCIS.

"Mr. Morrow," the young lady said, "I'll take you to the investigator's office if you two will follow me?"

The investigator was waiting and wasted no time in laying out all the evidence they had produced from the investigation.

"Was there a push to close this case fast?" Bobby asked.

The investigator paused then responded, "I would not normally say this, but I checked you out and you have quite a reputation, so I will tell you that, yes we had some pressure from above to quickly and quietly close the case as it appeared to be a suicide."

"And so you did not examine the blood spray pattern?"

"We did that, yes, and found it to be consistent with a shot in the right temple."

"But," Bobby said, "The Colonel was left-handed."

The investigator drew his left hand up to his left temple and a furrow developed on his forehead. Most people were right-handed. The Colonel was assumed to be right-handed and thus the blood spray pattern was consistent with a suicide. Why would someone change hands to commit suicide?

Bobby picked up the gun that was sealed in a clear plastic bag and asked, "Is this the weapon he used?"

"Yes, sir, and his prints were the only prints on it."

"It's a Taurus."

"Yes, sir, early vintage. Made in Brazil," the investigator thought for a moment then asked Bobby, "Is that a problem?"

"I have known the Colonel for way too many years than I care to remember. The Colonel had an extensive gun collection and we spent many hours talking about guns," Bobby said, "And one thing I remember the Colonel saying was he would never own a Taurus as they were so unreliable."

"What are you saying?" the investigator asked.

"The Colonel did not commit suicide," Bobby said. Bobby then looked at Amy and said to her, "We need to go."

"Mr. Morrow," the investigator asked, "Do you have an idea who did this?"

Bobby gave the investigator a half smile and again said to Amy, "We have to go."

Sarge and Sadie spent the morning soaking up sun. Venturing into the clear blue sea every few minutes and basically lounging away the morning. They walked the few steps to the poolside bar and ordered burgers for lunch then went right back to their chicki for more sand and sun. On one of their trips back to the chicki from the water, Sadie walked over to Becky's chicki to tell her, "If you were serious, we would like to take you up on your offer to go to the Lighthouse for dinner this evening."

"That's wonderful," Becky exclaimed.

"When do you want us to be ready?"

"We should go about 6:30 so we are there in time for the sunset."

"Perfect."

"We'll meet you in the lobby around 6:30," Becky said.

"We really appreciate you doing this for us."

"You are going to love this restaurant. It is so romantic."

Sadie blushed as she turned to tell Sarge they needed to be in the lobby at 6:30.

"No problem," Sarge said, "But for now, we need to take our towels and things to the room and get a taxi, because we promised Captain Cayce we would take his submarine ride this afternoon."

"Oh I almost forgot," Sadie said as she gathered up her belongings.

As they were leaving, Sadie said to Becky, "We have to run. We have an appointment for a submarine ride this afternoon."

"So you met Captain Cayce?" Steve asked.

A shocked Sadie stopped in her tracks and asked, "You know Captain Cayce?"

"Sure," Becky said, "Actually we are related. He's from Richmond also."

"Wow, small world," Sarge said as they held hands and walked to their room.

The submarine ride showed Sadie and Sarge a whole different world from what they were used to. Fifty feet under the Caribbean Sea and it was clear as a bell. You could actually see what was going on at the bottom of the Sea. The water was so clean and clear that light penetrated that far down. The sight was amazing. Elkhorn coral, barrel sponges, brain coral and of course, numerous fish. Fish of every size and color motoring around the coral. Parrot fish with their beak-like mouth were scraping the coral while tangs swam by in large schools changing color from deep blue to gray as they passed by. An octopus crawled out of a crack in the brain coral that did not look any where big enough to contain the eight legged brown ball. When the tour ended and they were leaving the submarine Captain Cayce approached the couple, "Thank you for taking time to enjoy our underwater world."

"We wouldn't have missed it for the world," Sadie said.

"You are too kind," the Captain said, "But I know how busy you newlyweds are and so I'm quite pleased that you chose to spend some time doing this."

Sadie gave the Captain a peck on the cheek as they left.

"He is such a nice man," Sadie said to Sarge.

"Yes he is," Sarge agreed, "We have only been here a day and we have already met several really nice people."

"Yes, and they are from the States."

"True, but the people at the Aruba Beach Club have been extremely nice also and they live here."

"Yes the Aruban people are unbelievably sweet and gracious."

"We better catch a cab and get back so we can get ready for our dinner this evening. We don't want to miss our ride."

Sadie was dressed in a light blue sundress with tropical flowers on it while Sarge had changed into tropical khaki pants and a red flowered shirt reminiscent of Magnum PI. When they met up with the Hughes in the lobby, Steve also had on khaki pants and a floral shirt while Becky looked stunning showing off her tan in a short white sundress with just a simple gold necklace glistening around her neck. When they arrived at the lighthouse, the Aruban waiter was dressed in his tuxedo and carried the large leather bound menus in the crook of his folded arm as he led the couples to a table for two down on the outdoor patio. After everyone was seated the waiter handed out the menus and the wine menu, advised the patrons of the catch of the day, and took their drink order. The couples talked but were all aware of the large bright ball of sun as it made its way across the sky to take its turn at swimming in the glistening Caribbean Sea. When the last remnants of the sun were still visible the patio came alive with cameras and cell phones all attempting to capture the final orange glow of the sun in perpetuity. The stars twinkled above, the candles on the tables began to glow and the waiters started serving the delicious Italian dishes that were the second reason why tourists flocked to this restaurant. With full bellies the foursome made the short drive down the coast past the high rise hotels to the low rise area where their rooms would welcome them for a night's sleep.

The sun poked its long yellow tendrils through Sarge's curtain again the next morning. And after consummating their marriage for the umpteenth time in just a few days, Sarge meandered to the beach to save what had now become his favorite chicki. Becky and Steve had arrived earlier to their favorite chicki and the couples became beach neighbors again.
"Thank you again for taking us to the Lighthouse last night," Sarge said.
"You are quite welcome," Becky said, "We enjoyed it also."
"Where's your bride?" Steve asked.
"She's doing those primping things that take up way too much beach time."
"What are you two planning to do today?" Becky asked.
"I think we are going to spend the whole day here on the beach," Sarge replied.
"You can't go wrong with that," Steve added.
"Tonight we may just walk over to Pizza Bob's. I get withdrawal angst if I don't have my pizza regular," said Sarge.
"You sound just like Steve," Becky said.
Steve rolled his eyes then said, "A man's got to have his pizza."
Sadie arrived showing off a new bikini and sarong and joined the conversation for a few minutes then Sarge grabbed her and carried her to the water. They frolicked in the water for a few minutes before walking back hand in hand to the waiting lounge chairs where they dried off and settled in to catch some rays from the glorious orb overhead.
Sarge was trying to read a new Jack Reacher novel but his eyelids were closed most of the time. Sadie asked him if he wanted to go back in the water but when he didn't answer and she saw the book covering his face, she decided to go

alone. Sadie took her time going out into the Sea and after she was out as far as she cared to go she bumped her toe on a large orange colored starfish. She stood still watching it for a few minutes but it did what starfish did, it just laid in the sand.

Sarge had awakened from his reading and noticing that Sadie was not on her lounge chair began scanning the water.

Steve said to Sarge, "I hate that those jetskis come down here and keep me awake with all their noise."

"Where do they come from?" Sarge inquired as he watched them come down the coast.

"Up at the high rise area," Steve said.

"Yes, they have every toy imaginable up there to rent," Becky said, "That's one more reason why we stay in this area."

"They sure get awfully close to the shore, don't they?" Sarge said.

"Yes, I'm sure somebody will get hurt one of these days."
The words were no sooner out of Steve's mouth when the jetski turned in extremely close to Sadie. The man on the back of the jetski reached out and grabbed Sadie by the arms pulling her onto the jetski as the driver made a sharp right turn and sped back up the coast. Sarge was off the lounge chair running full speed up the sandy beach with no hope of ever catching the speeding jetski as Sadie's words echoed off the water, "Sarge, help me!"

Sarge ran back to the chicki where Becky said to him, "Steve has gone to the room to get the car keys. He said for you to meet him out front."

Sarge ran to the lobby not bothering to put on his flip flops or even a shirt. The anger grew inside him and if he caught these two punks he was prepared to go off on them like the worst volcano they could ever imagine. Nobody harmed Sarge's new bride. Nobody.

Steve ran out the front entrance and motioned for Sarge to follow him. They ran to the car, jumped in and sped out of the parking lot onto the highway that ran up the coast. Sarge kept his eyes peeled to the water as Steve drove as fast as he could, passing every car on the highway and only slowing for the couple of stoplights they encountered. When they got to the high rise area, they still had not seen any sign of the jetski. Suddenly Steve made a sharp left turn and headed for the beach.

"Do you see them?" Sarge asked.

"No, but I see the booth where they rent jetskis. Let's check there."

Steve haphazardly parked the car and the two men ran to the booth. Sarge pushed a young couple out of the way and began questioning the attendant. The attendant smiled as Sarge babbled on until Sarge had enough and leapt over the counter where he grabbed the attendant around the throat shoving him up against the wall.

"Now what the hell do you think is so funny?" Sarge demanded.

"Nothing funny," the attendant tried to get out of his closing airway, "But man said you would be angry. He also said you would not harm me."

"What man?"

"Man that paid me to rent jetski then came back with blonde girl. He said he playing joke on you."

"I'm going to give him joke alright. Where is this man? Who is he?"

"I don't know his name. He come and pay extra, then he leave this envelope for you."

"Give me the envelope. What's taking you so long?" Sarge growled.

Sarge let go of the man's neck and he went back to the counter where he picked up an envelope that he handed to Sarge.

Sarge tore the envelope open and read it. Steve stood watching but after a moment asked, "What's it say Sarge?" Sarge being a man of few words handed the note to Steve while he asked the attendant, "Do you have a telephone?" "No have telephone." "Where is the nearest one?" The attendant pointed to the Marriott. Steve read the note: *Call your dense friend Bobby and tell him I left him enough clues. He is to come to me, otherwise I will be keeping your wife. If you call him immediately she will be back at the Aruba Beach Club when you get there. If Morrow fails to show, I will come back for her. Signed, Derrell Sherrod* Steve looked up from the note but Sarge was already running for the Marriott.

Steve waited near the car but it wasn't long before Sarge was piling into the passenger seat.

"What do you want me to do?" Steve asked.

"Let's go back to the resort and see if she is there, if she's not then maybe you can take me to the police station."

"Sure," Steve said as he started the little rental car and aimed it back down the coast, "Can I ask you something Sarge?"

"Sure, what would you like to know?"

"Exactly what line of work are you in? And who is Morrow?" Sarge looked over at Steve and answered him, "I used to be a federal undercover agent. Bobby Morrow trained me and I worked for him."

"So who is the guy that signed the note?"

"I don't know. That was before my time. It was a case that Bobby worked on."

"Were you able to call Morrow?"

"Yes. He was just on his way home from Washington, DC, where he was at the funeral of his friend and our former employer, the Colonel."

"What's the Colonel's name?"

"Just the Colonel. You would remember him from the Vietnam war where he was in command then he became the confidential advisor to several presidents."

"That Colonel? Everyone knows about him. You worked for him?"

"Yes."

Steve and Sarge arrived at the resort and they both loped down to the beach after checking for Sadie in the lobby. When they got to the chickis, Sadie and Becky were in a very animated conversation.

"Sadie was just telling me how those guys took her up the coast then put her in a car and brought her right back down," Becky said to Steve and Sarge.

"Did they hurt you?" Sarge asked Sadie.

"No. Other then rubbed my arm a little when they pulled me onto that stupid jetski," Sadie answered. Then continued, "What is this all about Sarge?"

"Apparently one of Bobby's past cases is trying to get him to go to Venezuela."

"What does that have to do with us? And how do they know you and me? And how do they know we are here?"

"The scum of the world have no problem keeping track of other people and they would have done their research to find out that Bobby and I worked together. Since our marriage was just in the newspaper, they probably found that on the internet also."

"Are we safe?"

"Yes, we're safe or they would not have let you go. Bobby is not safe though. They obviously are luring him to Venezuela for some kind of revenge or something."

Sarge looked to Steve and asked, "Do you still have the note?"

"Sure," he said as he pulled it from his pocket and handed it to Sarge. Sarge tucked the note inside his book.

"Take me back to the Colonel's office," Bobby said to Amy, "I have to get my car and head back home.

Bobby's cell phone rang and he answered it, "Sarge what are you calling me for? Aren't you on your honeymoon?"

"Yes, but I just had an incident."

"What kind of incident?"

"Sadie and I were on the beach. I fell asleep in the lounge chair and she went out into the water. Some guys came by on a jetski and snatched her..."

"Did you get her back? Is she alright?"

"Yes they brought her back on the condition that I phone you immediately and give you a message."

"What's the message?"

"They said they have given you enough clues. You are now to go meet a Derrell Sherrod."

Bobby was silent for a moment so Sarge asked, "Bobby who is Derrell Sherrod?"

"He's Cordell Sherrod's brother."

"And so who is Cordell Sherrod?"

"Before you came along, there was an undercover agent in Bonaire, only two islands away from where you are now. His name was Wildman Clint Armstrong. He was ready to nail Cordell for running drugs from Venezuela to Bonaire then onto Europe and the U.S.. Sherrod killed Armstrong. I caught Sherrod with Richard's help and he got sent to Guantanamo Bay where I believe he still is."

"And so Derrell wants revenge?"

"No doubt. After all his brother is rotting in a cell in Guantanamo."

"Bobby you can't go there alone," Sarge pleaded.

"I have to. They will know if anyone else is with me or in the background lurking."

"But you know they are going to kill you."

"You're probably right about that. Unless I can get them first."

"I'm just across the Caribbean from them. I'll meet you there."
"You will not! That is an order. You will finish your honeymoon and you will go home. I got this covered," Bobby said.
"That's what you said last Thanksgiving when you decided to not have your wife do all the cooking and you deep fried the turkey. You damn near burnt down your house."
"But I didn't. And I've done this before. That was my first time cooking a turkey. Who knew it would spit all that hot oil everywhere when you dropped the turkey in?"
"You weren't supposed to drop the turkey in. The directions specifically said, slowly place the turkey in the hot grease."
"I was in a hurry."
"Like you are now?"
Bobby ended the call then placed another call.
"Amy, I have to go to Venezuela."
"Does this have anything to do with the Colonel?" she asked.
"Yes. And it solves his murder. Derrell Sherrod, brother of Cordell Sherrod that we put away, the Colonel and I, has just contacted me through Sarge. He said he has left me enough clues, which would be the Taurus gun that the Colonel supposedly shot himself with. The Taurus was Sherrod's gun of choice and the Colonel would never own one. They shot the Colonel in the head from the right side knowing that the Colonel was left handed. Apparently they intend to take care of everyone that had anything to do with putting Cordell away. And I'm next on the list."
"You can't go there alone."
"I have to."

Chapter 9

Soaking up sunshine and playing in the Caribbean Sea was hard work and when the sun went down Sadie was ready for bed. She slept soundly while Sarge tossed and turned. After a while he thought he better get up before he woke Sadie so he pulled on some clothes and made his way down to the beach bar where Jimmy Buffet music was playing away while the bartender passed out cold beers and colorful drinks with umbrellas in them. Sarge found an open seat and with a slight motion to the bartender was quickly drinking a Bright beer. After all, while in Aruba, drink what the Arubans drink. Sarge was deep in thought as he fretted over what may happen to Bobby and how bad the timing was. If only he hadn't just got married, he could assist Bobby.

A quick slap on Sarge's broad shoulder made him jump.

"Sarge, what are you doing here? Don't you have a lovely new wife to snuggle up next to?"

"That I do Captain Cayce," Sarge said with a slight smile on his face.

"So what's the problem?"

"Not really anything I can discuss Captain," Sarge replied.

"Well you look like your favorite pet died."

Sarge studied a minute then answered, "That might be fairly accurate."

"Then allow me to help you," Captain Cayce said. "But first buy me a drink."

Cayce motioned for the bartender who without asking brought the Captain a shot and set it in front of him. Cayce tipped the shotglass up and after swiping his mouth with his hand said, "Sm-o-o-oth!", drawing the word out into a short sentence.

"I'm afraid there isn't anything you can do to help Captain. But I appreciate the thought."

The Captain pulled himself onto the high barstool and with a smirk on his face said to Sarge, "You may be surprised at what I can do?"

Sarge took a gulp of beer, "Like what? You want to lend me your submarine?"

Cayce slapped Sarge on the shoulder again, "That submarine's just for tourists, that thing wouldn't do you any good."

"Well the only way you could help me Captain is to smuggle me onto the beach in Venezuela and provide me with a map to the local druglord's lair," Sarge said as he took another gulp of beer and continued, "This isn't bad beer."

"It's the water."

"What?" Sarge asked shaking off the fog that was settling around his brain from the beer.

"It's the water. Aruba makes all of their own water from sea water so it's great water which makes good beer."

"Oh, I see."

"And I could get you onto the beach," the Captain said quietly, "And I can probably even get you a map to Sherrod's. I assume that's the druglord you are talking about?"

The fog disappeared from Sarge's brain as he concentrated on what he thought he had just heard the Captain say then he asked, "Did you just say..."

The Captain put his finger to his lips as a sign for Sarge to not speak. Sarge looked around then stared at Cayce and quietly asked, "Captain, who are you really?"

Cayce smiled and began singing, "Do, dat, da, diddy, de..."

"Captain?" Sarge asked again.

"Let's take a walk on the beach," Cayce said. "Not like you and your new bride would, but close enough to the water that only you and God can hear me."

Sarge motioned for the bartender and threw some money on the bar as he stood to leave. More money than was necessary including a handsome tip. The bartender smiled and said to Sarge as he was walking away with the Captain, "You come back now."

Neither spoke until they reached the water's edge where the surf was lapping onto the packed sand providing pleasant background music.

"I heard of Sherrod before I retired," the Captain said.

"Exactly what did you retire from?" Sarge asked.

"Government work," Cayce said meaning for that to be the end of that particular conversation.

"Someplace with Initials and not a name, I assume."

"Anyway," the Captain said as he pointed out into the dark Sea, "17 miles that direction, or 14.7 nautical miles, is the coast of Venezuela. Sherrod's compound is on the west side of the cape, north of the town of Punta Fijo, and it's situated along the coast."

"Then all we need is a boat," Sarge said.

Cayce held up his hand to stop Sarge, "It's not that easy. They have regular patrols along the coast plus they have a manned tower that scours the water for boats. A boat could not get near that place."

"Then how can I get there?"

"Have you ever heard of the Super Falcon?" the Captain asked.

Sarge shook his head negatively.

"The Super Falcon, is a two man, winged submersible made by Hawkes Ocean Technologies."

"I don't mean to be a wet blanket Captain," Sarge said, "But I'm rather sure I can't drive a submersible and if you go along that makes three people after we collect Bobby."

"I said they make a two man submersible. The one I have access to is slightly modified, it will hold three people. We've used it on a few occasions to take Navy Seals over to Colombia."

"We?" Sarge asked hoping to find out a bit more about the Captain.

"I'm a Captain. I drive boats and subs or anything that goes into the water."

"Bobby will be there tomorrow morning," Sarge stated.

"We will have no choice but to wait until nightfall to go in after him. I'll pick you up outside the lobby tomorrow night about one o'clock a.m., and that will put us there around two in the morning when they should start getting lackadaisical. But you have to realize, I'm a lover not a fighter. I'll get you there and I'll get you back but it will be up to you to spring your Mr. Morrow."

"I hope he's not dead by then or too badly beaten."

"I'm afraid it's the best we can do."

"He is a tough guy so we'll assume he'll still have all his body parts intact and can walk out of the compound. You wouldn't happen to have a map of the compound would you?"

The Captain snickered, "What do you think I am, a travel agent? No, I don't have a map but I will bring along a little something that will help you."

"What's that?"

"Night vision binoculars with heat imaging recognition. You will at least be able to tell where the bodies are located."

"That will be fabulous," Sarge said, "I suppose I shouldn't ask how you happen to have them?"

"It's probably best you don't ask. But let me ask you, Is your major medical insurance paid up? Because you are walking into a regular viper's nest."

"He's my friend," Sarge said, "There is nothing I wouldn't do to help Bobby. Nothing!"

The finality of Sarge's statement left no doubt in Cayce's mind that Sarge was a warrior and true to his word. Nothing would stop him.

The Captain turned and walked away singing, "Tomorrow. Dum, da dee, da, doo, …scooby dooby doo….."

Sarge was able to quietly reenter his room and slide under the covers next to his beautiful bride without waking her. When sleep finally came to him, it was quickly chased away by intruding rays of glorious sunshine. Sarge looked over at Sadie. Sadie smiled back at him.

While Sarge and Sadie were frolicking between the sheets, then soaking up sunshine while occasionally cooling their bodies with salt water, Bobby Morrow willingly stepped off an airplane, went through Venezuelan Customs and was met at the airport entrance by several of the meanest looking men in South America. The gruffly grabbed Bobby, one man on each side, and practically drug him across the concrete into a waiting car with blacked-out windows. After roughly throwing him into the backseat another ruffian began to search him.

"I just got off an airplane," Bobby said, "exactly where the hell do you think I would be able to conceal a weapon? Have you been through airport security in the United States lately? Hell, they wouldn't even allow me to bring my toenail clippers so I could give you a pedicure."

"Shut up Gringo," one of the men said in broken english, "You talk too much."

"You think this is bad, you should see my daughter."

The ruffian next to Bobby slapped duct tape over Bobby's mouth then grabbed his wrists and bound them with a plastic zip-tie as tightly as he could.

Bobby saved his energy. The car ride was not very long and under different circumstancesthe scenery would have been very pleasing. Especially when they drove out onto the neck of the cape where you could see the shimmering blue Caribbean Sea on both sides of the highway. Shortly after that they passed through the rusty metal gates of a compound which was overloaded with shirtless men bearing guns of all sizes and shapes. The ruffian pulled Bobby out of the backseat as soon as the car slid to a stop and held him up while Derrell Sherrod strode up like a four star general. Sherrod punched Bobby in the stomach as hard as he could while two men firmly held onto Bobby's arms. Bobby spat something out which was indecipherable due to the duct tape on his mouth. Derrell reached over and roughly pulled the duct tape from Bobby's mouth, "Did you say something Mr. Morrow?"

"I merely asked if that was your best punch. You hit like a girl," Bobby said with a snicker on his face.

Immediately another punch struck Bobby in the gut.

"How about you tell the goons to go away then you and I can get to it?" Bobby asked Derrell.

"You insist on being a tough guy," Derrell said, "Well we're going to take some of the tough out of you." Derrell placed a finger in front of his mouth while holding up his arm with the other arm then said, "Correction, we are going to take *all* of the tough out of you. Every last breath."

"I hope you packed a lunch Derrell because if you're doing the beating it's going to be a long day."

"Take that piece of gringo dung into the shed and string him up. I'll be there after I have a nice leisurely lunch. It's hot, perhaps I'll also have a nice mojito."

"Have one of your goons bring a mojito out to me," Bobby shouted to Derrell as they carried him off with his feet dragging in the red dirt causing dust to fly into the air.

Derrell Sherrod entered the building where Bobby hung, patting his stomach after his delicious lunch of conch salad and mojitos, and carrying an electric cattle prod.

"Not getting enough, you have to use an artificial stimulator?" Bobby asked.

"I intend to stimulate you, my friend," said a calm Sherrod. "Then you better hope I don't get loose Sherrod because if I do the first item on my agenda will be to stick that cattle prod where the sun don't shine."

"We'll see how tough you are in a minute," Sherrod said with a smile on his face.

Sherrod took his time rolling up the sleeves of his fine silk shirt then admired the cattle prod and watching the sparks fly as he pressed the button for show. Slowly he advanced towards Bobby with the cattle prod held out in front of himself.

It was extremely easy for Sarge to fall asleep under the chicki. All comfortable on the lounge chair and with the intention of reading a few more chapters of the Jack Reacher book but with the long night talking with Captain Cayce and worrying about Bobby sleep was only now advancing upon him. Sadie would get up from her sun worshipping every now and then to ask Sarge if he wanted to join her in the deep blue Sea, but each time her request was met with snores coming from under the book covering Sarge's face, so she went in alone to enjoy the water on her hot tanned body. Sarge did awake around lunchtime and said to Sadie, "Wow, I must have fell asleep, do you want to get something to eat?"

"Sure, what did you have in mind?"

"I think I'd like a fresh Wahoo sandwich from the beach bar," Sarge said.

"That sounds good," answered Sadie. "Do you want me to go get them?"

"I'll go," Sarge said, "I need the exercise."

"I thought maybe I was wearing you out," Sadie said as she smiled up at Sarge.

Sarge was at a loss for words so he put down his book, rounded up his plastic sandwich bag with his cash and credit cards in it, or as it is called here on the island, his Aruban wallet, slipped into his flip flops and headed for the beach bar. After lunch a few more exhausting hours of playing in the sun, sand, and sea, plus chatting with their chicki neighbors, the couple decided to go to their room and shower for dinner. As the couple passed their chicki neighbors, Sarge stopped to quietly speak with Steve.

"Will you please check on Sadie in the morning? We are in room 219," Sarge asked Steve.

"Sure. Of course," Steve said with concern emanating from his face, "Is anything wrong?"

"I have to go somewhere late tonight and I just need to know that someone will look after her," Sarge said as he handed Steve a folded piece of paper. "Here are some numbers in case there are any problems. Please contact her father and the other number."

Steve looked at the paper as he responded, "Is there anything else I can do?"

"Thanks, but no."

"Is this about the note you received the other day when the jetskiers snatched Sadie?"

"Yes, but you will be better off not knowing too much."

"I looked that Sherrod name up on the internet last night," Steve said, "I saw that there are drug dealers in Venezuela by that name."

"You should forget that you know that," Sarge advised Steve.

Steve stared at Sarge for a few moments before saying, "You're going there aren't you?"

Sarge turned to walk away when Steve grabbed Sarge's beefy arm to stop him and asked, "Can I go with you?"

"I need you here," Sarge said as he walked away to catch up with Sadie who was standing at the edge of the patio using the outdoor shower to wash the sand off her feet before putting on her flip flops.

Becky was good at reading body language and immediately asked Steve, "What's going on Steve?"
"We need to keep an eye on Sadie. There's a storm brewing in the Caribbean."

Sarge hailed a taxi in front of the resort and he and Sadie climbed in the backseat.
"Where to?" the taxi driver asked.
"Iguana Moe's" Sarge replied.
"Very good," said the taxi driver as he checked his mirrors and pulled out from the resort. They arrived in just a few minutes and after Sarge paid the taxi driver the couple walked up the steps to the second floor restaurant that overlooked the downtown area and the cruise ships that were in the harbor. The waitress seated the couple, brought menus, and asked for their drink order.
"Cactus colada for me," said Sarge. "What would you like Sadie?"
"I'll try the same thing. No, on second thought, I want a Mango daiquiri."
"I'll be back in a minute with your drinks," said the waitress as she left the table.
The ambience of the open air restaurant with the cruise ships anchored on the shimmering blue sea and the trade winds carrying the smells of exotic plants and whatever was cooking in the kitchen was exciting. The waitress returned with their drinks and took their food order. The couple clinked glasses as the couple said in unison, "You and me. May we always be - Together!"
Sarge put his hand on top of Sadie's and told her he loved her.

When they returned to the Aruba Beach Club, Sarge let out a yawn while stretching his muscular arms up in the air. "I think we should go to bed early tonight," he said. And they did.

Sarge woke after midnight and quietly moved out of the bed, pulled on some black clothes and snuck out of the room while Sadie slept peacefully. The Captain, being a man of his word, was waiting in his car in front of the resort with the motor running. Sarge jumped in and the vehicle sped off. When they reached the Captain's office they climbed on board a small boat. Sarge looked questioningly at the Captain but he merely motored the boat out of the slip and headed for the dark Sea. When the Captain passed the outer small islands that ring the downtown harbor he made a sharp left turn and sped along the coast past the airport and the brewery which were both lit up like a ball park on the night of a big game. Cayce slowed as he came upon an old steel sided shed that jutted out into the water. He pulled up next to the connected dock and turned off the boat motor, motioned to Sarge to follow him and he jumped from the boat with a rope in his hand to tie up the motor boat. After a quick glance around Cayce put a key into the lock on the steel covered door and entered the shed. He motioned for Sarge to follow into the darkness as he again glanced around the perimeter. After Sarge was inside Cayce closed the door and turned on the lights. The Super Falcon looked to Sarge like something out of a James Bond movie, it was a submersible, or maybe an airplane, or possibly a mixture of both. It had three round glass tops lined up on the slender body which also had short wings on the sides. Sarge stared in amazement.

"She's a beauty, isn't she?" Cayce asked.

"Are you sure this thing will hold three of us?" Sarge asked.

"Of course," Cayce said as he began to lower the custom built submersible into the water. The glass hatches opened when Cayce pushed a remote and he said to Sarge, "You sit in the middle hatch." Sarge gingerly stepped off the interior dock and into the open cockpit while clinging tightly to the sides as it rocked slightly on the water.

Captain Cayce then climbed into the front cockpit and closed the glass hatches. Sarge experienced a moment of anxiety then he heard Cayce's voice over an intercom, "It's just like being in an airplane except this one flies under the water. It is very safe because it is positively buoyant...."

Sarge interrupted, "What the hell does that mean?"

Cayce answered with a laugh in his voice, "It means that it remains floating unless some mechanical device or additional weight is used. In other words we force it under water the same way a whale would dive or you would dive under water. Saying that, the captain massaged the controls and said to Sarge, "Here we go."

Sarge hung on tight to the seat rails as he watched the water rise up and over the glass hatch. In a matter of seconds he was under water. Under the dark black water where the only thing he could see was what was lit up by the bright lights on the front of the craft. By the time they reached their stopping point Sarge had relaxed and was almost enjoying the sights of the underwater nightlife where the octopus, shrimp, lobster, and other marine life came out to feed. Cayce raised the submersible so that only the three glass hatches were above the water line then he said to Sarge, "When I open the hatch grab the waterproof bag at your feet and jump out quick. I can't stay here long or eventually they will spot us. Remember the spot on the beach where you go ashore and when you come back just swim out a few yards. I'll be waiting." The hatch opened, Sarge grabbed the black waterproof bag and jumped over the side into the refreshing sea water and swam towards shore. He looked back after a minute but there was nothing to see. The captain and his craft were gone. Sarge crawled onto the beach on his belly dragging the bag for a few yards then jumped up and sprinted into the palm trees on the other side of the beach where he immediately took cover and listened for any sounds that he may have alerted someone. He then opened the bag to see what Cayce had given him. Two Glock pistols and a Ka-bar knife along with the night vision that he had told Sarge about. Sarge stuck the knife in his waistband, and checked the clips on both Glocks. Full clips. "Thanks Captain," Sarge said under his breath, "You're a life saver."

Sarge placed the night vision on his head then like an Indian watching each footfall he headed out in the direction of the compound. At the edge of the compound Sarge scanned each of the buildings with the heat imaging feature of the night vision goggles. Several of the buildings showed bodies in a horizontal position. People sleeping. In the far building he saw a deformed body that appeared to be standing but not quite so and it was giving off large amounts of heat. Plus there were two people outside the building walking back and forth. Sarge was sure that would be where Bobby was and he moved in that direction. When he got close he quietly approached the building from the side. He waited a few minutes and eventually a guard with an assault rifle came to the edge of the building to look down the side. The guard never saw the flick of the Ka-bar as it sliced his throat open. Sarge grabbed the body before it fell over and pulled it around the side of the building then he took the assault rifle, bent over to appear smaller and walked quickly across the front of the building to the other guard. The other guard was walking straight at him and was about to question his strange appearance when the Ka-Bar knife flew through the air with tremendous speed and accuracy and sank into his chest cavity. The man reached for his chest while blood poured out from between his fingers as he slowly sank to the ground. Sarge wasted no time entering the building where he stopped to get a good look around him before he moved on. The night vision showed a weary, bloody

Bobby hanging from his arms in the center of the room. Sarge ran to him and untied the ropes that held him up.

"Are you going to make it?" Sarge asked Bobby.

"I was saving my strength so I could open a can of whip-ass on these guys in the morning."

"Sure you were," said Sarge. "How about we get the hell out of here?"

"Let me get my legs under me first," Bobby said. "Then I have to have a word with Sherrod. It wouldn't be polite to leave without expressing my gratitude for his hospitality."

"Or we could just get out of here!"

"It will only take a second. He's in the next building, probably sleeping."

"Then we should let him sleep," Sarge said to Bobby's back as Bobby walked unsteadily to the door. Sarge followed and when they went out the door, Sarge scanned the area with the night vision checking for more guards. Bobby picked up his pace as he went to the next building where he strode up to the door, turned the knob and strolled in making his way through the house until he came to the bedroom. He opened the bedroom door and walked up to the side of the bed. Derrell was sound asleep with his arm around a slender long haired female. Bobby slapped Derrell lightly across the face. Derrell awoke and panic swept over his face.

"I didn't want to leave without thanking you for your hospitality," Bobby said as Derrell tried to slide up the bed away from Bobby. "I especially enjoyed the shock therapy. I was sort of in a funk and that put new spark in my life. And the beatings reminded me that I may have let myself go a little so I'm going to get back to the gym when I get home and get in shape."

Derrell lunged for the nightstand pulling open the drawer and reaching for a gun. Bobby grabbed his hand with the gun in it and summoning his testosterone he overpowered Derrell. Bobby placed the gun against Derrell's head then asked him,

"Is this how you shot the Colonel?"

Derrell spit at Bobby. Bobby pulled the trigger. The frightened woman that had been lying next to Derrell was now screaming.

Bobby tried to comfort her, "One day you'll thank me for this."

"Can we go now?" Sarge asked.

Bobby turned and said, "Maybe you better lead the way. I had a chauffeur when I arrived."

Sarge scanned the exterior then led Bobby out of the compound the same way he entered. When they reached the beach before they left the shelter of the palms, Bobby whispered, "I assume you have a plan big guy?"

"Sure, when you're ready we are going to swim out into sea."

"I'm not sure I have the strength to swim to Aruba," Bobby said.

"It's only seventeen miles. You must be getting soft in your old age."

Bobby punched Sarge in the shoulder.

"Trust me," Sarge said.

Sarge found the waterproof bag, placed the guns and night vision equipment back in it, took one last look around and ran across the sand into the water with Bobby right on his heels. Sarge dove into the water and began swimming so Bobby followed. A few yards from shore the glass hatches arose out of the water a mere couple feet in front of the swimmers. The hatches opened, Sarge jumped into the center one and motioned for Bobby to get in the last one. Bullets started whizzing past their heads. The glass hatches closed and the submersible sank under the water. As the submersible turned away the bullets zipped past the submersible under water leaving trails.

"Welcome aboard, mates," Cayce said over the intercom.

"Captain Cayce," Bobby said excitedly, "Is that you?"

"Aye, it's me," Cayce said, "I see you are still having a problem staying out of trouble?"

"It seems to follow me Captain."

"You know you owe me a drink when we get back to Aruba."

"It will be a pleasure to buy you a drink Captain," Bobby said.

"You still drink that hundred and fifty proof rum?"

"Good memory."

Sarge interjected, "You mean you two know each other?"

"Sarge how long have you known Bobby?" Cayce asked.

"For a few years now."

"Then you should know that someone has to be available to pull his butt out of the predicaments he gets into."

"I should have guessed. Maybe you can tell me some stories when we get back Captain."

"Oh, I could, but, as they say, then I'd have to kill you."

The submersible pulled into the old steel shack and rose above the water level. The hatches opened and the trio jumped out of the submersible onto the interior dock. The Captain pushed the remote and the submersible was raised above the water.

"Sarge, we better get you back before your bride misses you and Bobby you can stay at my place tonight since your flight doesn't leave until tomorrow," the Captain stated as he led them out of the old steel shed and locked the door.

Sarge quietly entered the room, undressed and slipped under the covers.

"You're not going to make a habit of this are you?" Sadie whipered.

"No dear. Please go back to sleep."

"I will but first......"

Chapter 10

Sarge was not only prepared for the early morning sunshine to penetrate his room, he was welcoming it. He kissed his bride, got the towels, books, and sunscreen and said to Sadie, "I'll get us a chicki. Then I'll meet you at the beach restaurant for breakfast."

"Sounds good to me," Sadie answered.

Sarge strode through the sand to his favorite chicki and spread the towels on the lounge chairs then went back to the restaurant at the edge of the sand. He picked a table at the edge of the sand where he could watch the calm blue sea and waited for Sadie. The Hughes came into the restaurant and Sarge motioned for them to join him.

"Sarge," an elated Steve said, "I'm glad to see you. How was your evening?"

Sarge nodded his head while saying, "It was good."

Becky looked at Steve feeling left out of the conversation and asked Steve, "I thought you said there was a storm brewing, look at this beautiful day."

Steve winked at Sarge and said, "Apparently the storm has passed Becky."

Sadie came in showing off another new bikini and sarong as the waitress appeared with the menus and water. The couples ordered breakfast when from behind Sarge a voice said, "Do you like that as well as what they are wearing this year?"

Sarge turned and smiled, "What, Captain, you don't like my flowered shirt?"

"It's fine," Cayce said, "Did it come with a whistle?"

"Please join us, Captain," Sadie said. "I believe you already know Steve and Becky? Sarge you may need to introduce Bobby to the Hughes."

Sarge made the introductions as he and Steve pulled another table over to theirs to make room for everyone.

"Bobby," Sadie asked, "Where did you take my husband last night?"

Bobby looked at Sarge who shrugged his shoulders.

Cayce interjected, "I'm afraid that was my fault, dear, I took them on a late night boat ride. Some of the marine life only comes out at night and I wanted them to see it."

"I wish I could have gone," Steve said.

"The next time you come to Aruba, Steve, you and I will go out at night," Cayce said, "If that's alright with Becky."

"Steve can go," Becky said, "But you're not getting me out there in the dark on a boat."

Sarge elbowed Bobby and then pointed, "There's that beautiful woman that was at Richard St.Clair's funeral."

"Nanita," Bobby shouted to her as he stood from the table. Everyone turned to see who Bobby was talking to.

"She is pretty," Sadie said. "Who is she?"

Captain Cayce eyed her up and down and said, "She doesn't affect me,....doesn't affect me,....doesn't affect me." Leaving no doubt that he was affected by her beauty.

Sarge said to Cayce, "She is beautiful, but maybe too young for you."

Cayce said to Bobby's back in his best Australian accent, "Give her a go mate, she's eighteen." With the eighteen coming out more like a-deen.

Everyone at the table laughed until tears formed in their eyes.

"Where do you get this stuff?" Sarge asked Cayce.

"Back in the big war, when we got off the ship in Australia, that was what we heard a lot of: give her a go mate she's eighteen."

Sarge then looked to Sadie and told her, "To answer your question, she is the manager here and apparently she knew Senator St.Clair very well."

Nanita said to Bobby, "I had no idea that you were here, but I just received a message for Sarge and it mentioned your name. Which one is Sarge," she asked the group.

"I am," said Sarge as he stood up and Nanita handed him the message. Sarge read it then handed it to Bobby.

Bobby read the message to himself, "Sarge, if you can locate Bobby Morrow, please have him call Attorney General Ellwood Sine at his earliest convenience. His cell phone appears to be out of order."

It's more than out of order Bobby thought to himself, Derrell Sherrod's men took it and he will never get it back. Then Bobby addressed the group at the table, "Excuse me please I have to make a phone call. Nanita, do you have a telephone that I can use?"

"Of course Bobby," she said, "Please come with me." She intertwined her arm around Bobby's and they walked to her office where she had him sit at her desk and instructed him on how to reach the United States.

"Ellwood," Bobby said when the Attorney General came on the line. "What's up?"

"I've been trying to locate you. Where are you?"

"I'm in Aruba at the moment but will be taking a flight home in a couple hours."

"Dare I ask what you are doing in Aruba?"

"You probably don't want to know Ellwood," Bobby said.

"I'll just assume that it had something to do with the Colonel's death and the fact that we received word that Derrell Sherrod is dead."

Bobby did not say anything. Sometimes the unsaid speaks volumes.

"Right," Ellwood said, "Anyway I was about to ask if you could go to Aruba to do some protective work for us. Since you are already there, would you be willing to stay a few days?"

"I guess. I will need to contact my wife."

"I have already contacted her and she said you would insist on doing this detail for us."

"Really? What detail are we talking about?"

"We have a Senator's daughter that may be a prime kidnapping candidate."

"I hope you don't mean Senator Snead's daughter," Bobby said as he looked back towards the restaurant.

"I'm afraid so. We have some intel from our feet on the ground in China that they may attempt a kidnapping to coerce the Senator to relinquish the codes to the star wars satellites."

"Will you call Claire and tell her I'll be home in a few days?"

"Of course. I also need to ask you, do you need any…. shall we say….*tools*?"

"I happen to know a man who is here at breakfast with me that has some *tools* that I can borrow," Bobby replied.

"Looks like you are back on the federal payroll Bobby."

"Looks like," he said as he hung up the telephone and hurried back to the restaurant.

"What's up?" Sarge asked him as he was sitting back down to his steaming breakfast.

"Seems my plane has been delayed," Bobby said. Then he turned to Cayce and whispered, "Can I borrow your waterproof bag of goodies?"

"Certainly Bobby," Captain Cayce said, "When we leave here I'll drive you over and you can get the bag of goodies plus you may use my car while you're here. Is there anything else I can do to assist?"

"I'm going to need a cell phone and your phone number in case I get in another sticky situation. Oh, and do you have any connections here, I need a room. Preferably close to Sarge's room."

"Do I have connections?" Cayce asked. "You know I do. I'll go get you a room key now." Cayce pushed back from the table and strutted to the front desk coming back with a key to room 217 which he passed off to Bobby."

"You do have connections," said Bobby.

Cayce winked the nbegan singing, "doot ..da deet,.. scooby , dooby, …".

When Bobby came back to the resort after he and Cayce went for the *"tools"*, Bobby got Sarge alone and handed him a neatly wrapped beach towel.

"Keep this with you Sarge," he whispered.

Sarge took the towel and guessing at its contents due to the weight of the towel asked Bobby, "Is there anything I should know?"

"Stay alert and don't allow your lovely bride away from your side."

Sarge stowed the towel with its contents in his bag with his sunscreen and book and immediately assumed his position next to Sadie.

Bobby took up residence in a chicki behind Sarge and Sadie and started working on his tan. When they gathered their belongings and departed the beach Bobby did likewise at a discreet distance. Knowing the couple was having dinner at the Old Cunuchu House, Bobby discreetly followed them there and back. And when they retired to their room Bobby finally went to his room and collapsed on the bed. Assuming any good kidnapper worth his salt would wait until the wee hours of the morning when their prey would be barely coherent, Bobby laid on the bed for a quick nap, setting the alarm clock for midnight when he would resume his babysitting.

Bobby had just fallen off to sleep when he heard a light knock on the next room's door. Bobby jumped off the bed, grabbed the Glock he had placed under his pillow, ran to the door, and slowly opened his door just enough to see who was knocking on Sarge's door. Seeing that it was Steve and Becky, Bobby closed his door and flopped back on the bed.

"Oh, hi, Steve and Becky," Sarge said as he opened the door while sticking his Glock in his waistband behind his back.

"Your friend asked us to stop by," Steve said. "And take you to our room for the night. He thought it would be much safer if anyone came for you that you weren't here."

"Sarge," Sadie asked, "What is going on?"

"I didn't want to alarm you but the call that Bobby got this morning was to ask him to stay and guard us because the Chinese might be attempting to kidnap you to coerce your father to give them the star wars satellite codes."

Becky gasped, "You're kidding me."

"I'm afraid not," Sarge said, "But don't worry. Bobby is the best." Looking to Steve, Sarge said, "That's probably not a bad idea, but we sure hate to put you two out."

"You wouldn't be putting us out," Becky said, "We have a two bedroom suite. You would have your own room. And we could play Farkle."

"Farkle?" Sadie asked, "What is Farkle?"

"It's a dice game. It's really fun."

Steve whispered to Sarge, "I would ask though that you didn't bring any guns into our room. Becky is deathly afraid of them."

"I guess we won't need one when we aren't even where we're supposed to be," Sarge said as he slipped the Glock out of his waistband and placed it in the safe in the closet along with their passports and extra money.

"We don't want anyone thinking you are moving to a different room," Steve said, "So just put your night clothes in Sadie's purse."

"Good idea," said Sadie as she stuffed her nightie into her purse.

"If you're ready, we may as well head for our room."

The Hughes room was on the first floor at the end of the resort facing the ocean.

After they entered Sadie looked out the glass sliding doors at the Sea and proclaimed, "You two have an awesome suite. I would love to wake up to this each morning!"

"Your room will be this one," Becky said as she glided across the room and opened the door.

Sarge and Becky ambled into their new room. The door shut behind them and the lights went on. Two Chinese men dressed in tan suits were each training pistols on them.

"Search him," one of them said in barely understandable English.

The other carefully patted Sarge down then did the same to Sadie. It took all of Sarge's self control to not attack the man as he put his hands on Sarge's new bride.

"You will come with us," the first man said.

"You will walk in front of us and remember any wrong move and I will shoot the woman first. You understand me big man?"

Sarge nodded his head.

"Say the words," the man persisted, "Say you understand me."

"I understand you," Sarge said through gritted teeth.

"Go. Slowly. No sudden moves!"

The couple left the bedroom they didn't have time to get acquainted with passing Steve and Becky standing close together in the living room holding each other.

The first man said to Steve and Becky, "Your free Aruba vacation is now earned. Congratulations!"

Steve and Becky lowered their heads and stared at the floor.

When Sarge and Sadie reached the door the first man said, "Wait." Then to his companion he ordered, "Check the hallway."

The other man opened the door just a crack and scanned the hallway.

"Anyone there?" the first one asked?

"Only janitor scrubbing hallway."

"Remember you two, be quiet. No sudden moves. Now, go."

Sarge and Sadie led the two men out the door and down the hallway.

The janitor never looked up at them he was engrossed in swinging the big mop back and forth across the hallway as he sang "da, doot, dadoot, diddle e dee…"

Sarge and Sadie passed the janitor as he paused and stepped aside to let them by while he stared at the fresh footprints on his just washed floor and shook his head.

When the two men were directly in front of the janitor, the mop handle came down with such speed that neither man knew what happened until it had cracked across their arms knocking their guns to the floor where they skittered across the wet tile. Sarge wasted no time when he heard the gun skittering across the floor, he turned and while he was turning he pulled the long muscular arm back then unloaded a punch that had all his weight behind it knocking the first man back down the hall on his backside. The long handle of the mop then smacked the other man on the back of his head knocking him forward. Sarge grabbed him and slammed him head first into the wall. The janitor threw a ziptie to Sarge who roughly placed it on the wrists of the man who was bleeding profusely from his skull. The janitor rolled the man on the floor over and ziptied his wrists behind him as he said to the man, "You dirtied my clean floor!" For good measure he kicked him in the leg.

Steve came running out of his room when he heard the commotion. Sarge charged towards Steve but the janitor grabbed him and held him back.

"Whoa Sarge," the janitor said, "take it easy."

"But they lured us down here to get taken by these idiots. And by the way, Captain Cayce, since when are you a janitor."

"You'd be surprised where you might find me," Cayce said. "And as for Steve and Becky, they had contacted the FBI in Virginia when they were approached by men that claimed they would kill their children if they didn't do what they were ordered to do. The FBI has been watching all their children."

Steve approached Sarge, "I'm really sorry man."

"Not your fault," said Sarge as they shook hands.

Cayce pulled out his cell phone and made a call, "Clean up on aisle three."

Several police officers immediately filled the hallway and picked up the two bound men.

"Well," said Cayce, "How about a drink. The beach bar is still open."

Steve said "No thanks. I've had all the excitement I can stand for one vacation and he sauntered back his room. Cayce looked at Sarge and Sadie.

Sadie spoke, "We'd love to Captain." She grabbed his arm and off they went with Sarge following behind.

The bartender brought Captain Cayce his usual and two blue iced drinks for the newlyweds. Captain Cayce raised his glass to the couple. The three of them touched glasses as Cayce said, "Sm-o-o-o-th! Re-e-e-al Sm-o-o-o-o-th!"

The flatscreen television behind the bar was showing a newscaster from the United States.

"This just in," the talking head said, "We are being told by a reliable source that the son of a chief of police in Ganister, Pennsylvania was found dead in a field from a single gunshot wound. It is believed the victim had been deer hunting and was probably killed by a stray bullet or another hunter mistook him for a deer. The victim was wearing the required bright orange coat and hat. We will keep you updated on this as we learn more."

Sarge shook his head when he heard the news. Bobby arrived at the bar and said, "What are you all doing here?"

"Celebrating," Cayce said, "Would you like a drink?"

"How did you know we were here?" Sarge asked Bobby.

"The commotion in the hall downstairs woke me so I checked your room and you weren't there, then as I was looking out the window I see the three of you traipsing over to the beach bar.

"Some bodyguard you are," Sarge said to Bobby. "Maybe the government should pay Cayce instead of you."

Bobby smiled and said, "The government probably does pay Cayce."

"Ahh yes," Cayce said, "I get my social security check every month. Well, I must be going. Goodbye all. And remember, Tempest fugits. Tempest fugits!"

<u>Thank you</u>

First to those who take the time to read these stories and Secondly to my friends that allow me to use their names.

Cayce was one of those rare men that you meet in life who was intelligent, witty, and a true gentleman. I'm glad that I had the opportunity to know him. He will be greatly missed by everyone that knew him
Tempest Fugits, Cayce!.

Please support your favorite charity. If you need one to support here are my favorites:
www.shrinershospitalsforchildren.org
www.woundedwarriorsproject.org
www.coralrestoration.org

Made in the USA
Charleston, SC
08 April 2014